MOBILE SUIT GUNDAM 0079

BY KAZUHISA KONDO

Based on the anime TV series MOBILE SUIT GUNDAM created by Hajime YATATE and Yoshiyuki TOMINO

Cover Illustration/Kazuhisa Kondo
Layout & Design/Sean Lee
Translation/William Flanagan
Script Consultant/Mark Simmons
Touch-Up Art & Lettering/Bill Schuch
Contributing Editor/Mark Simmons
Editor/Ian Robertson

Managing Editor/Annette Roman
V.P. of Sales & Marketing/Rick Bauer
Editor-in-Chief/Hyoe Narita
Publisher/Seiji Horibuchi

Printed in Canada

Published by Viz Communications, Inc.
P.O. Box 77010 • San Francisco, CA 94107
www.viz.com • www.j-pop.com

10 9 8 7 6 5 4 3 2 1
First printing, June 2002

**MOBILE SUIT GUNDAM 0079
GRAPHIC NOVELS TO DATE:**
MOBILE SUIT GUNDAM 0079 Vol.1
MOBILE SUIT GUNDAM 0079 Vol.2
MOBILE SUIT GUNDAM 0079 Vol.3
MOBILE SUIT GUNDAM 0079 Vol.4
MOBILE SUIT GUNDAM 0079 Vol.5

D0617766

VIZ GRAPHIC NOVEL

MOBILE SUIT
GUNDAM
0079
VOL. 5

VIZ GRAPHIC NOVEL

MOBILE SUIT GUNDAM 0079

VOL. 5

By KAZUHISA KONDO

MOBILE SUIT
GUNDAM 0079

The official adaptation of the anime series Mobile Suit Gundam

A 43-episode animated series that began airing in Japan in 1979, *Mobile Suit Gundam* was unusual for a Japanese "giant robot" show in its grim war story and its then-revolutionary concept of using the robots (or "mobile suits," in this case) as mass-produced war machines, like tanks or planes, rather than more colorful, superhero-like, transforming robots. Edited together into three two-hour movies (*Gundam I, II* and *III*), the *Gundam* saga was released in theaters in 1981 and 1982 to enthusiastic crowds. The resulting boom in toy model kits from the series elevated *Gundam* to legendary status, and animated sequels, comics, and merchandise have been continuously produced for over 20 years to this day.

In condensing the series into six hours, the movie editions removed many of the nuance of the TV series version, as well as several of the more colorful machines. *Gundam 0079*, by using the TV series continuity for much of its story, gives readers who may have only seen the movie editions a look at the whole story with which Japanese viewers are familiar. The *Mobile Suit Gundam* TV series is still often rerun on Japanese TV.

STORY

In the not-so-far-off future, Earth's increasing population forces mankind to emigrate into space. Gigantic, orbiting space colonies are built around the Earth to house humanity's billions, and within half a century, entire nations of human beings call these space colonies their homeland.

In the calendar year of the Universal Century 0079, the furthest group of colonies from Earth, Side 3, under the name "Principality of Zeon," began a war of independence against the Earth Federation government. In slightly over a month of battle, both the Principality of Zeon and the Federation saw half their populations die. The Zeon forces' use of a new weapon, a humanoid-shaped fighting unit called a "mobile suit," gave it the advantage in battle. A temporary truce was called, a treaty was signed to prevent the use of nuclear weapons and poison gas, and the war came to a stalemate for a little more than eight months.

A Zeon attack on the space colony of Side 7 forced many of the colonists to seek refuge on the Federation mobile suit carrier *White Base*. Some of those civilians are called upon to help the Earth Federation defend itself against the Zeon enemy. Piloting a mobile suit salvaged from the Side 7 colony, the Earth Federation's new "Gundam," 15-year-old Amuro Ray finds himself on the front line of battle.

CHARACTERS

AMURO RAY

A 15-year-old civilian from the Side 7 space colony. The son of the Federation engineer who designed the Gundam, Amuro has demonstrated a knack for piloting this prototype mobile suit.

BRIGHT NOAH

One of the few surviving crew members of the Federation mobile suit carrier *White Base*, this former cadet has become the ship's acting captain.

SAYLA MASS

A mysterious refugee from Side 7, who now serves as the *White Base*'s communications officer. She appears to have some connection to enemy ace Char Aznable.

MIRAI YASHIMA

A member of the influential Yashima family, and part of the Federation's social elite. After the escape from Side 7, Mirai becomes the *White Base*'s pilot.

SEKI

A Federation technical officer dispatched, along withMatilda's supply corps, to carry out field repairs on the damaged White Base.

KAI SHIDEN

A cynical civilian from Side 7, and the pilot of the mobile suit Guncannon.

HAYATO KOBAYASHI

Amuro's hot-tempered Side 7 neighbor, who teams up with Ryu to operate the mobile suit Guntank.

FRAW BOW

Amuro's would-be girlfriend helps out by serving food and riding herd on the younger refugees.

MARKER CLAN AND OSCAR DUBLIN

The White Base's ever-reliable bridge operators.

CHARACTERS

GENERAL REVIL

One of the Earth Federation's highest-ranking generals, Revil is keeping a careful eye on the progress of the *White Base*.

MATILDA AJAN

An officer of the Federation's supply corps. Her transport planes serve as the *White Base*'s lifeline during its journey through enemy territory.

OMUR FANG

A White Base crew member who was originally a trainee mechanic, and now serves as the ship's de facto chief engineer.

ELRAN

A high-ranking Federation commander involved in the planning of the Odessa offensive. Elran is secretly collaborating with enemy commander M'Quve.

JUDOCK

A Zeon spy who masquerades as a Federation officer, and serves as a messenger between M'Quve and the traitorous Admiral Elran.

FEDERIC BRAUN

This young Zeon pilot is the protagonist of artist Kazuhisa Kondo's first Gundam comic, "MS Senki."

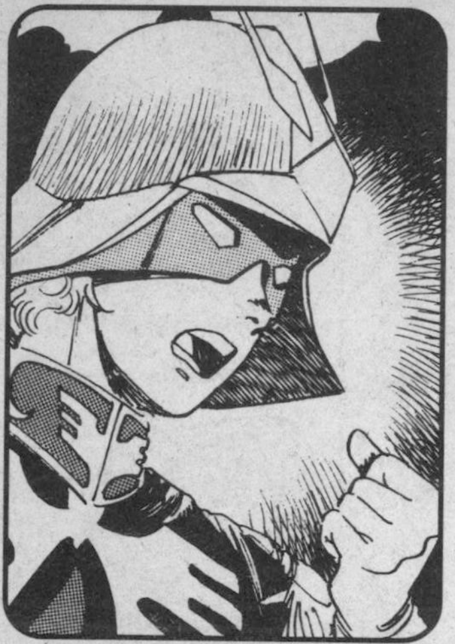

CHAR AZNABLE

Zeon's famous "Red Comet" is a legendary ace mobile suit pilot, with a sinister secret agenda of his own. Char's dismissal from the Space Attack Force, for his failure to protect Garma Zabi, complicates both his career and his private schemes.

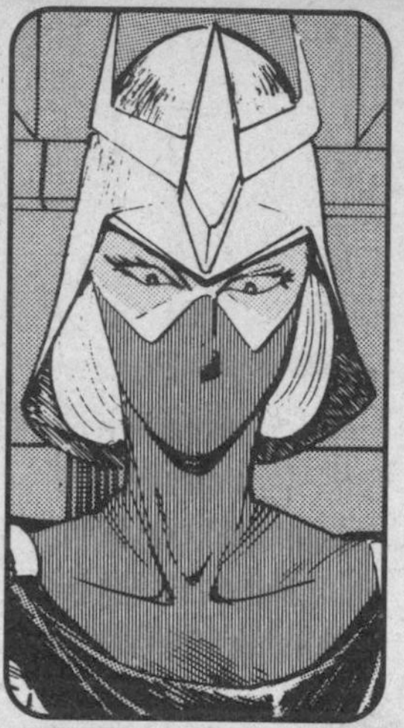

KYCILIA ZABI

The eldest daughter of Zeon's ruling Zabi family. Kycilia commands the Mobile Assault Force from her headquarters on the moon.

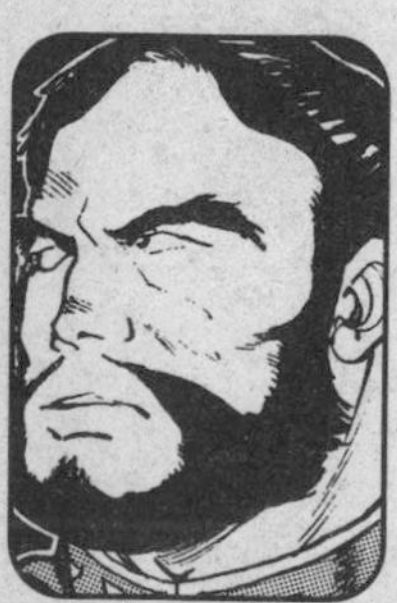

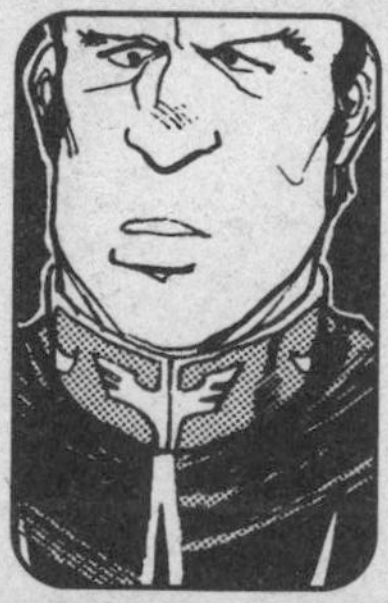

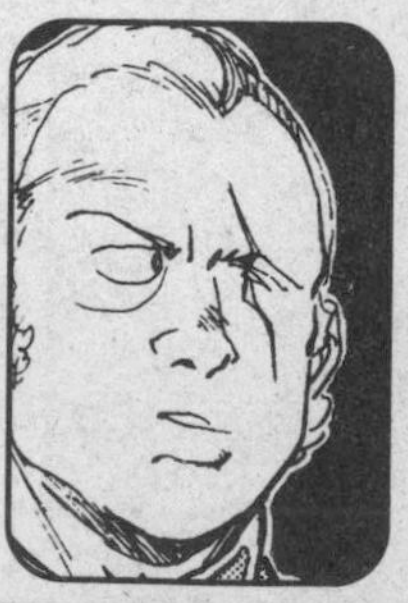

GAIA, ORTEGA, AND MASH

A trio of Zeon ace pilots, famous for capturing General Revil during the battle of Loum. Kycilia sends these "Black Tri-Stars" to Earth to aid M'Quve.

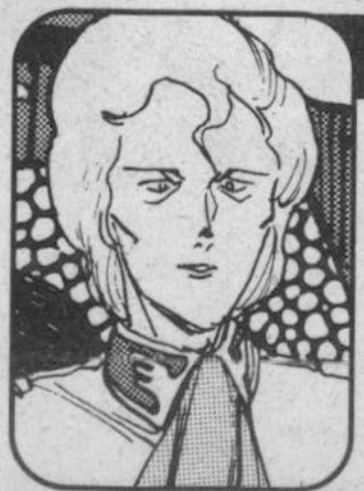

M' QUVE

The commander of Zeon's Odessa mining base. M'Quve reports directly to Kycilia Zabi, and is thus reluctant to assist Dozle's envoy Ramba Ral.

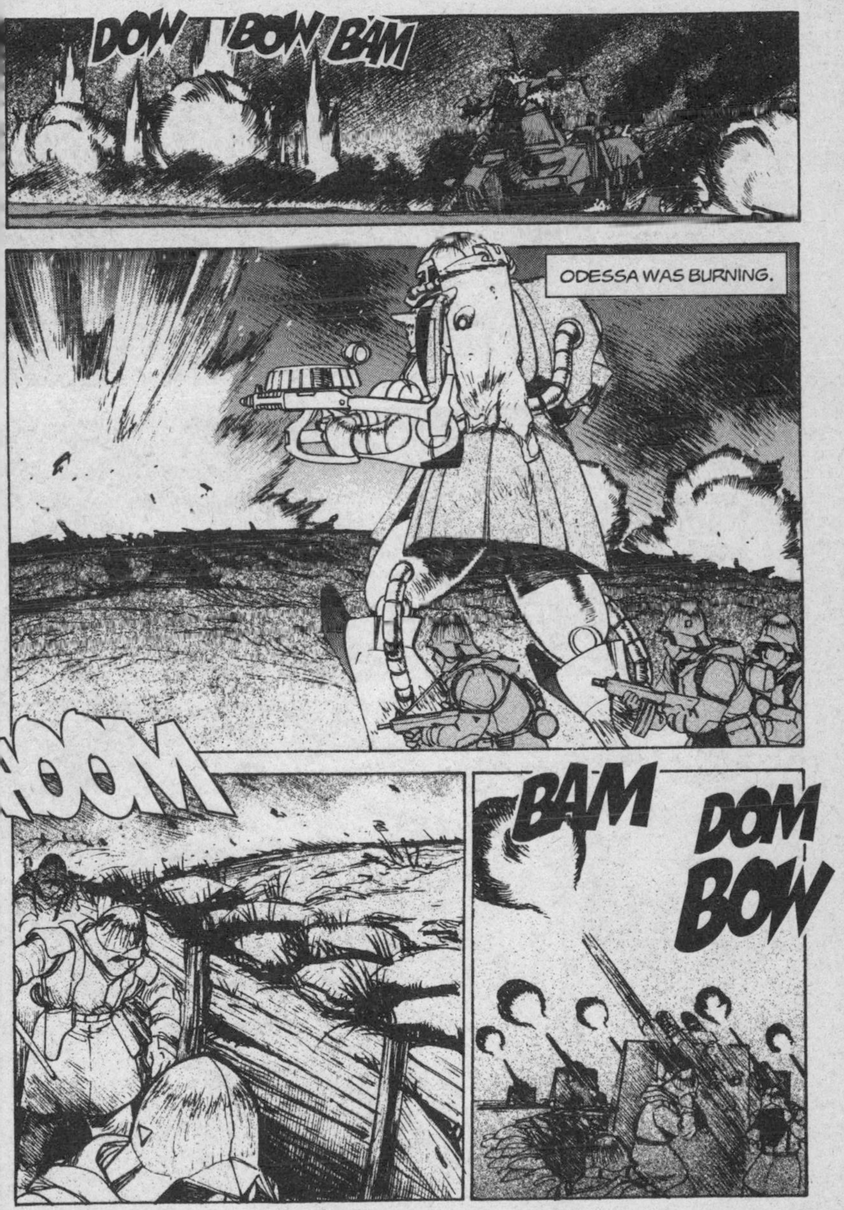
DOW BOW BAM
ODESSA WAS BURNING.
OOM
BAM
DOM
BOW

THE ODESSA DEFENSE FORCES, LED BY CAPTAIN M'QUVE OF ZEON'S EARTH EXPEDITIONARY FORCE, WERE DRIVEN BACK BY A THREE-PRONGED ATTACK OF EARTH FEDERATION GROUND FLEETS.

ALL OF THE FEDERATION FLEETS WITH THE EXCEPTION OF ADMIRAL ELRAN'S NORTHERN FLEET MANAGED TO BREAK THROUGH ZEON'S FIRST DEFENSIVE LINE.

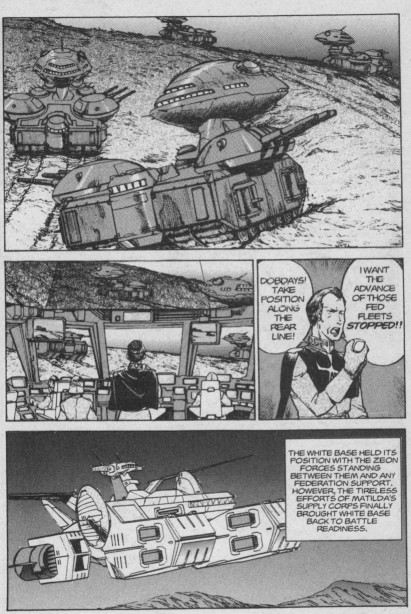

DOBDAYS! TAKE POSITION ALONG THE REAR LINE!

I WANT THE ADVANCE OF THOSE FED FLEETS *STOPPED*!!

THE WHITE BASE HELD ITS POSITION WITH THE ZEON FORCES STANDING BETWEEN THEM AND ANY FEDERATION SUPPORT. HOWEVER, THE TIRELESS EFFORTS OF MATILDA'S SUPPLY CORPS FINALLY BROUGHT WHITE BASE BACK TO BATTLE READINESS.

11

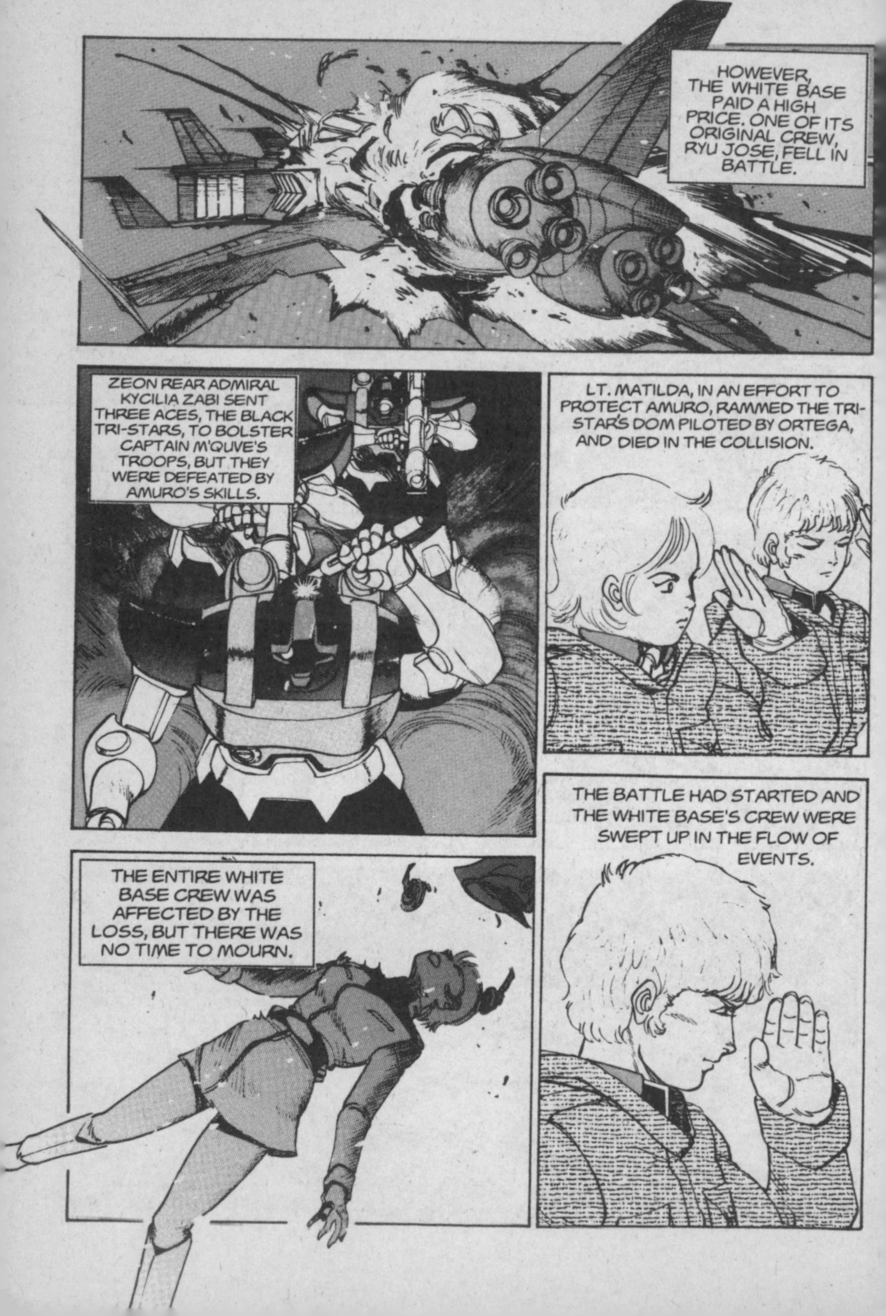
HOWEVER, THE WHITE BASE PAID A HIGH PRICE. ONE OF ITS ORIGINAL CREW, RYU JOSE, FELL IN BATTLE.
ZEON REAR ADMIRAL KYCILIA ZABI SENT THREE ACES, THE BLACK TRI-STARS, TO BOLSTER CAPTAIN M'QUVE'S TROOPS, BUT THEY WERE DEFEATED BY AMURO'S SKILLS.
LT. MATILDA, IN AN EFFORT TO PROTECT AMURO, RAMMED THE TRI-STAR'S DOM PILOTED BY ORTEGA, AND DIED IN THE COLLISION.
THE ENTIRE WHITE BASE CREW WAS AFFECTED BY THE LOSS, BUT THERE WAS NO TIME TO MOURN.
THE BATTLE HAD STARTED AND THE WHITE BASE'S CREW WERE SWEPT UP IN THE FLOW OF EVENTS.

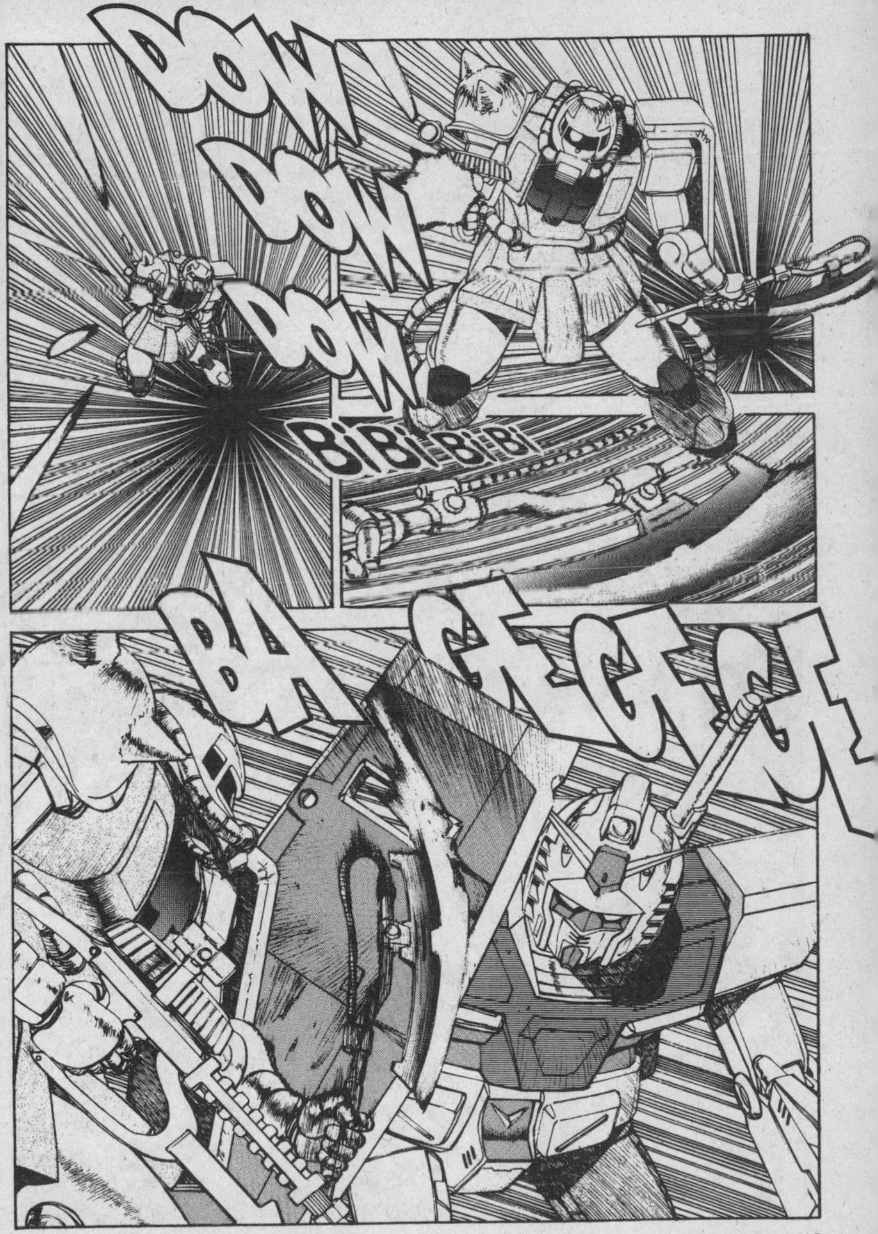
DOW
DOW
DOW
BiBiBiBi
BA CHCHCH

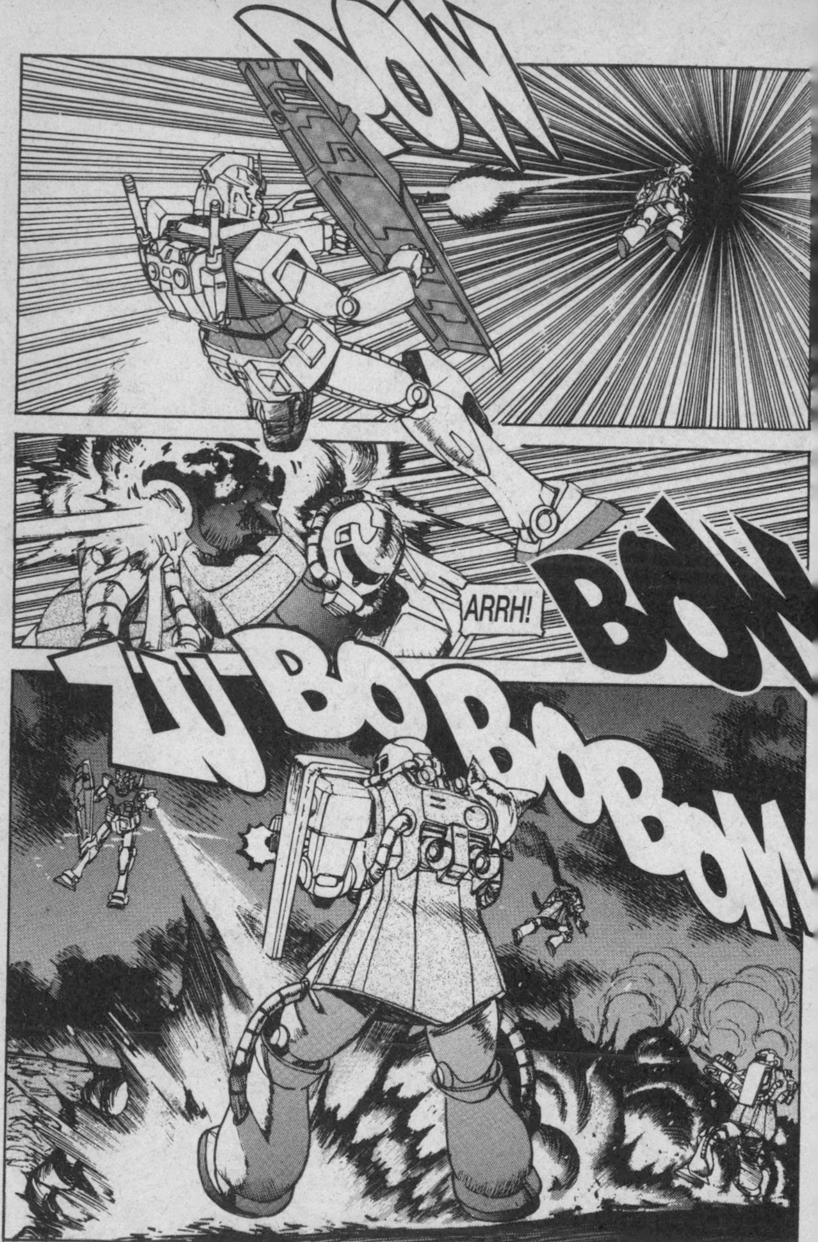
DOW
ARRH!
BOBOBOM

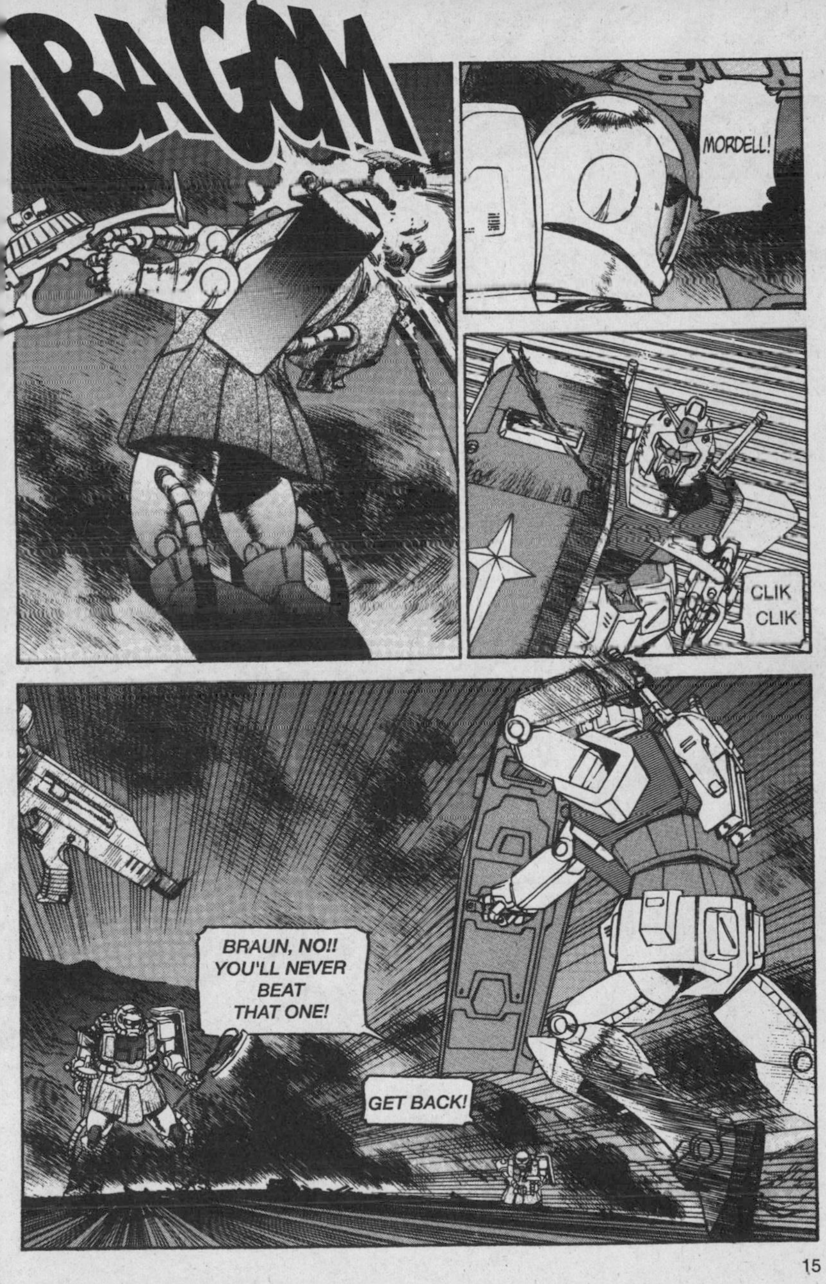
BAGOM
MORDELL!
CLIK CLIK
BRAUN, NO!! YOU'LL NEVER BEAT THAT ONE!
GET BACK!

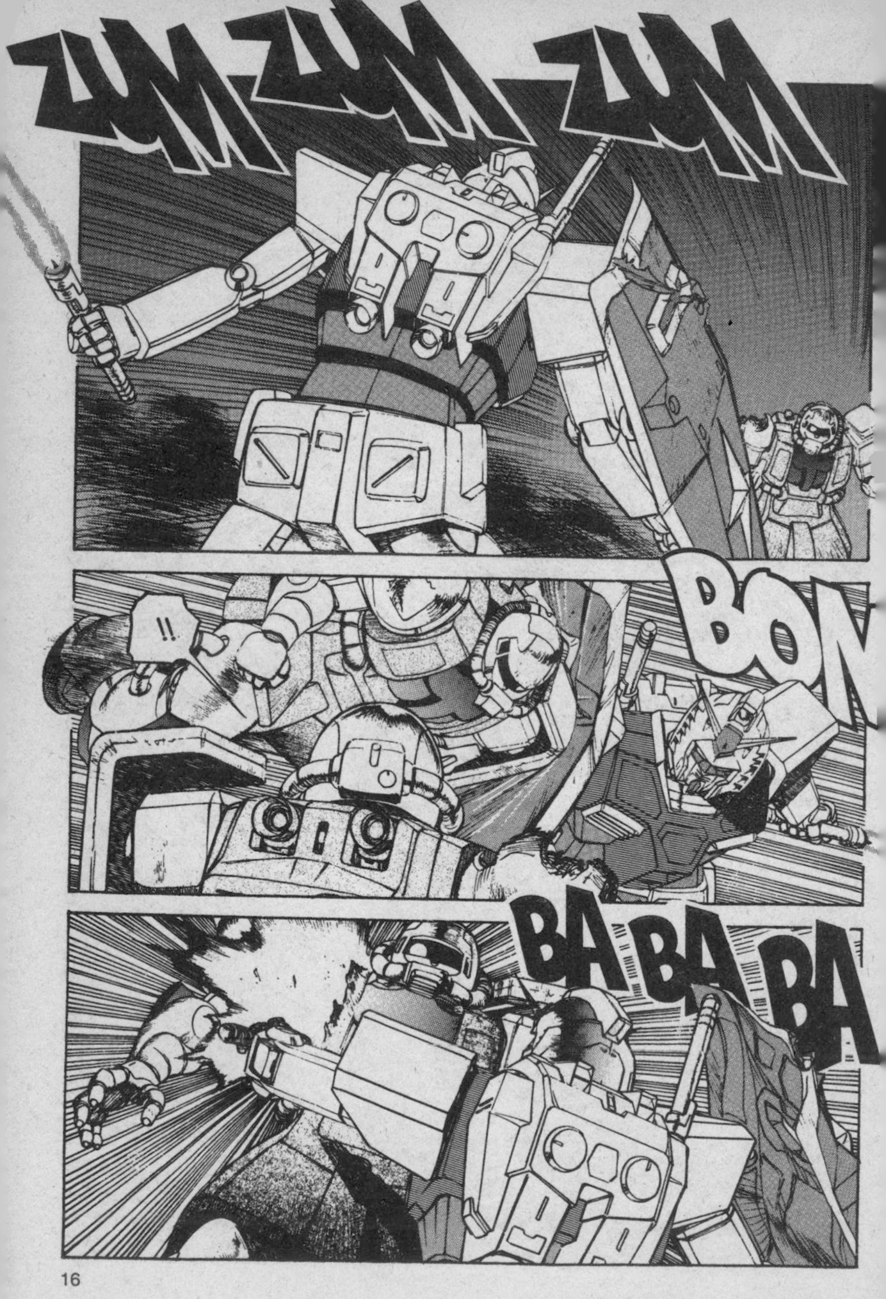
ZUM-ZUM-ZUM
!!
BON
BABABA

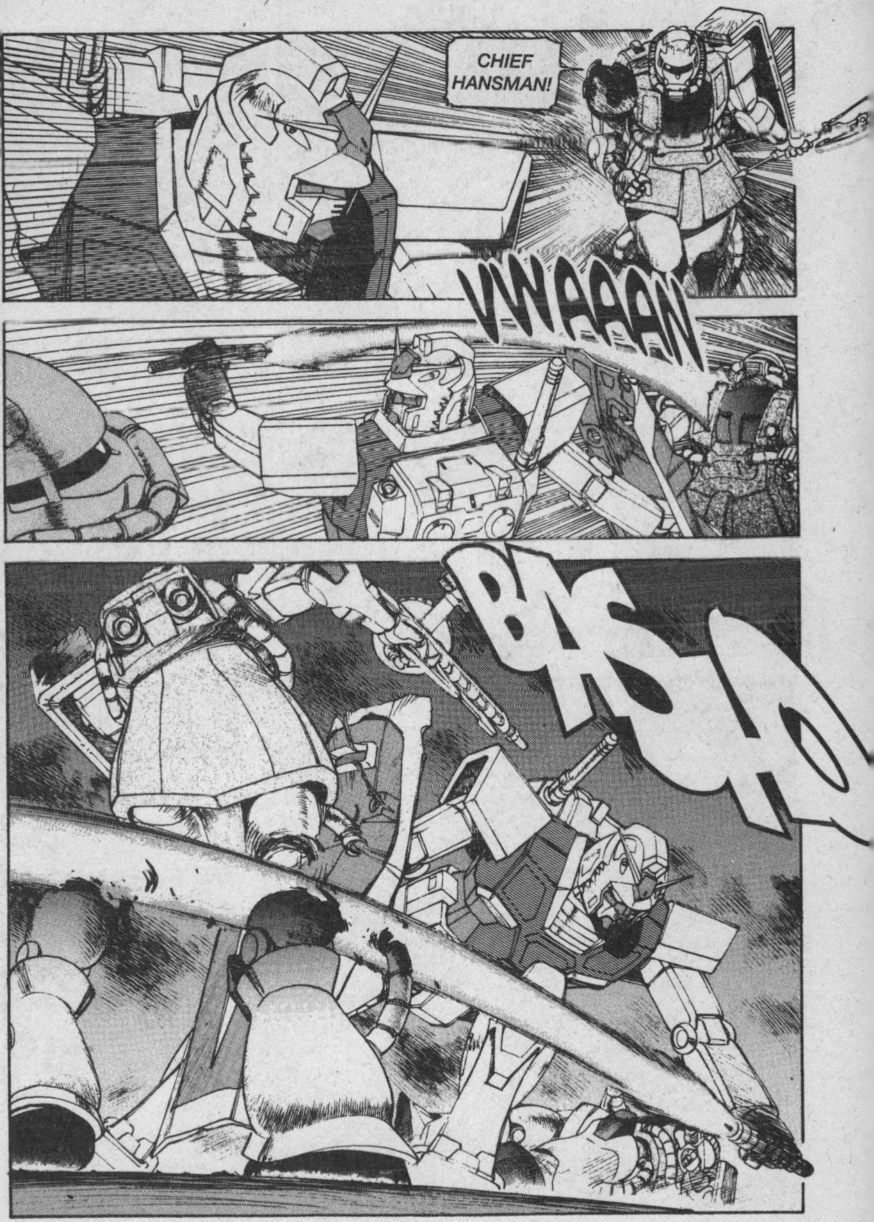
CHIEF HANSMAN!
VWAAAN
BASHA

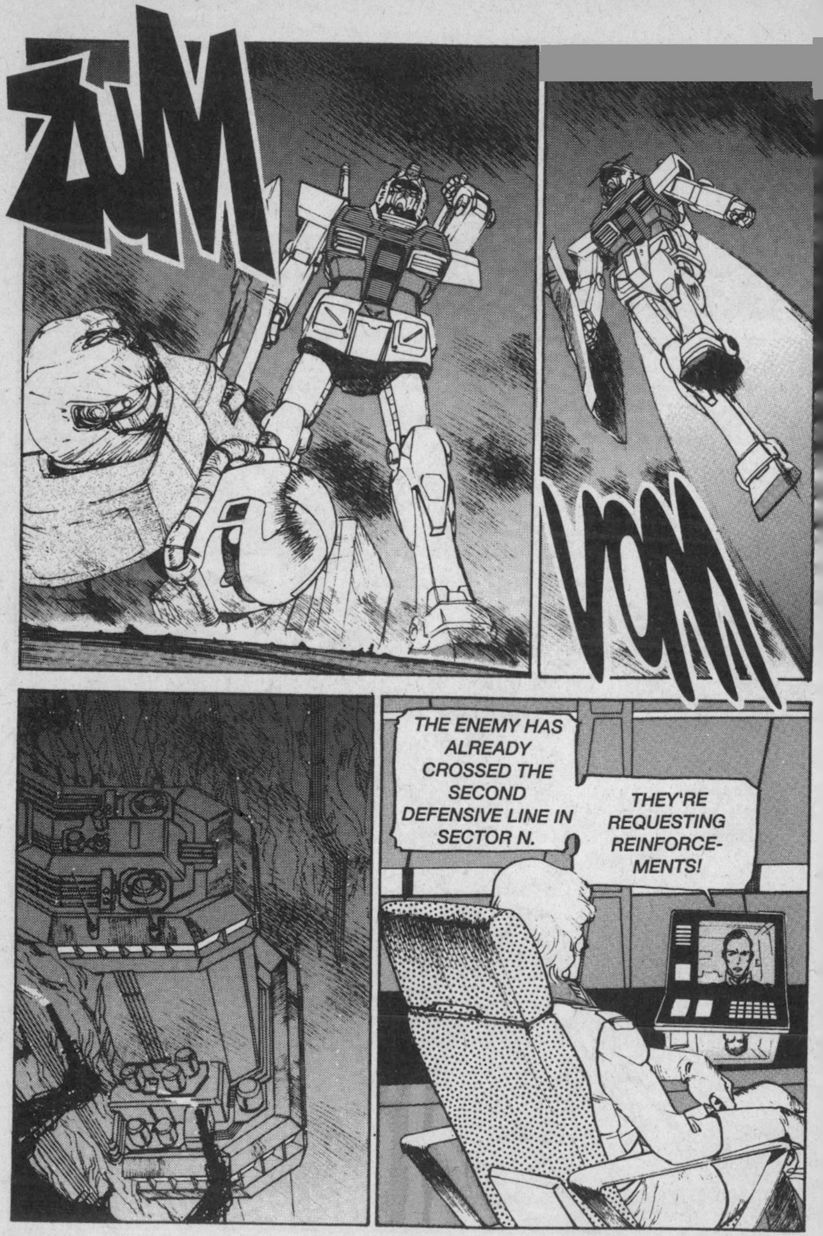
ZUM
VOM
THE ENEMY HAS ALREADY CROSSED THE SECOND DEFENSIVE LINE IN SECTOR N.
THEY'RE REQUESTING REINFORCE-MENTS!

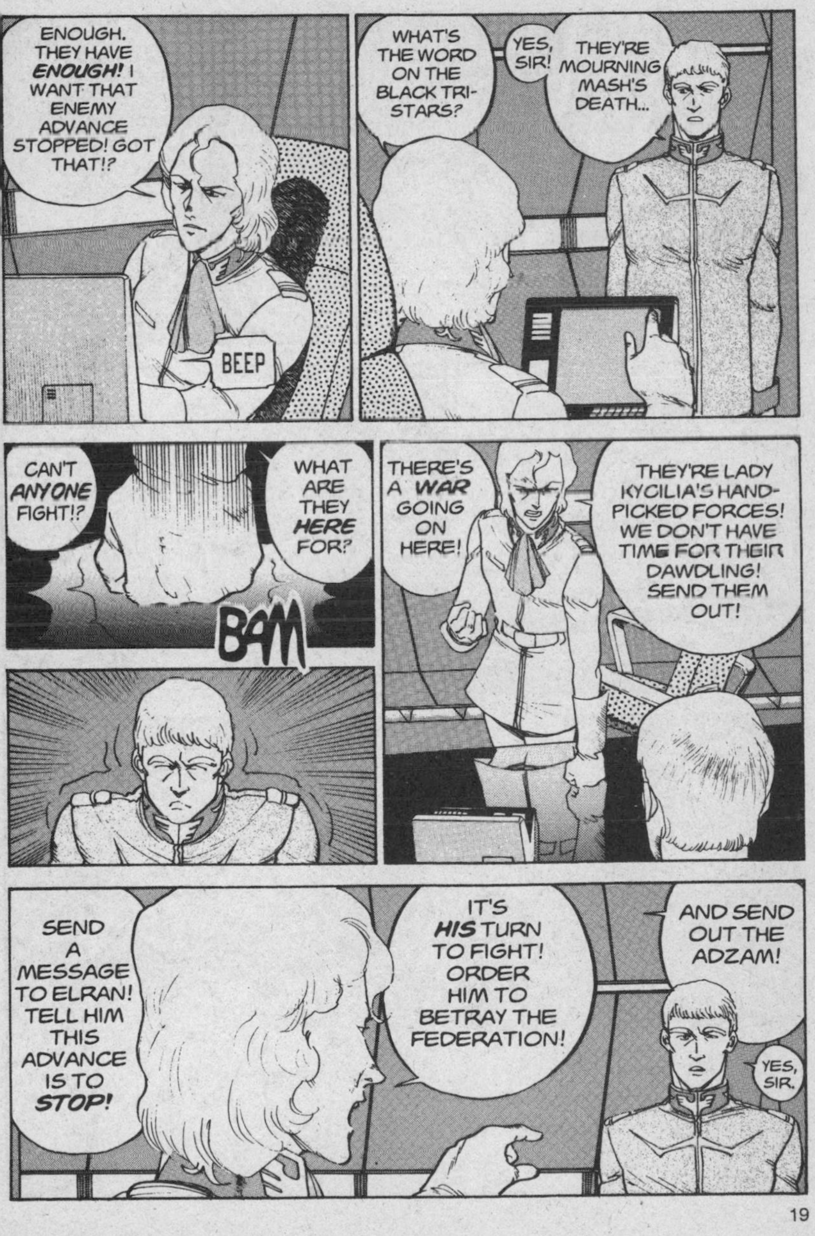
ENOUGH. THEY HAVE ENOUGH! I WANT THAT ENEMY ADVANCE STOPPED! GOT THAT!?
BEEP
WHAT'S THE WORD ON THE BLACK TRI-STARS?
YES, SIR!
THEY'RE MOURNING MASH'S DEATH...
CAN'T ANYONE FIGHT!?
WHAT ARE THEY HERE FOR?
BAM
THERE'S A WAR GOING ON HERE!
THEY'RE LADY KYCILIA'S HAND-PICKED FORCES! WE DON'T HAVE TIME FOR THEIR DAWDLING! SEND THEM OUT!
SEND A MESSAGE TO ELRAN! TELL HIM THIS ADVANCE IS TO STOP!
IT'S HIS TURN TO FIGHT! ORDER HIM TO BETRAY THE FEDERATION!
AND SEND OUT THE ADZAM!
YES, SIR.

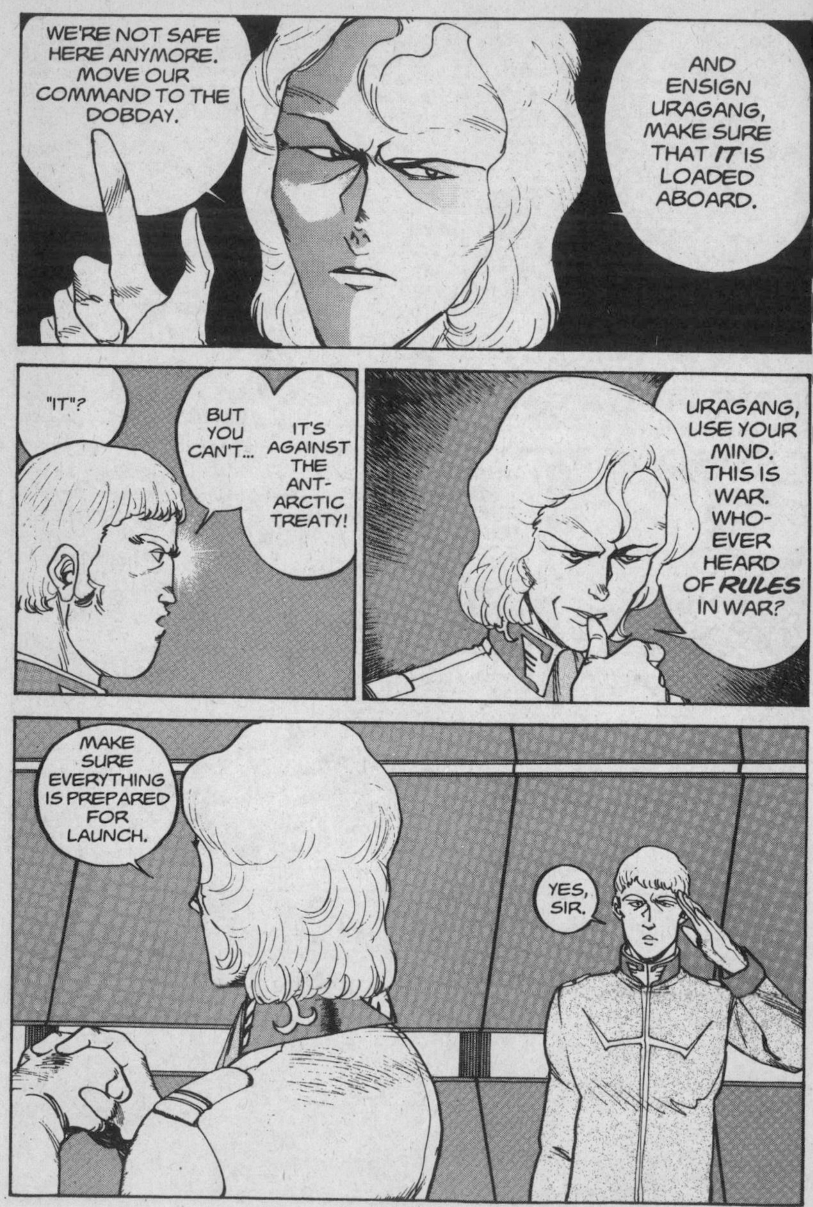
WE'RE NOT SAFE HERE ANYMORE. MOVE OUR COMMAND TO THE DOBDAY.
AND ENSIGN URAGANG, MAKE SURE THAT IT IS LOADED ABOARD.
"IT"?
BUT YOU CAN'T...
IT'S AGAINST THE ANT-ARCTIC TREATY!
URAGANG, USE YOUR MIND. THIS IS WAR. WHO-EVER HEARD OF RULES IN WAR?
MAKE SURE EVERYTHING IS PREPARED FOR LAUNCH.
YES, SIR.

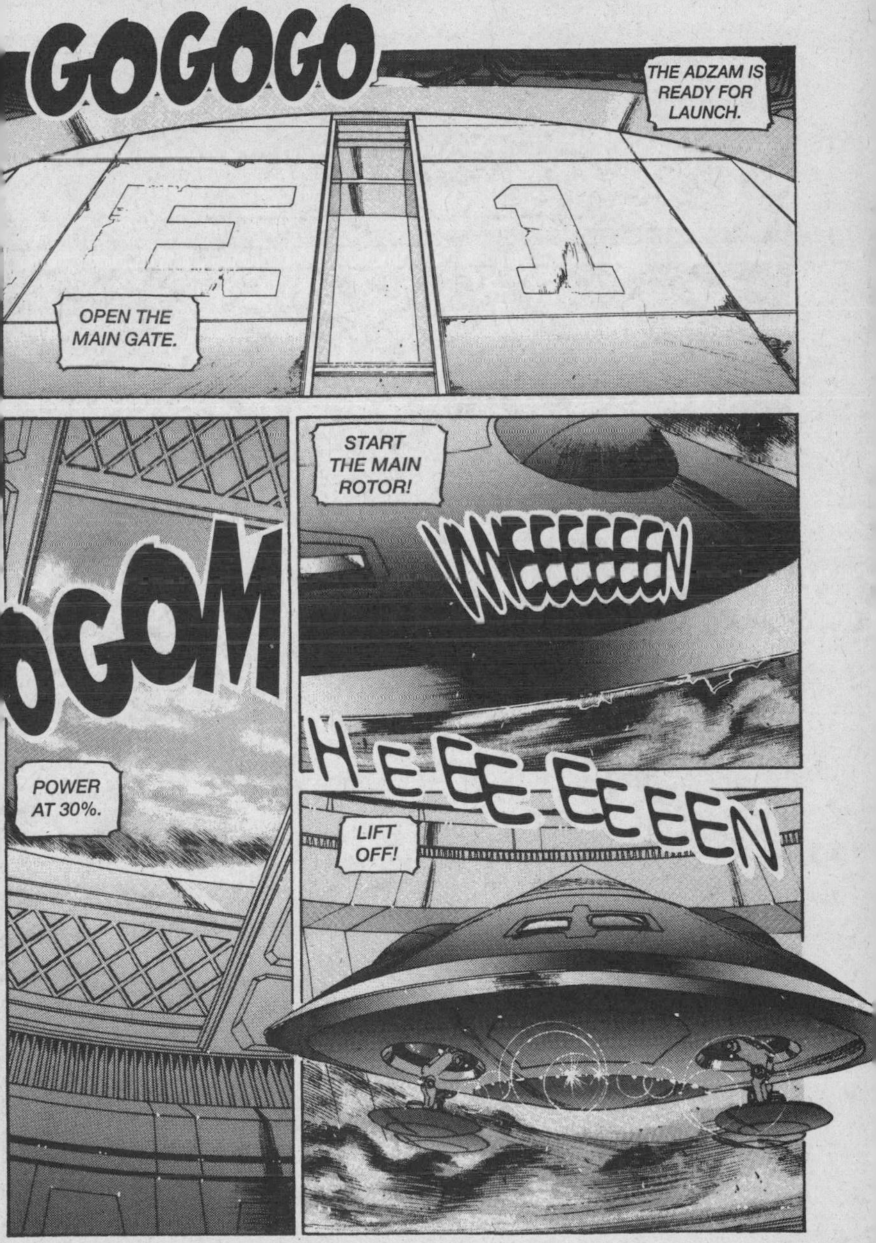
GOGOGO
THE ADZAM IS READY FOR LAUNCH.
OPEN THE MAIN GATE.
GOGOM
POWER AT 30%.
START THE MAIN ROTOR!
WEEEEEEN
HEEEEEEEN
LIFT OFF!

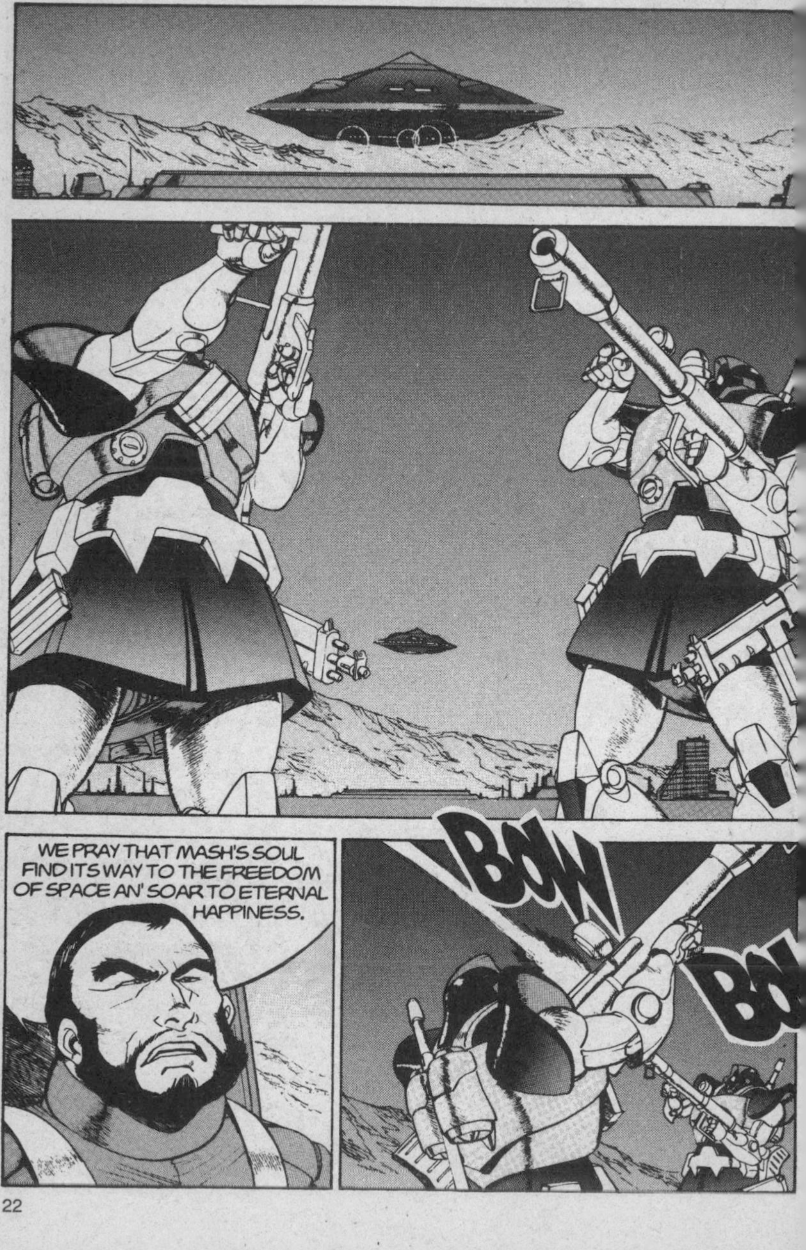
WE PRAY THAT MASH'S SOUL FIND ITS WAY TO THE FREEDOM OF SPACE AN' SOAR TO ETERNAL HAPPINESS.
BOW
BO

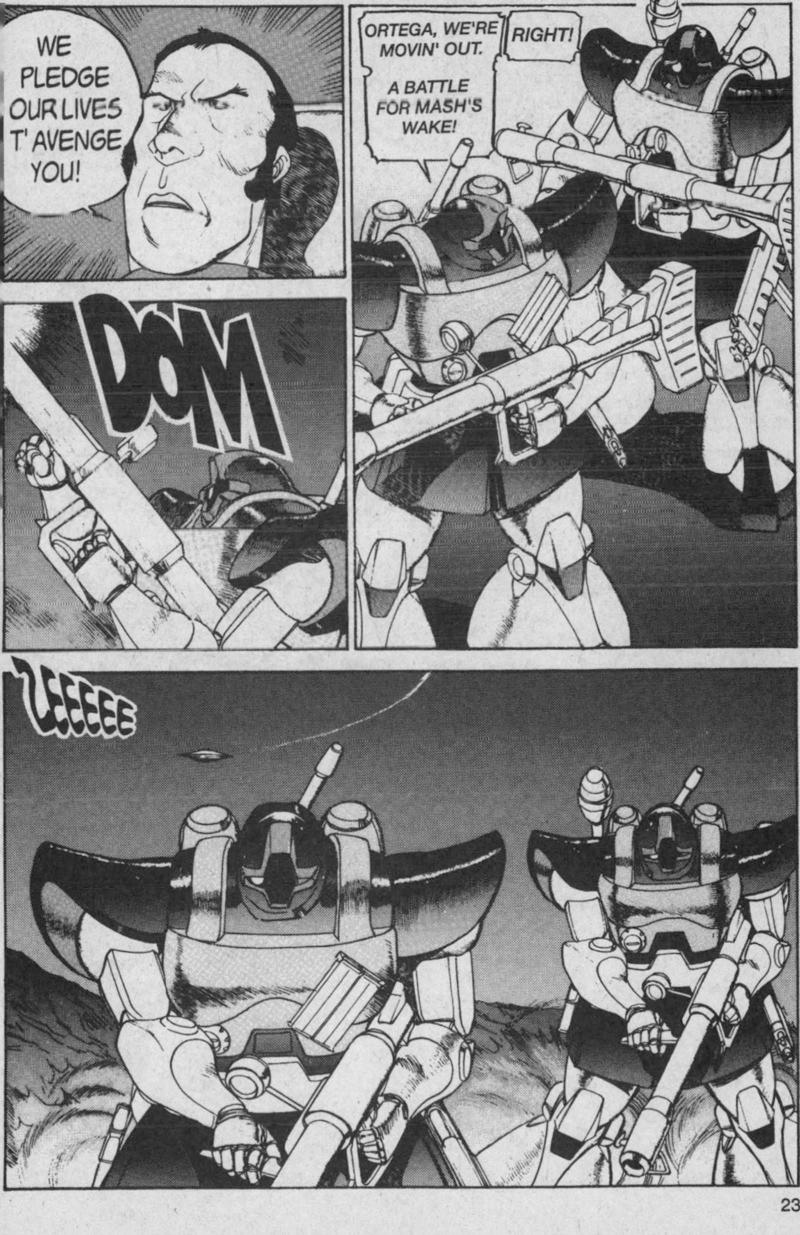
WE PLEDGE OUR LIVES T' AVENGE YOU!
DOM
ORTEGA, WE'RE MOVIN' OUT.
A BATTLE FOR MASH'S WAKE!
RIGHT!
ZEEEEEE

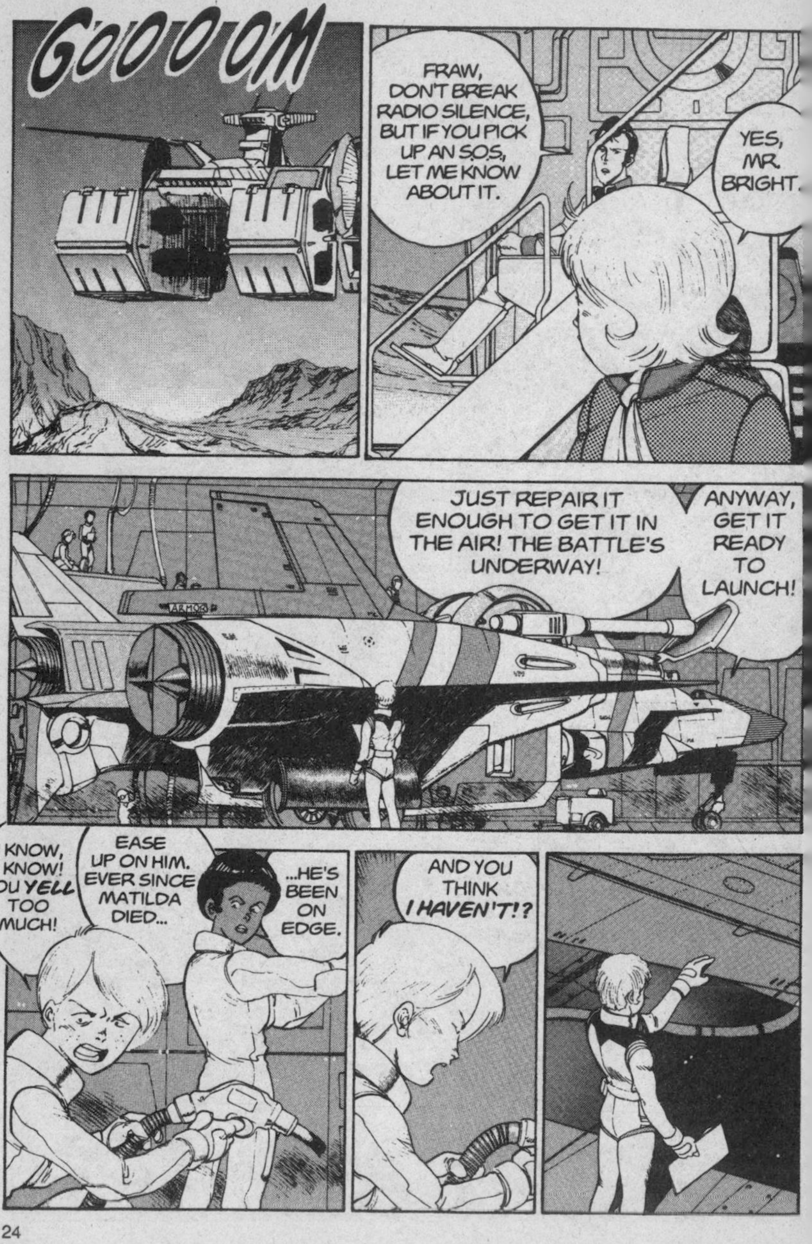
GOOOOM
FRAW, DON'T BREAK RADIO SILENCE, BUT IF YOU PICK UP AN S.O.S., LET ME KNOW ABOUT IT.
YES, MR. BRIGHT.
JUST REPAIR IT ENOUGH TO GET IT IN THE AIR! THE BATTLE'S UNDERWAY!
ANYWAY, GET IT READY TO LAUNCH!
I KNOW, I KNOW! YOU YELL TOO MUCH!
EASE UP ON HIM. EVER SINCE MATILDA DIED...
...HE'S BEEN ON EDGE.
AND YOU THINK I HAVEN'T!?

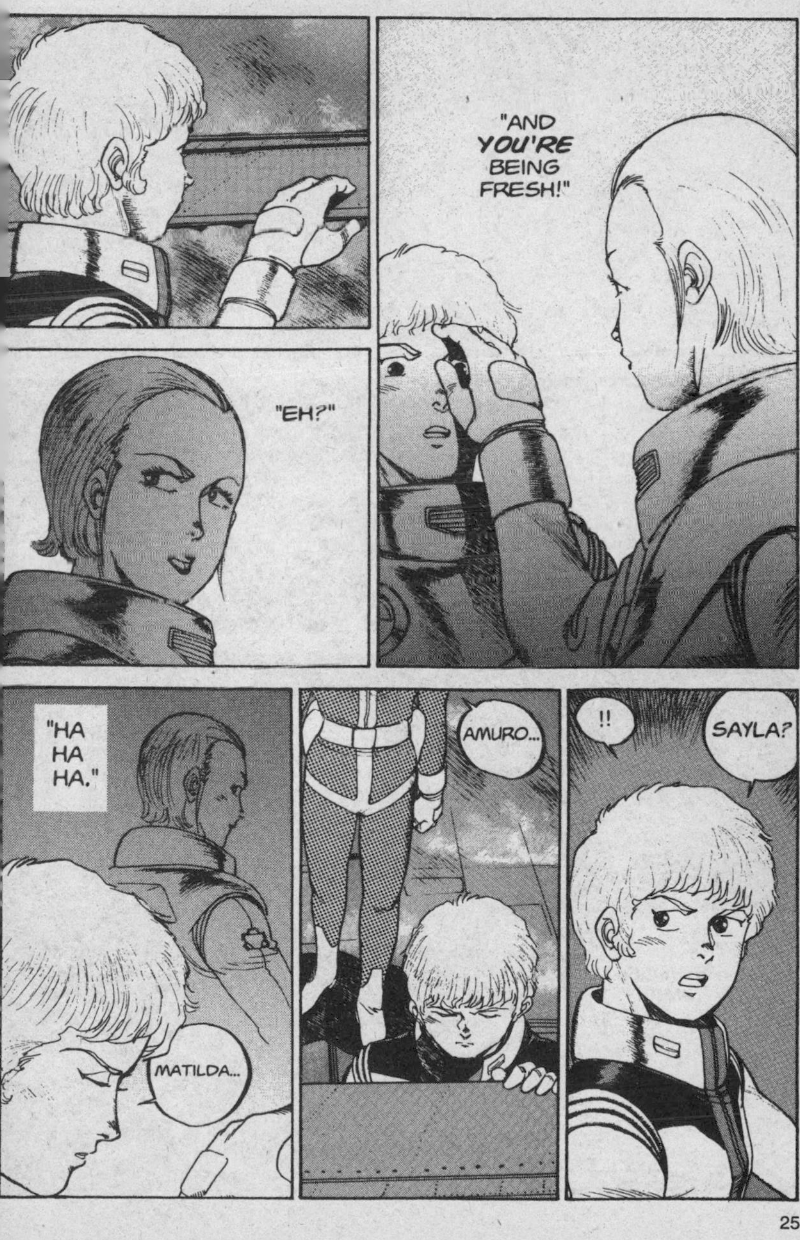
"AND YOU'RE BEING FRESH!"
"EH?"
"HA HA HA."
MATILDA...
AMURO...
!!
SAYLA?

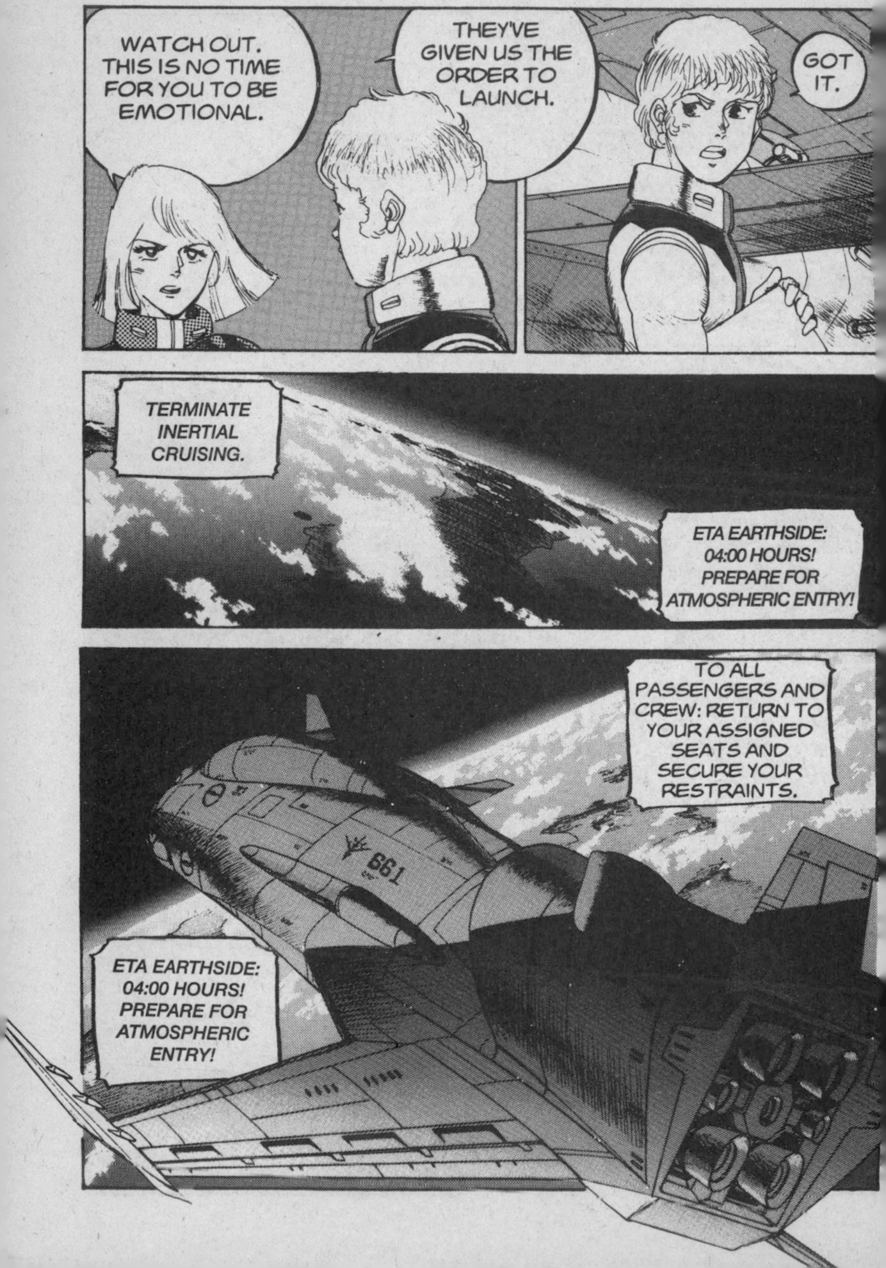
WATCH OUT. THIS IS NO TIME FOR YOU TO BE EMOTIONAL.
THEY'VE GIVEN US THE ORDER TO LAUNCH.
GOT IT.
TERMINATE INERTIAL CRUISING.
ETA EARTHSIDE: 04:00 HOURS! PREPARE FOR ATMOSPHERIC ENTRY!
TO ALL PASSENGERS AND CREW: RETURN TO YOUR ASSIGNED SEATS AND SECURE YOUR RESTRAINTS.
ETA EARTHSIDE: 04:00 HOURS! PREPARE FOR ATMOSPHERIC ENTRY!

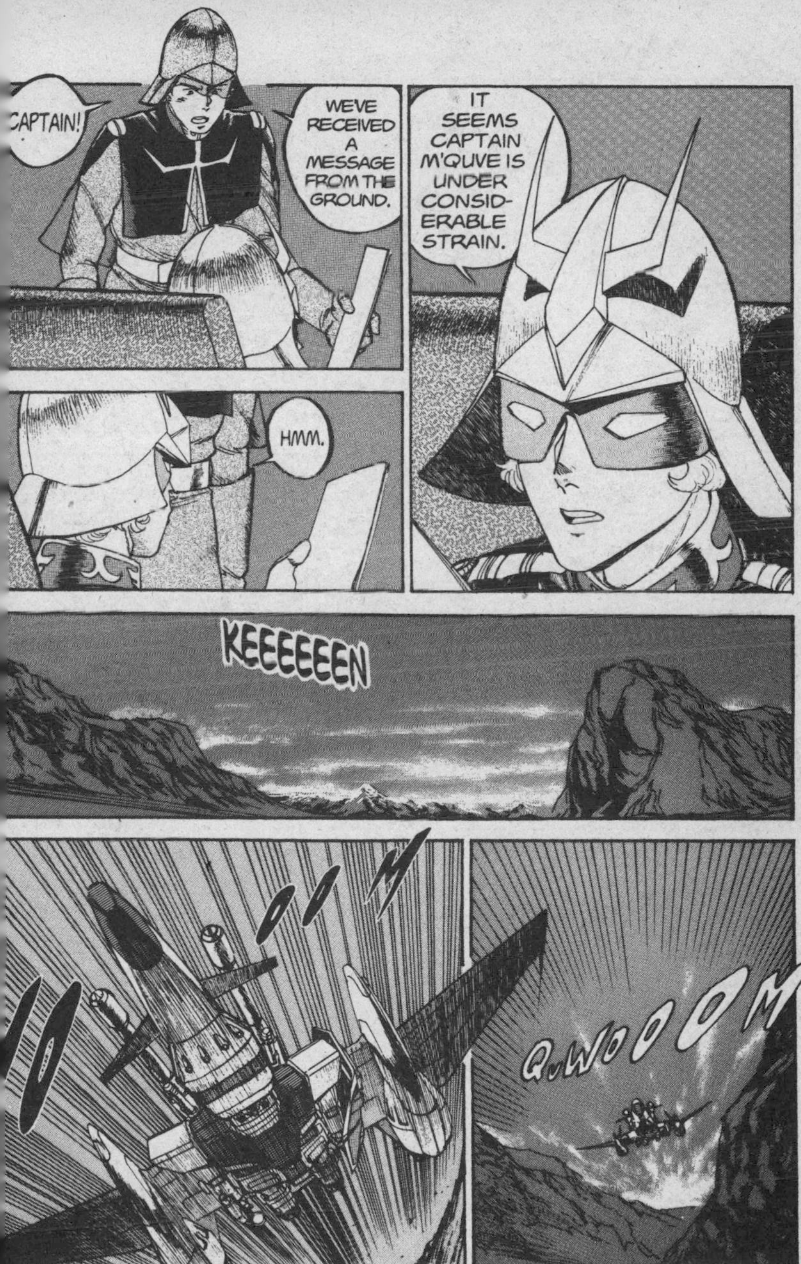
CAPTAIN!
WE'VE RECEIVED A MESSAGE FROM THE GROUND.
IT SEEMS CAPTAIN M'QUVE IS UNDER CONSIDERABLE STRAIN.
HMM.
KEEEEEEN
OOOM
QWOOOOM

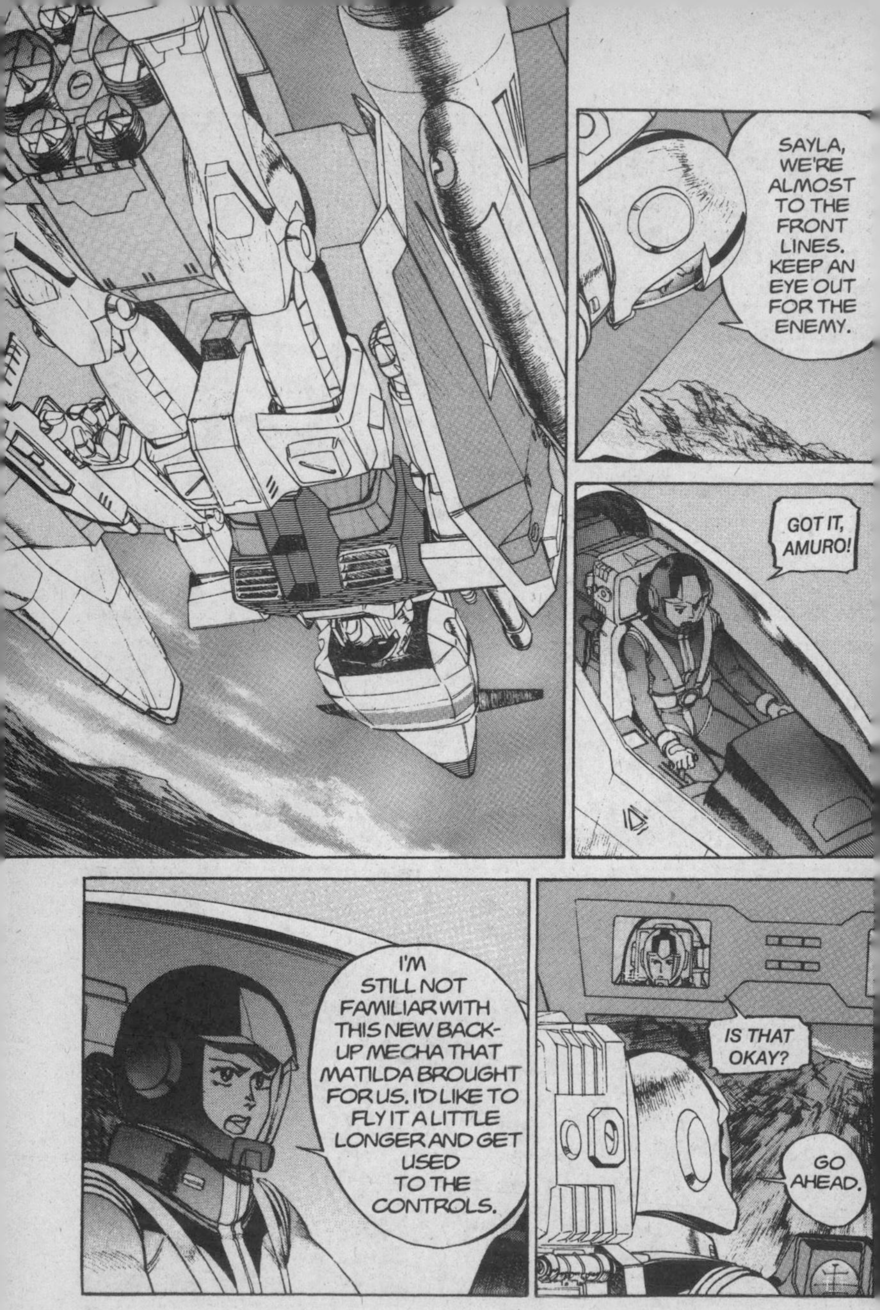
SAYLA, WE'RE ALMOST TO THE FRONT LINES. KEEP AN EYE OUT FOR THE ENEMY.
GOT IT, AMURO!
I'M STILL NOT FAMILIAR WITH THIS NEW BACK-UP MECHA THAT MATILDA BROUGHT FOR US. I'D LIKE TO FLY IT A LITTLE LONGER AND GET USED TO THE CONTROLS.
IS THAT OKAY?
GO AHEAD.

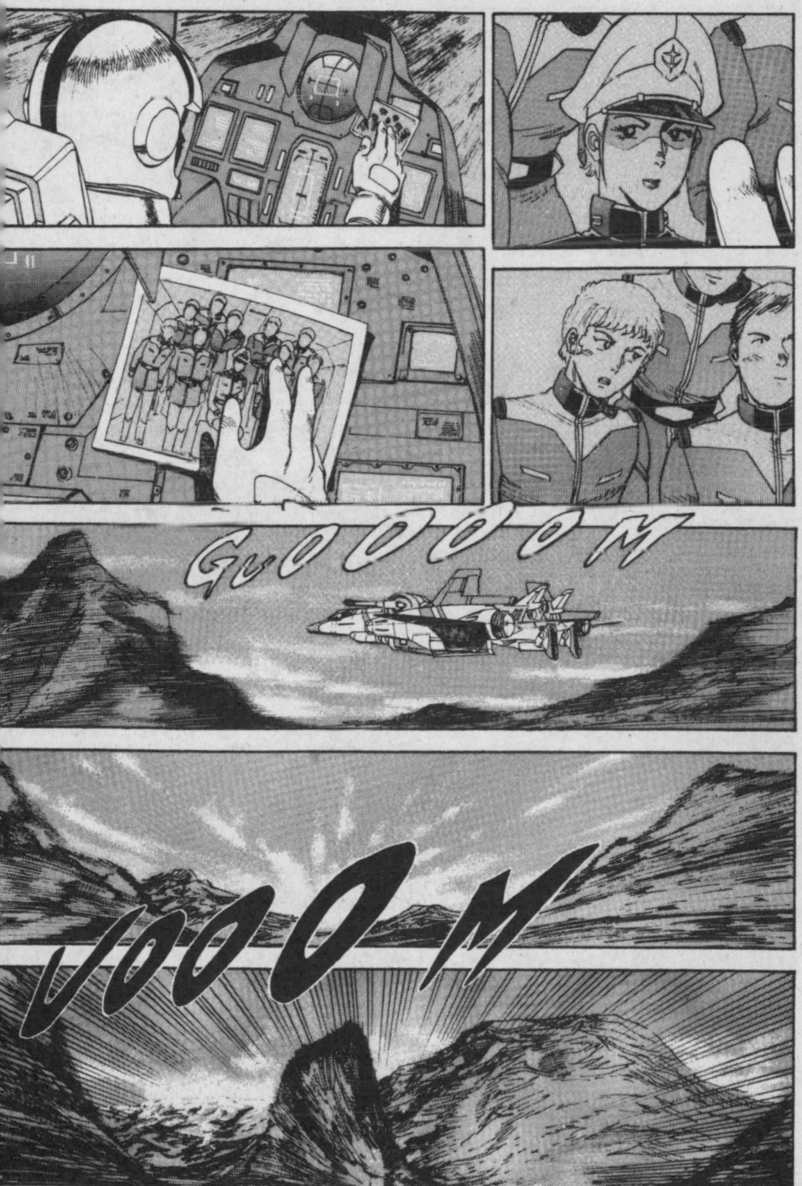
GUOOOOM
JOOOM

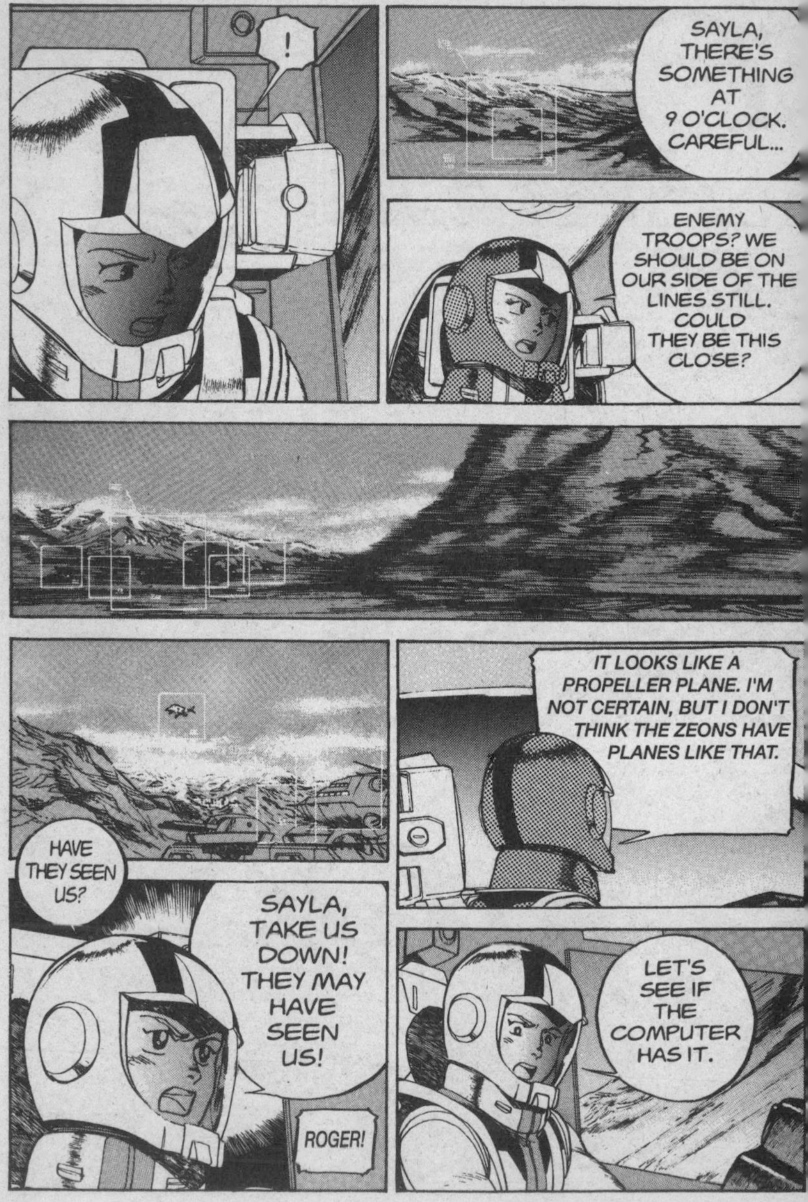
!
SAYLA, THERE'S SOMETHING AT 9 O'CLOCK. CAREFUL...
ENEMY TROOPS? WE SHOULD BE ON OUR SIDE OF THE LINES STILL. COULD THEY BE THIS CLOSE?
HAVE THEY SEEN US?
IT LOOKS LIKE A PROPELLER PLANE. I'M NOT CERTAIN, BUT I DON'T THINK THE ZEONS HAVE PLANES LIKE THAT.
SAYLA, TAKE US DOWN! THEY MAY HAVE SEEN US!
ROGER!
LET'S SEE IF THE COMPUTER HAS IT.

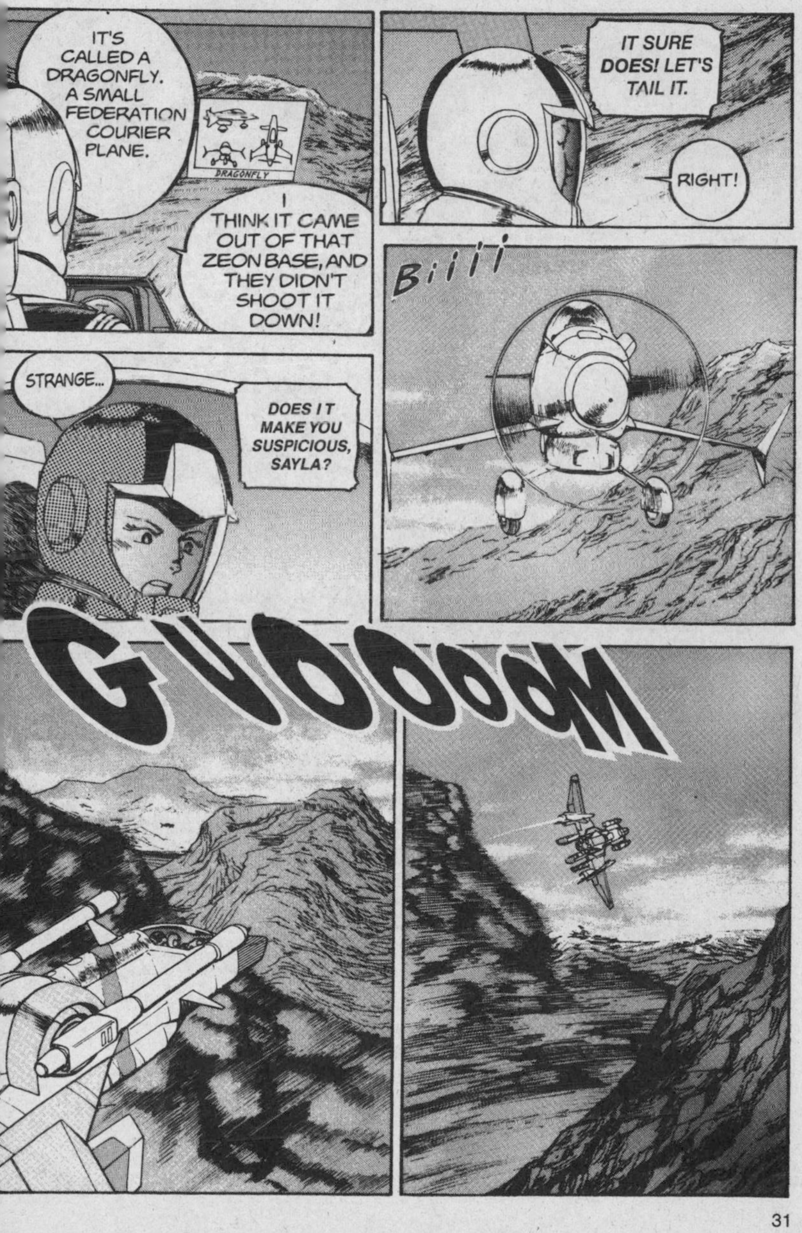
IT'S CALLED A DRAGONFLY. A SMALL FEDERATION COURIER PLANE.
DRAGONFLY
I THINK IT CAME OUT OF THAT ZEON BASE, AND THEY DIDN'T SHOOT IT DOWN!
IT SURE DOES! LET'S TAIL IT.
RIGHT!
STRANGE...
DOES IT MAKE YOU SUSPICIOUS, SAYLA?
Biiii
GVOOOOM

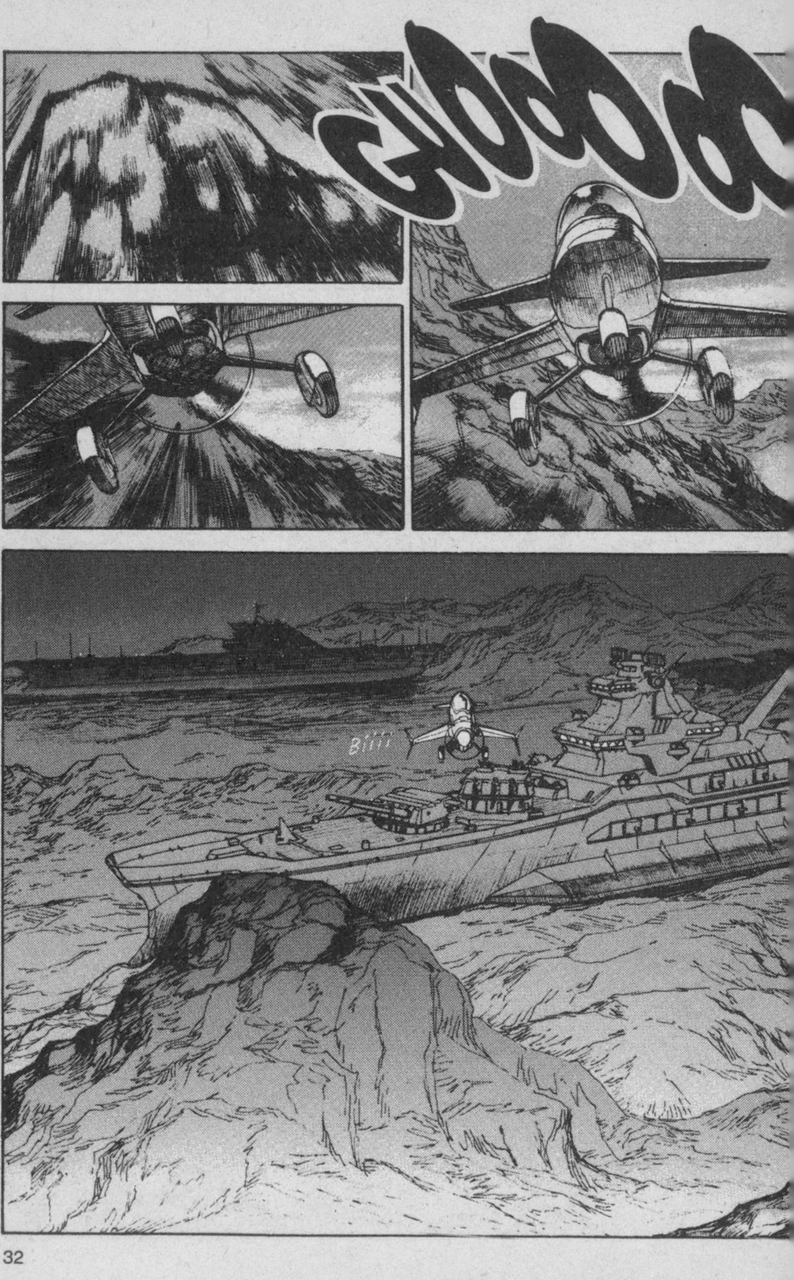
GYOOOO
Biiii

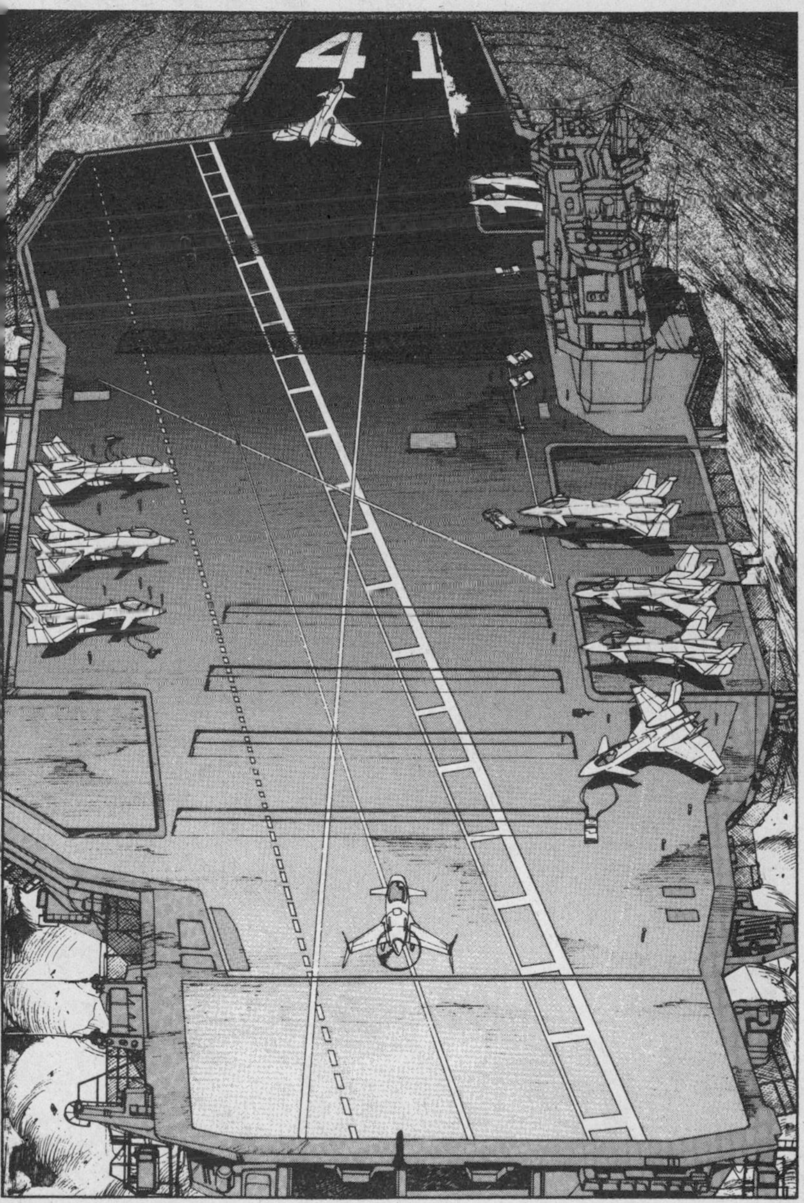
41

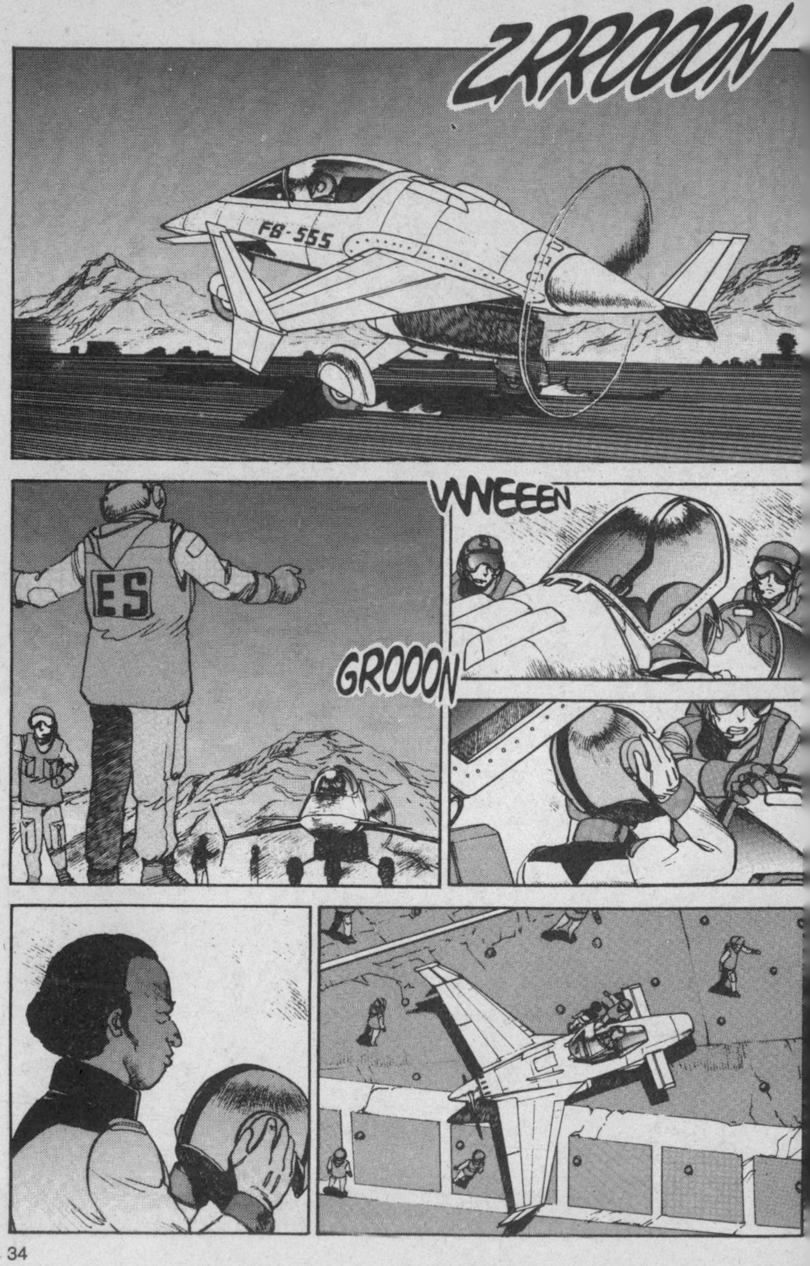
ZRROOON
FB-555
ES
VWEEEN
GROOON

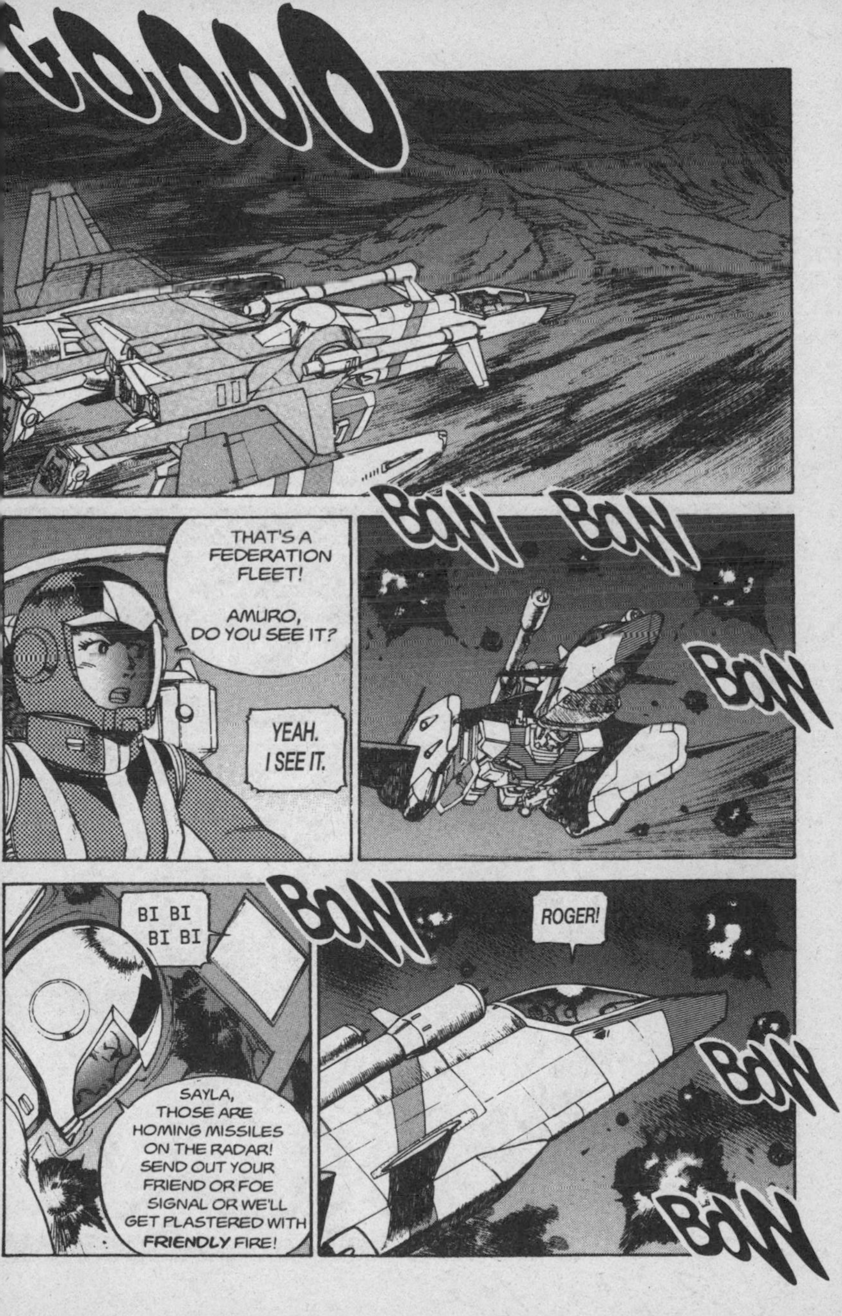
GOOOO
BOW BOW
THAT'S A FEDERATION FLEET!
AMURO, DO YOU SEE IT?
YEAH. I SEE IT.
BOW
BI BI BI BI
SAYLA, THOSE ARE HOMING MISSILES ON THE RADAR! SEND OUT YOUR FRIEND OR FOE SIGNAL OR WE'LL GET PLASTERED WITH FRIENDLY FIRE!
BOW
ROGER!
BOW
BOW

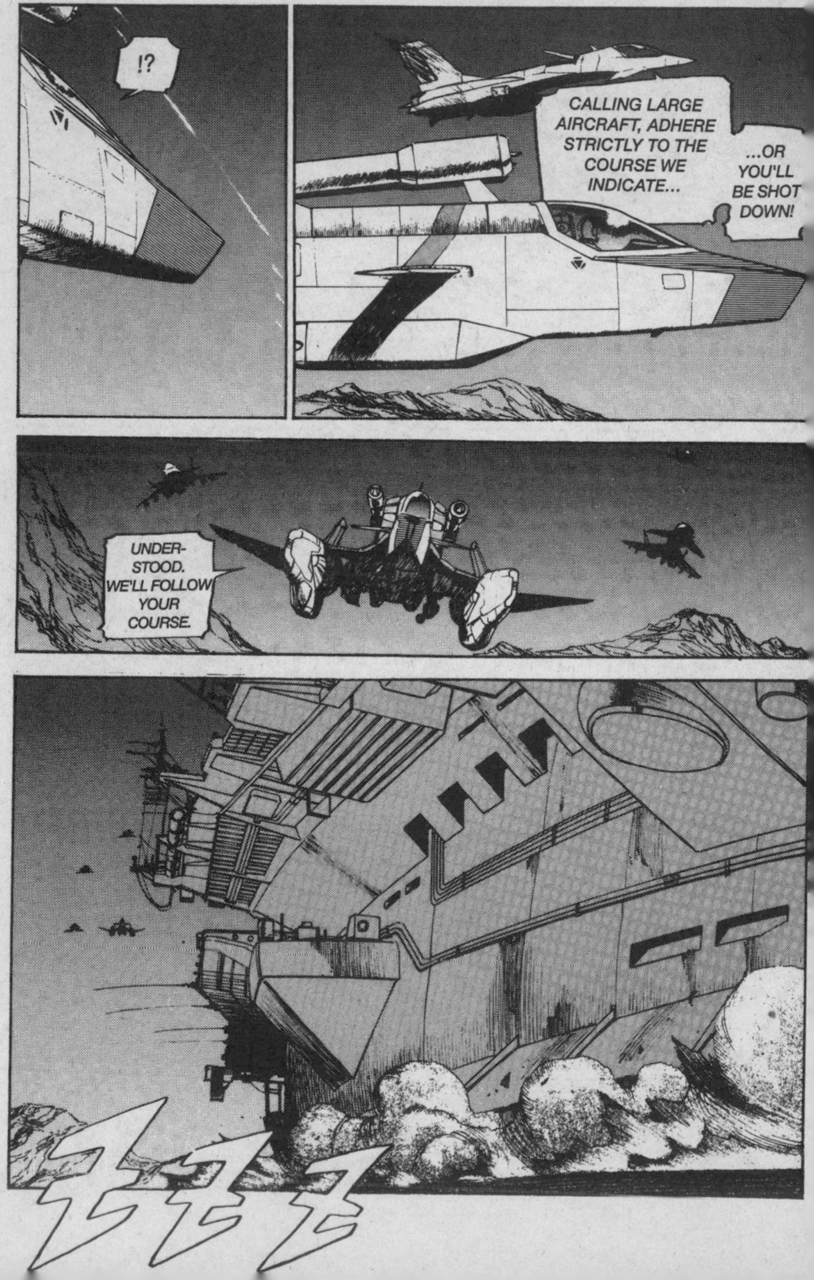
!?
CALLING LARGE AIRCRAFT, ADHERE STRICTLY TO THE COURSE WE INDICATE...
...OR YOU'LL BE SHOT DOWN!
UNDER-STOOD. WE'LL FOLLOW YOUR COURSE.

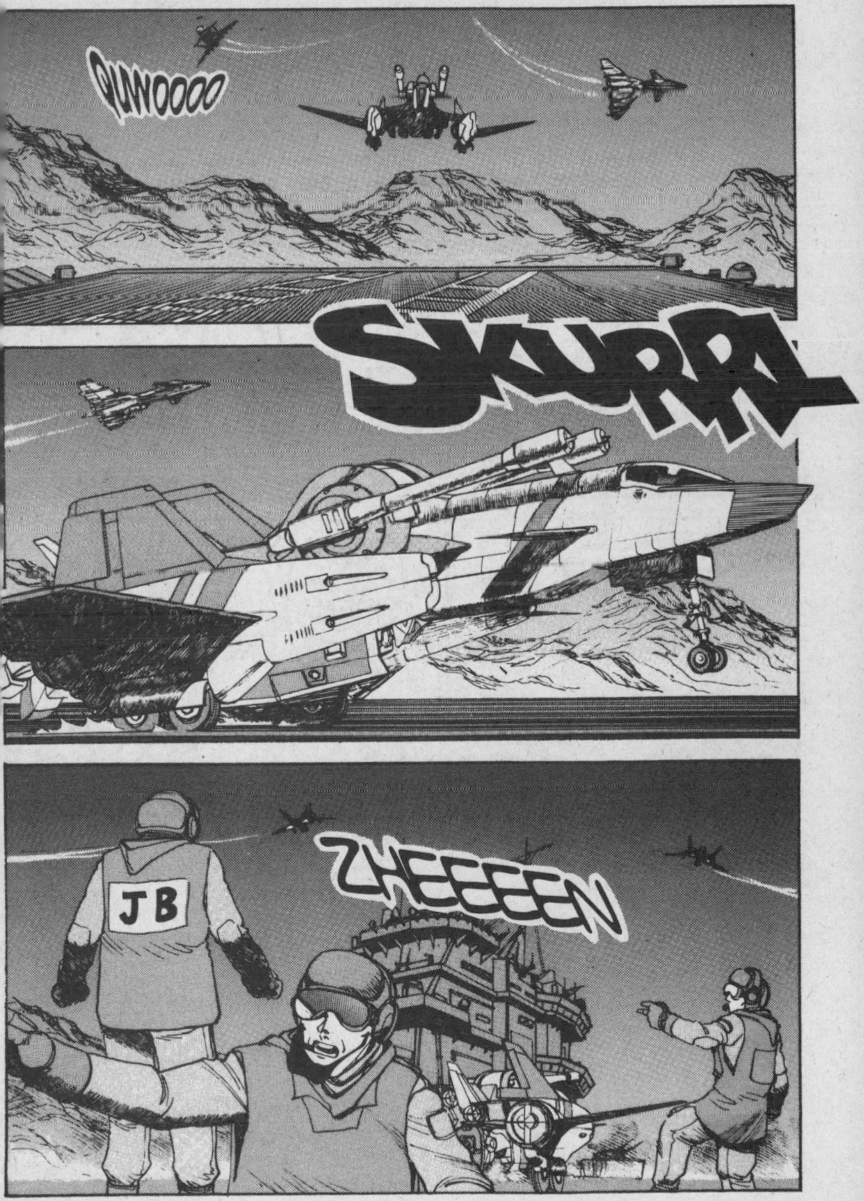
GUWOOOO
SKURR
JB
ZHEEEEEN

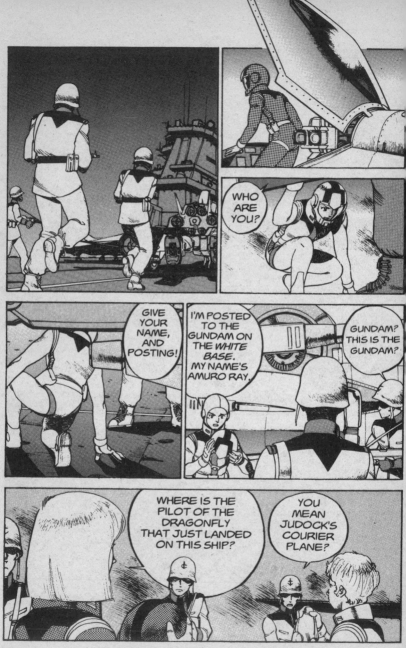

WHO ARE YOU?

GIVE YOUR NAME, AND POSTING!

I'M POSTED TO THE GUNDAM ON THE *WHITE BASE*. MY NAME'S AMURO RAY.

GUNDAM? THIS IS THE GUNDAM?

WHERE IS THE PILOT OF THE DRAGONFLY THAT JUST LANDED ON THIS SHIP?

YOU MEAN JUDOCK'S COURIER PLANE?

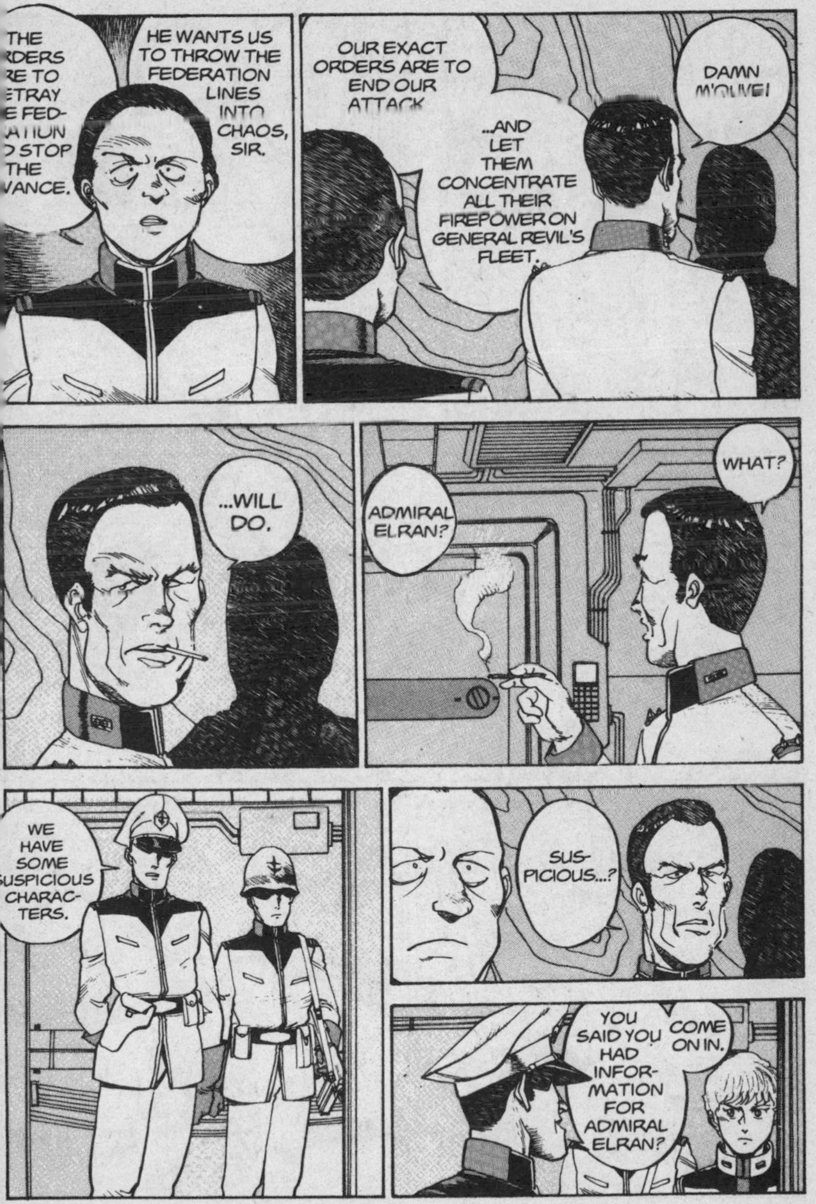

THE RDERS RE TO ETRAY E FED- ATION D STOP THE VANCE.
HE WANTS US TO THROW THE FEDERATION LINES INTO CHAOS, SIR.
OUR EXACT ORDERS ARE TO END OUR ATTACK
...AND LET THEM CONCENTRATE ALL THEIR FIREPOWER ON GENERAL REVIL'S FLEET.
DAMN M'QUVE!
...WILL DO.
ADMIRAL ELRAN?
WHAT?
WE HAVE SOME SUSPICIOUS CHARAC-TERS.
SUS-PICIOUS...?
YOU SAID YOU HAD INFOR-MATION FOR ADMIRAL ELRAN?
COME ON IN.

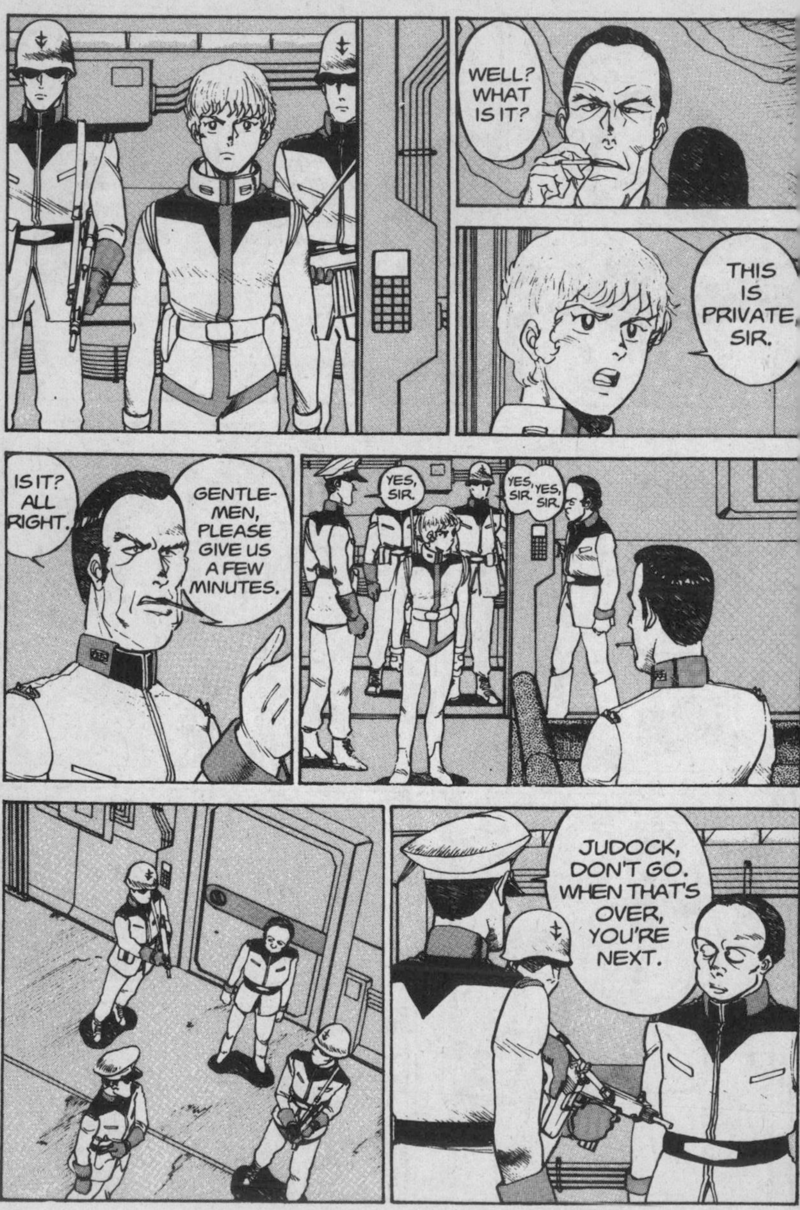
WELL? WHAT IS IT?
THIS IS PRIVATE, SIR.
IS IT? ALL RIGHT.
GENTLEMEN, PLEASE GIVE US A FEW MINUTES.
YES, SIR.
YES, SIR.
YES, SIR.
JUDOCK, DON'T GO. WHEN THAT'S OVER, YOU'RE NEXT.

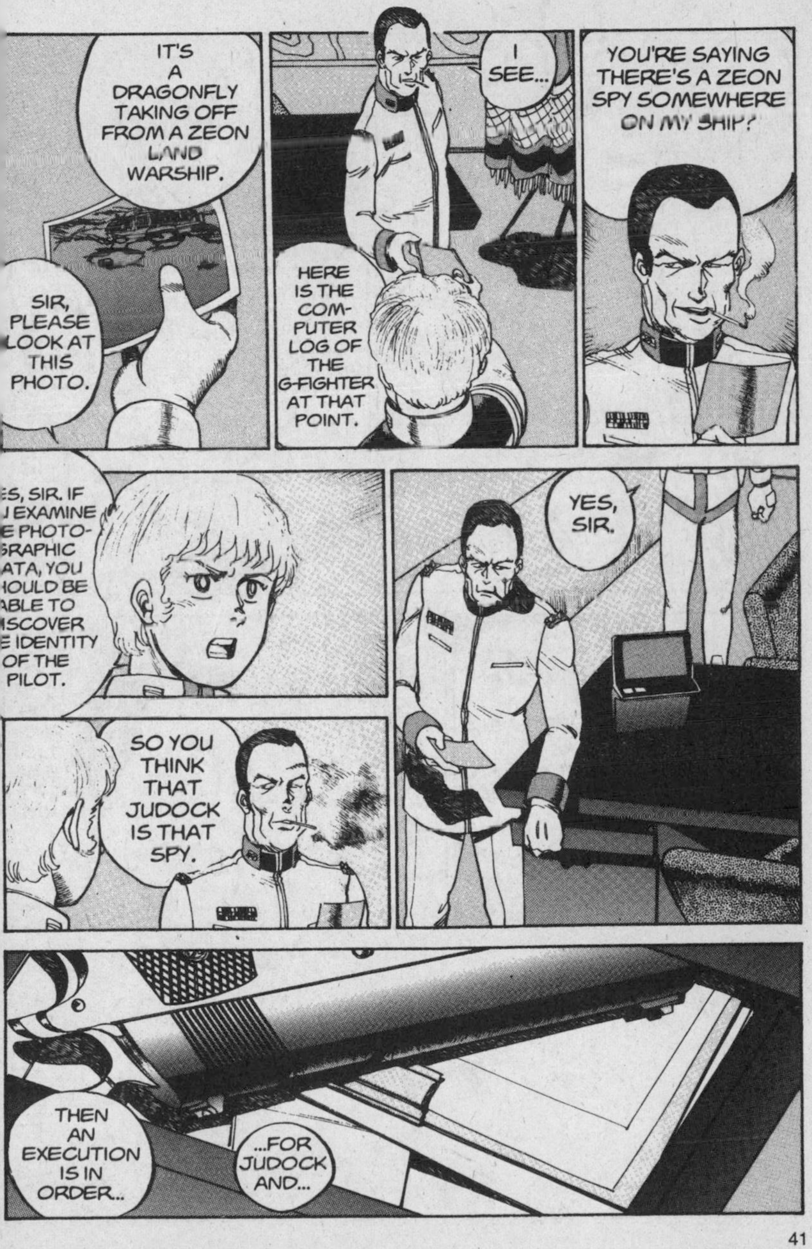
IT'S A DRAGONFLY TAKING OFF FROM A ZEON LAND WARSHIP.
SIR, PLEASE LOOK AT THIS PHOTO.
I SEE...
HERE IS THE COM-PUTER LOG OF THE G-FIGHTER AT THAT POINT.
YOU'RE SAYING THERE'S A ZEON SPY SOMEWHERE ON MY SHIP?
ES, SIR. IF U EXAMINE E PHOTO-GRAPHIC ATA, YOU HOULD BE ABLE TO ISCOVER E IDENTITY OF THE PILOT.
SO YOU THINK THAT JUDOCK IS THAT SPY.
YES, SIR.
THEN AN EXECUTION IS IN ORDER..
...FOR JUDOCK AND...

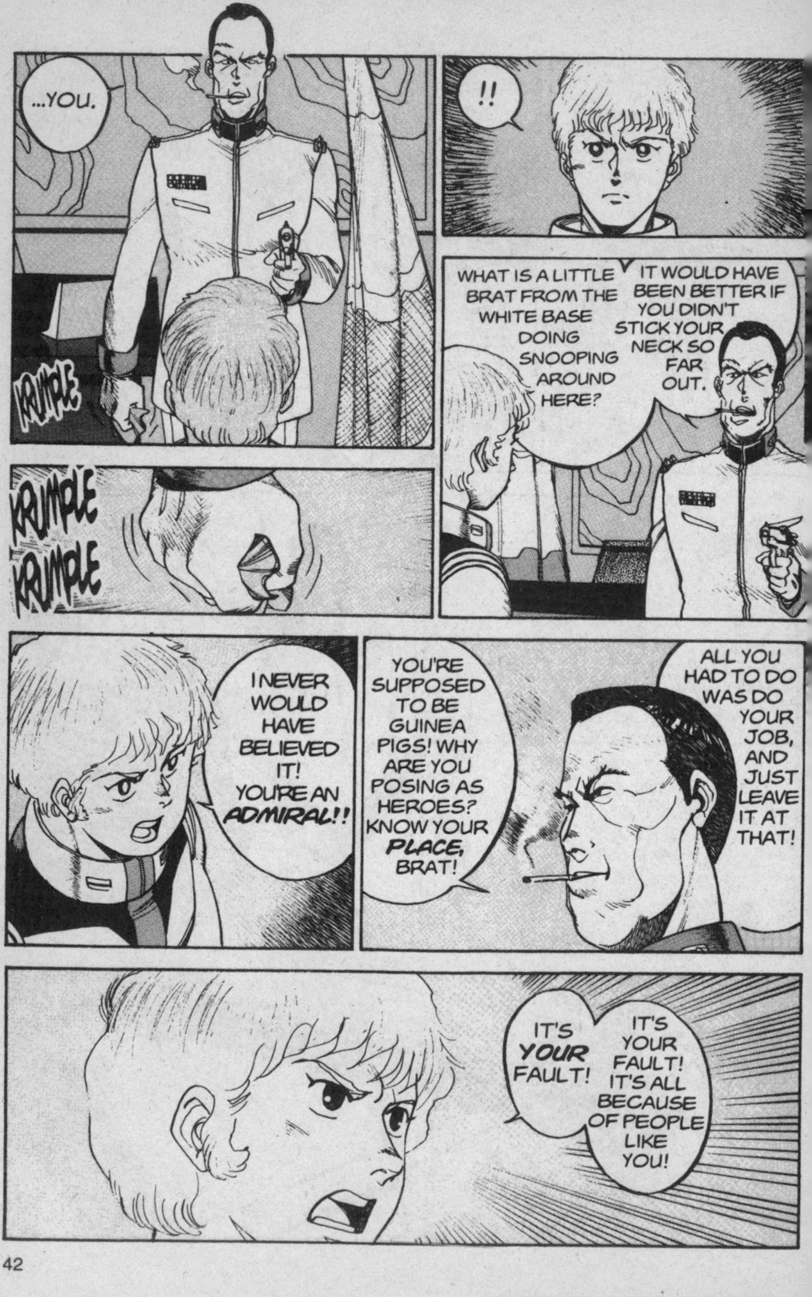
...YOU.
KRUMPLE
!!
KRUMPLE KRUMPLE
WHAT IS A LITTLE BRAT FROM THE WHITE BASE DOING SNOOPING AROUND HERE?
IT WOULD HAVE BEEN BETTER IF YOU DIDN'T STICK YOUR NECK SO FAR OUT.
I NEVER WOULD HAVE BELIEVED IT! YOU'RE AN ADMIRAL!!
YOU'RE SUPPOSED TO BE GUINEA PIGS! WHY ARE YOU POSING AS HEROES? KNOW YOUR PLACE, BRAT!
ALL YOU HAD TO DO WAS DO YOUR JOB, AND JUST LEAVE IT AT THAT!
IT'S YOUR FAULT!
IT'S YOUR FAULT! IT'S ALL BECAUSE OF PEOPLE LIKE YOU!

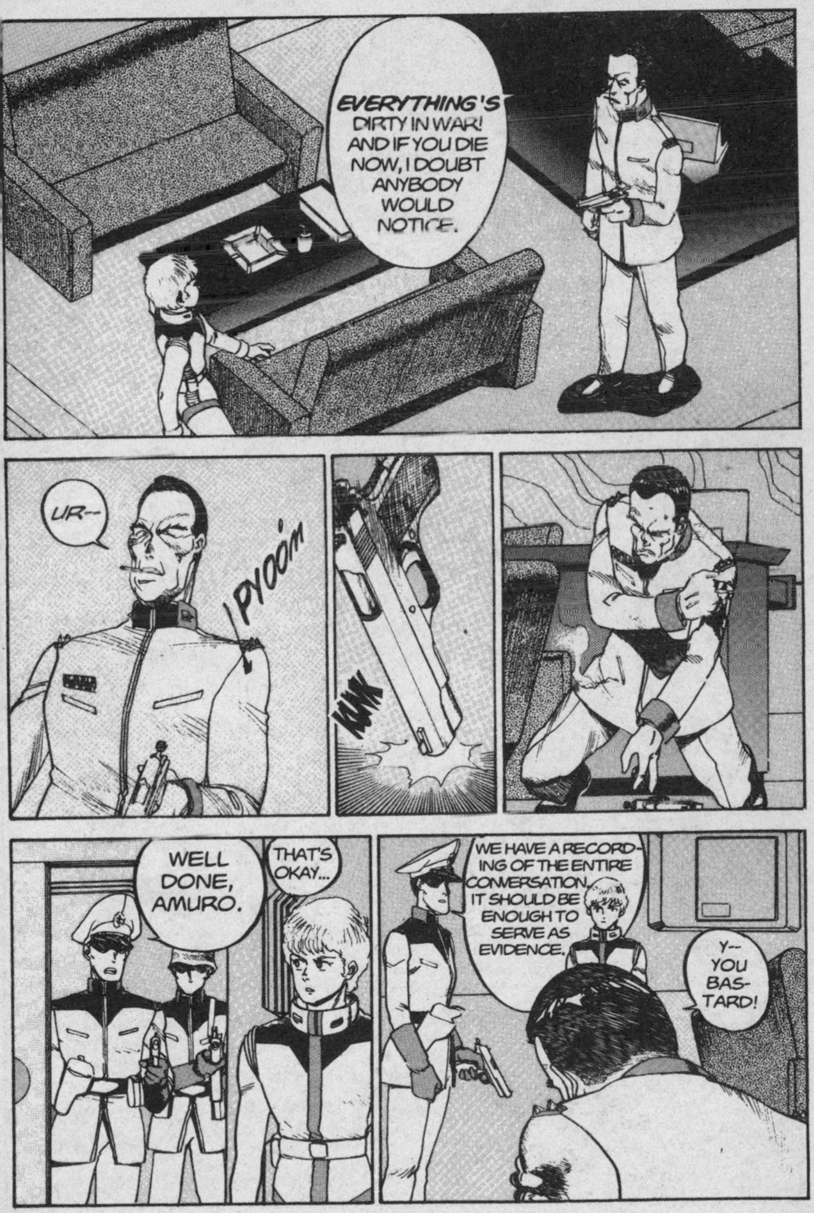
EVERYTHING'S DIRTY IN WAR! AND IF YOU DIE NOW, I DOUBT ANYBODY WOULD NOTICE.
UR--
PYOOM
KLINK
WELL DONE, AMURO.
THAT'S OKAY...
WE HAVE A RECORDING OF THE ENTIRE CONVERSATION. IT SHOULD BE ENOUGH TO SERVE AS EVIDENCE.
Y-- YOU BASTARD!

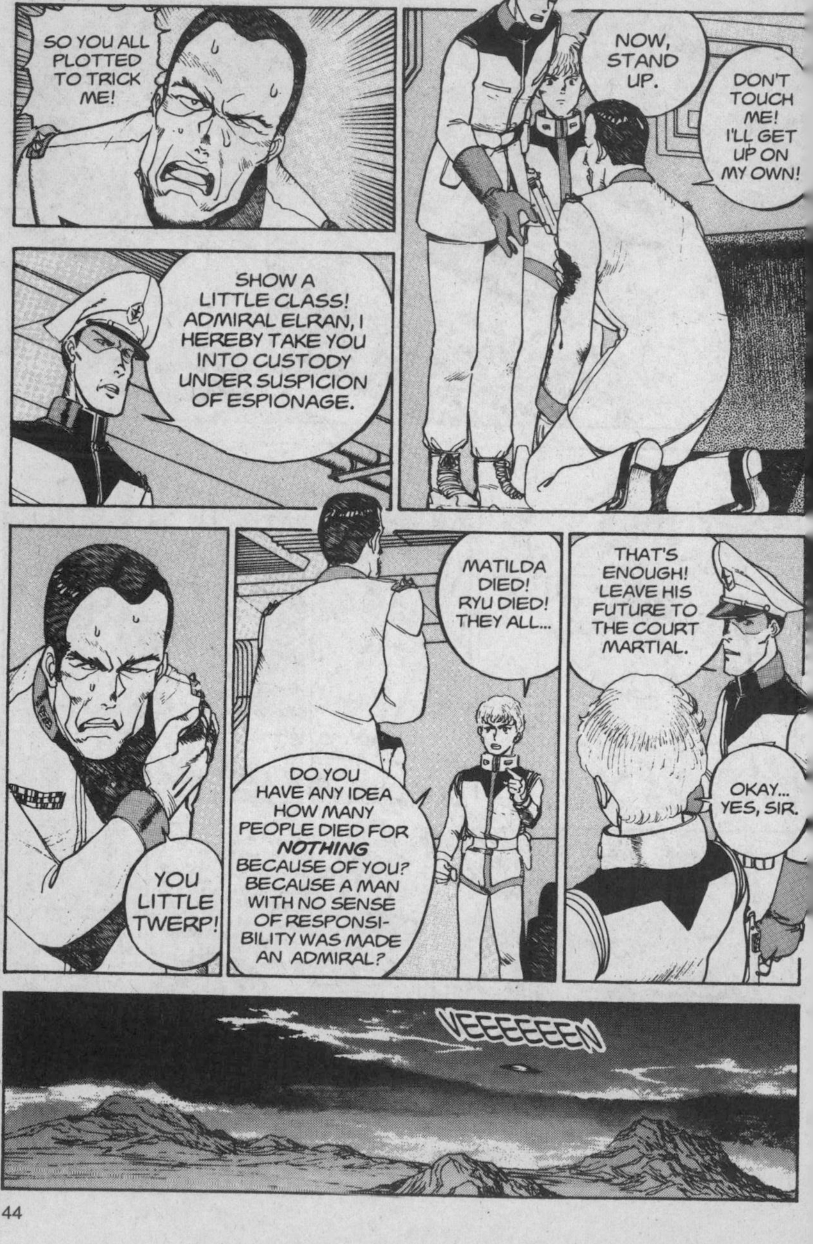
SO YOU ALL PLOTTED TO TRICK ME!
NOW, STAND UP.
DON'T TOUCH ME! I'LL GET UP ON MY OWN!
SHOW A LITTLE CLASS! ADMIRAL ELRAN, I HEREBY TAKE YOU INTO CUSTODY UNDER SUSPICION OF ESPIONAGE.
YOU LITTLE TWERP!
MATILDA DIED! RYU DIED! THEY ALL...
DO YOU HAVE ANY IDEA HOW MANY PEOPLE DIED FOR ***NOTHING*** BECAUSE OF YOU? BECAUSE A MAN WITH NO SENSE OF RESPONSIBILITY WAS MADE AN ADMIRAL?
THAT'S ENOUGH! LEAVE HIS FUTURE TO THE COURT MARTIAL.
OKAY... YES, SIR.
VEEEEEEEN

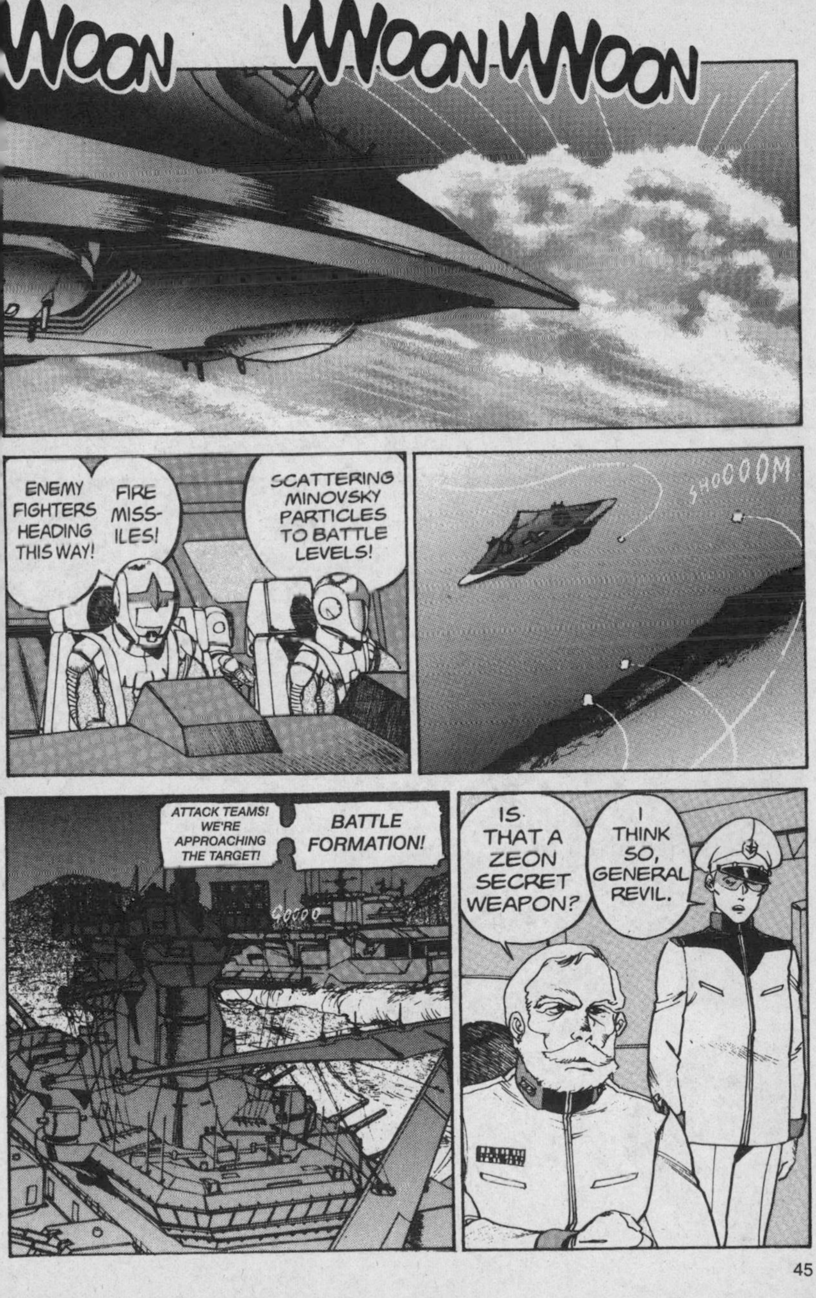
WOON
WOON WOON
ENEMY FIGHTERS HEADING THIS WAY!
FIRE MISS-ILES!
SCATTERING MINOVSKY PARTICLES TO BATTLE LEVELS!
SHOCOOM
ATTACK TEAMS! WE'RE APPROACHING THE TARGET!
BATTLE FORMATION!
GOOOO
IS THAT A ZEON SECRET WEAPON?
I THINK SO, GENERAL REVIL.

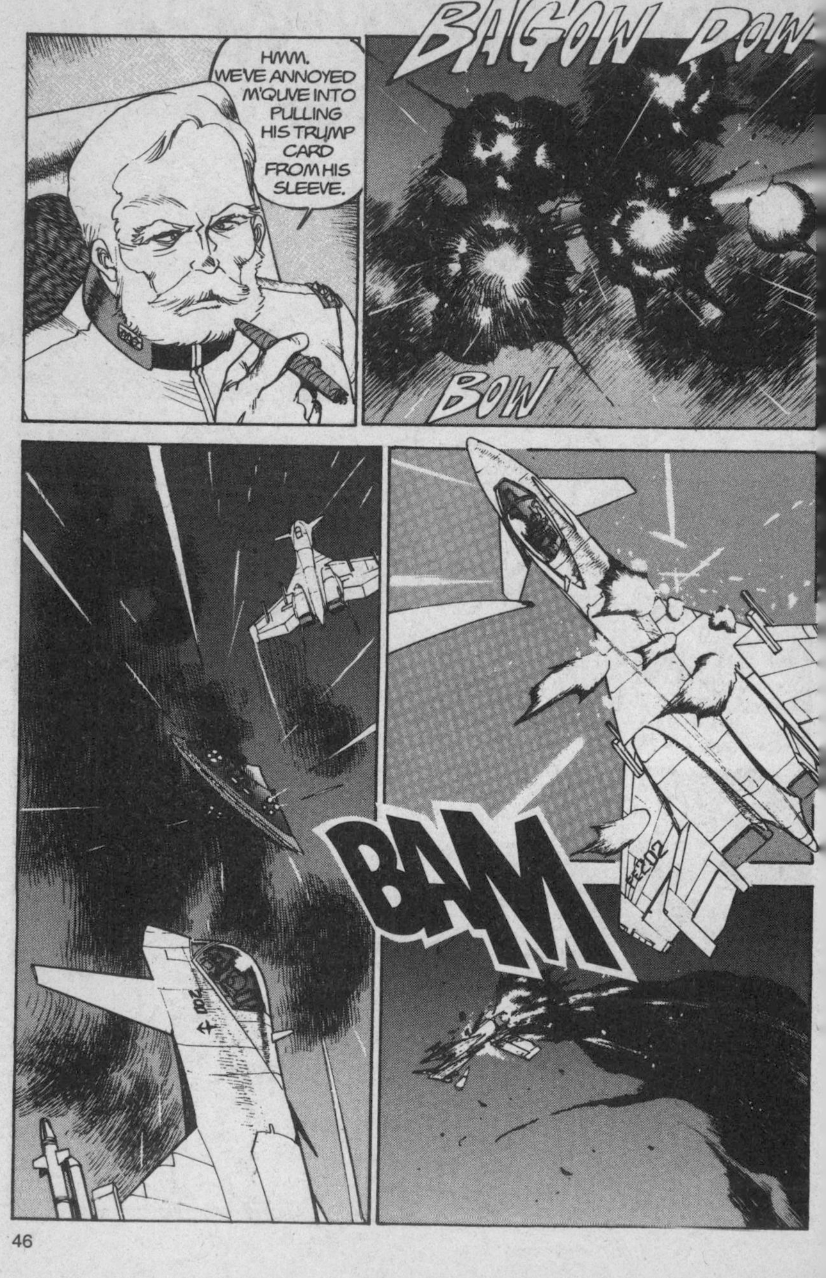
HMM. WEVE ANNOYED M'QUVE INTO PULLING HIS TRUMP CARD FROM HIS SLEEVE.
BAGOW DOW
BOW
BAM

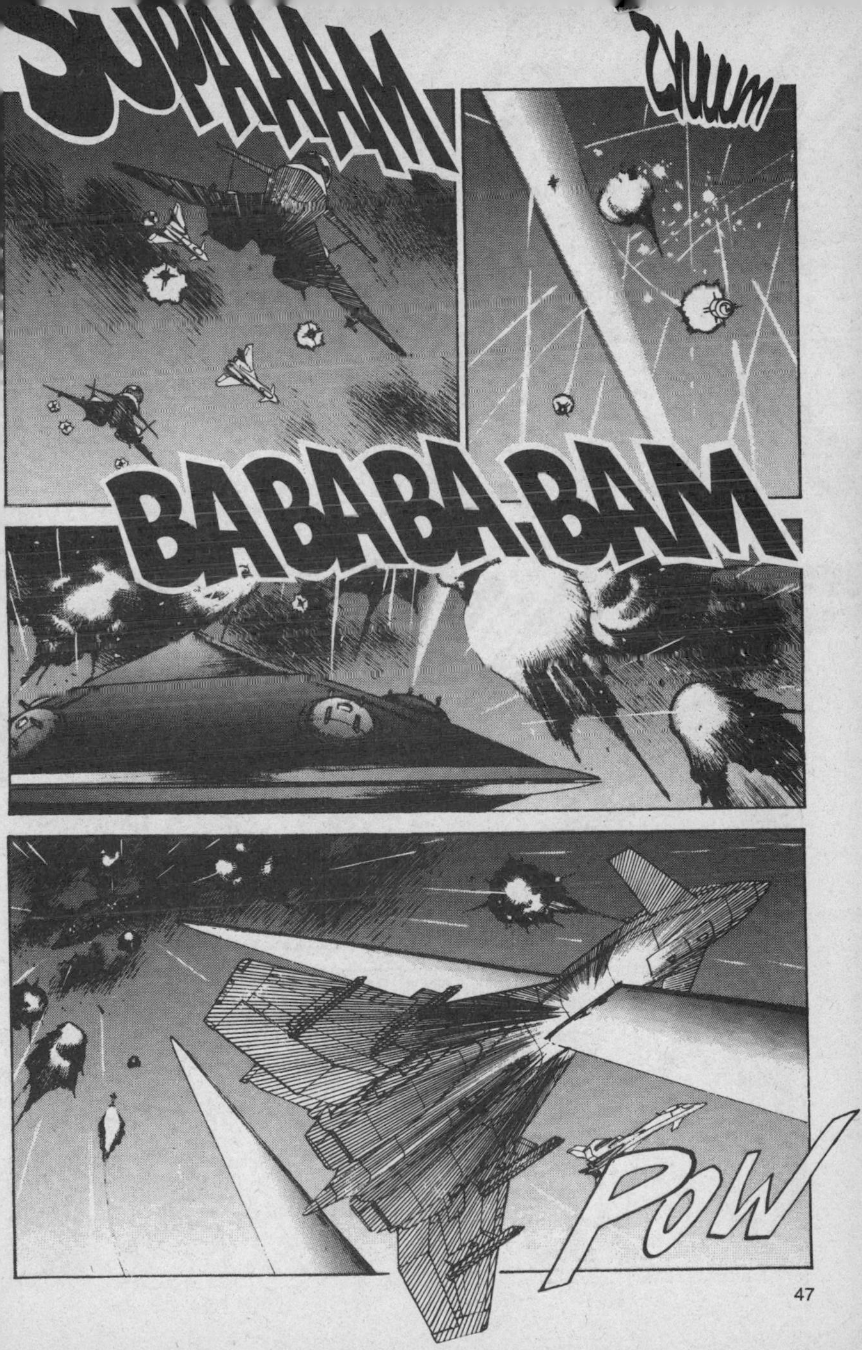
SUPAAAM
BABABA-BAM
POW

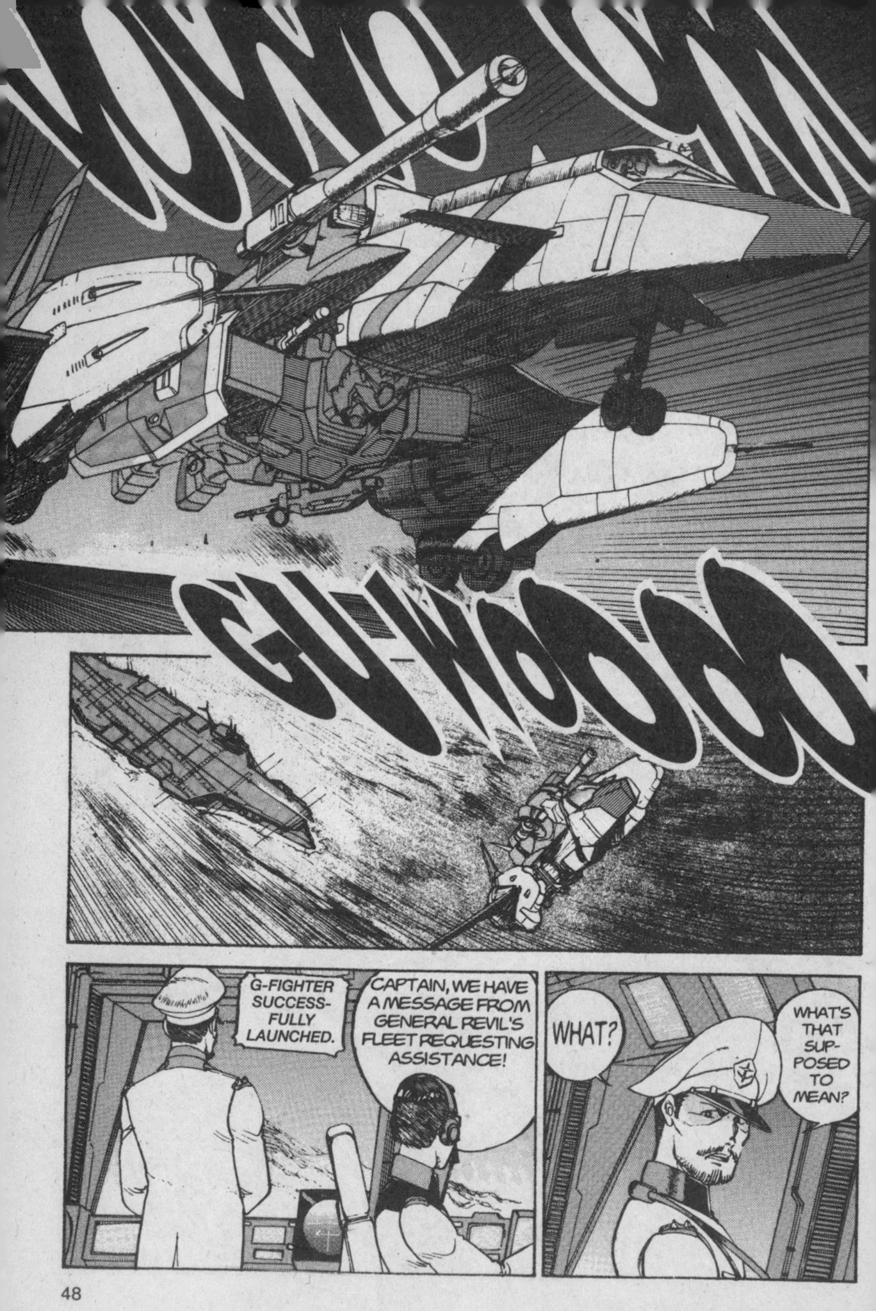
G-FIGHTER SUCCESS-FULLY LAUNCHED.
CAPTAIN, WE HAVE A MESSAGE FROM GENERAL REVIL'S FLEET REQUESTING ASSISTANCE!
WHAT?
WHAT'S THAT SUP-POSED TO MEAN?

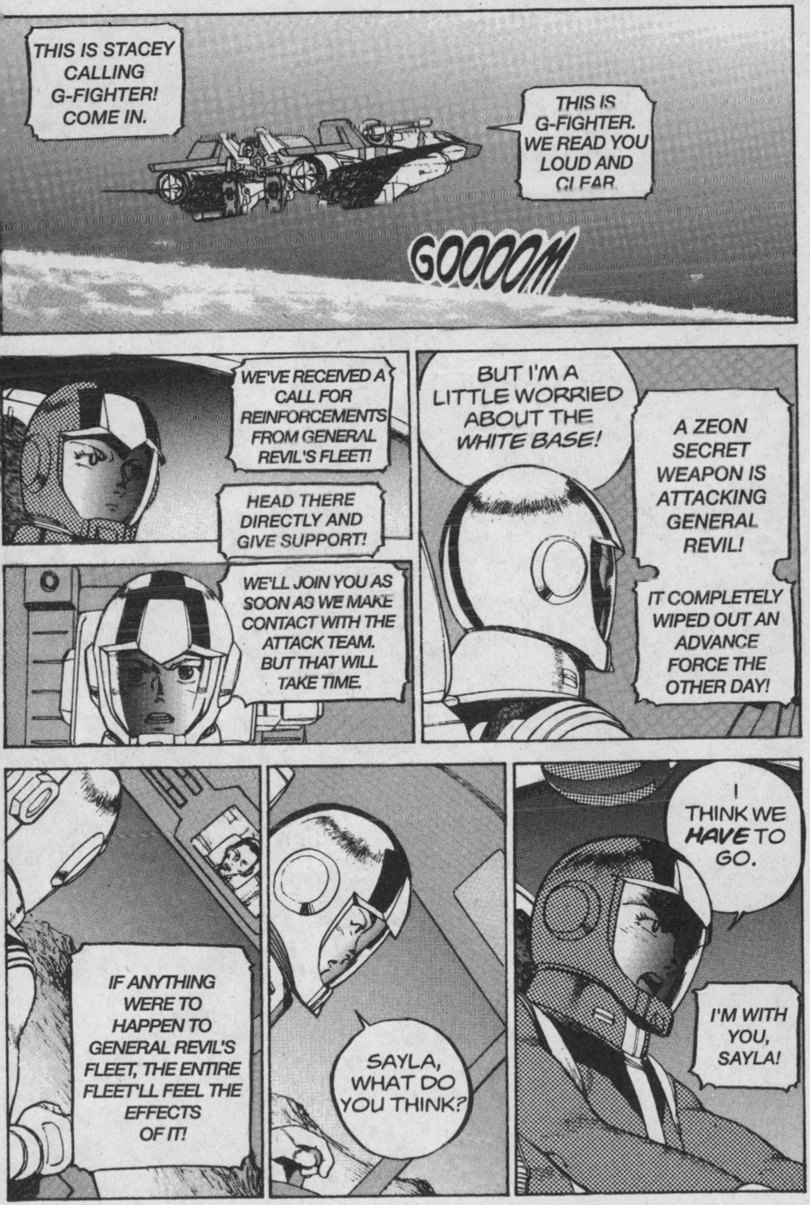
THIS IS STACEY CALLING G-FIGHTER! COME IN.
THIS IS G-FIGHTER. WE READ YOU LOUD AND CLEAR.
GOOOOM
WE'VE RECEIVED A CALL FOR REINFORCEMENTS FROM GENERAL REVIL'S FLEET!
HEAD THERE DIRECTLY AND GIVE SUPPORT!
WE'LL JOIN YOU AS SOON AS WE MAKE CONTACT WITH THE ATTACK TEAM. BUT THAT WILL TAKE TIME.
BUT I'M A LITTLE WORRIED ABOUT THE WHITE BASE!
A ZEON SECRET WEAPON IS ATTACKING GENERAL REVIL!
IT COMPLETELY WIPED OUT AN ADVANCE FORCE THE OTHER DAY!
IF ANYTHING WERE TO HAPPEN TO GENERAL REVIL'S FLEET, THE ENTIRE FLEET'LL FEEL THE EFFECTS OF IT!
SAYLA, WHAT DO YOU THINK?
I THINK WE HAVE TO GO.
I'M WITH YOU, SAYLA!

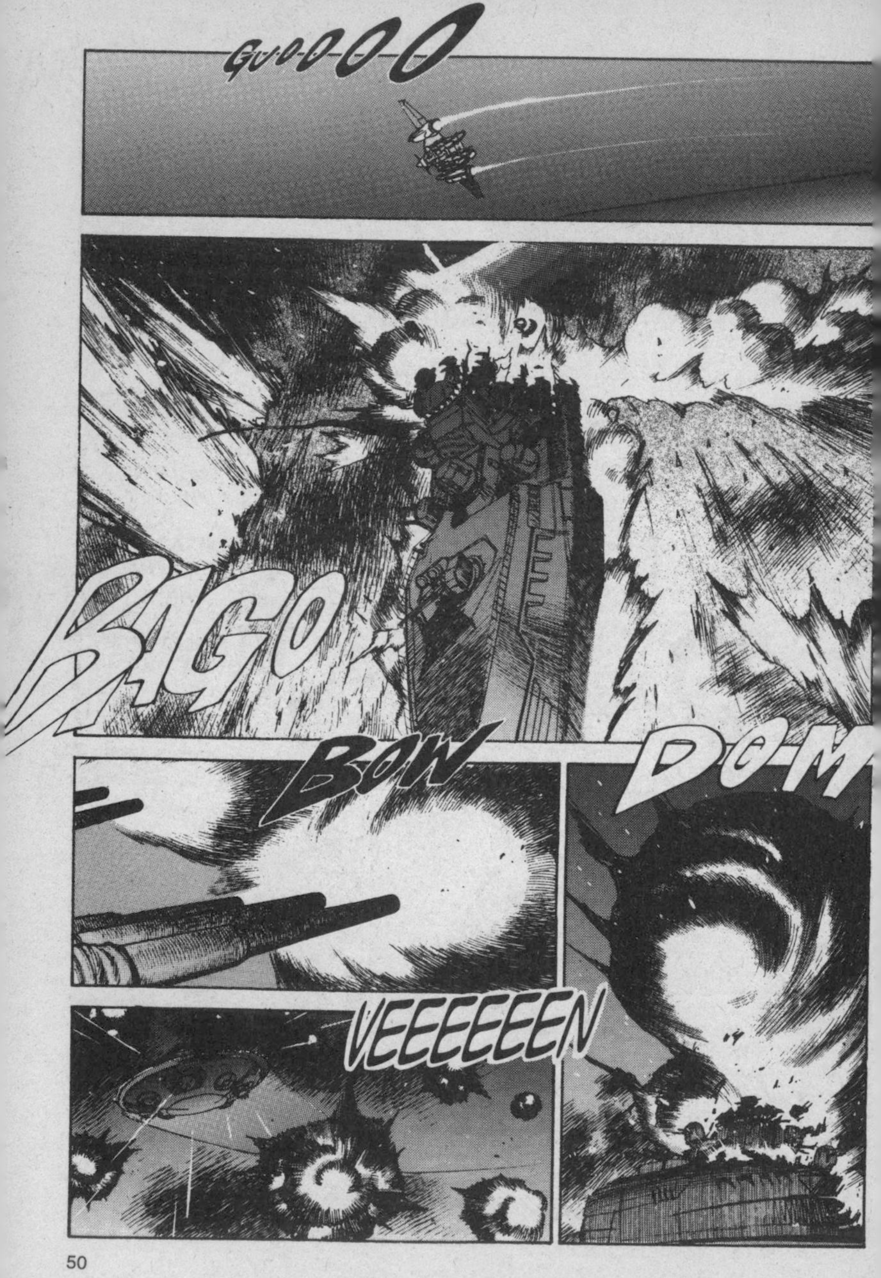
GU-O-O-O-O
BAGO
BOW
DOM
VEEEEEEN

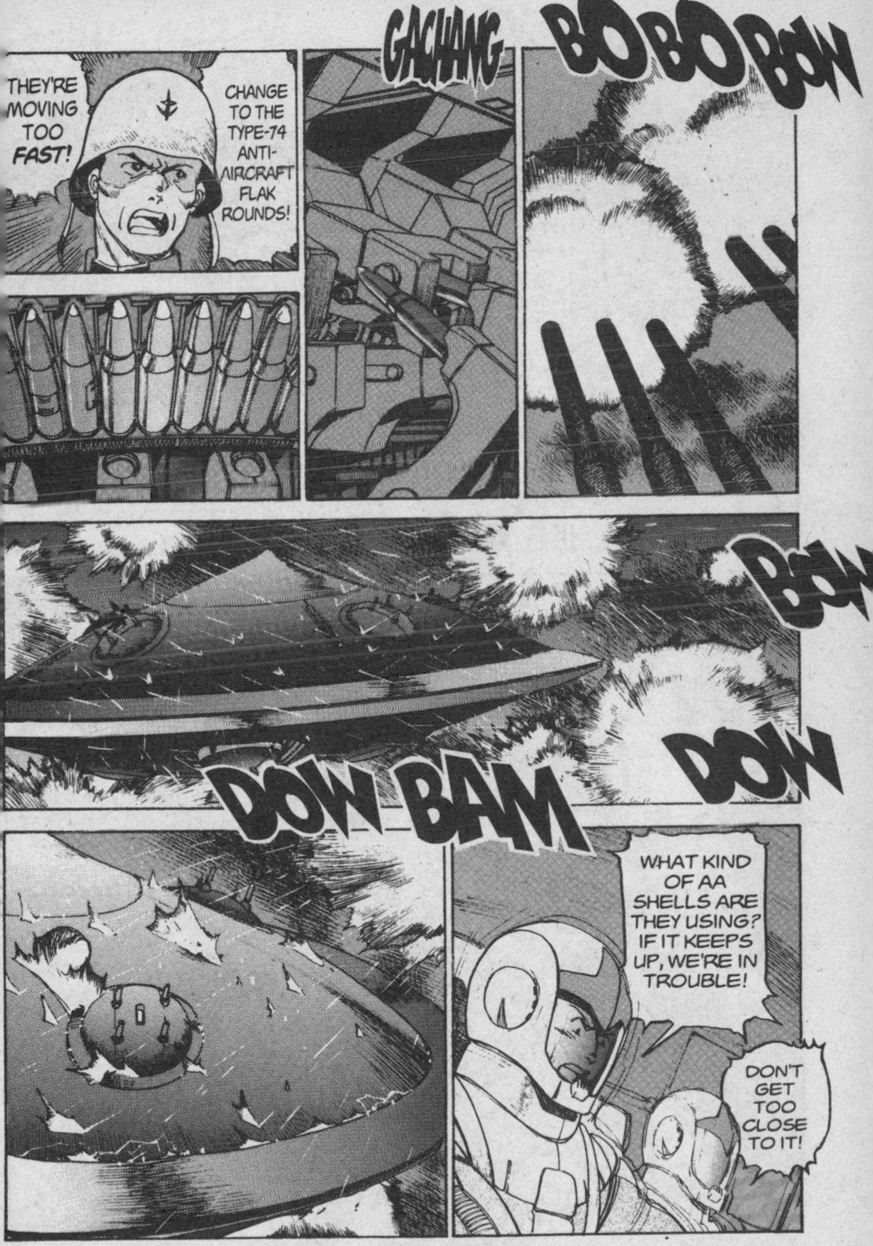

THEY'RE MOVING TOO FAST!
CHANGE TO THE TYPE-74 ANTI-AIRCRAFT FLAK ROUNDS!
GACHANG
BOBOBOW
BOW
DOW BAM DOW
WHAT KIND OF AA SHELLS ARE THEY USING? IF IT KEEPS UP, WE'RE IN TROUBLE!
DON'T GET TOO CLOSE TO IT!

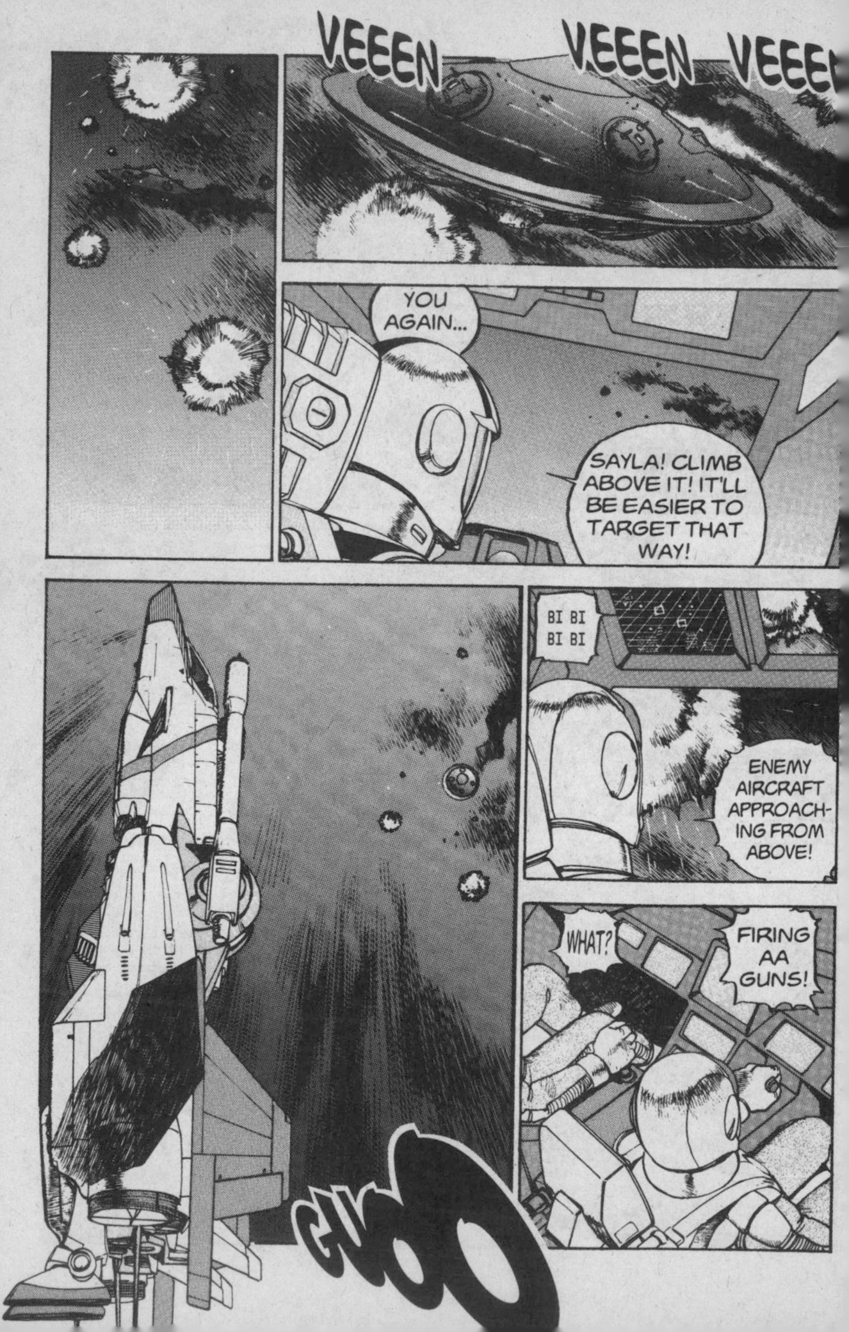
VEEEN VEEEN VEEE
YOU AGAIN...
SAYLA! CLIMB ABOVE IT! IT'LL BE EASIER TO TARGET THAT WAY!
GUOO
BI BI BI BI
ENEMY AIRCRAFT APPROACHING FROM ABOVE!
WHAT?
FIRING AA GUNS!

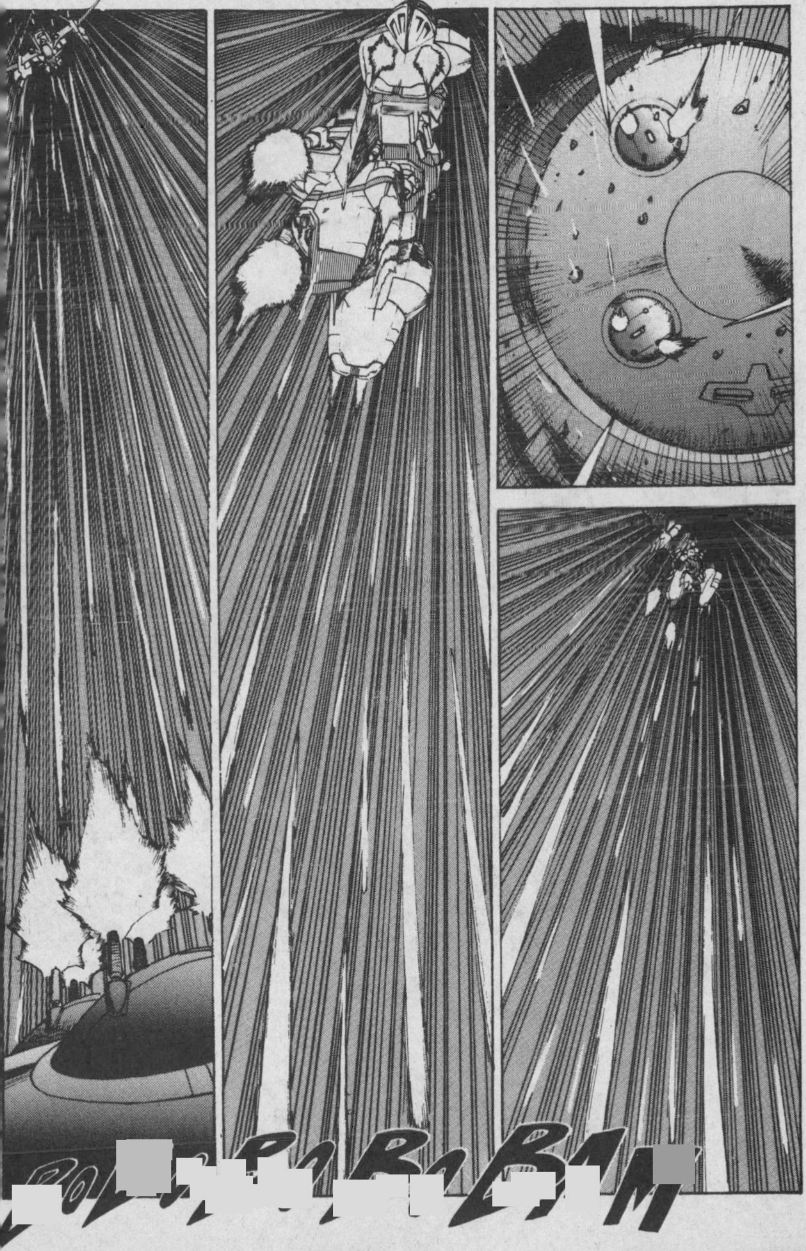
BAM

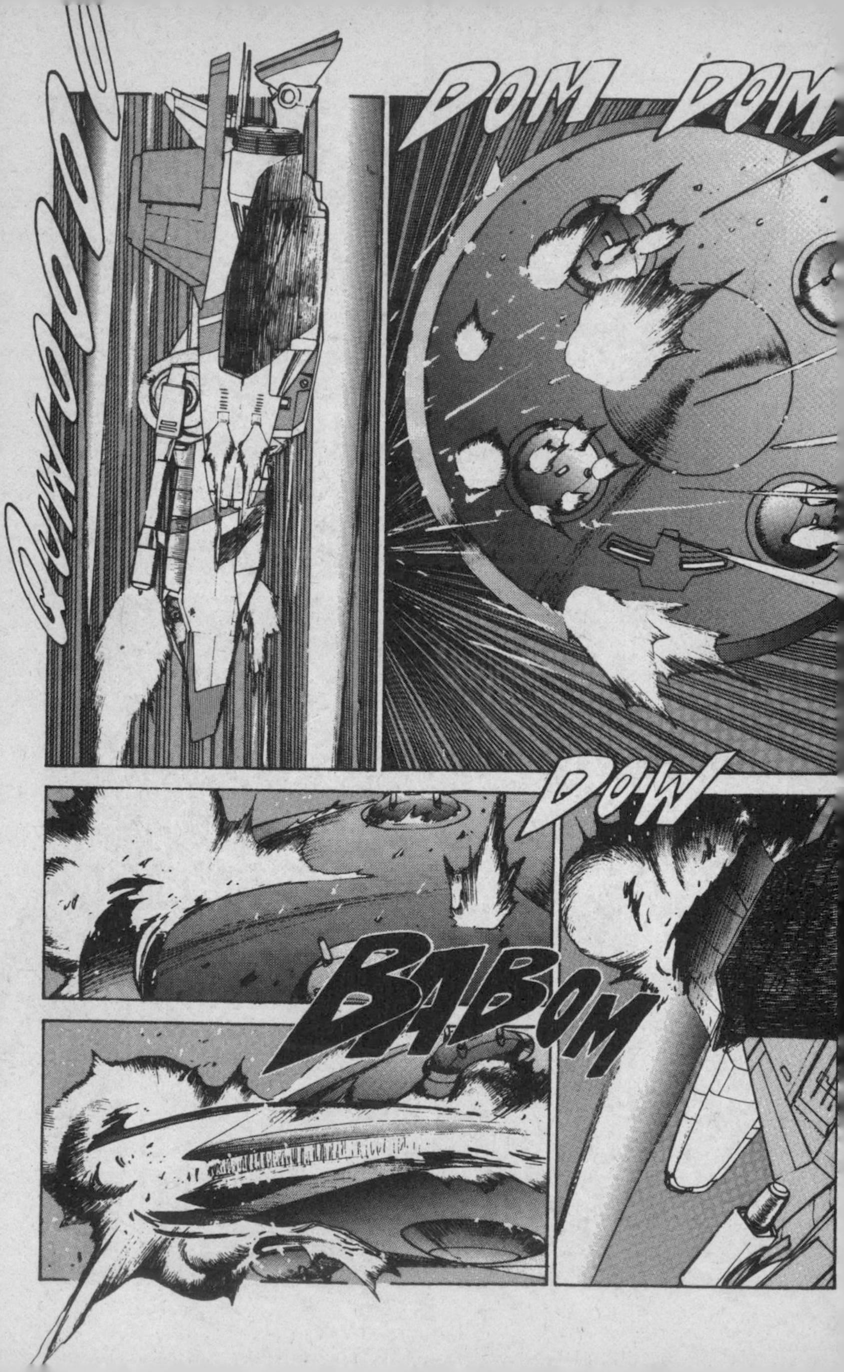

DOM DOM
DOW
BABOM

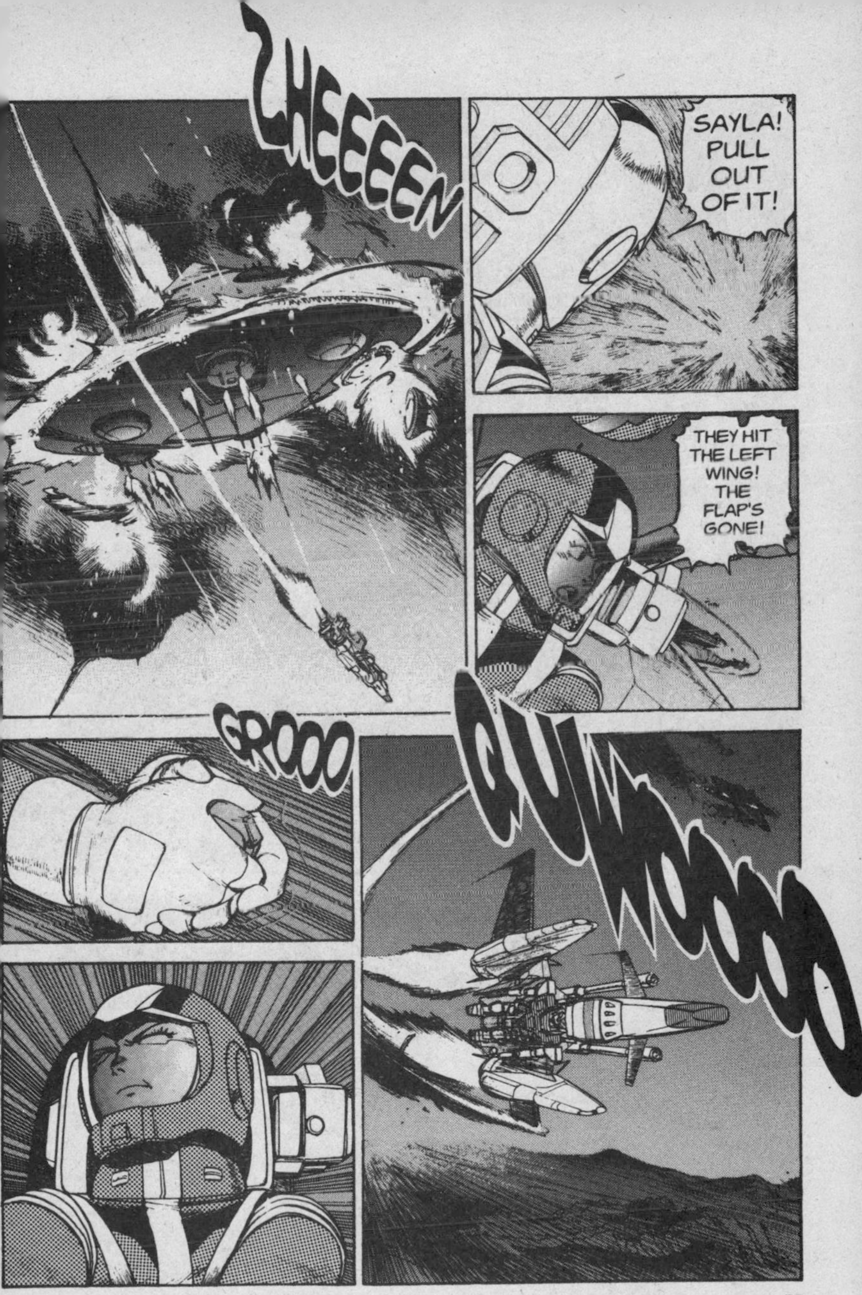

ZHEEEEN
SAYLA! PULL OUT OF IT!
THEY HIT THE LEFT WING! THE FLAP'S GONE!
GROOO
GUWOOOOO

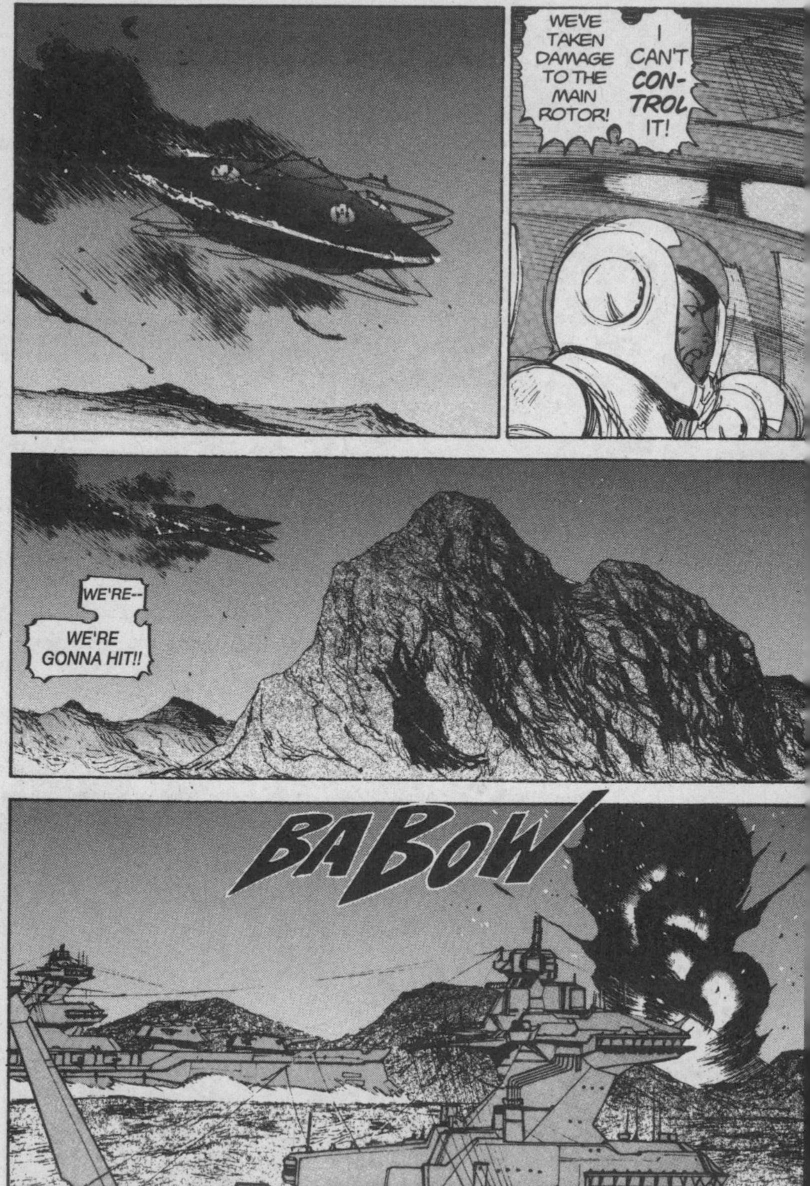
WE'VE TAKEN DAMAGE TO THE MAIN ROTOR!
I CAN'T CONTROL IT!
WE'RE--
WE'RE GONNA HIT!!
BABOW

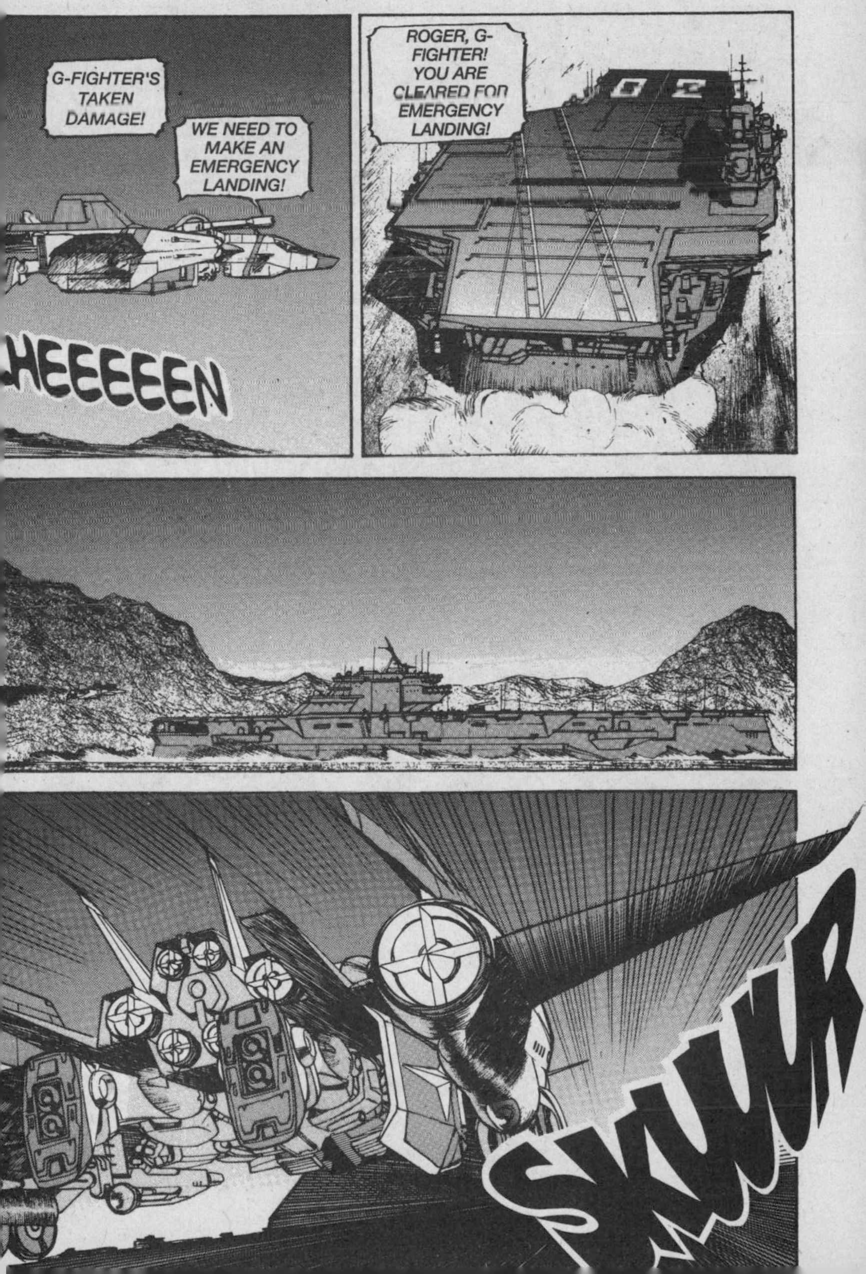
G-FIGHTER'S TAKEN DAMAGE!
WE NEED TO MAKE AN EMERGENCY LANDING!
HEEEEEN
ROGER, G-FIGHTER! YOU ARE CLEARED FOR EMERGENCY LANDING!
SKUUR

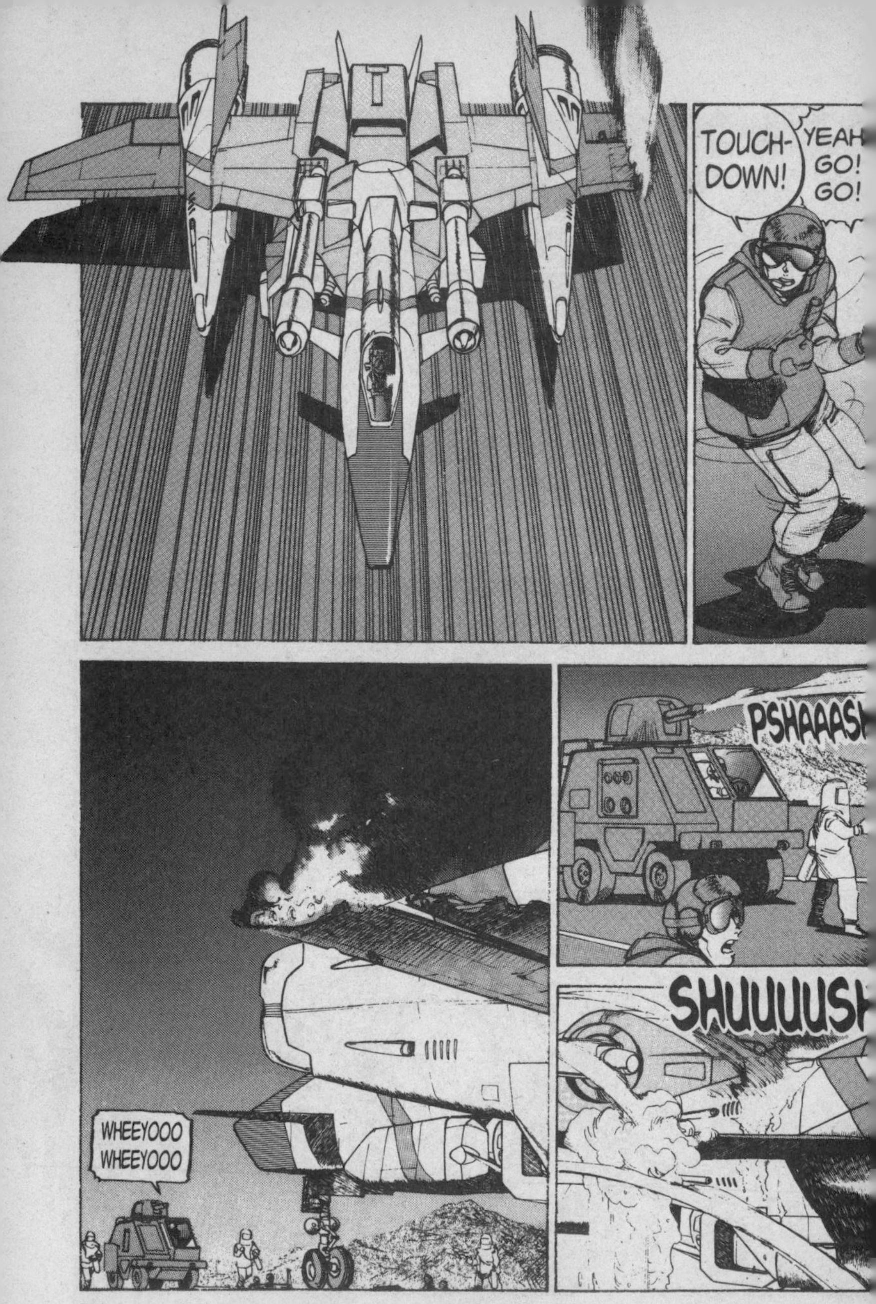
TOUCH-DOWN!
YEAH GO! GO!
WHEEYOOO WHEEYOOO
PSHAAAS
SHUUUUS

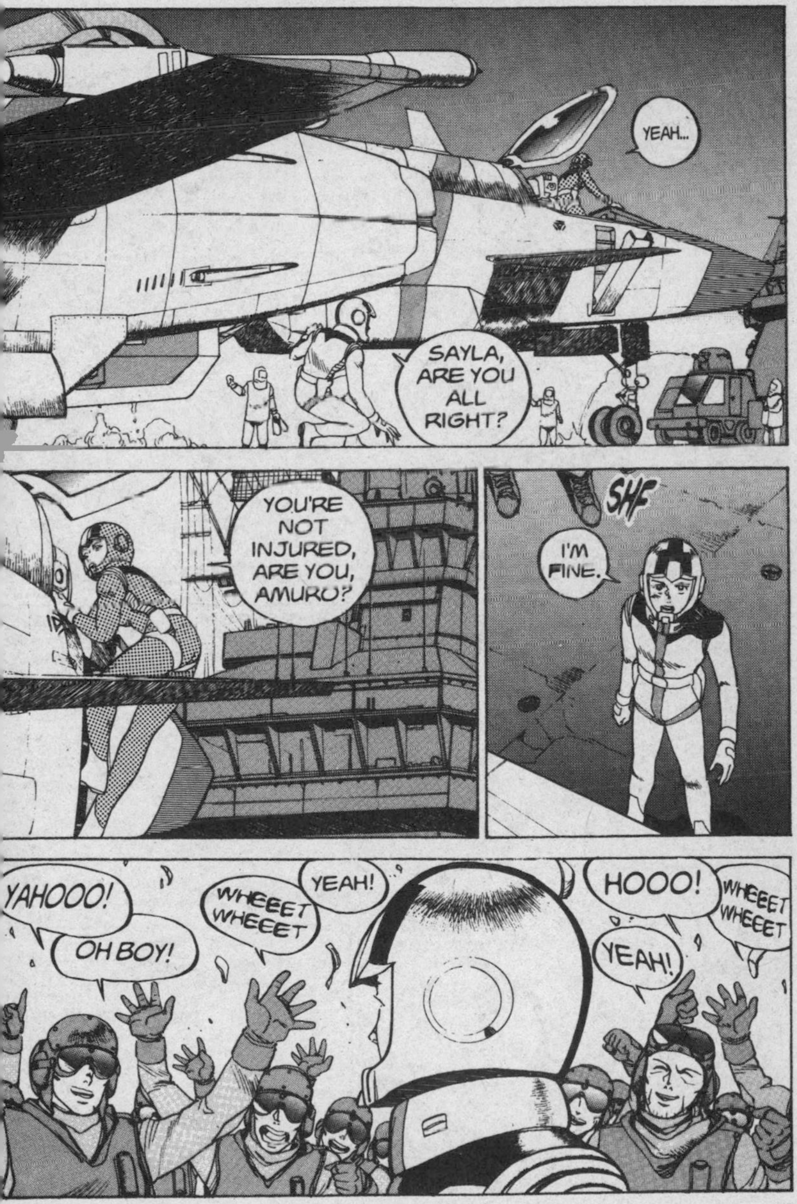
YEAH...
SAYLA, ARE YOU ALL RIGHT?
YOU'RE NOT INJURED, ARE YOU, AMURO?
SHF
I'M FINE.
YAHOOO!
OH BOY!
WHEEET WHEEET
YEAH!
HOOO!
YEAH!
WHEEET WHEEET

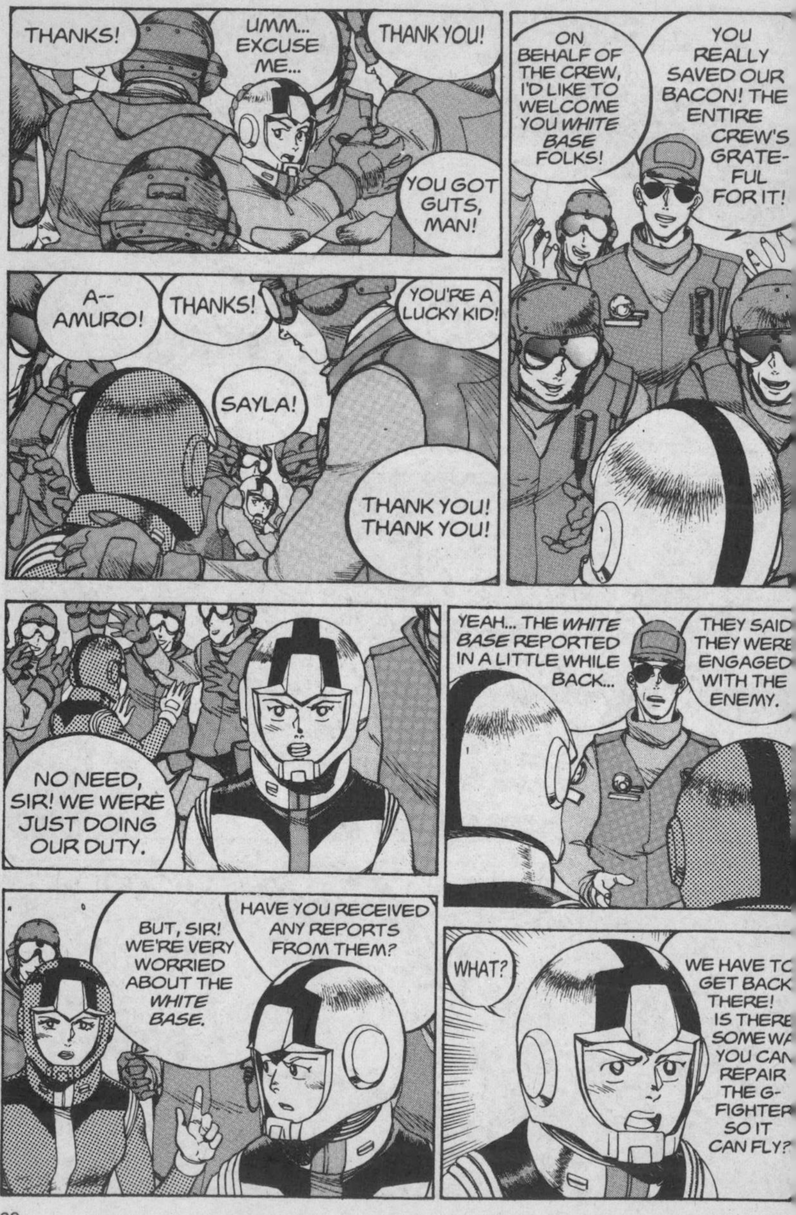
THANKS!
UMM... EXCUSE ME...
THANK YOU!
YOU GOT GUTS, MAN!
A-- AMURO!
THANKS!
YOU'RE A LUCKY KID!
SAYLA!
THANK YOU! THANK YOU!
ON BEHALF OF THE CREW, I'D LIKE TO WELCOME YOU *WHITE BASE* FOLKS!
YOU REALLY SAVED OUR BACON! THE ENTIRE CREW'S GRATEFUL FOR IT!
NO NEED, SIR! WE WERE JUST DOING OUR DUTY.
YEAH... THE *WHITE BASE* REPORTED IN A LITTLE WHILE BACK...
THEY SAID THEY WERE ENGAGED WITH THE ENEMY.
BUT, SIR! WE'RE VERY WORRIED ABOUT THE *WHITE BASE.*
HAVE YOU RECEIVED ANY REPORTS FROM THEM?
WHAT?
WE HAVE TO GET BACK THERE! IS THERE SOME WA YOU CAN REPAIR THE G-FIGHTER SO IT CAN FLY?

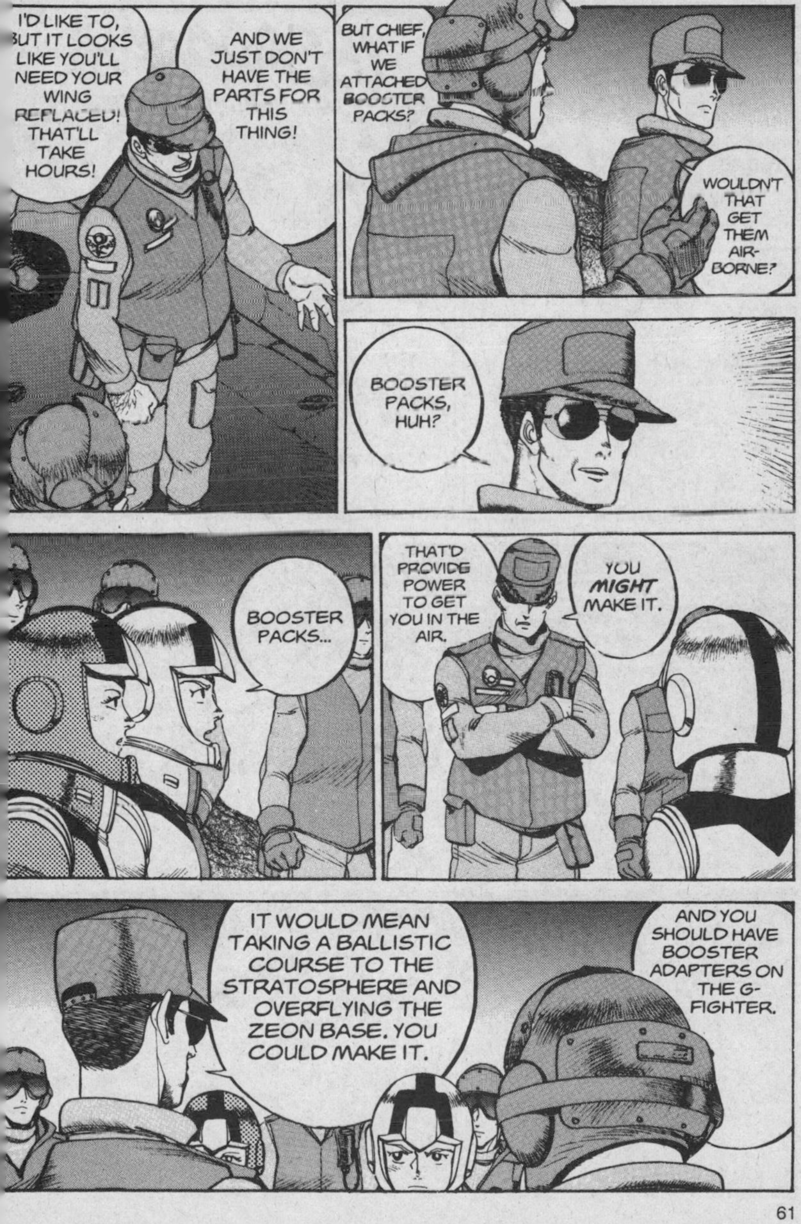
I'D LIKE TO, BUT IT LOOKS LIKE YOU'LL NEED YOUR WING REPLACED! THAT'LL TAKE HOURS!
AND WE JUST DON'T HAVE THE PARTS FOR THIS THING!
BUT CHIEF, WHAT IF WE ATTACHED BOOSTER PACKS?
WOULDN'T THAT GET THEM AIR-BORNE?
BOOSTER PACKS, HUH?
BOOSTER PACKS...
THAT'D PROVIDE POWER TO GET YOU IN THE AIR.
YOU *MIGHT* MAKE IT.
IT WOULD MEAN TAKING A BALLISTIC COURSE TO THE STRATOSPHERE AND OVERFLYING THE ZEON BASE. YOU COULD MAKE IT.
AND YOU SHOULD HAVE BOOSTER ADAPTERS ON THE G-FIGHTER.

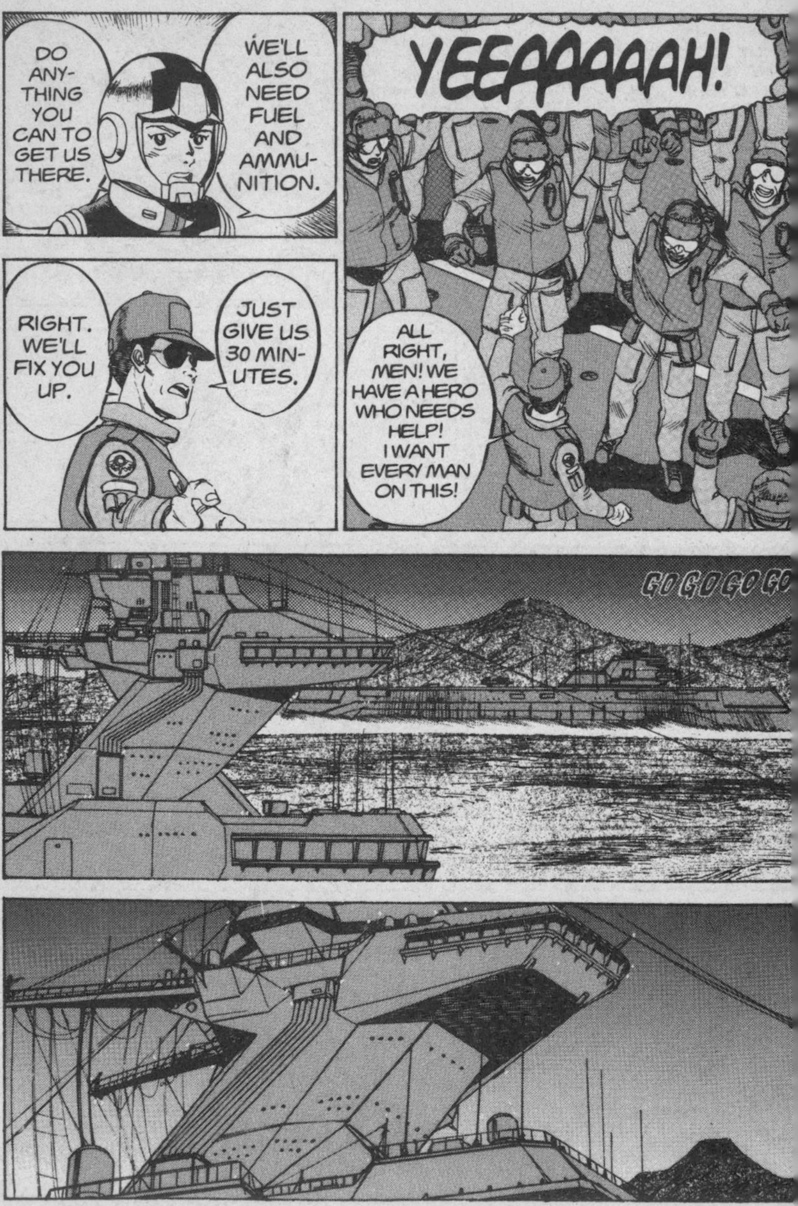
DO ANY-THING YOU CAN TO GET US THERE.
WE'LL ALSO NEED FUEL AND AMMU-NITION.
RIGHT. WE'LL FIX YOU UP.
JUST GIVE US 30 MIN-UTES.
YEEAAAAAAH!
ALL RIGHT, MEN! WE HAVE A HERO WHO NEEDS HELP! I WANT EVERY MAN ON THIS!
GOGOGOGO

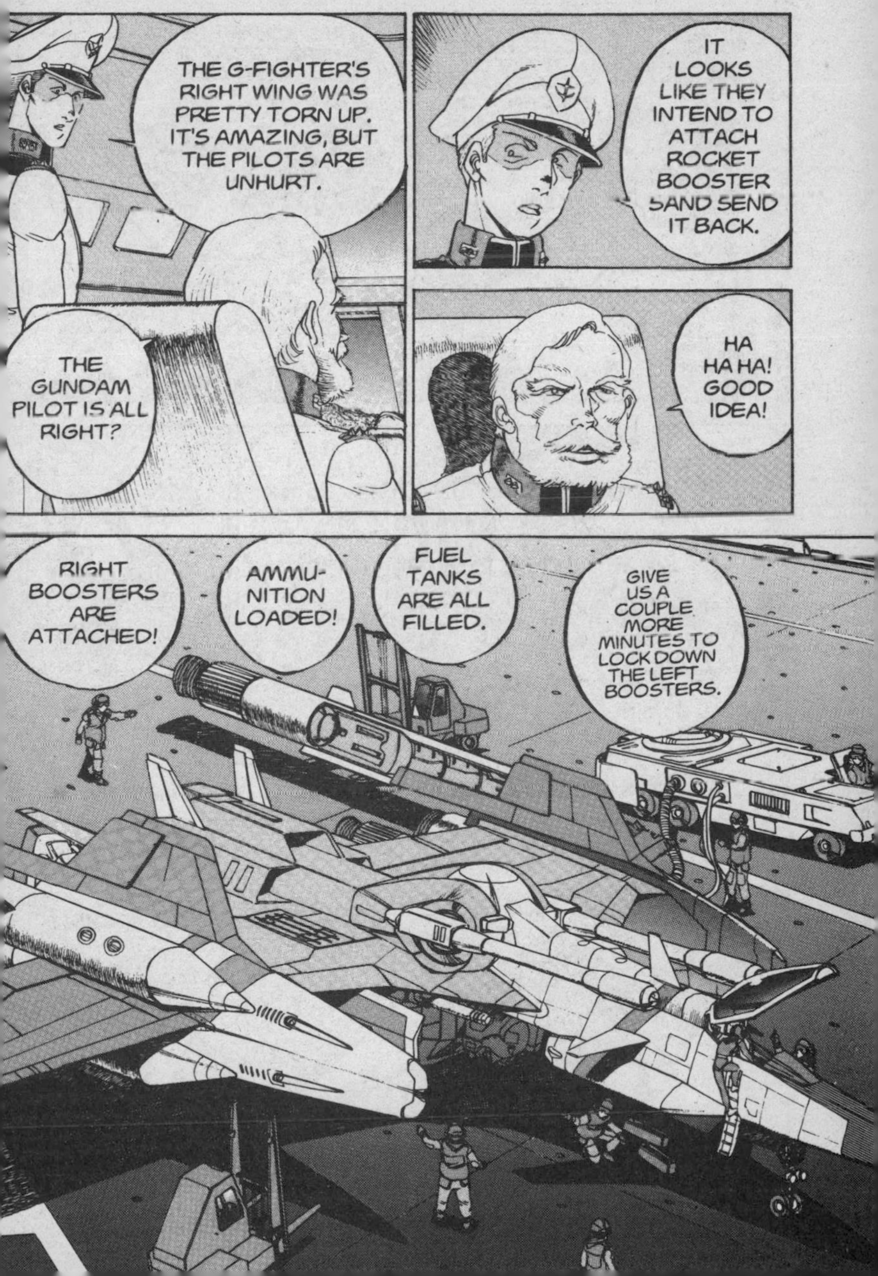
THE G-FIGHTER'S RIGHT WING WAS PRETTY TORN UP. IT'S AMAZING, BUT THE PILOTS ARE UNHURT.
THE GUNDAM PILOT IS ALL RIGHT?
IT LOOKS LIKE THEY INTEND TO ATTACH ROCKET BOOSTER SAND SEND IT BACK.
HA HA HA! GOOD IDEA!
RIGHT BOOSTERS ARE ATTACHED!
AMMU-NITION LOADED!
FUEL TANKS ARE ALL FILLED.
GIVE US A COUPLE MORE MINUTES TO LOCK DOWN THE LEFT BOOSTERS.

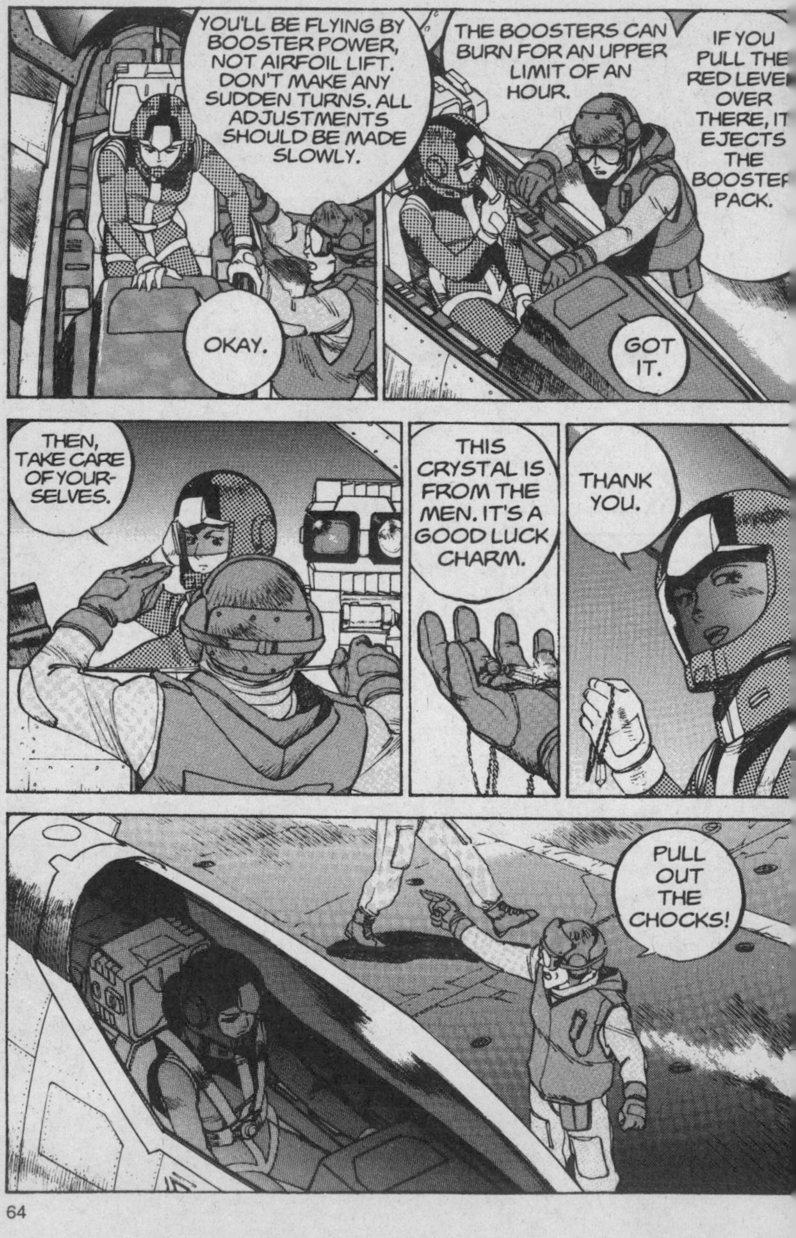
YOU'LL BE FLYING BY BOOSTER POWER, NOT AIRFOIL LIFT. DON'T MAKE ANY SUDDEN TURNS. ALL ADJUSTMENTS SHOULD BE MADE SLOWLY.
OKAY.
THE BOOSTERS CAN BURN FOR AN UPPER LIMIT OF AN HOUR.
IF YOU PULL THE RED LEVE OVER THERE, IT EJECTS THE BOOSTER PACK.
GOT IT.
THEN, TAKE CARE OF YOUR-SELVES.
THIS CRYSTAL IS FROM THE MEN. IT'S A GOOD LUCK CHARM.
THANK YOU.
PULL OUT THE CHOCKS!

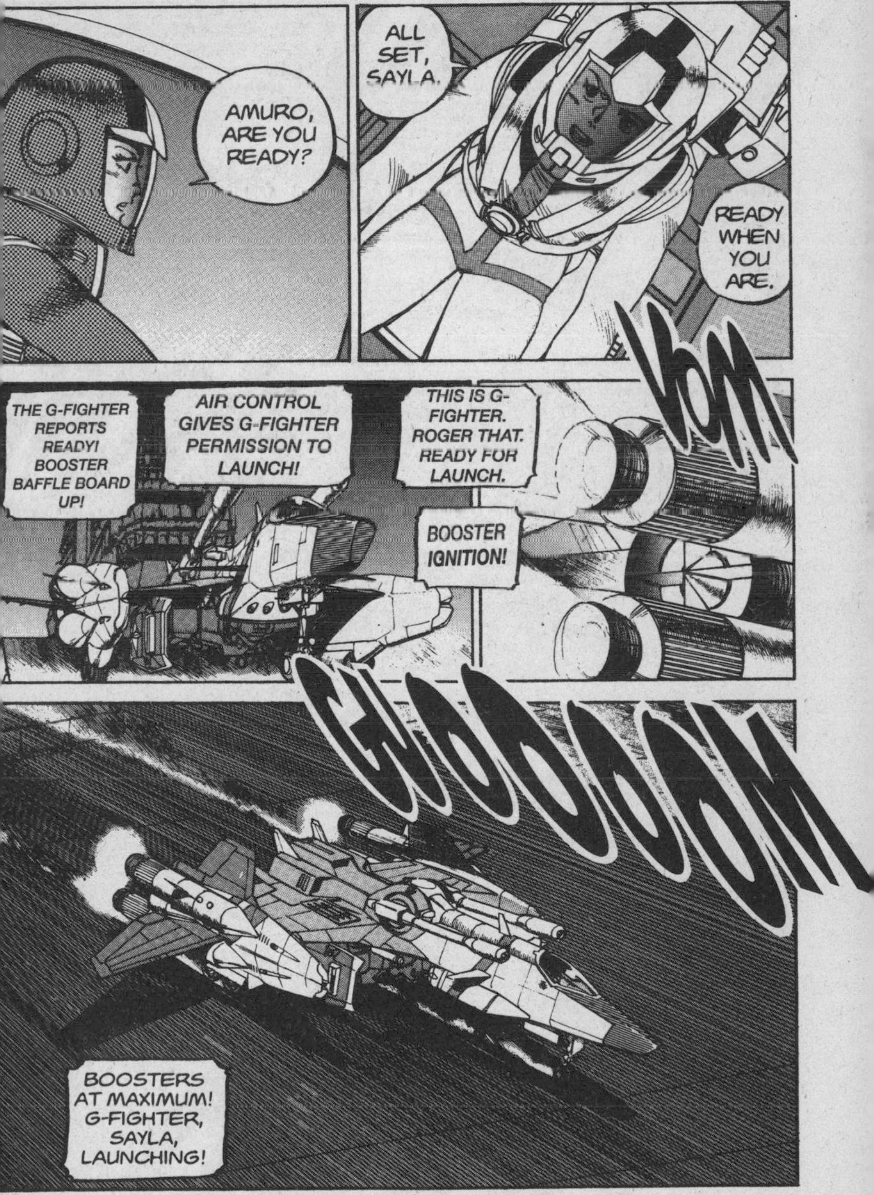
AMURO, ARE YOU READY?
ALL SET, SAYLA.
READY WHEN YOU ARE.
VOM
THE G-FIGHTER REPORTS READY! BOOSTER BAFFLE BOARD UP!
AIR CONTROL GIVES G-FIGHTER PERMISSION TO LAUNCH!
THIS IS G-FIGHTER. ROGER THAT. READY FOR LAUNCH.
BOOSTER IGNITION!
CHOOOOOM
BOOSTERS AT MAXIMUM! G-FIGHTER, SAYLA, LAUNCHING!

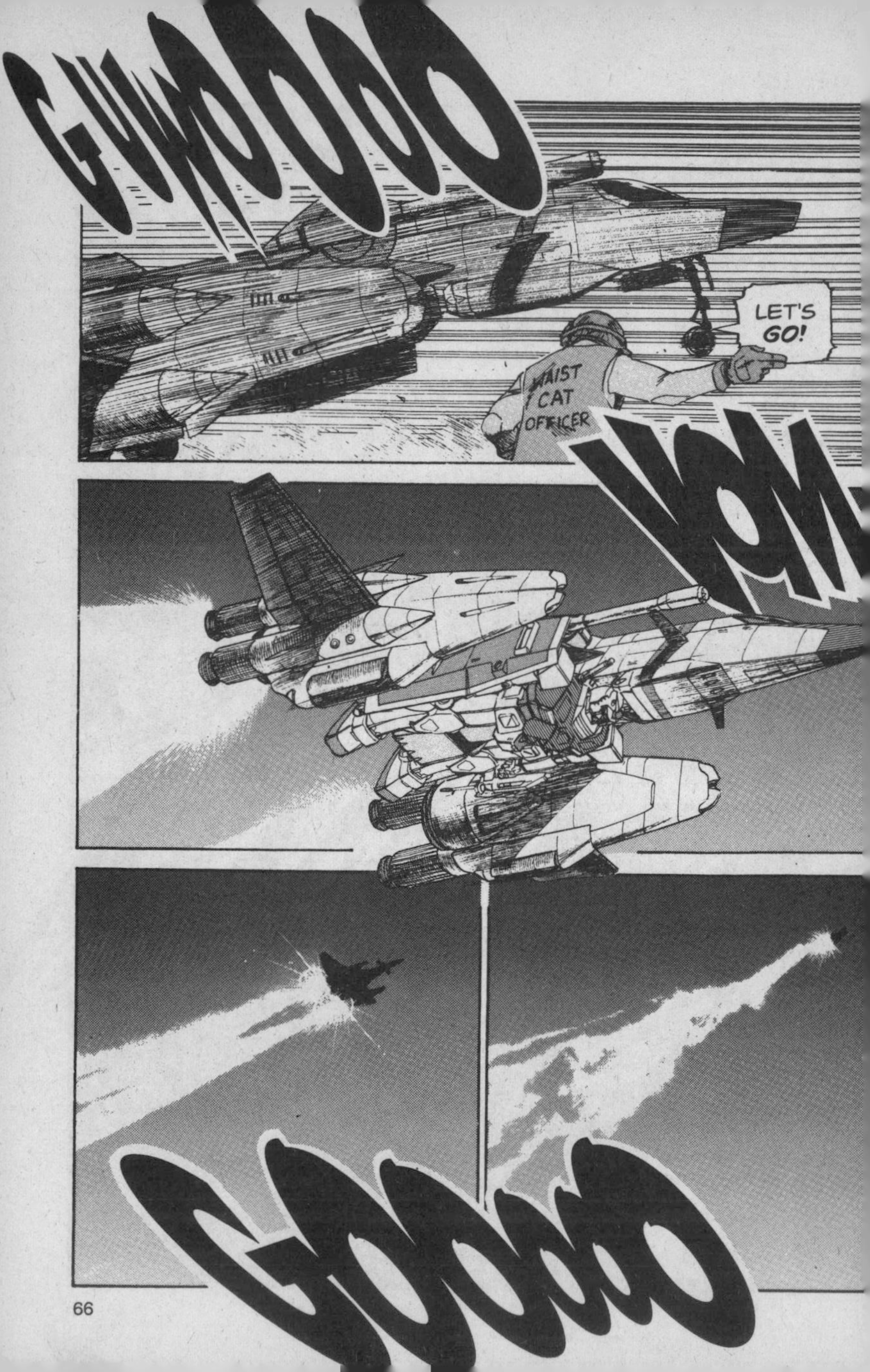
GUWOOOO
LET'S GO!
WAIST CAT OFFICER
GOOOOO

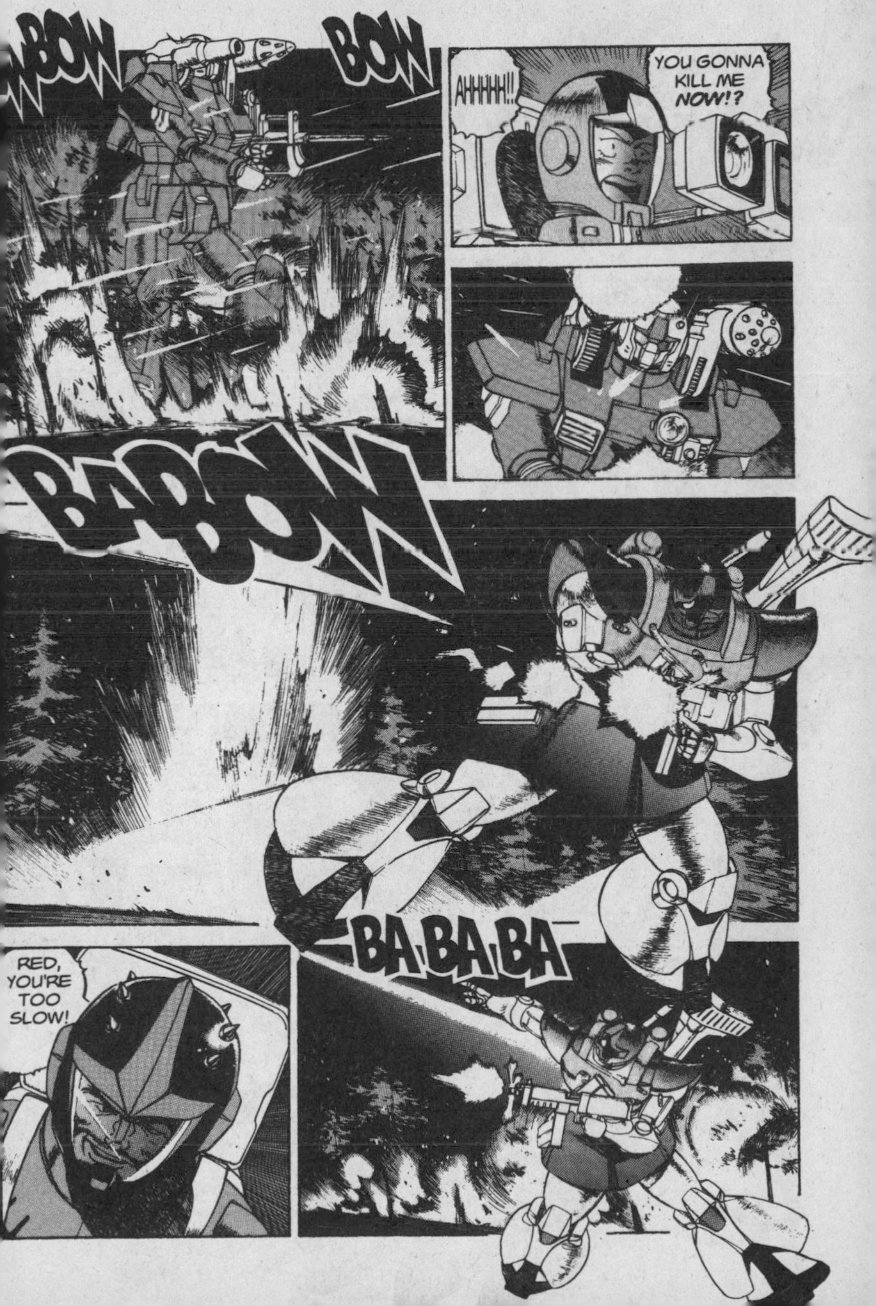
BOW
BOW
AHHHHH!!
YOU GONNA KILL ME NOW!?
BABOW
BA BA BA
RED, YOU'RE TOO SLOW!

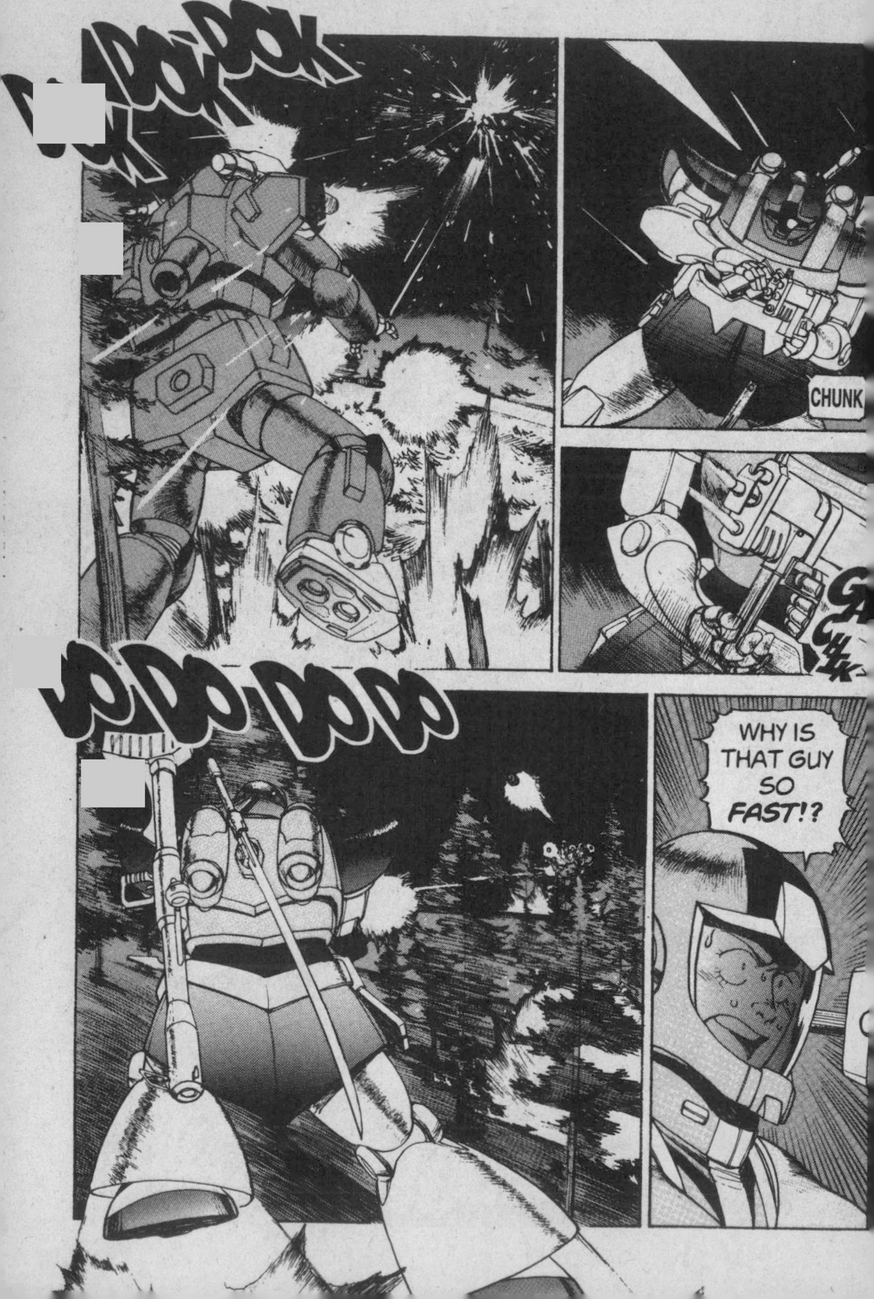
CHUNK
WHY IS THAT GUY SO FAST!?

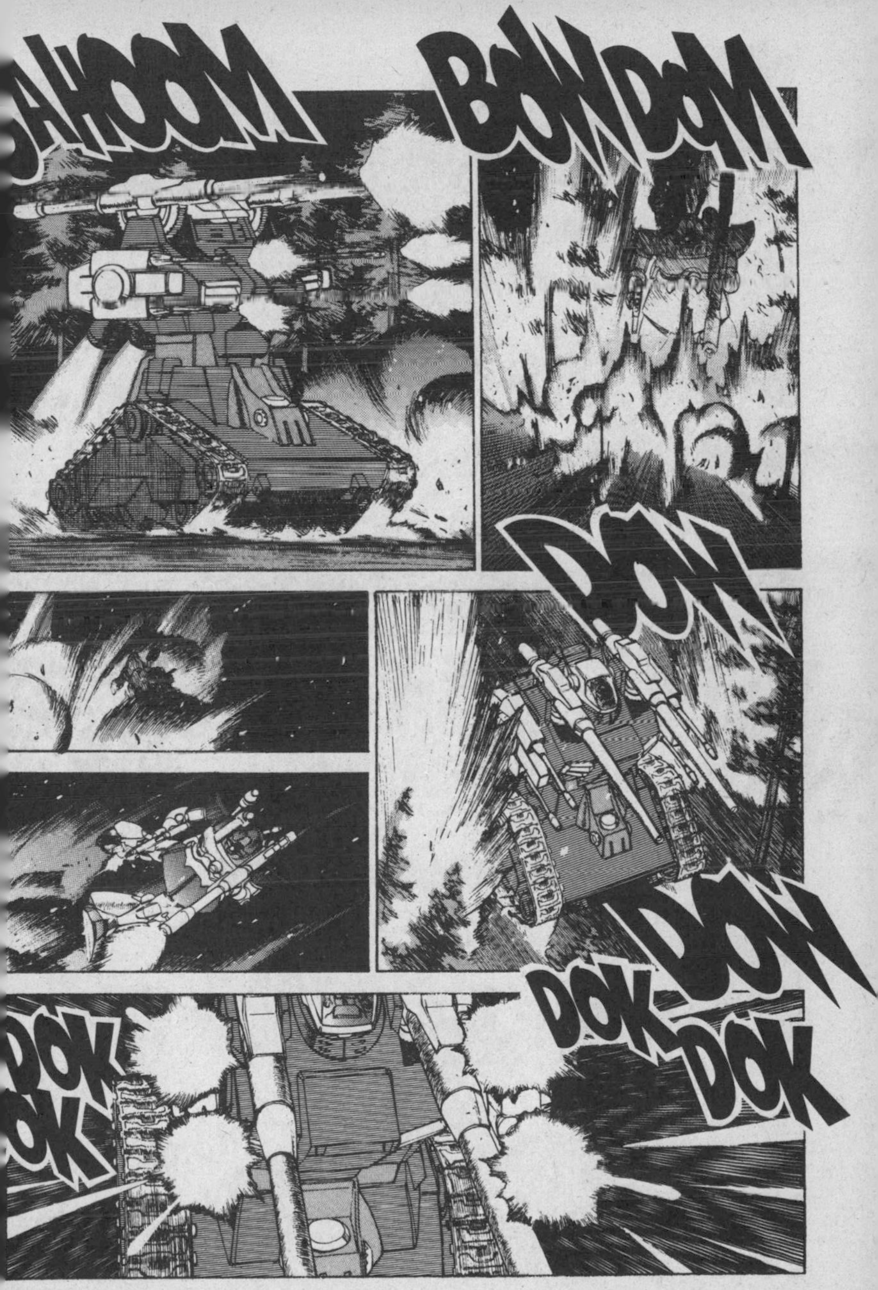
SHOOM
BONDOM
DON
DON
DOK-DOK
DOK
OK

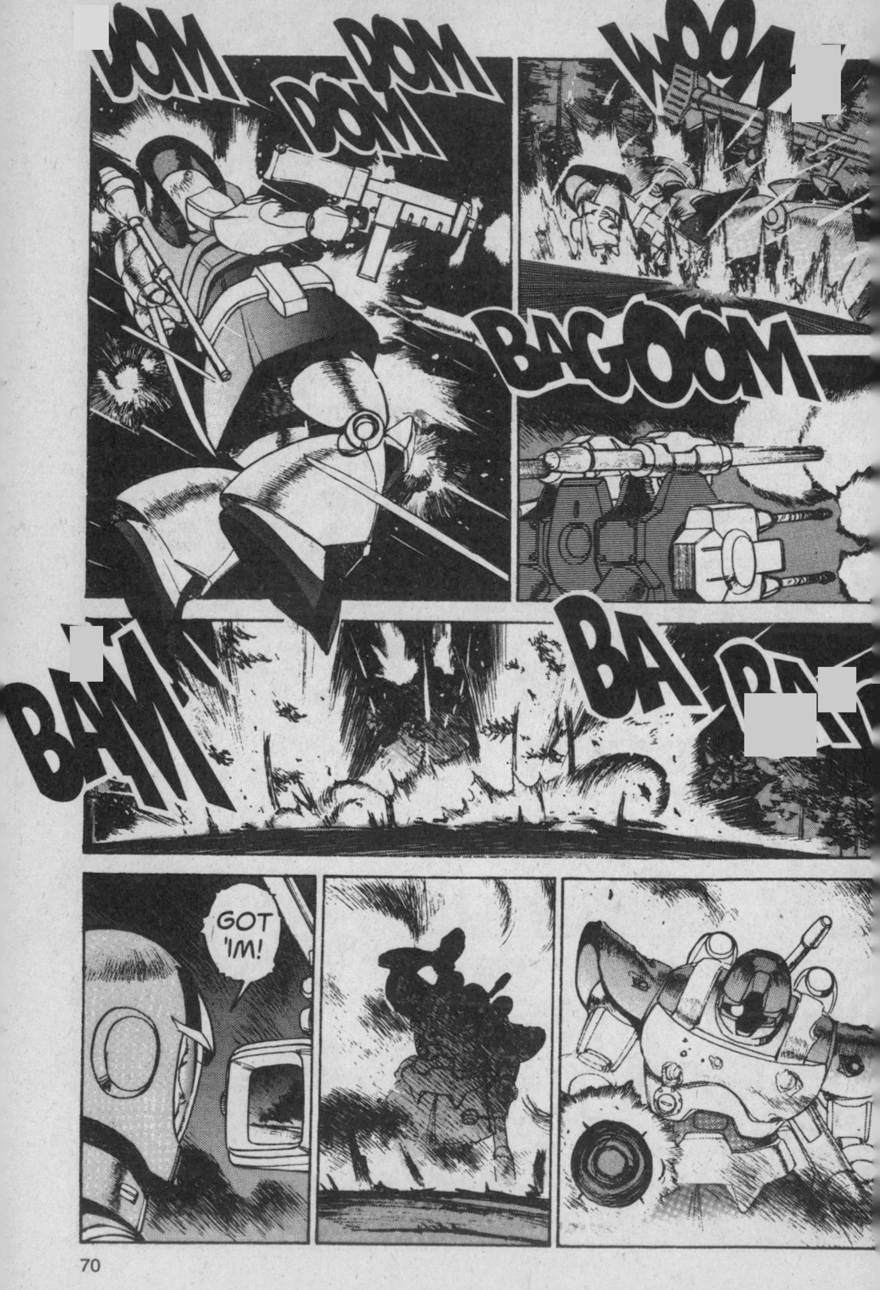
OM
DOM
DOM
WOOM
BAGOOM
BAM
BA
GOT 'IM!

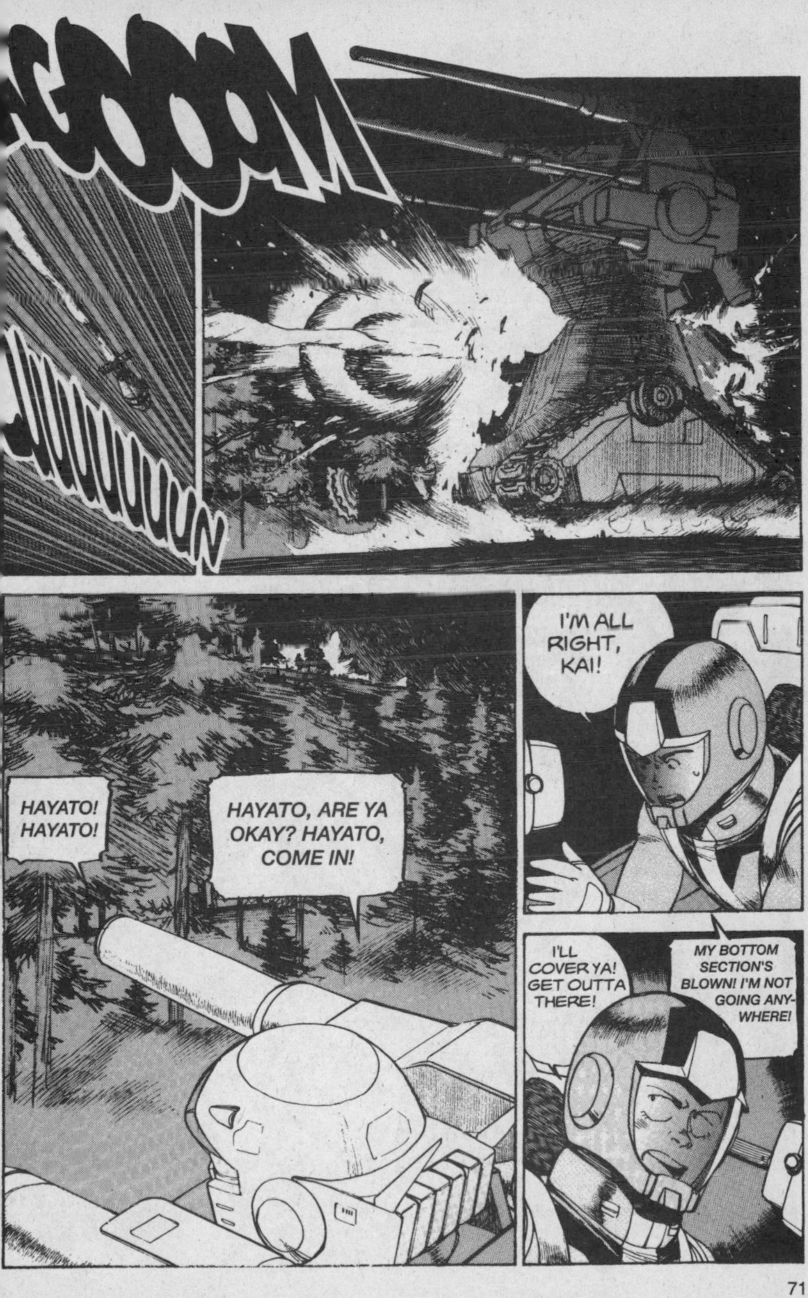
GOOOM
GUUUUUUUN
HAYATO! HAYATO!
HAYATO, ARE YA OKAY? HAYATO, COME IN!
I'M ALL RIGHT, KAI!
I'LL COVER YA! GET OUTTA THERE!
MY BOTTOM SECTION'S BLOWN! I'M NOT GOING ANY-WHERE!

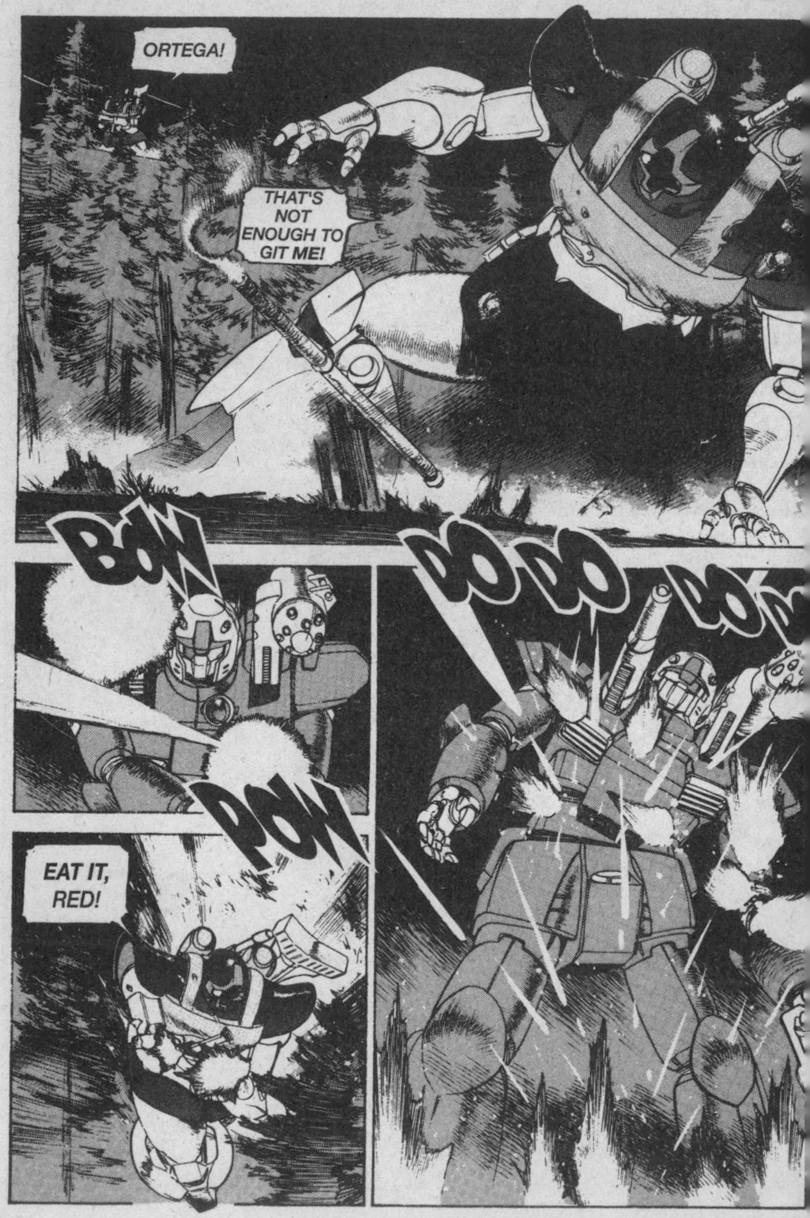

ORTEGA!
THAT'S NOT ENOUGH TO GIT ME!
BOW
DO DO
POW
EAT IT, RED!

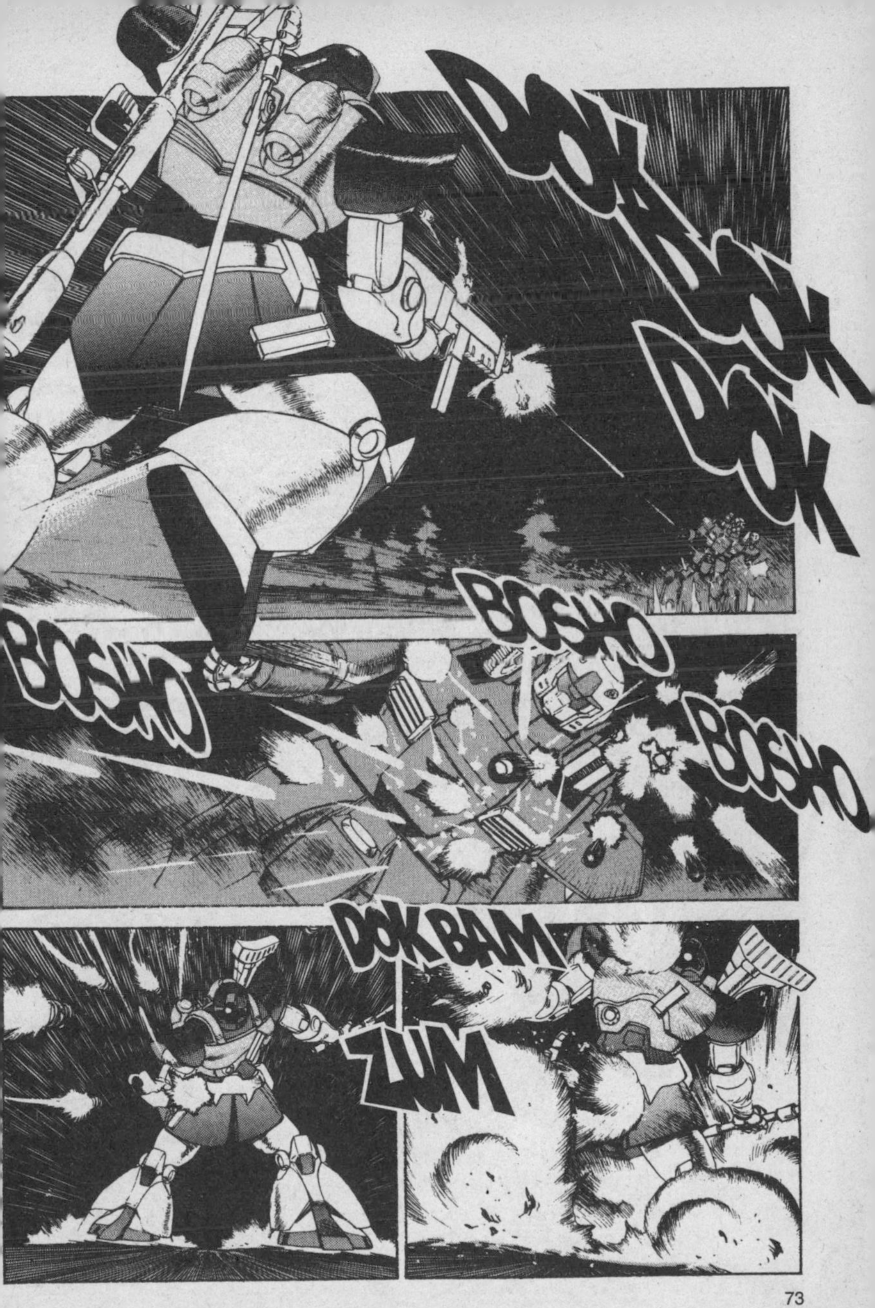
DOK
DOK
DOK
DOK
BOSHO
BOSHO
BOSHO
DOK BAM
ZUM

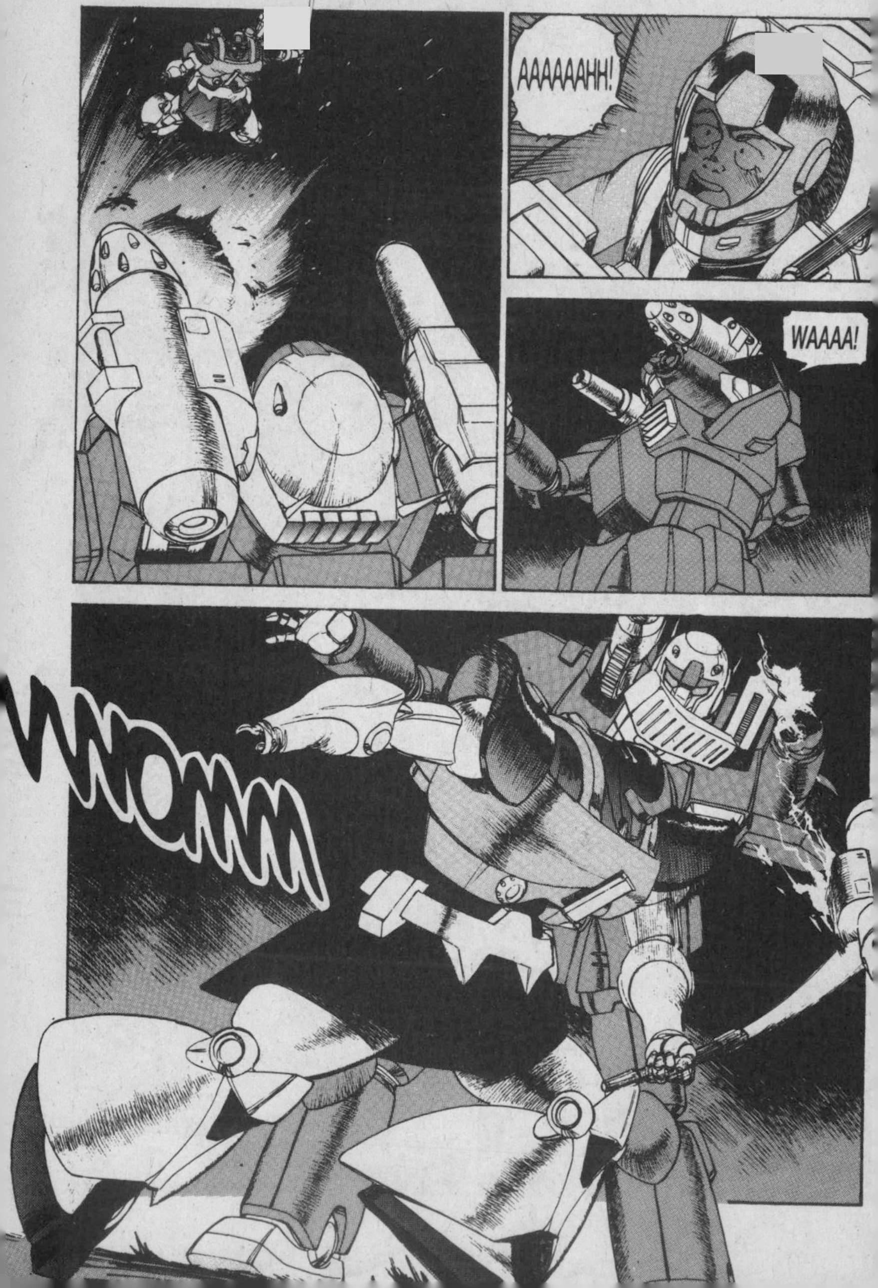
AAAAAAHH!
WAAAA!
WHOMM

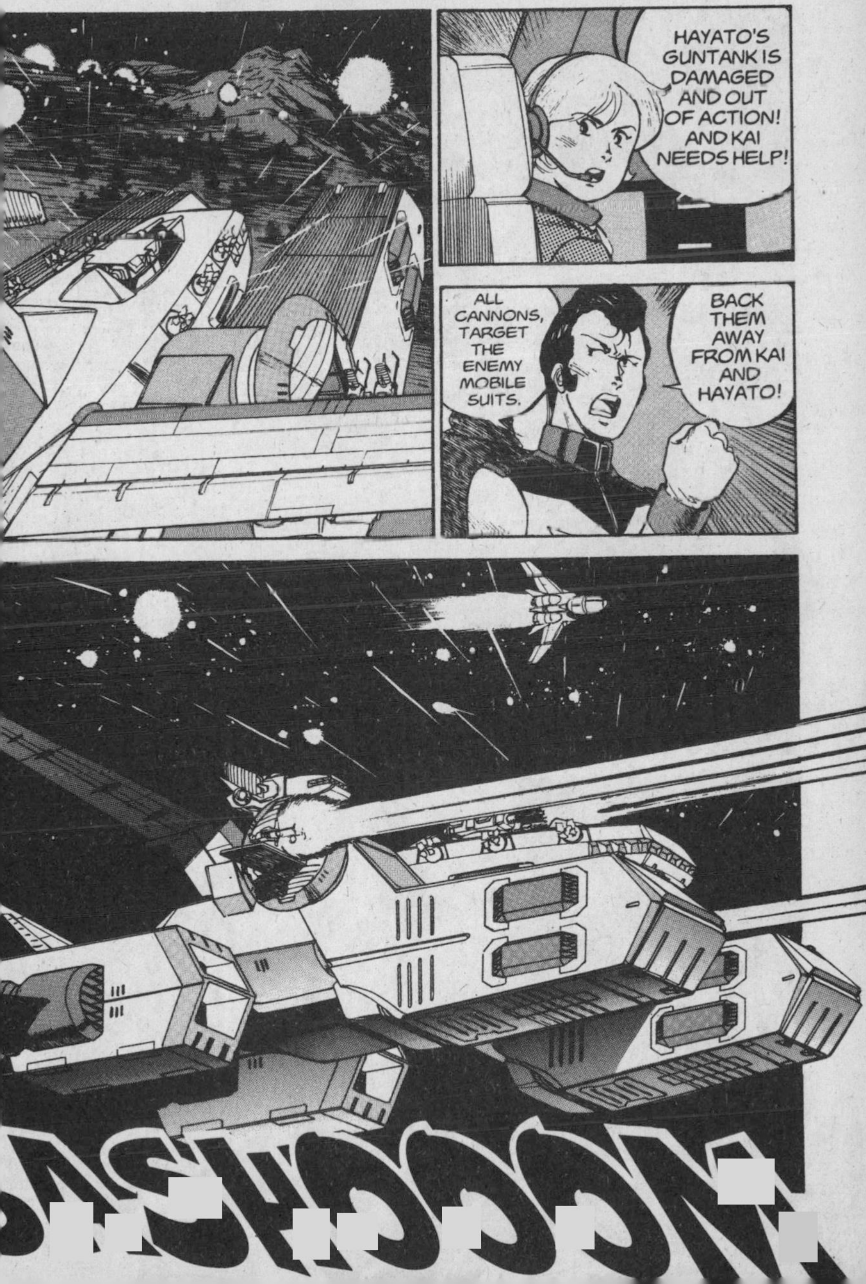
HAYATO'S GUNTANK IS DAMAGED AND OUT OF ACTION! AND KAI NEEDS HELP!
ALL CANNONS, TARGET THE ENEMY MOBILE SUITS.
BACK THEM AWAY FROM KAI AND HAYATO!

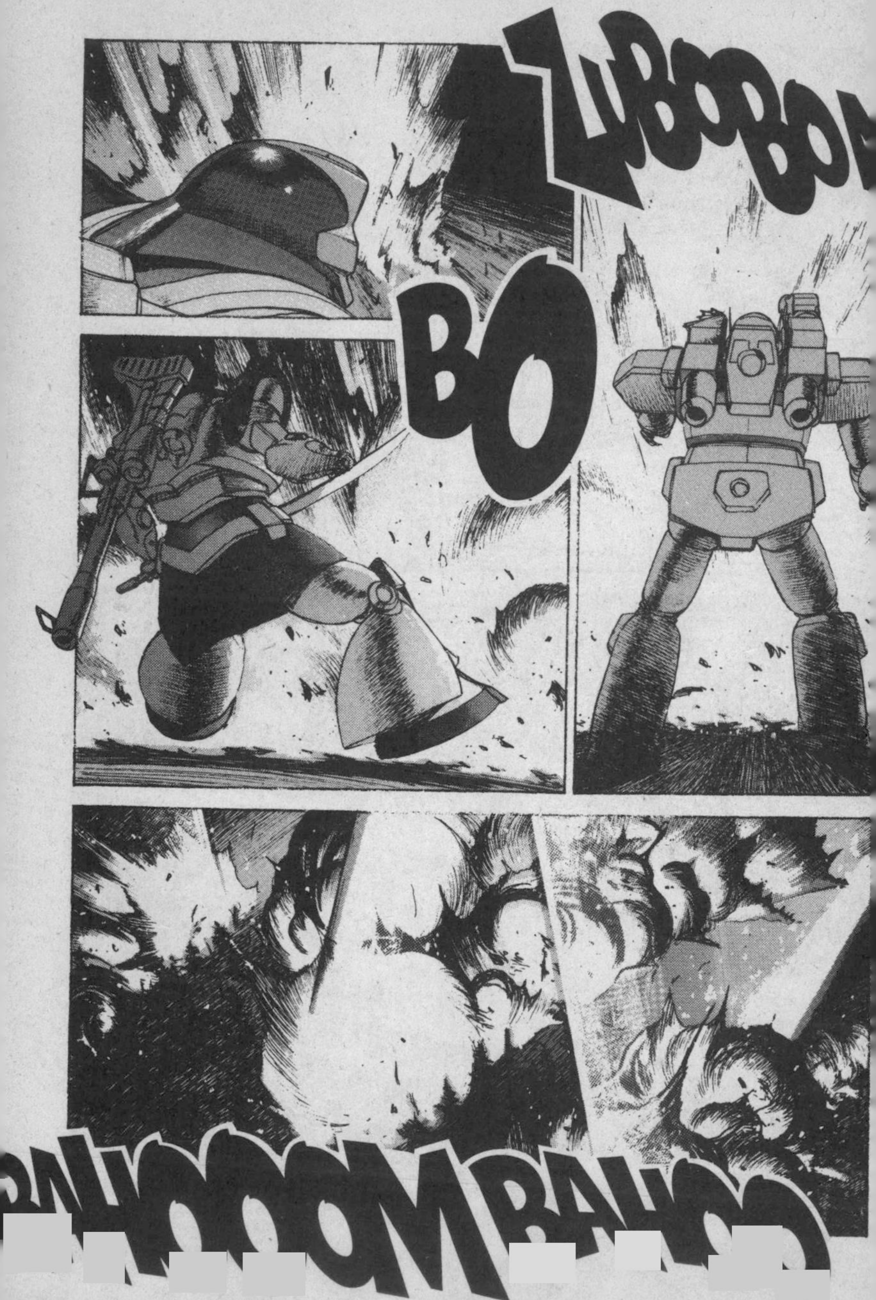
ZUBOOBO
BO
BAHOOOOM
BAHOO

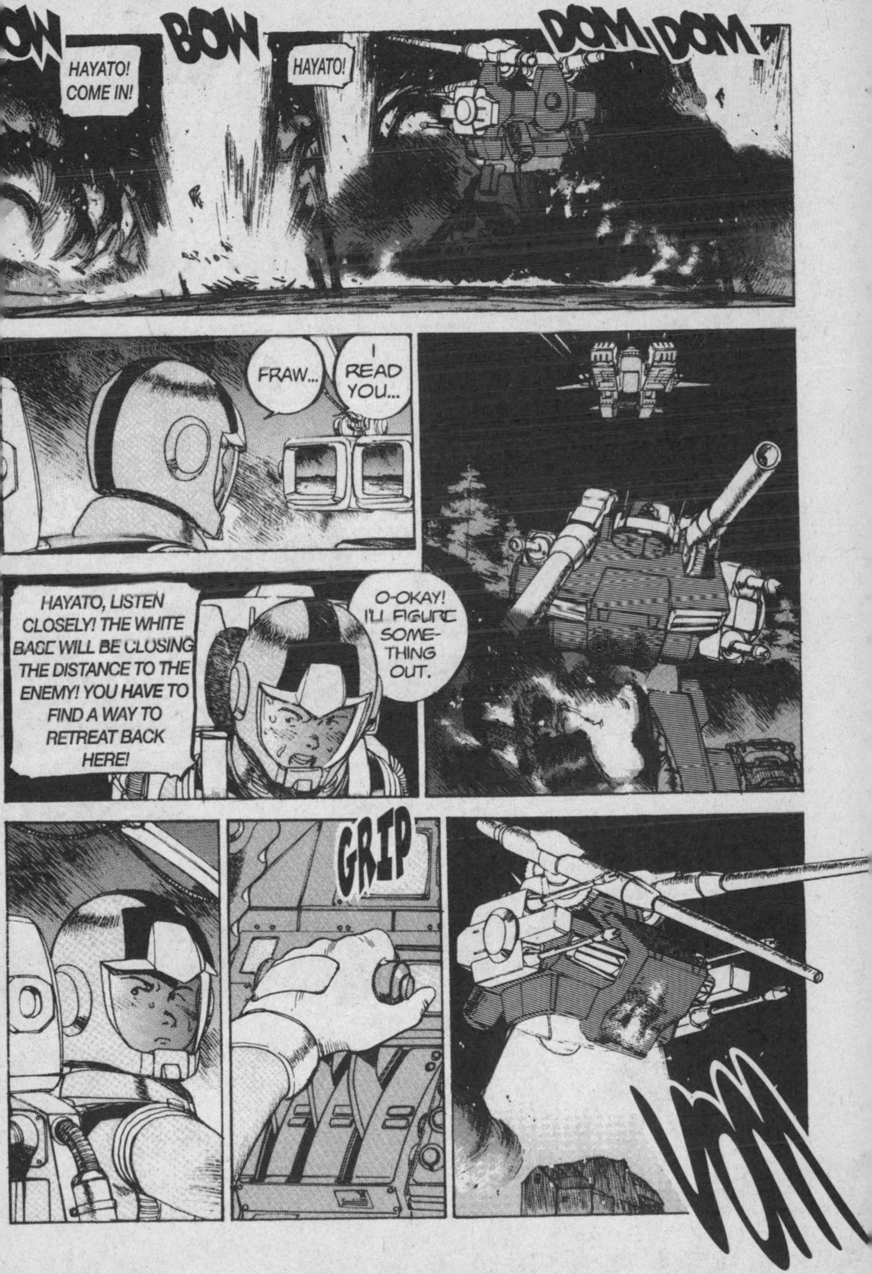

BOW
BOW
HAYATO! COME IN!
HAYATO!
DOM DOM
FRAW...
I READ YOU...
HAYATO, LISTEN CLOSELY! THE WHITE BASE WILL BE CLOSING THE DISTANCE TO THE ENEMY! YOU HAVE TO FIND A WAY TO RETREAT BACK HERE!
O-OKAY! I'LL FIGURE SOME-THING OUT.
GRIP
VOOM

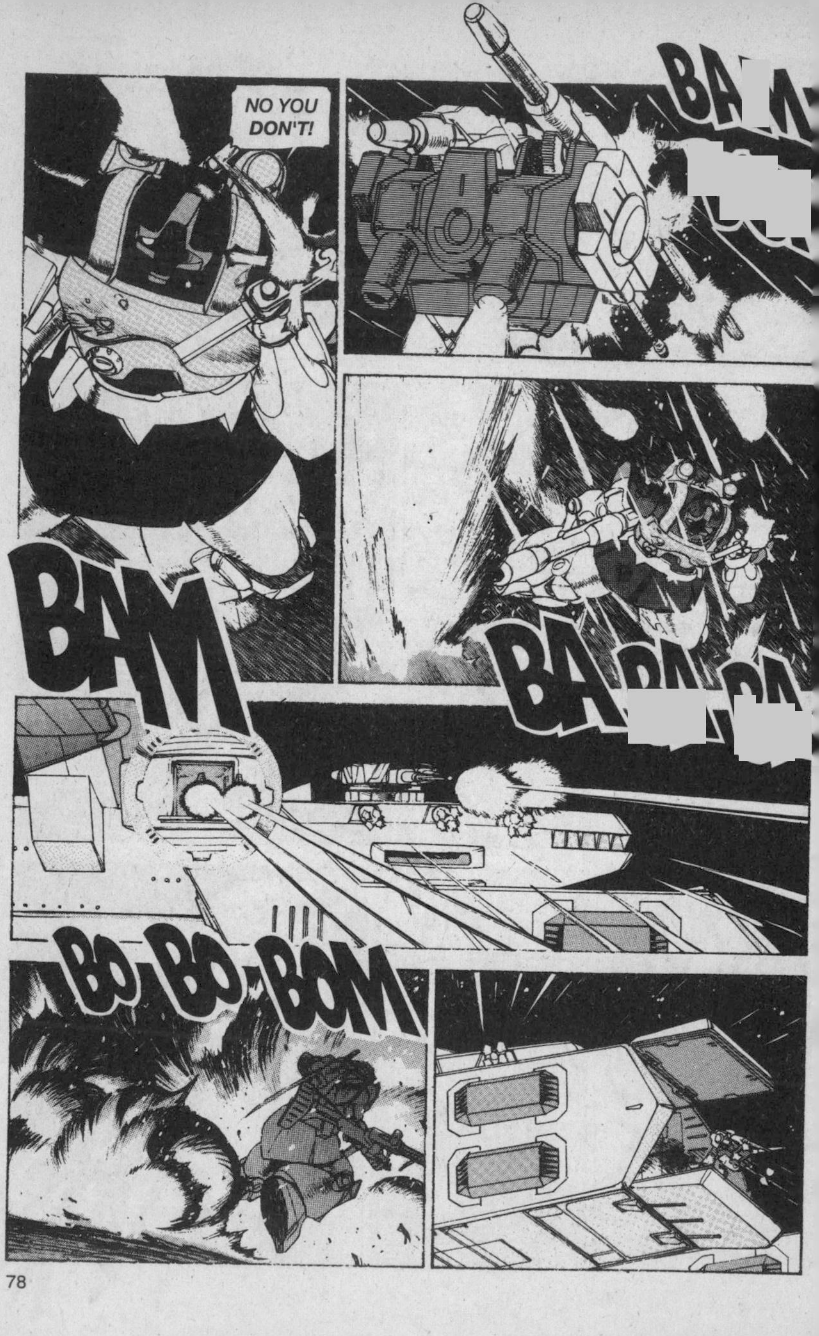
NO YOU DON'T!
BAM
BO-BO-BOM

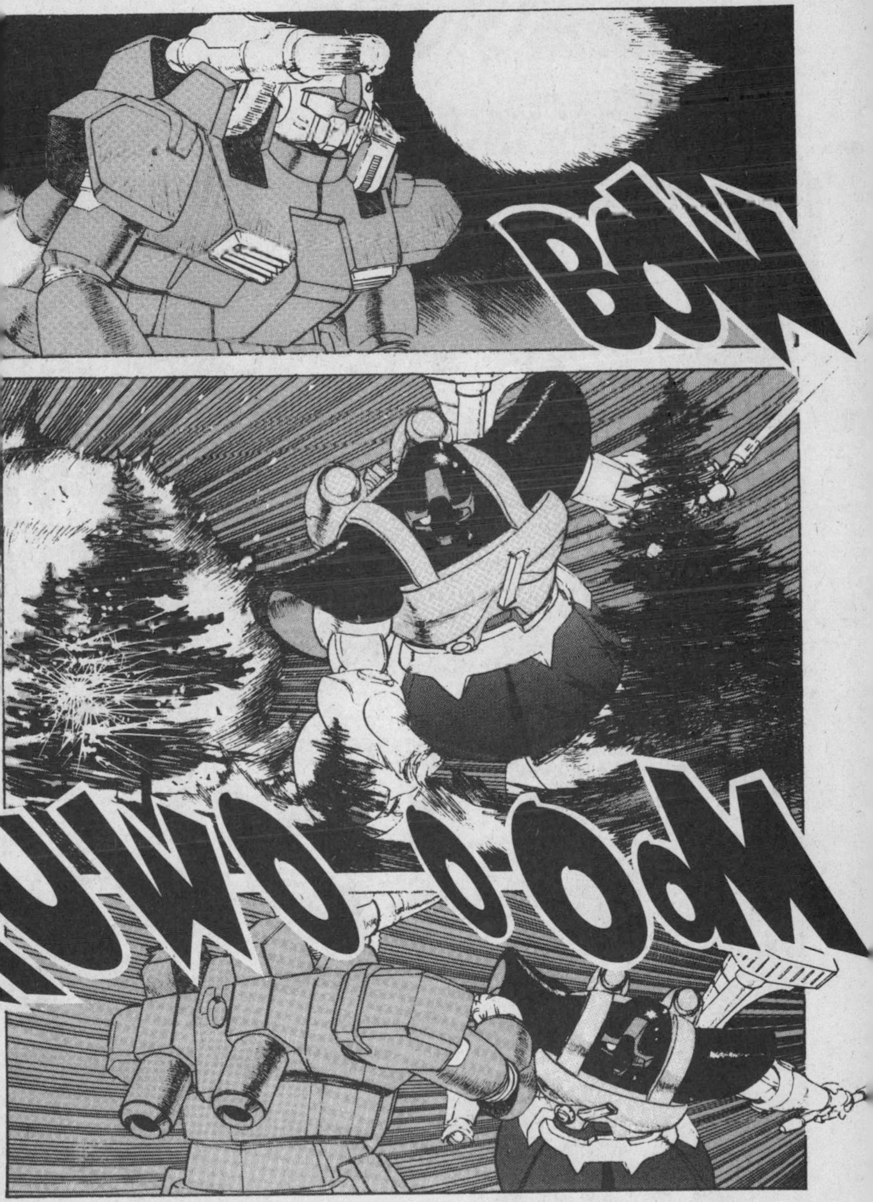
BOM
WO-O-OOM

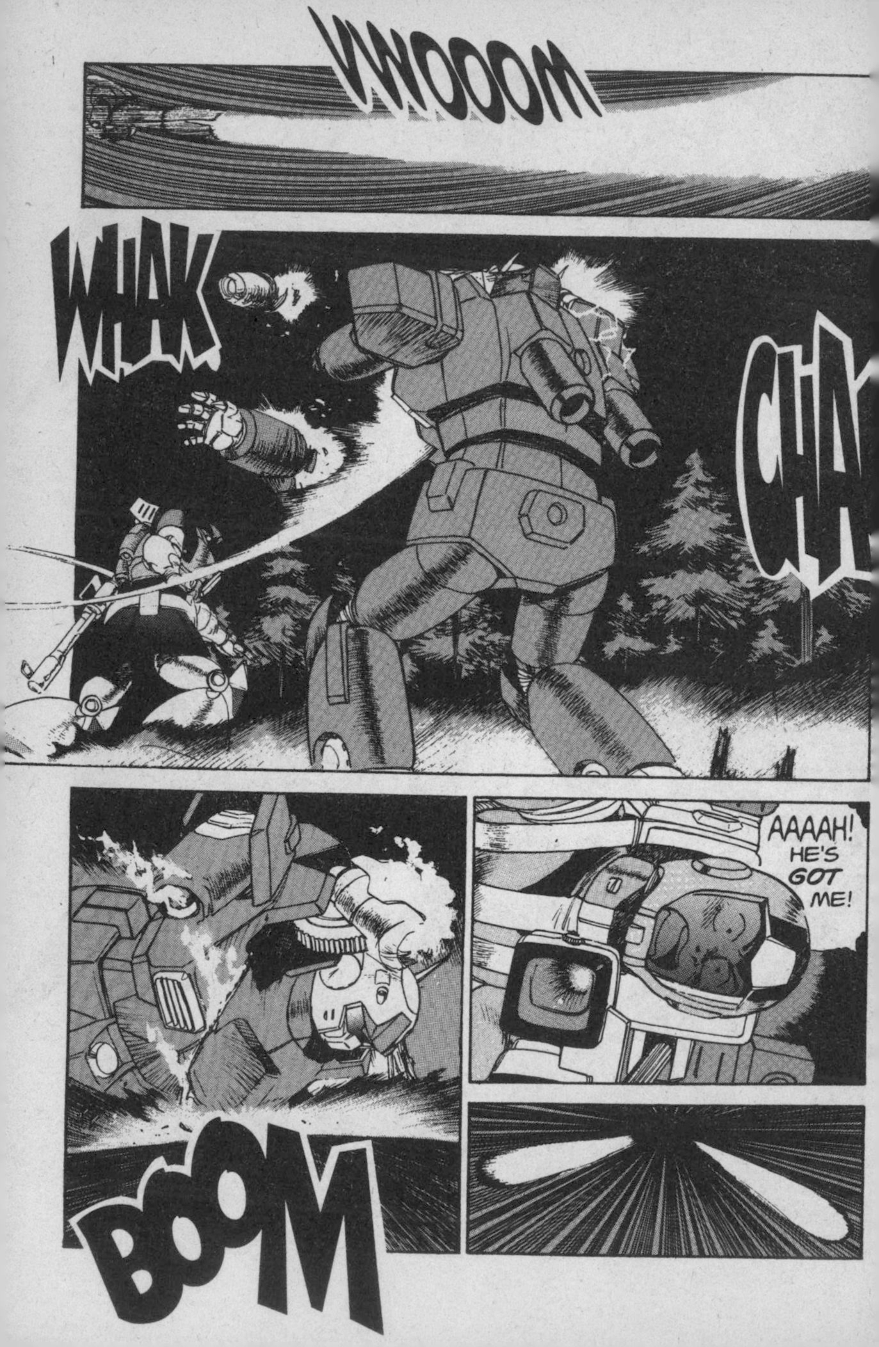
VWOOOM
WHAK
CHA
BOOM
AAAAH! HE'S GOT ME!

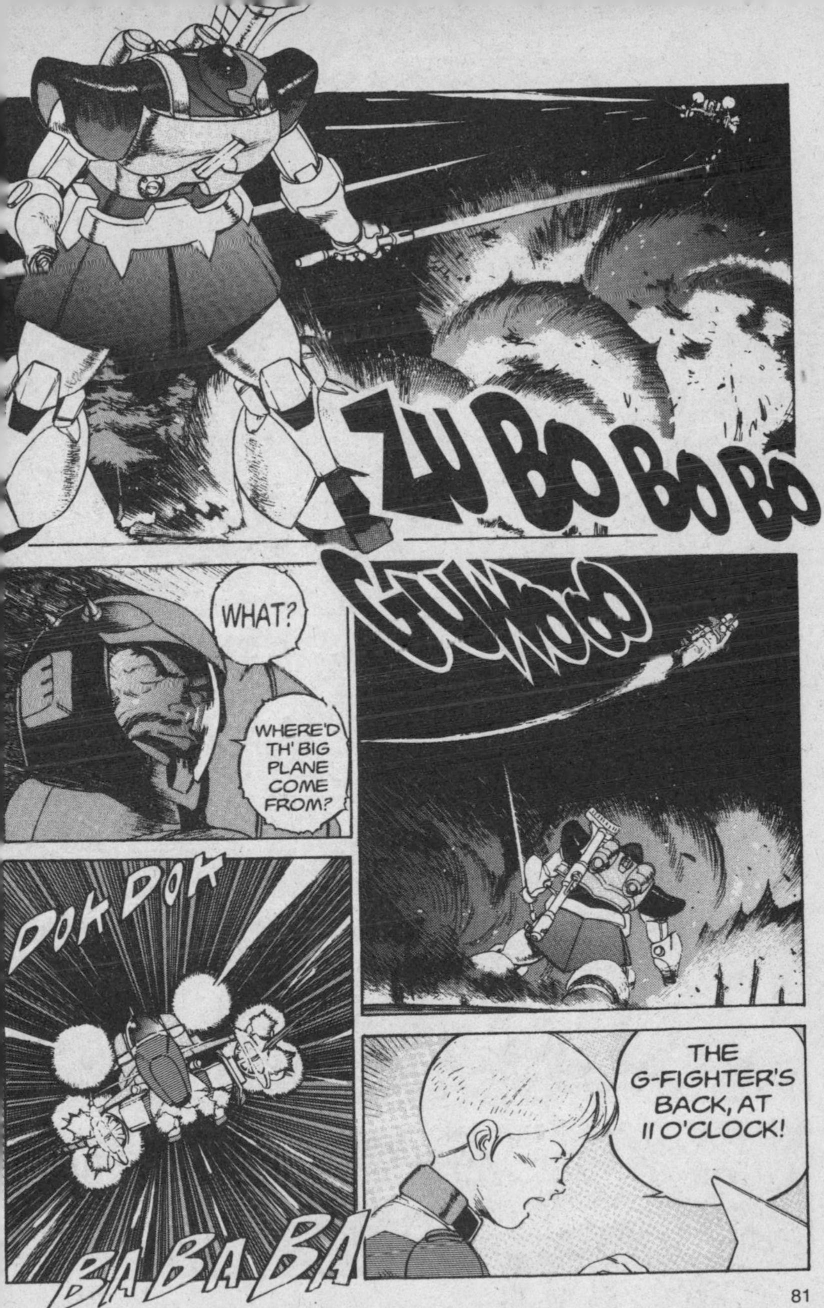
ZU BO BO BO
WHAT?
WHERE'D TH' BIG PLANE COME FROM?
GUWOOO
DOK DOK
BA BA BA BA
THE G-FIGHTER'S BACK, AT 11 O'CLOCK!

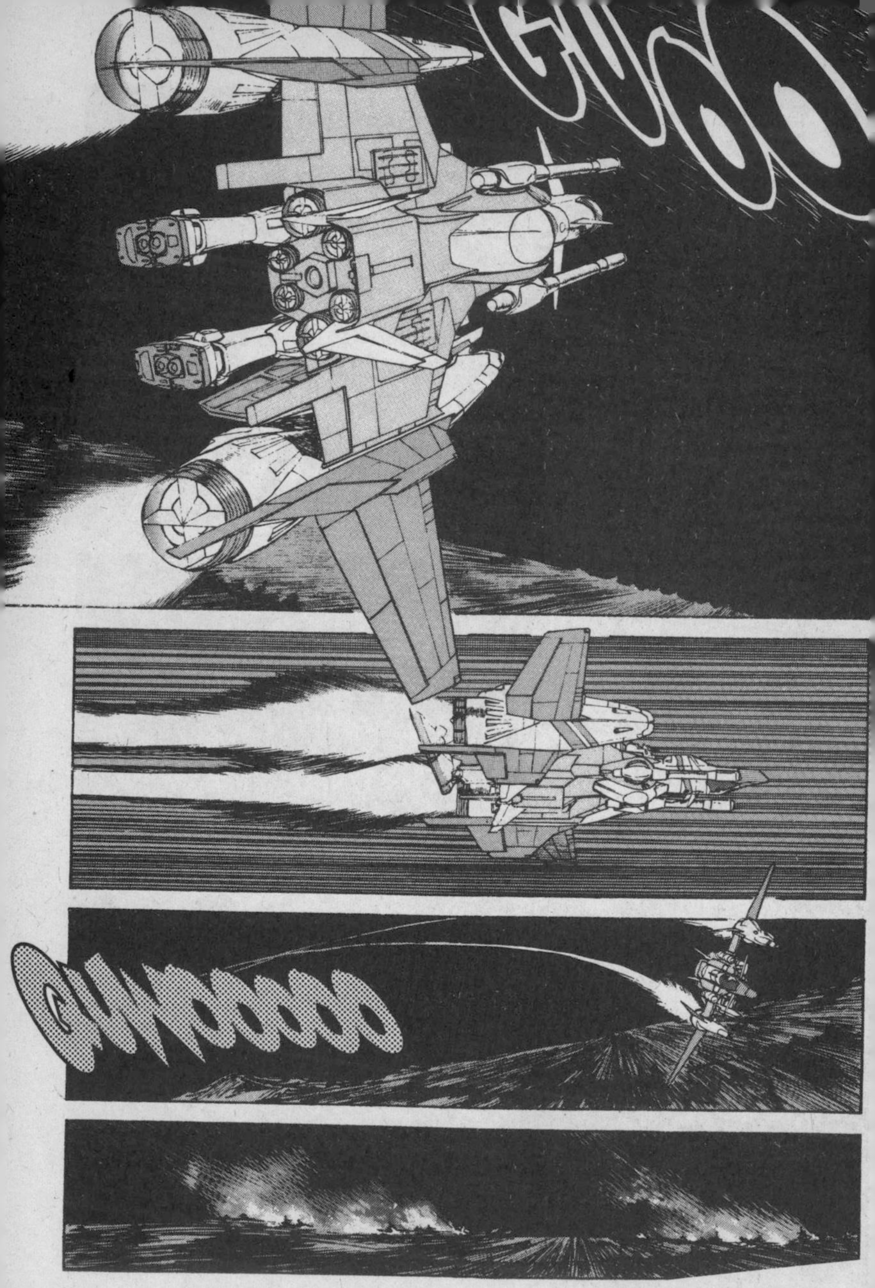
GWOO
GWOOOOO

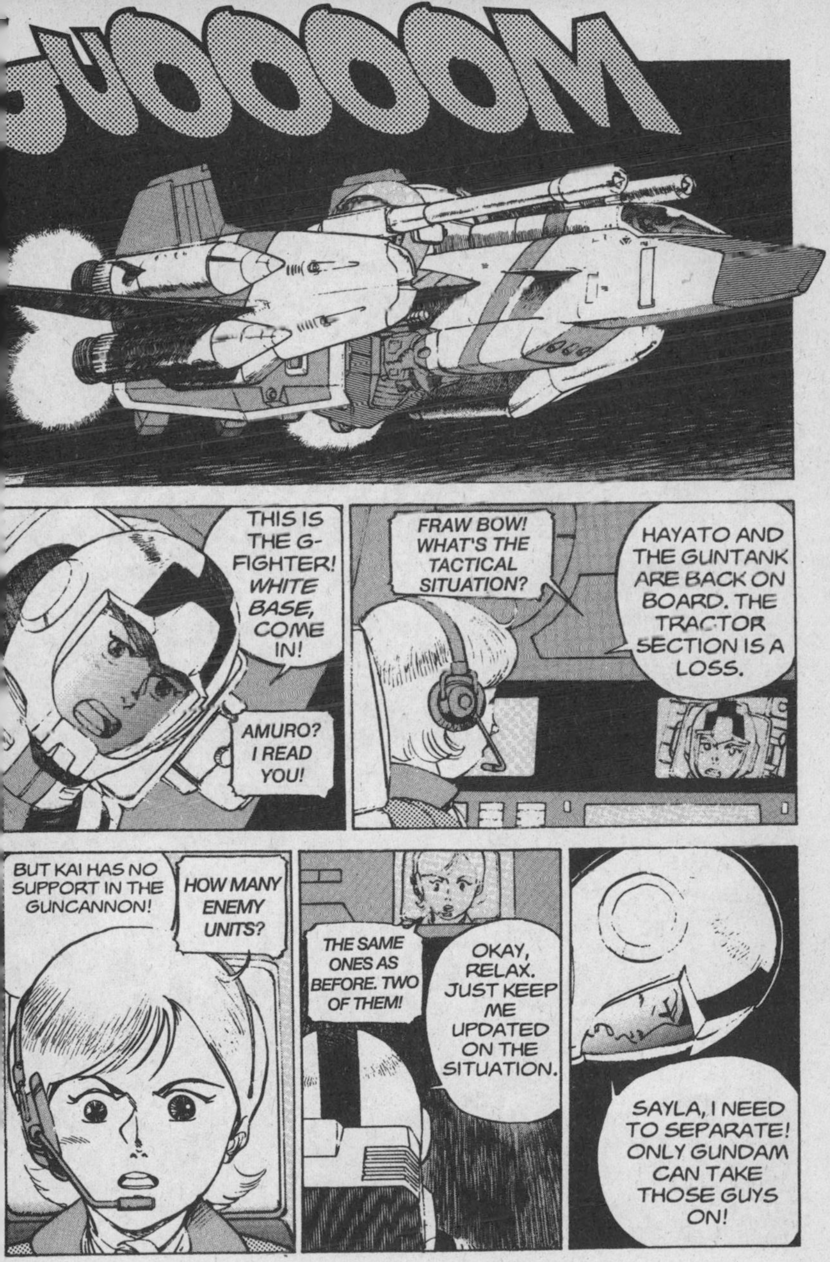
GUOOOOM
THIS IS THE G-FIGHTER! WHITE BASE, COME IN!
AMURO? I READ YOU!
FRAW BOW! WHAT'S THE TACTICAL SITUATION?
HAYATO AND THE GUNTANK ARE BACK ON BOARD. THE TRACTOR SECTION IS A LOSS.
BUT KAI HAS NO SUPPORT IN THE GUNCANNON!
HOW MANY ENEMY UNITS?
THE SAME ONES AS BEFORE. TWO OF THEM!
OKAY, RELAX. JUST KEEP ME UPDATED ON THE SITUATION.
SAYLA, I NEED TO SEPARATE! ONLY GUNDAM CAN TAKE THOSE GUYS ON!

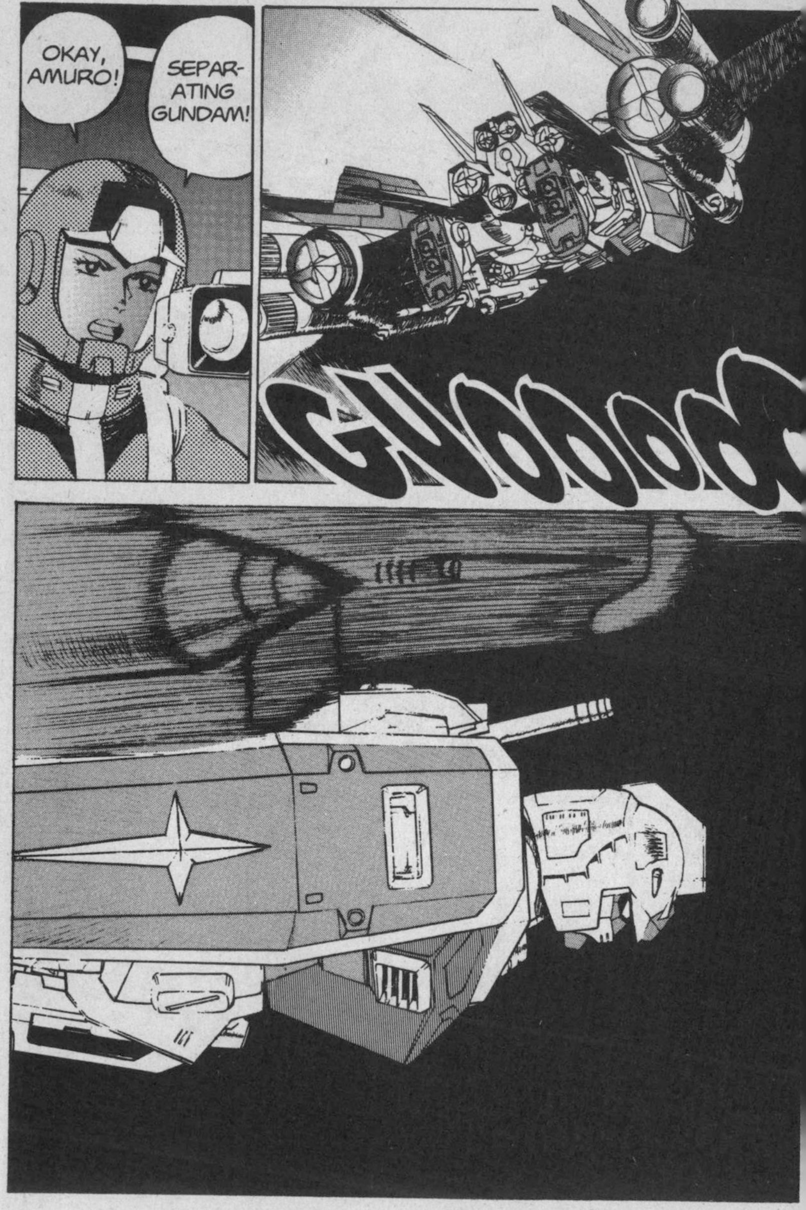
OKAY, AMURO!
SEPAR-ATING GUNDAM!

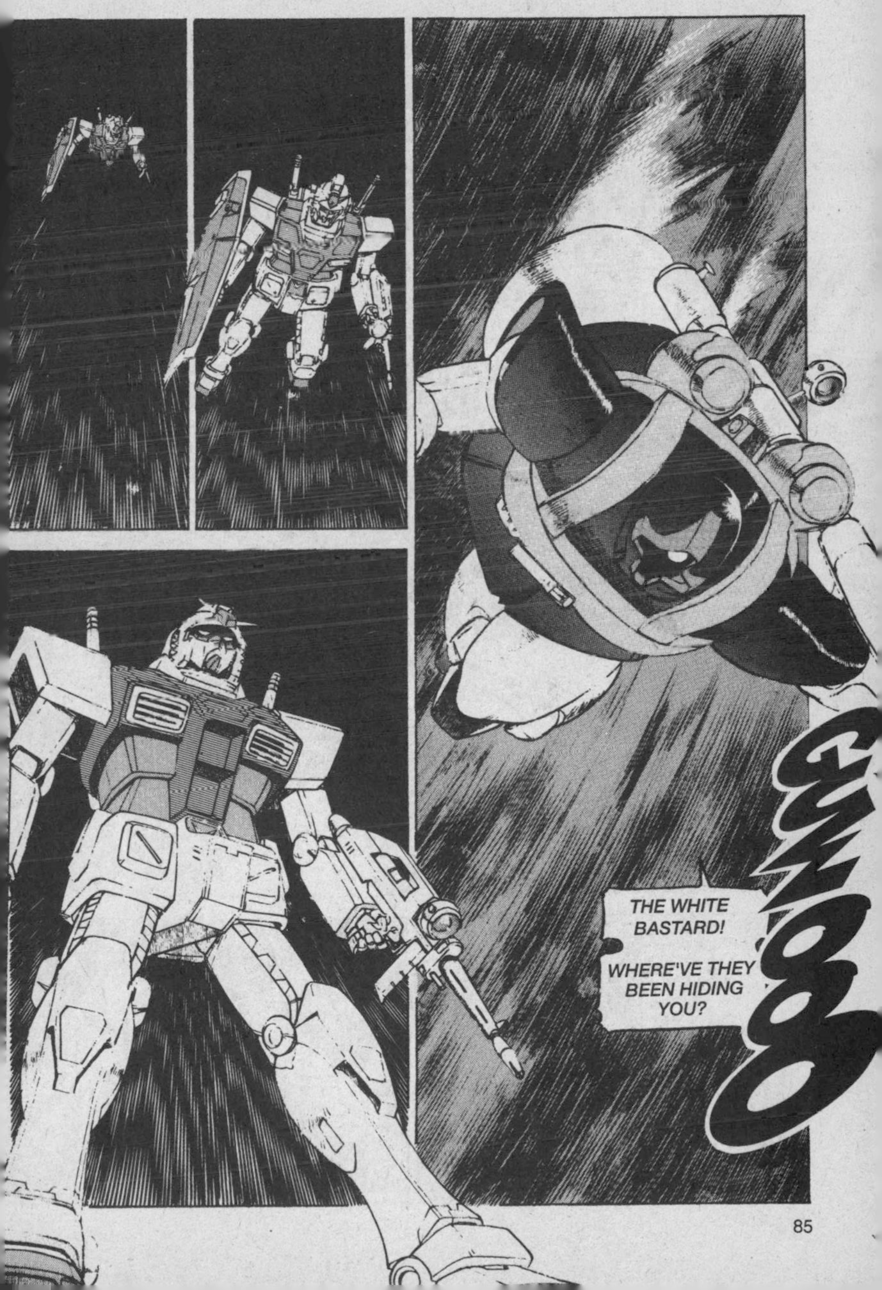
THE WHITE BASTARD!
WHERE'VE THEY BEEN HIDING YOU?
GUWOOO

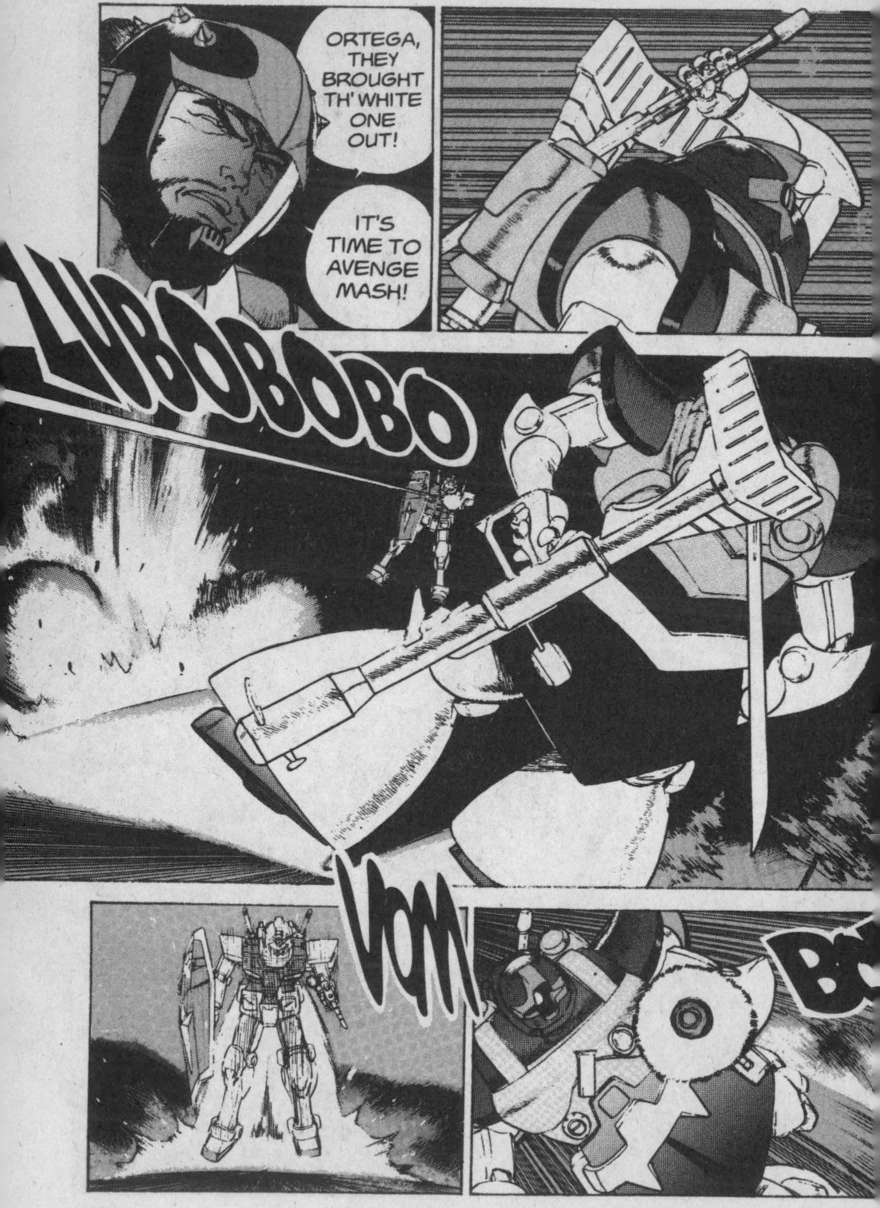
ORTEGA, THEY BROUGHT TH' WHITE ONE OUT!
IT'S TIME TO AVENGE MASH!
ZUBOBOBO
VOM

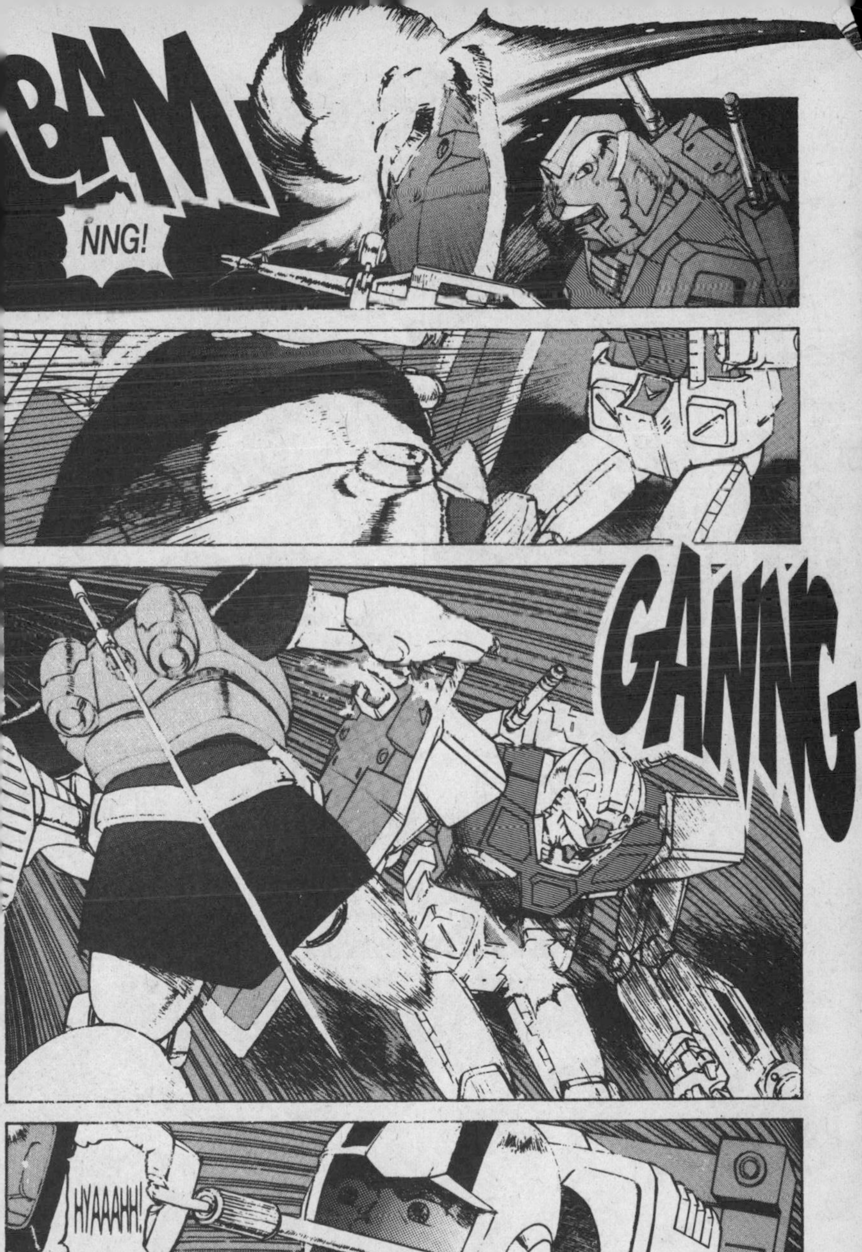
BAM
NNG!
GAMNG
HYAAAHH!

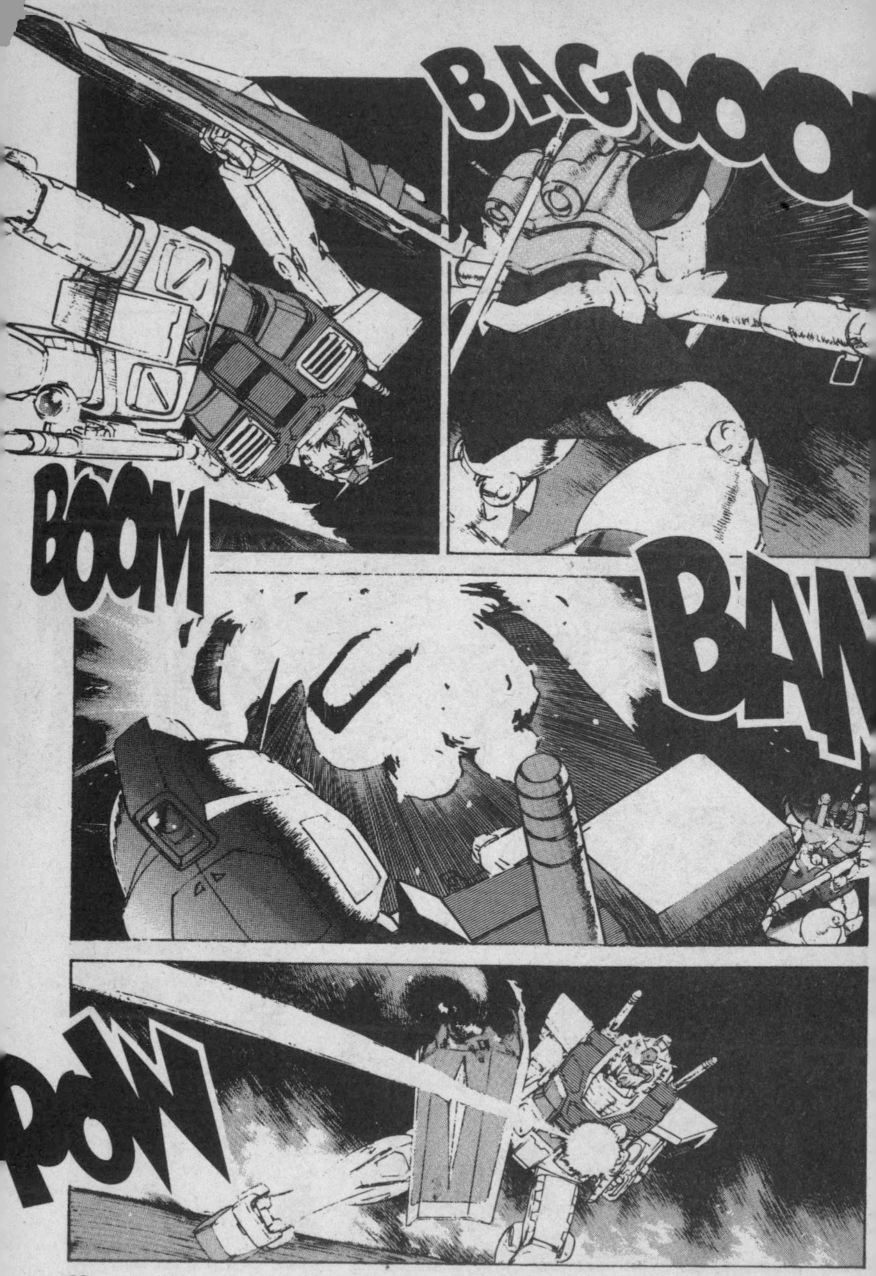
BOOM
BAGOOO
BA
POW

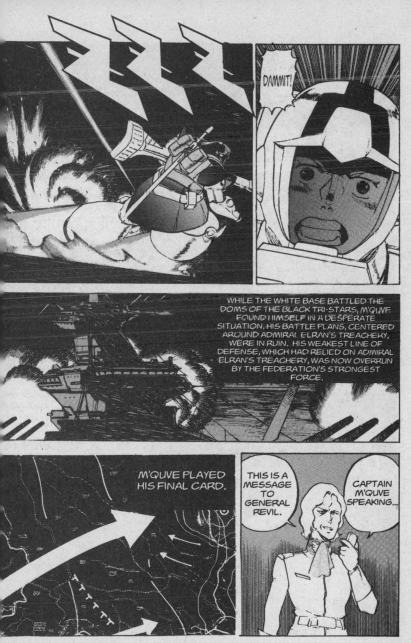

DAMMIT!

WHILE THE WHITE BASE BATTLED THE DOMS OF THE BLACK TRI-STARS, M'QUVE FOUND HIMSELF IN A DESPERATE SITUATION. HIS BATTLE PLANS, CENTERED AROUND ADMIRAL ELRAN'S TREACHERY, WERE IN RUIN. HIS WEAKEST LINE OF DEFENSE, WHICH HAD RELIED ON ADMIRAL ELRAN'S TREACHERY, WAS NOW OVERRUN BY THE FEDERATION'S STRONGEST FORCE.

M'QUVE PLAYED HIS FINAL CARD.

THIS IS A MESSAGE TO GENERAL REVIL.

CAPTAIN M'QUVE SPEAKING...

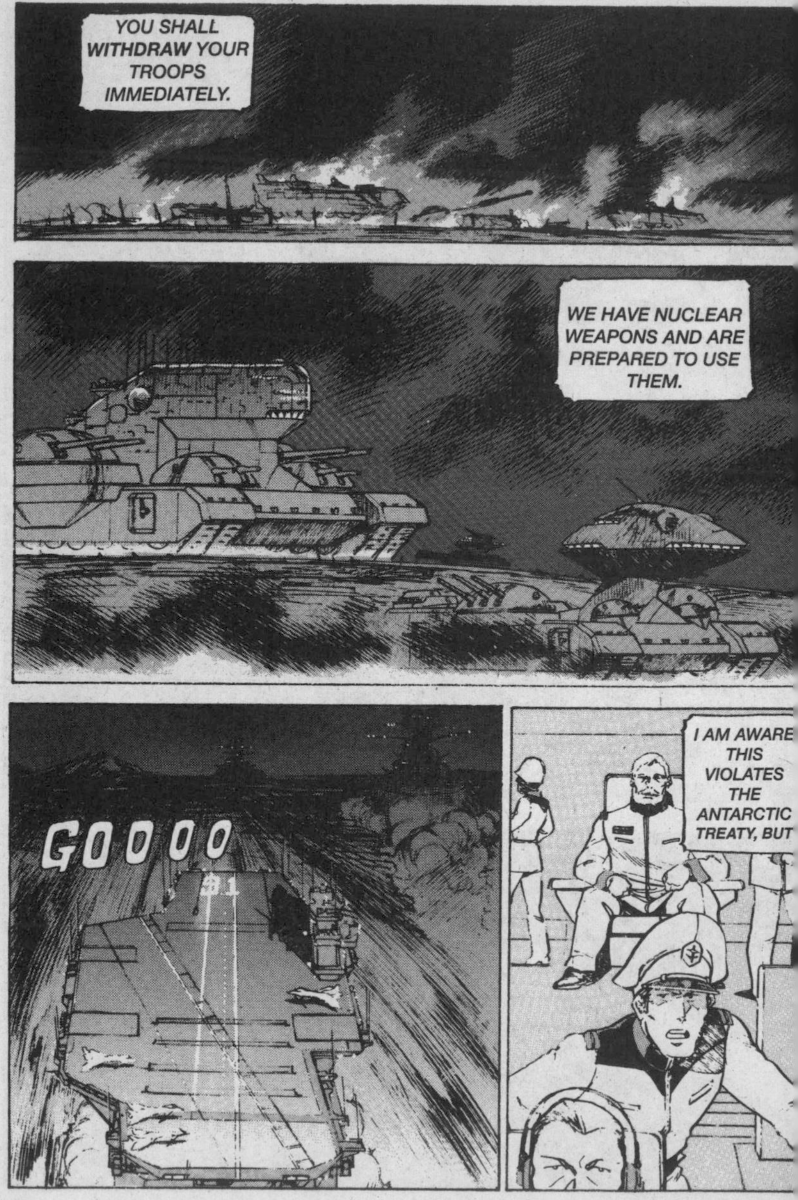
YOU SHALL WITHDRAW YOUR TROOPS IMMEDIATELY.
WE HAVE NUCLEAR WEAPONS AND ARE PREPARED TO USE THEM.
GOOOO
I AM AWARE THIS VIOLATES THE ANTARCTIC TREATY, BUT

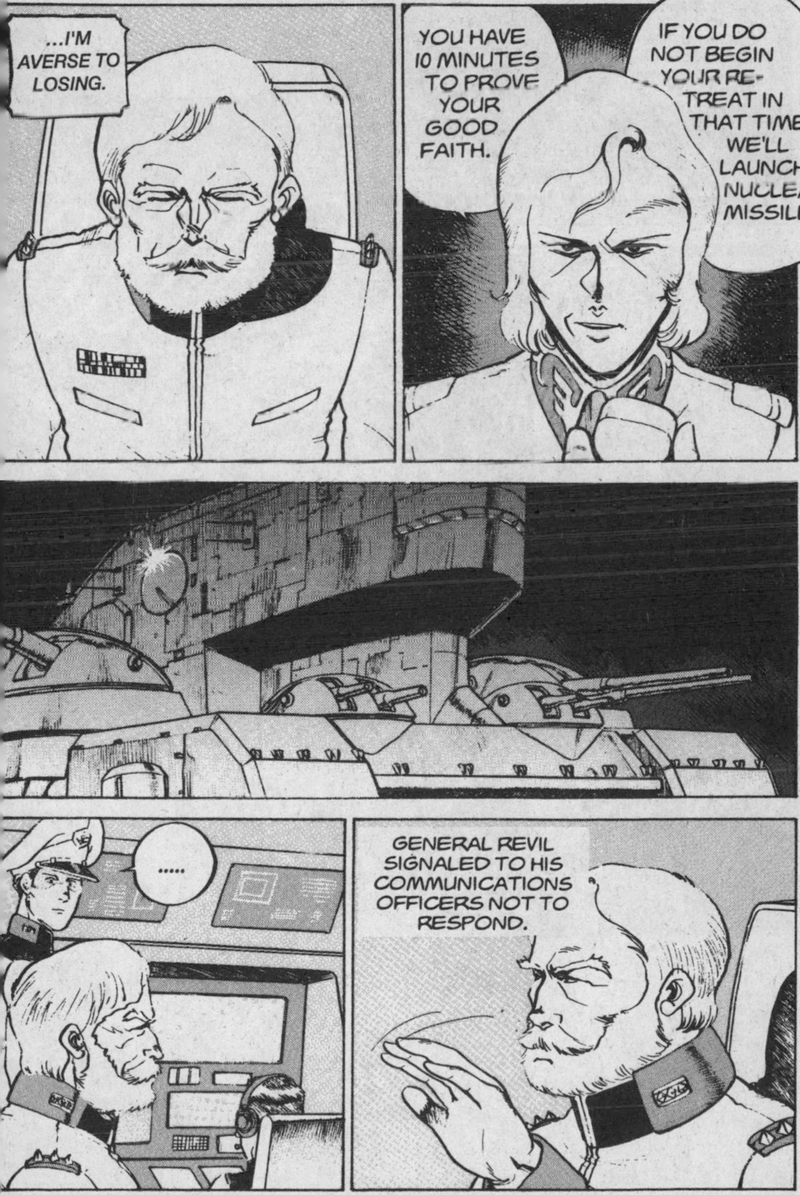
...I'M AVERSE TO LOSING.
YOU HAVE 10 MINUTES TO PROVE YOUR GOOD FAITH.
IF YOU DO NOT BEGIN YOUR RE-TREAT IN THAT TIME, WE'LL LAUNCH NUCLEAR MISSILES.
......
GENERAL REVIL SIGNALED TO HIS COMMUNICATIONS OFFICERS NOT TO RESPOND.

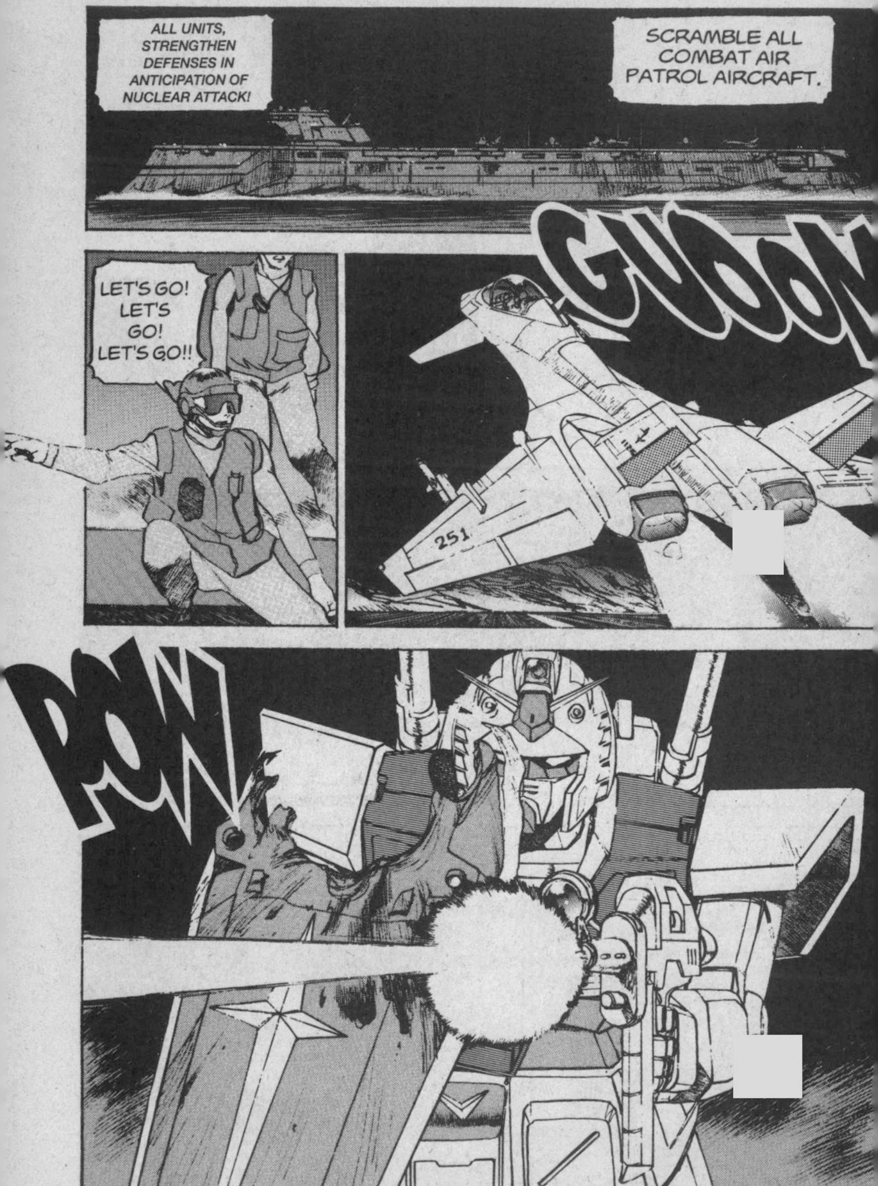
ALL UNITS, STRENGTHEN DEFENSES IN ANTICIPATION OF NUCLEAR ATTACK!
SCRAMBLE ALL COMBAT AIR PATROL AIRCRAFT.
GUOOM
LET'S GO! LET'S GO! LET'S GO!!
251
POW

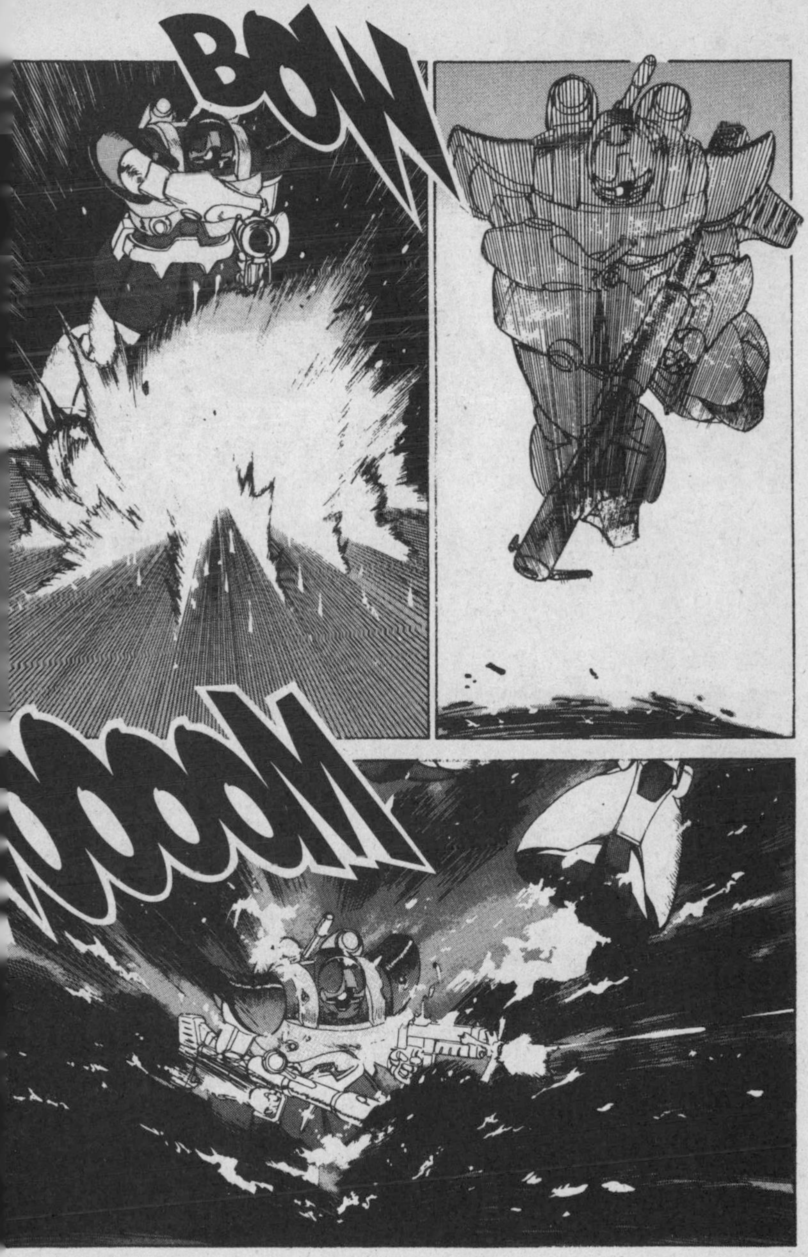
BOW
WOOOOM

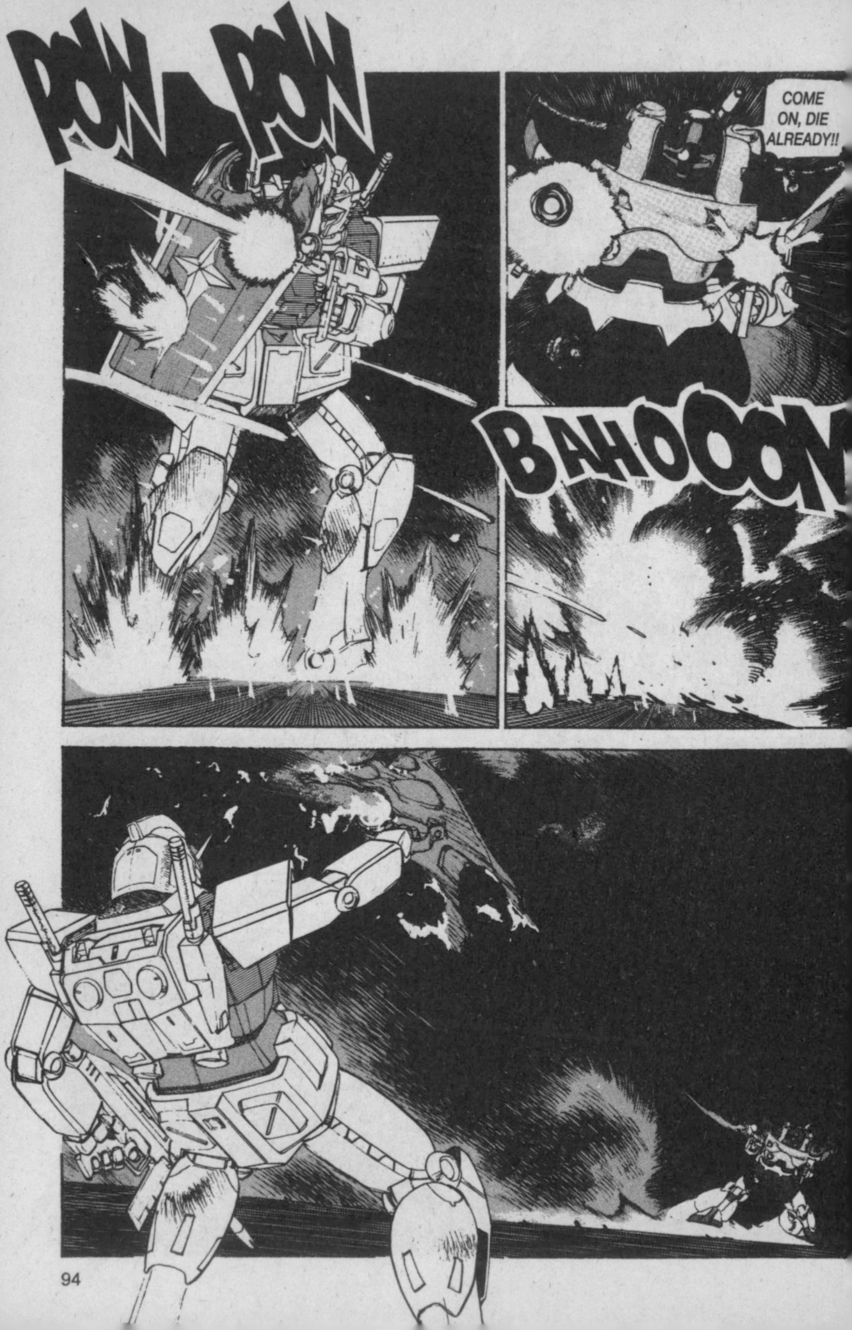
POW POW
COME ON, DIE ALREADY!!
BAHOOOM

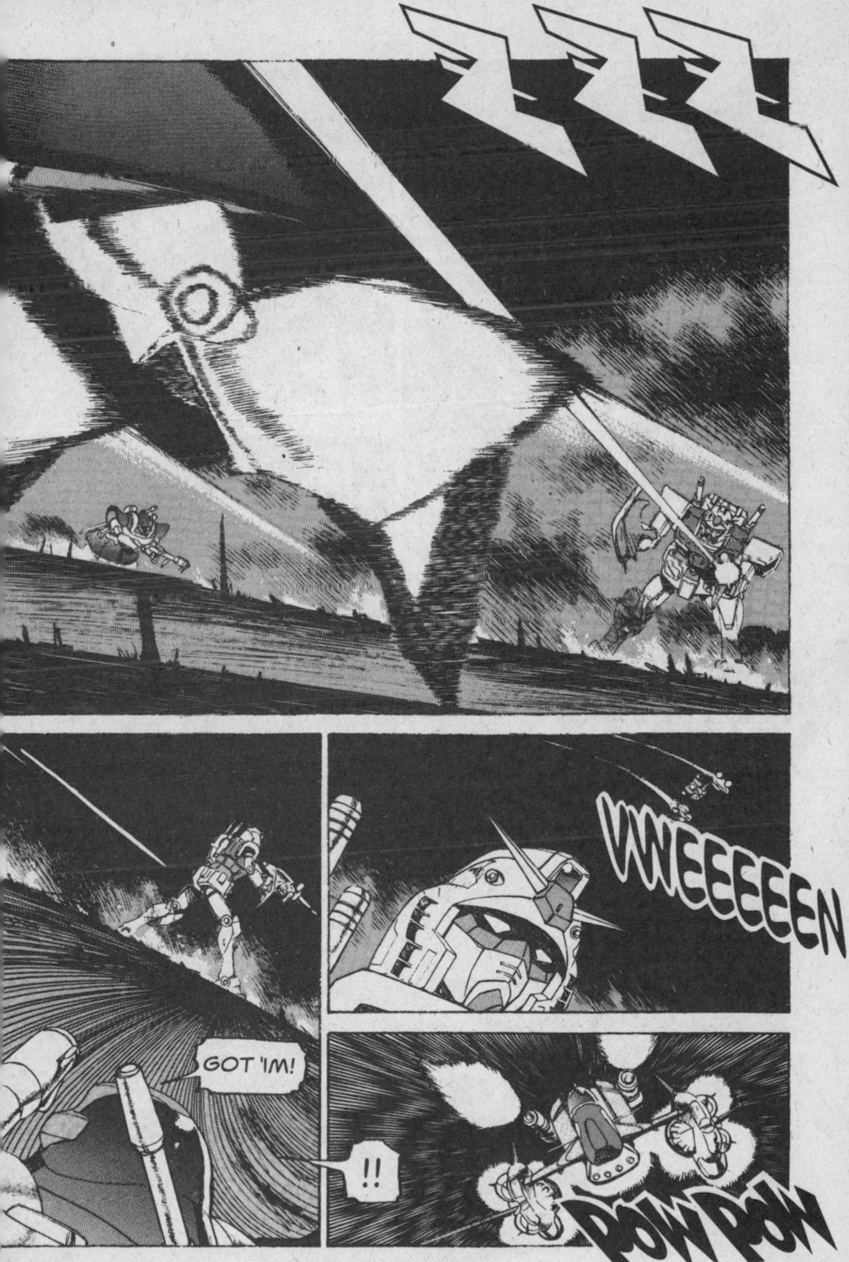
ZZZ
GOT 'IM!
VWEEEEEN
!!
POW POW

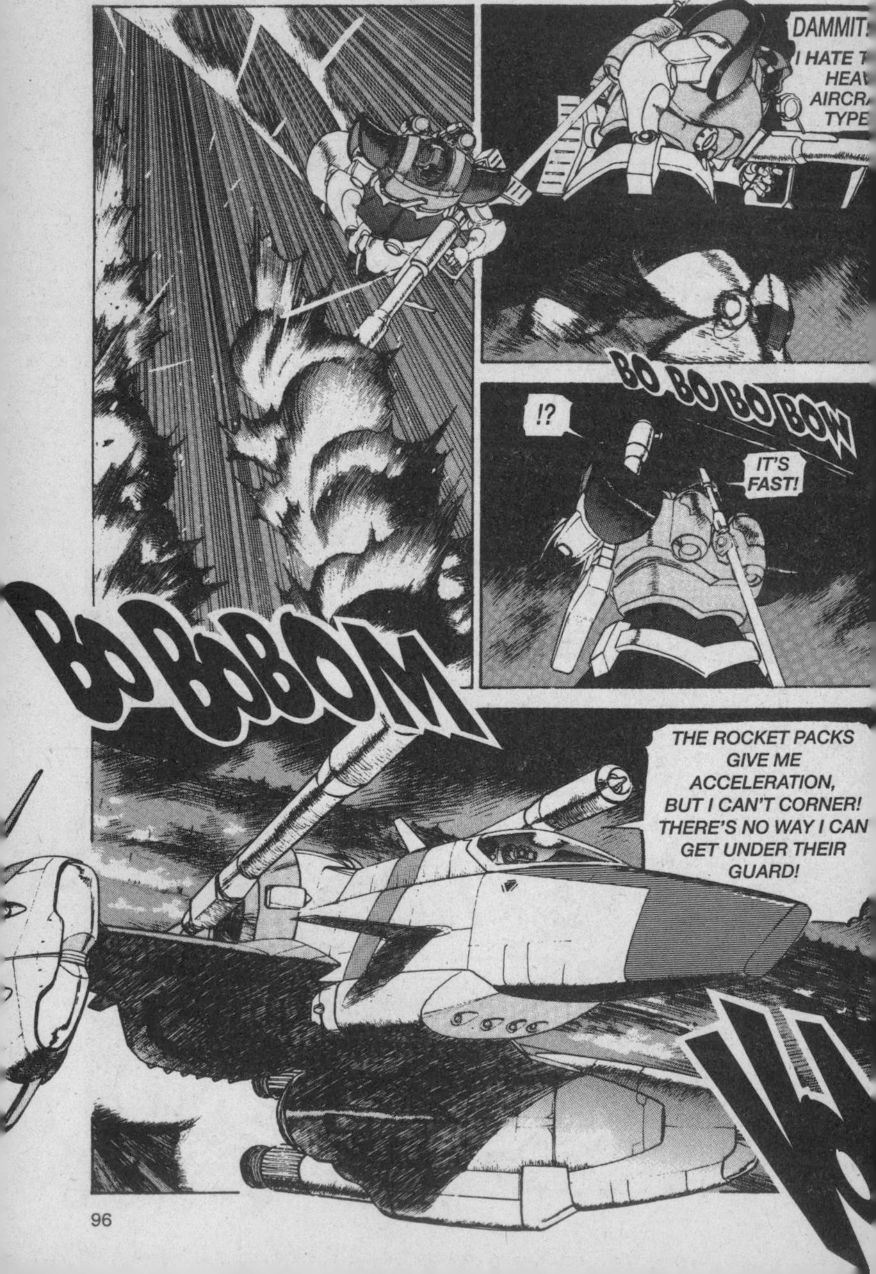
BOBOBOM
DAMMIT!
I HATE T HEAV AIRCRA TYPE
BO BO BO BOW
!?
IT'S FAST!
THE ROCKET PACKS GIVE ME ACCELERATION, BUT I CAN'T CORNER! THERE'S NO WAY I CAN GET UNDER THEIR GUARD!

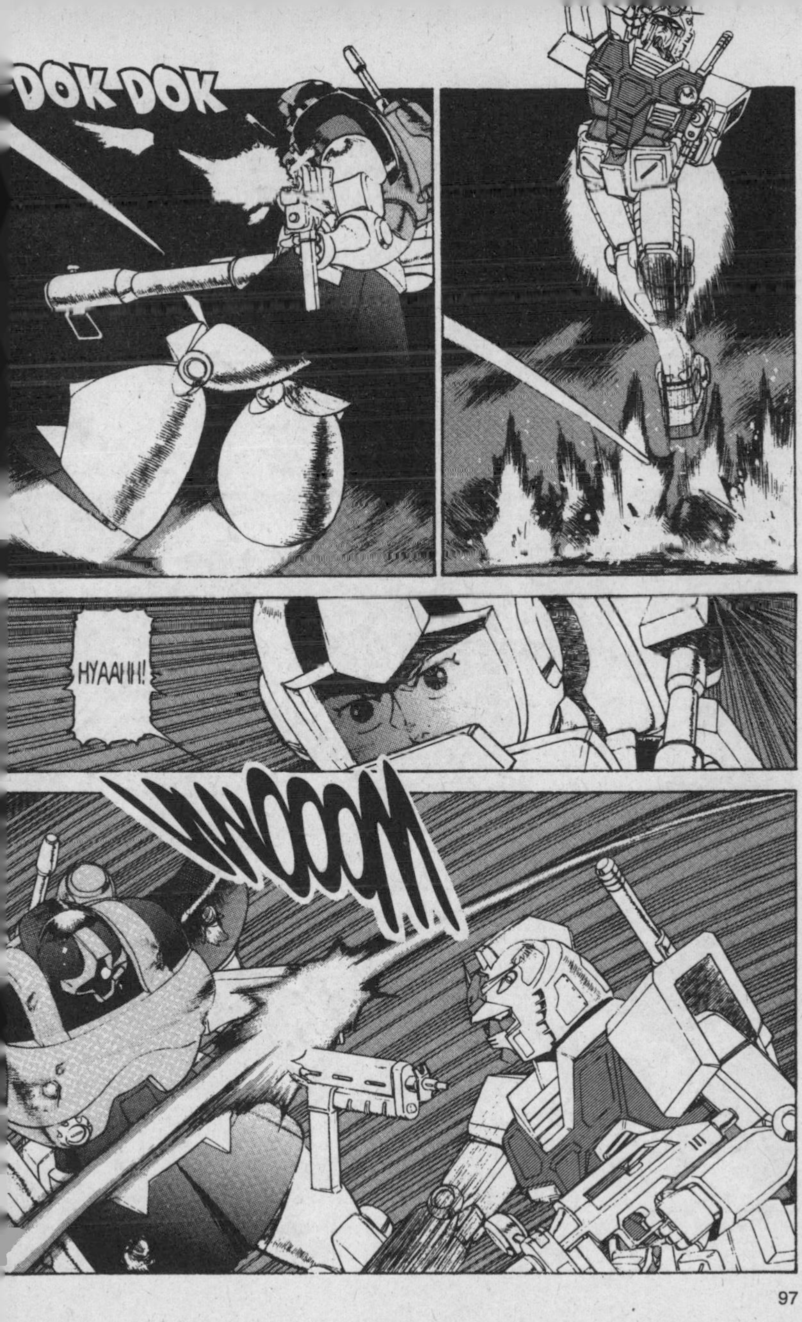
DOK DOK
HYAAHH!
WHOOOM

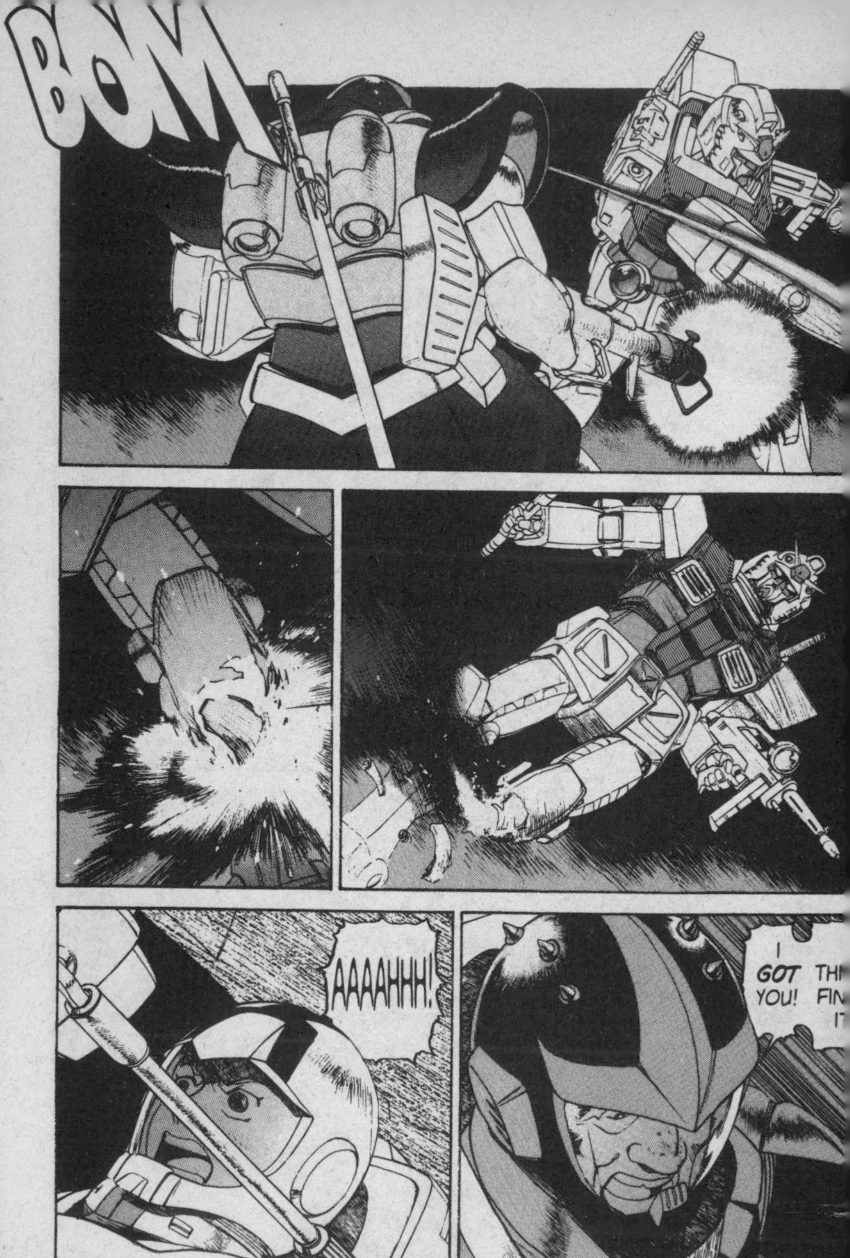
BOOM
AAAAHHH!
I GOT YOU!

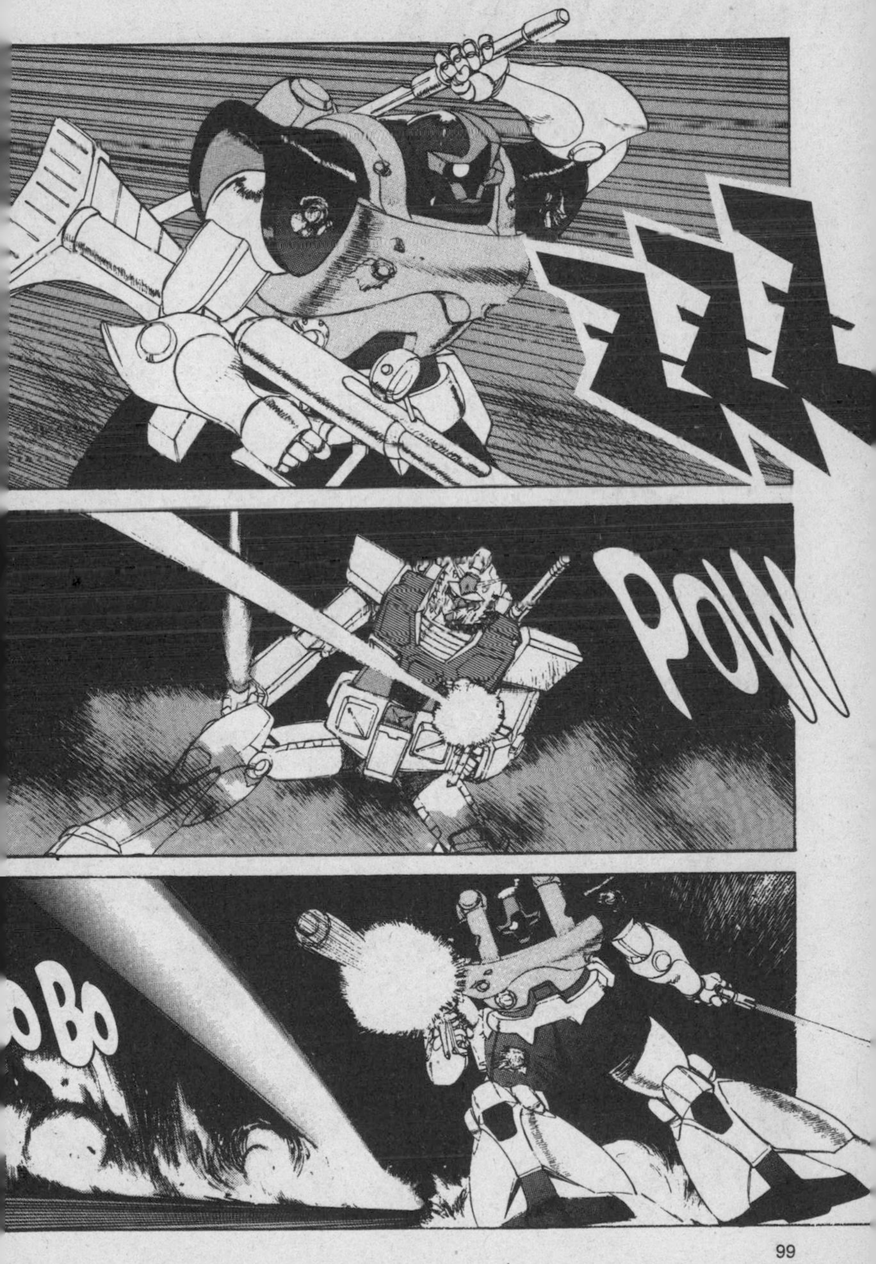
POW

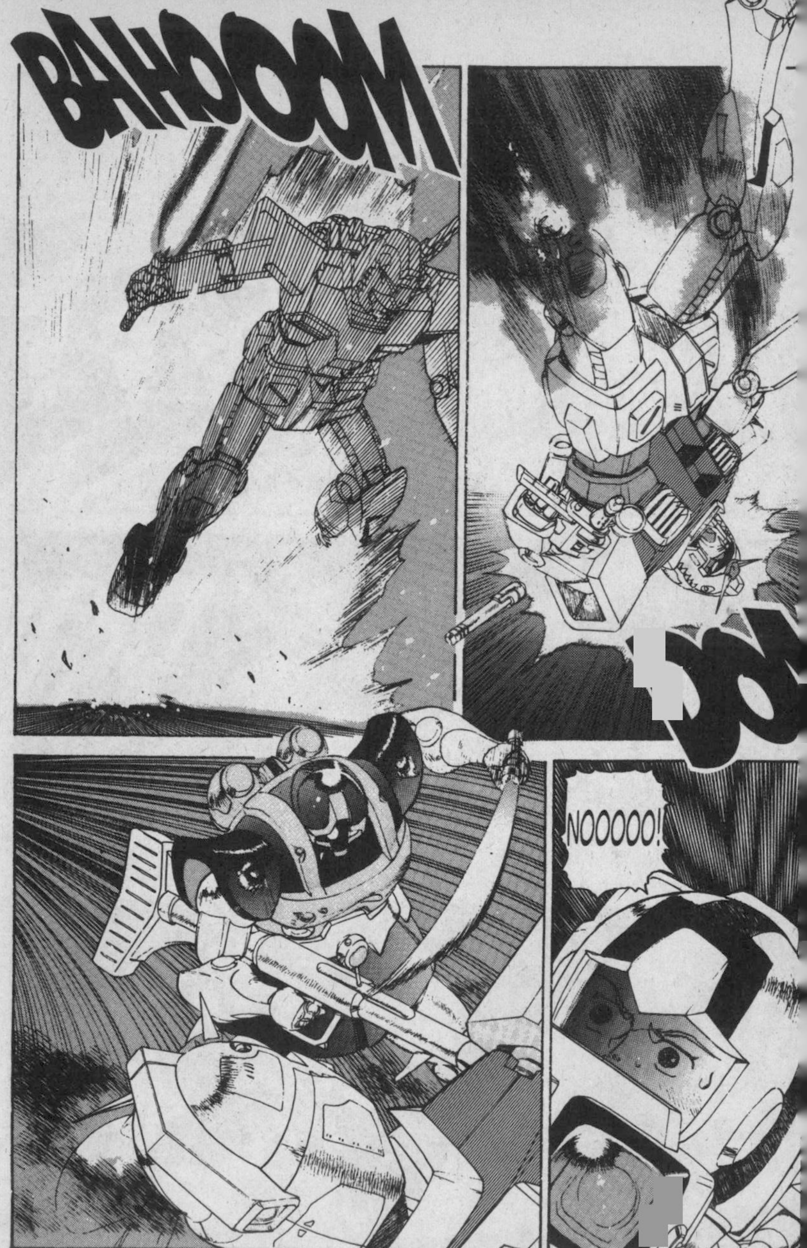
BAHOOOM
NOOOOO!

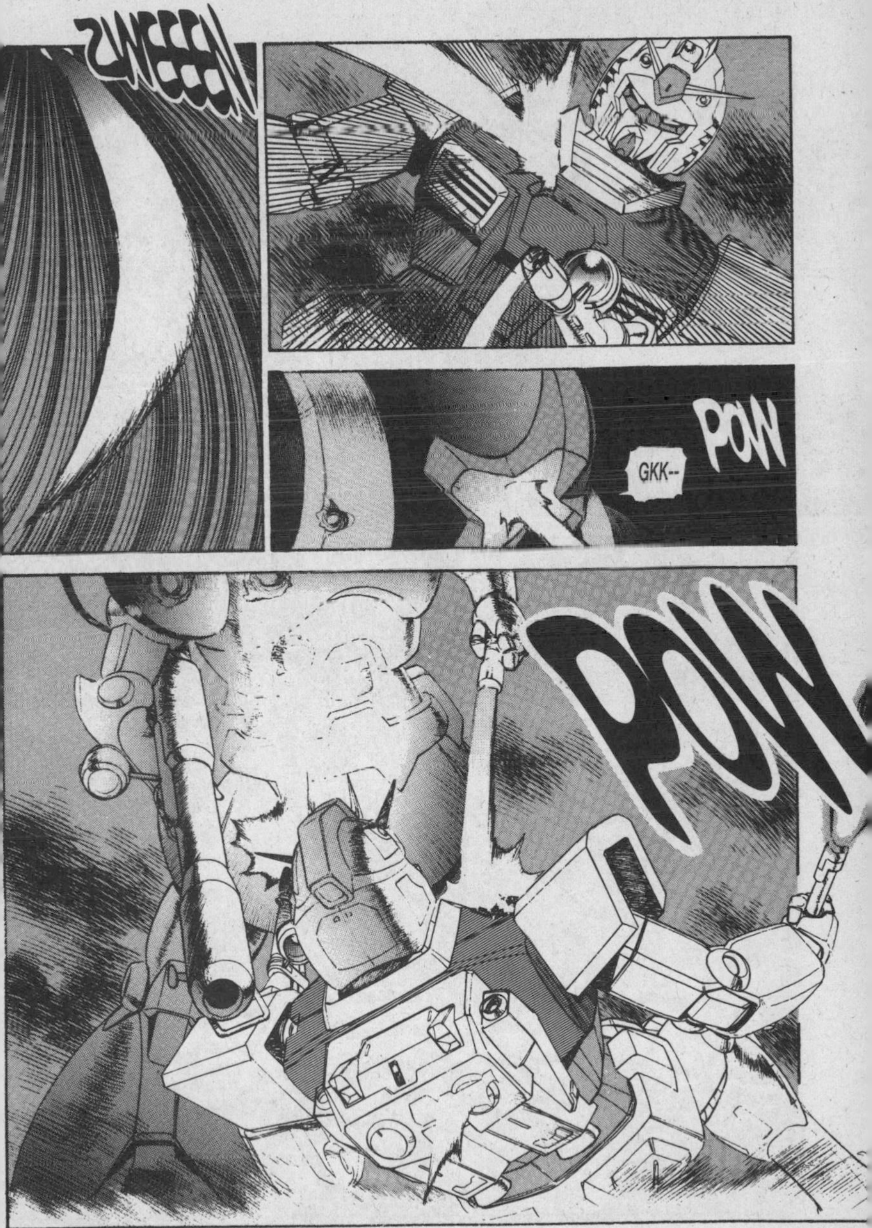
GKK--
POW
POW

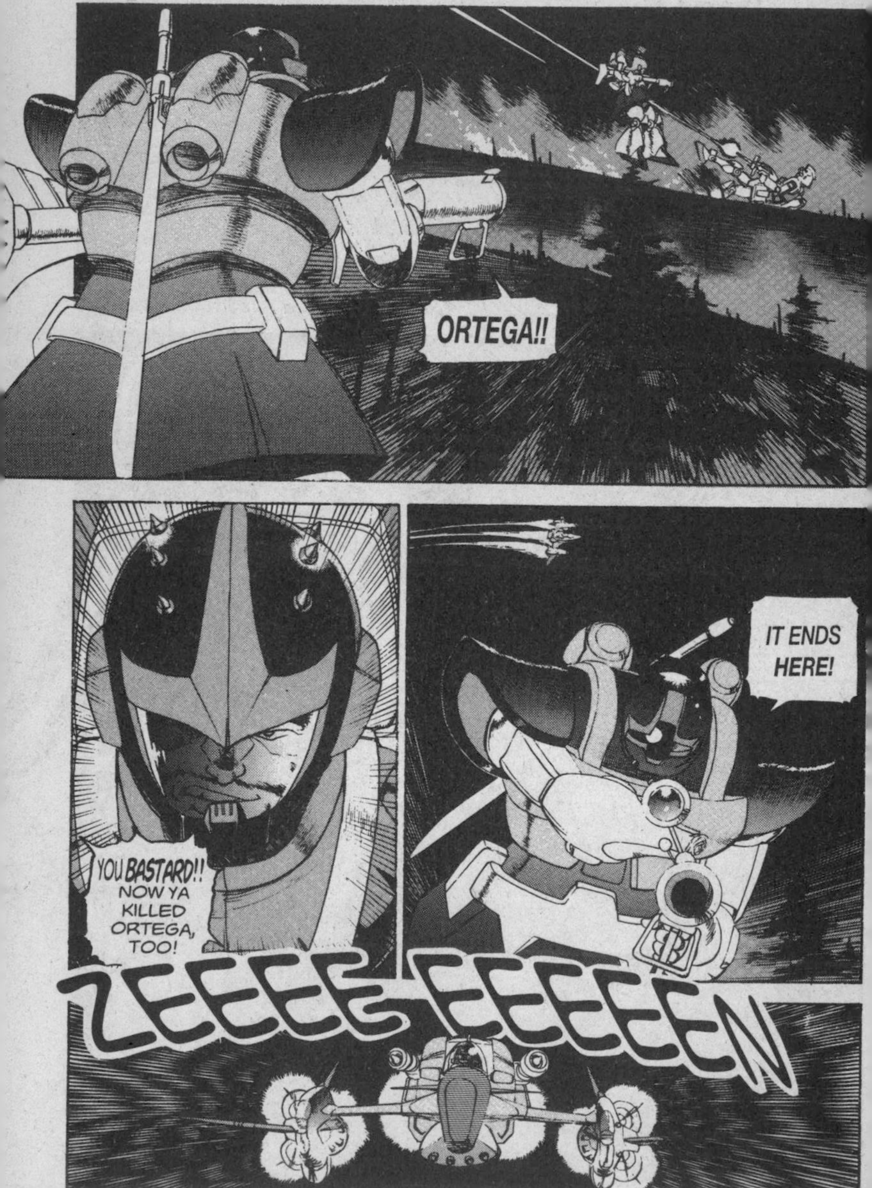
ORTEGA!!
YOU BASTARD!! NOW YA KILLED ORTEGA, TOO!
IT ENDS HERE!
ZEEEEE EEEEEEN

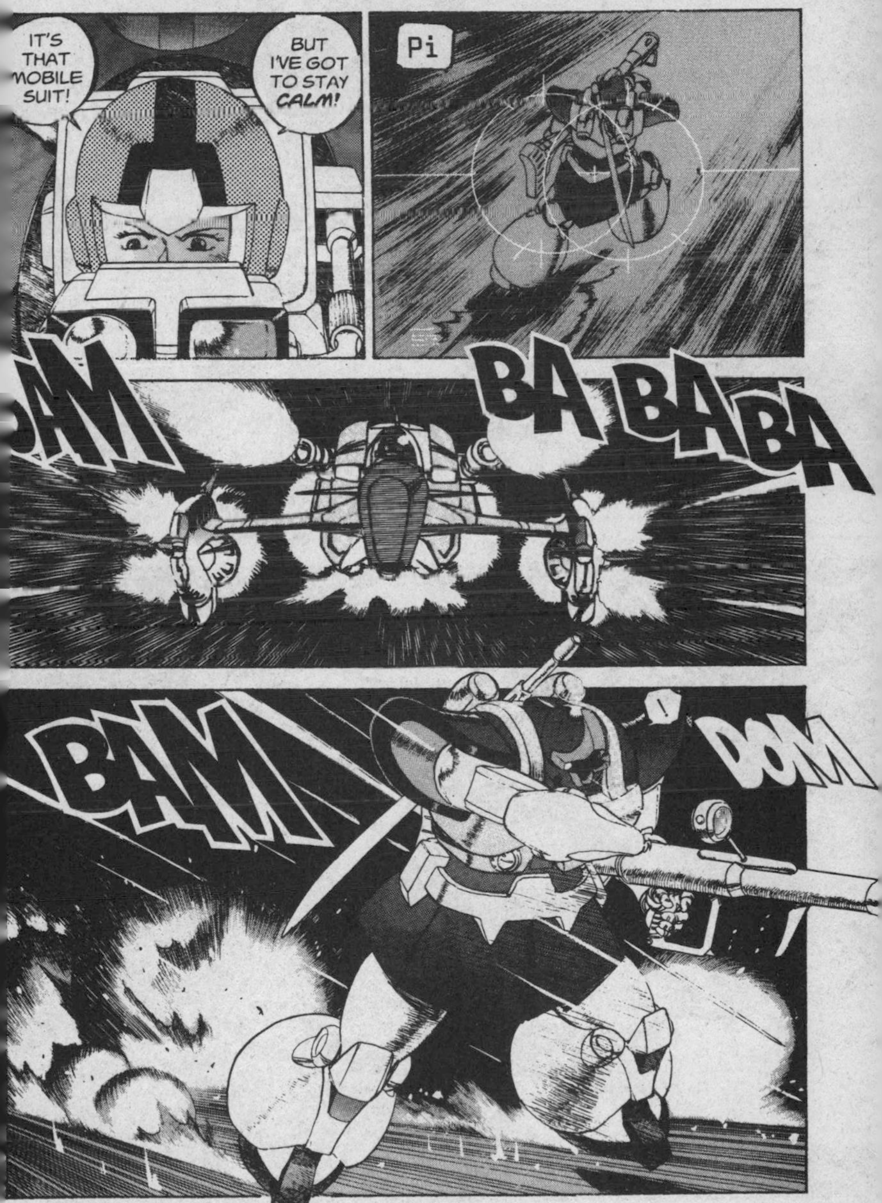
IT'S THAT MOBILE SUIT!
BUT I'VE GOT TO STAY CALM!
Pi
BAM
BA BA BA BA
BAM
!
DOM

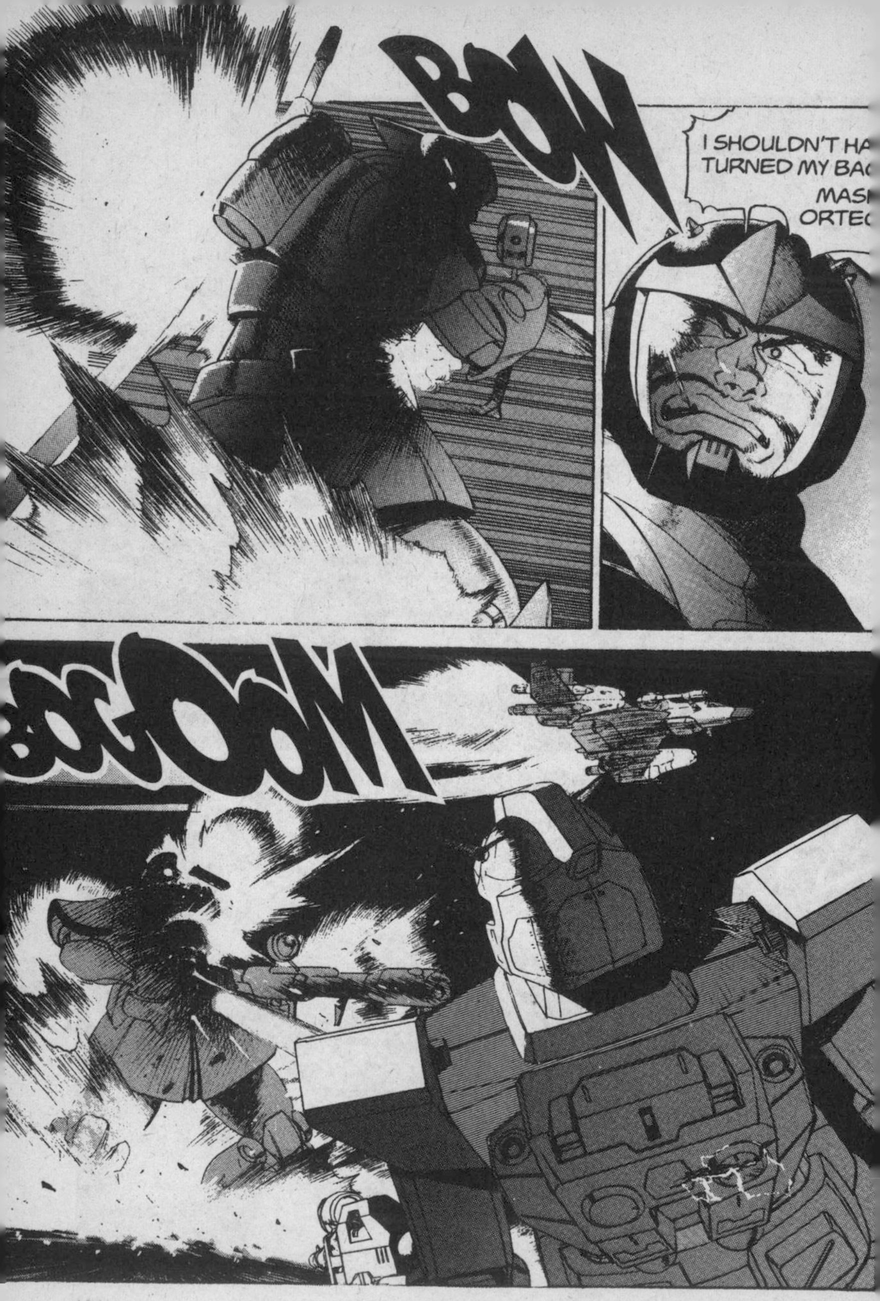
BOOM
I SHOULDN'T HA
TURNED MY BAC
MASI
ORTEC
BOGOOM

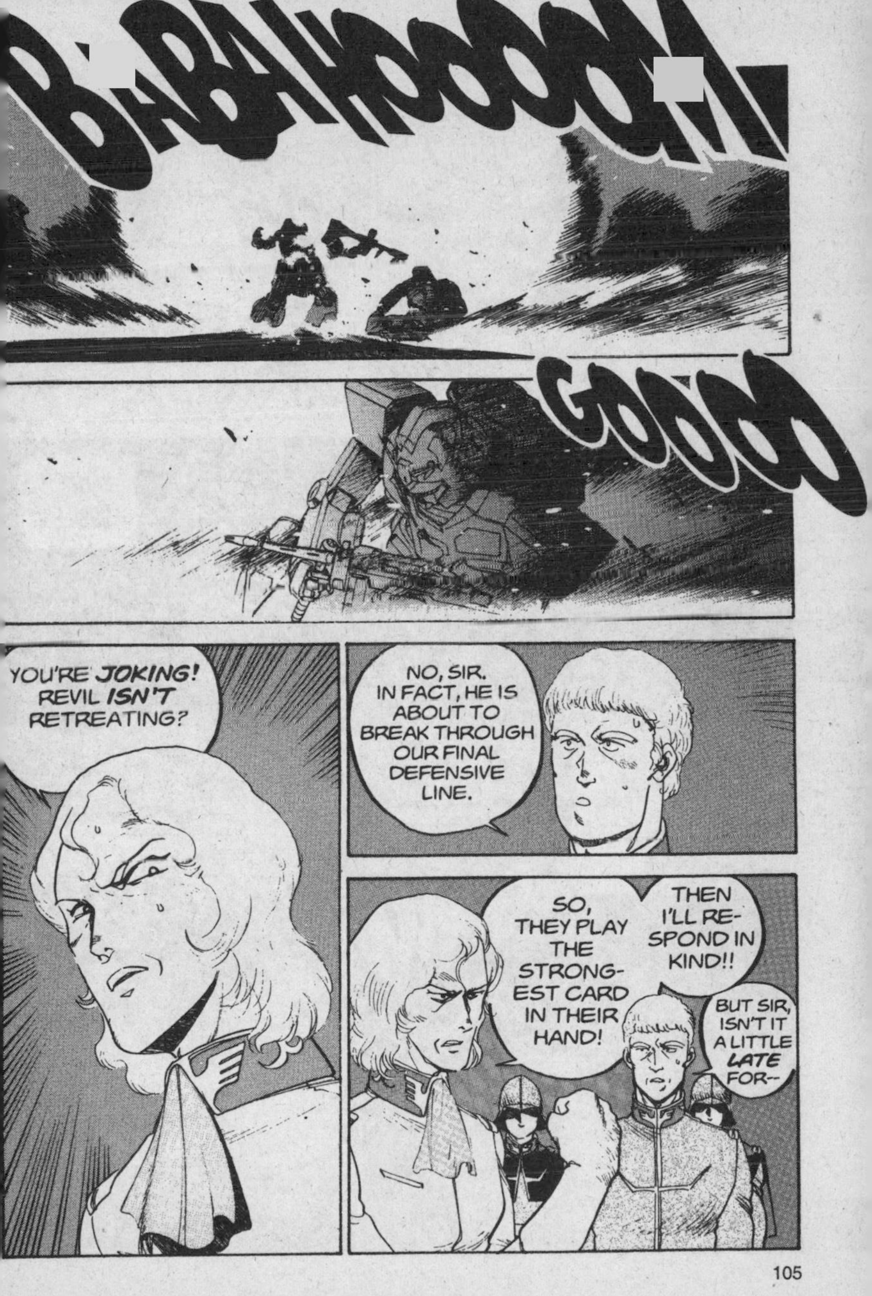
B-BAHOOOOM!!
GOOO
YOU'RE *JOKING!* REVIL *ISN'T* RETREATING?
NO, SIR. IN FACT, HE IS ABOUT TO BREAK THROUGH OUR FINAL DEFENSIVE LINE.
SO, THEY PLAY THE STRONG-EST CARD IN THEIR HAND!
THEN I'LL RE-SPOND IN KIND!!
BUT SIR, ISN'T IT A LITTLE *LATE* FOR--

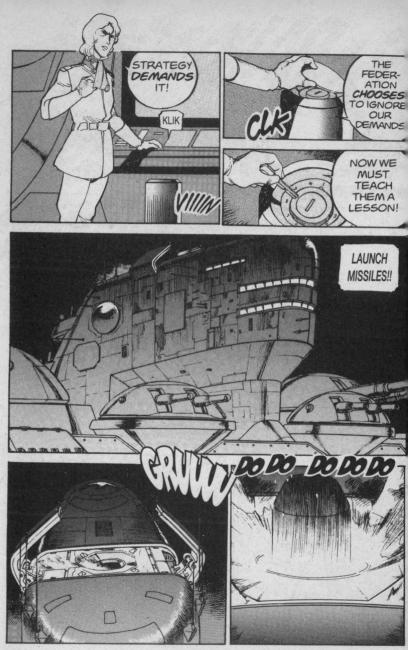

STRATEGY **DEMANDS** IT!

KLIK

THE FEDER- ATION **CHOOSES** TO IGNORE OUR DEMANDS

CLK

NOW WE MUST TEACH THEM A LESSON!

VIIIIN

LAUNCH MISSILES!!

GRUUUU DO DO DO DO DO

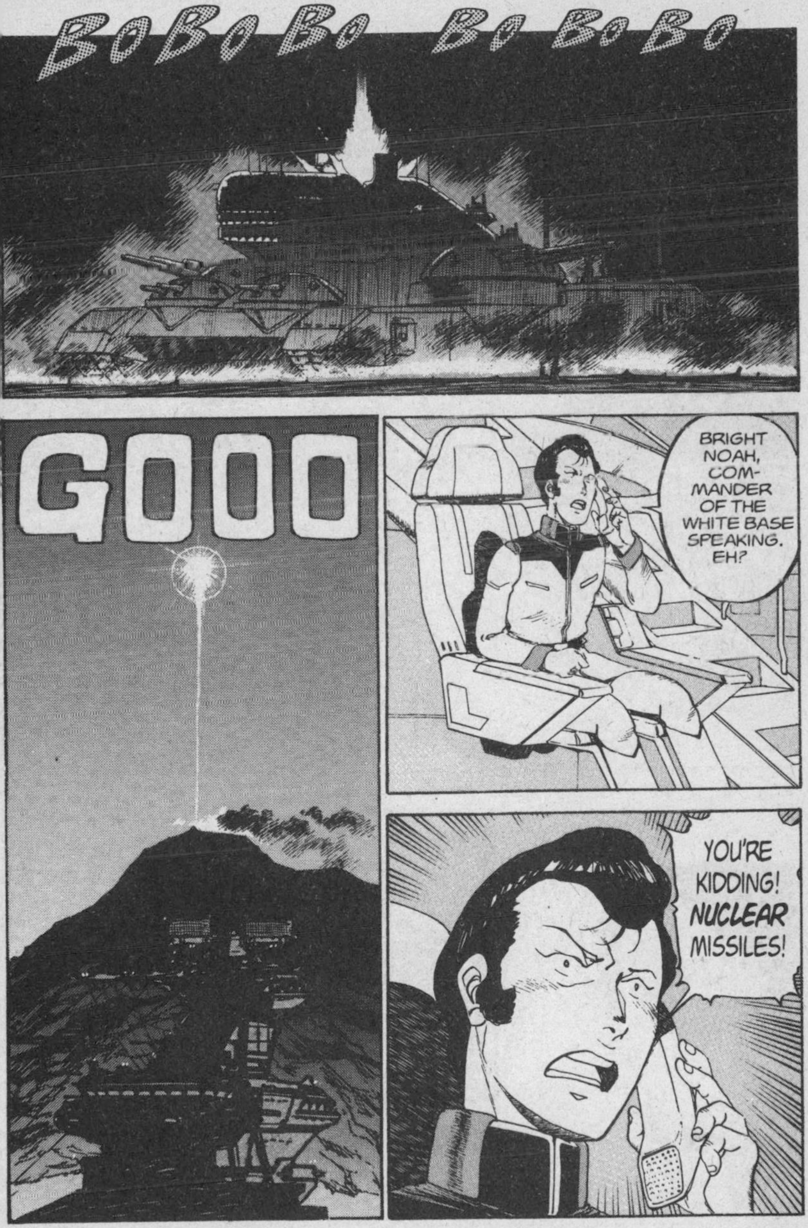
BoBoBo BoBoBo
GOOO
BRIGHT NOAH, COM-MANDER OF THE WHITE BASE SPEAKING. EH?
YOU'RE KIDDING! NUCLEAR MISSILES!

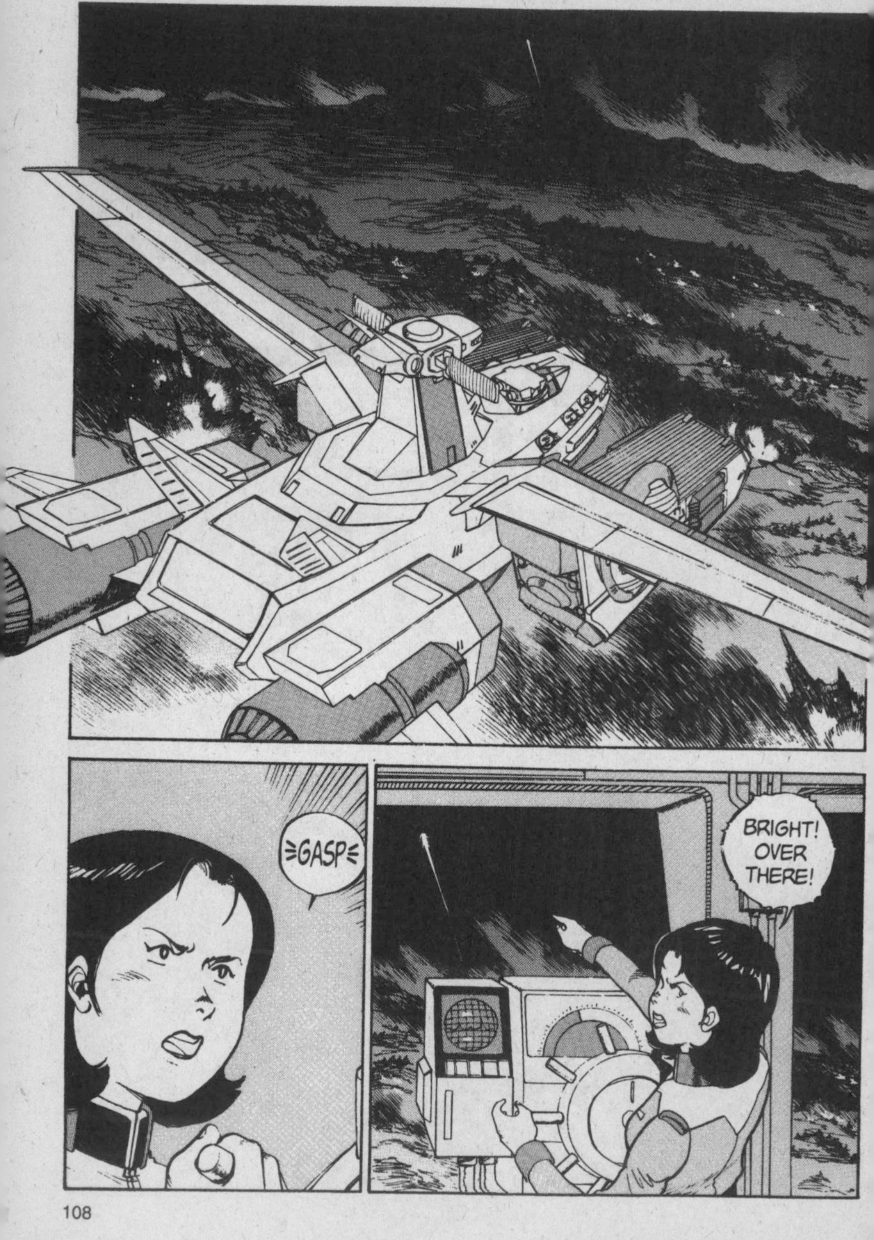
GASP
BRIGHT! OVER THERE!

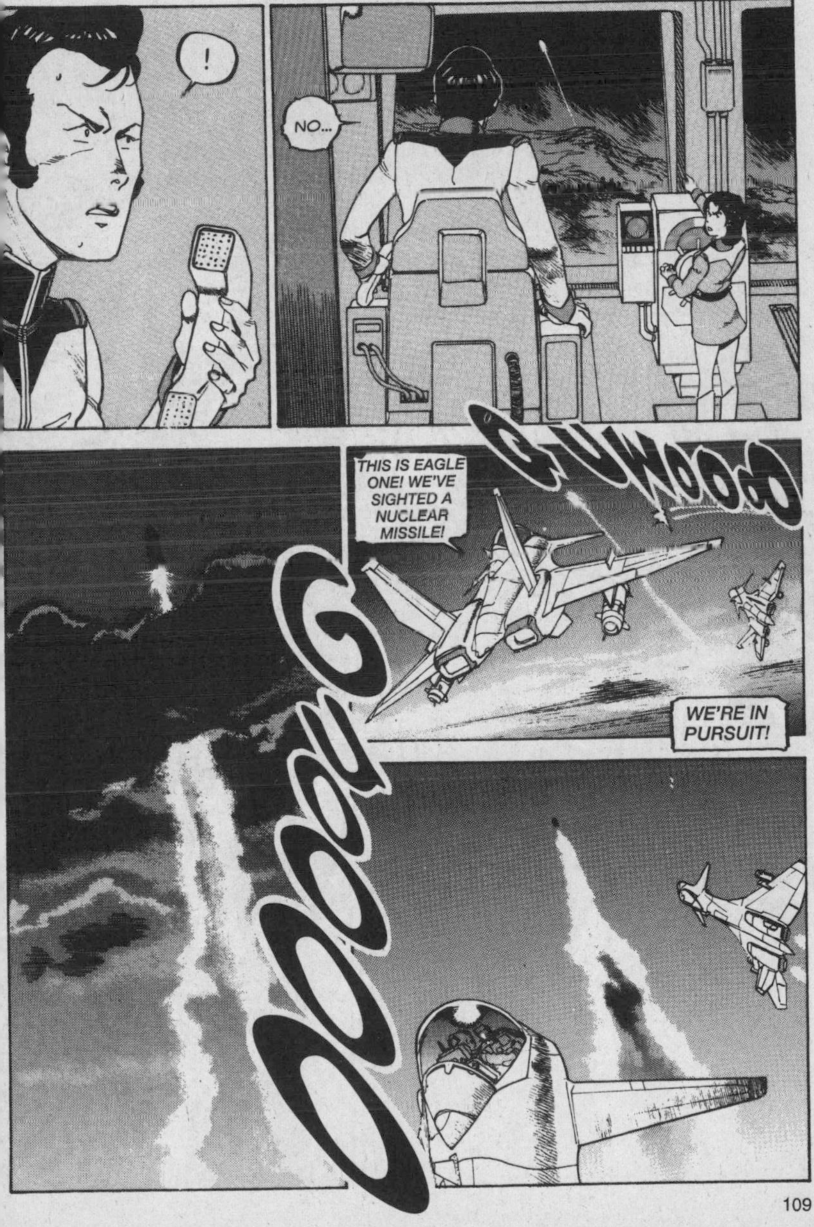
!
NO...
THIS IS EAGLE ONE! WE'VE SIGHTED A NUCLEAR MISSILE!
WE'RE IN PURSUIT!

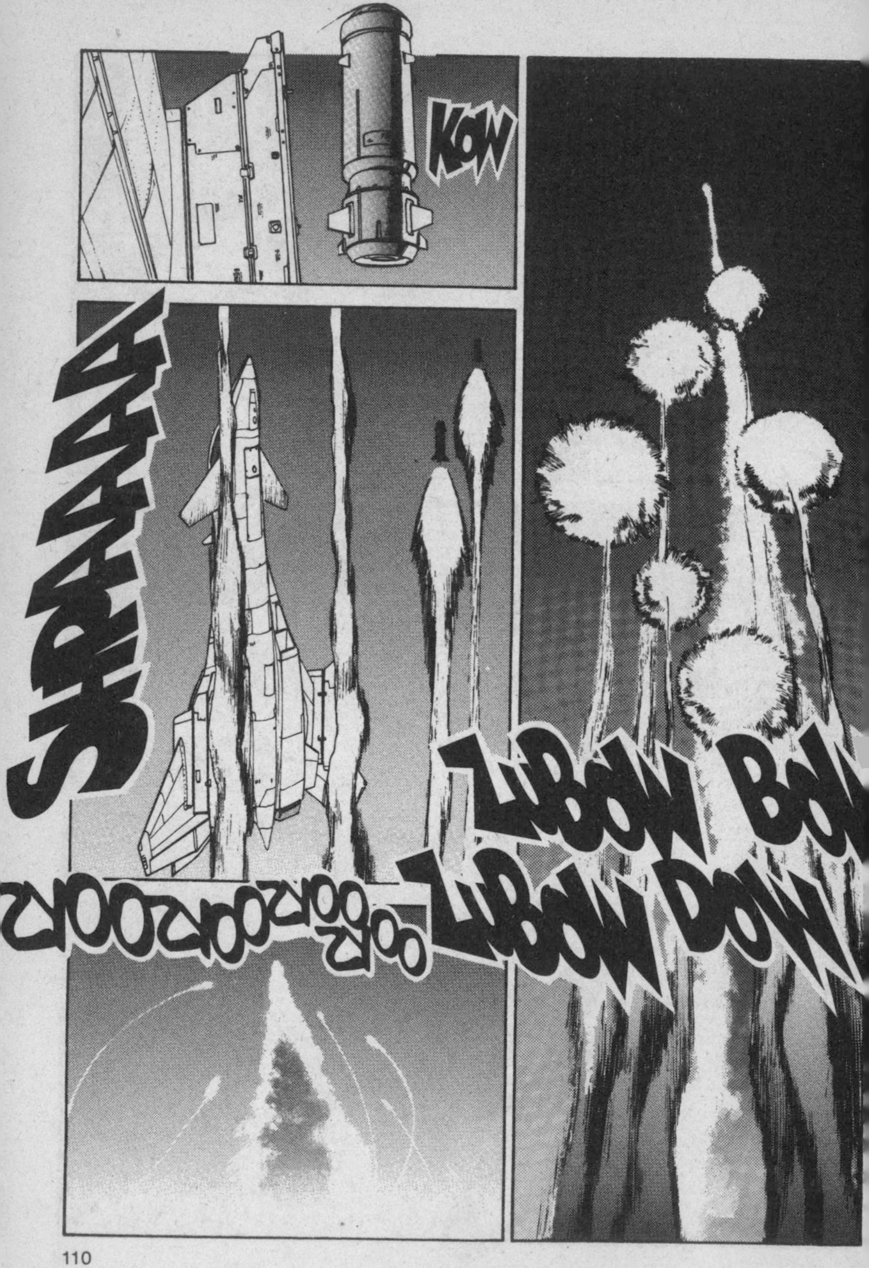
KOW
SHPAAAA
ZUBOW
ZUBOW DOW

GAM

BE SHOOW

GUNDAM: DOCKED!!

AMURO, DO YOU READ?

LOUD AND CLEAR, LT. BRIGHT.

THE ENEMY SENT UP A MISSILE WITH A HYDROGEN BOMB WARHEAD! YOU NEED TO *DESTROY IT.*

A HYDROGEN BOMB!?

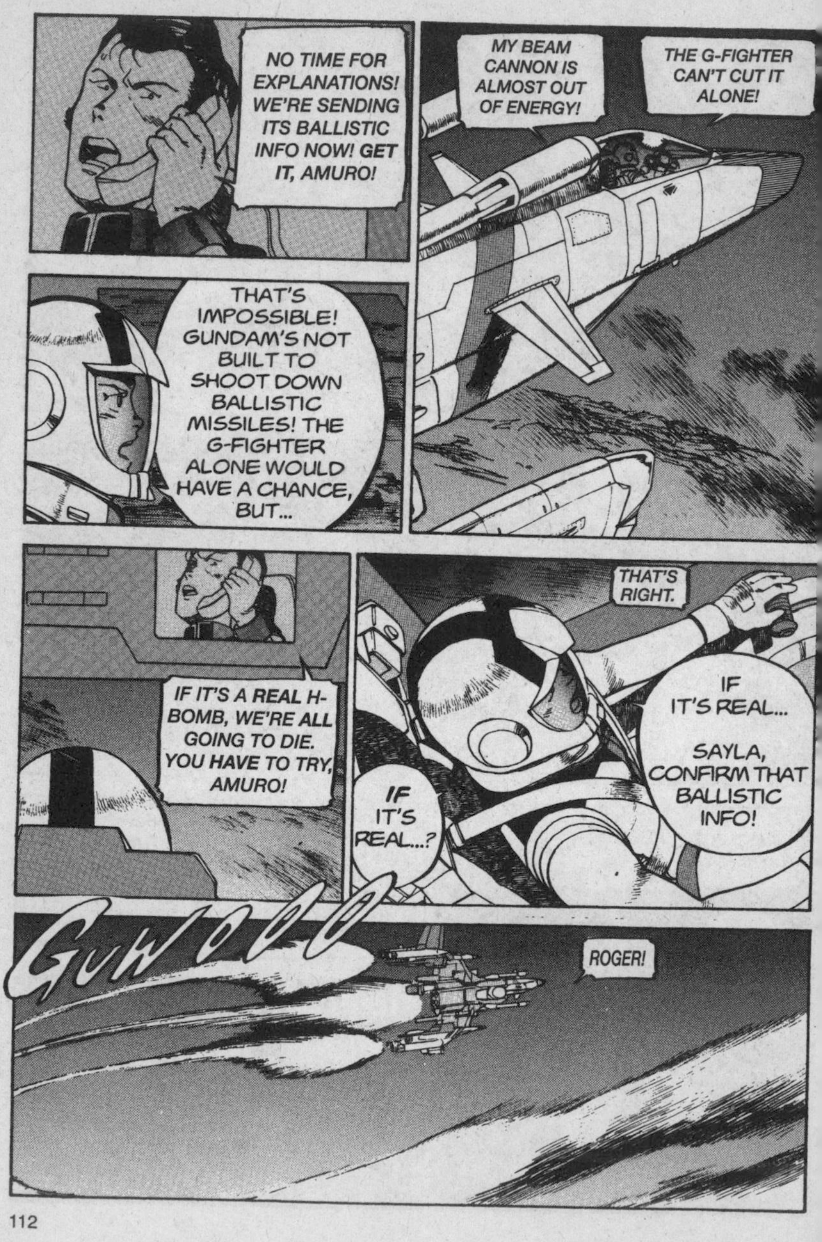

NO TIME FOR EXPLANATIONS! WE'RE SENDING ITS BALLISTIC INFO NOW! GET IT, AMURO!
THAT'S IMPOSSIBLE! GUNDAM'S NOT BUILT TO SHOOT DOWN BALLISTIC MISSILES! THE G-FIGHTER ALONE WOULD HAVE A CHANCE, BUT...
MY BEAM CANNON IS ALMOST OUT OF ENERGY!
THE G-FIGHTER CAN'T CUT IT ALONE!
IF IT'S A REAL H-BOMB, WE'RE ALL GOING TO DIE. YOU HAVE TO TRY, AMURO!
THAT'S RIGHT.
IF IT'S REAL...
SAYLA, CONFIRM THAT BALLISTIC INFO!
IF IT'S REAL...?
GWOOO
ROGER!

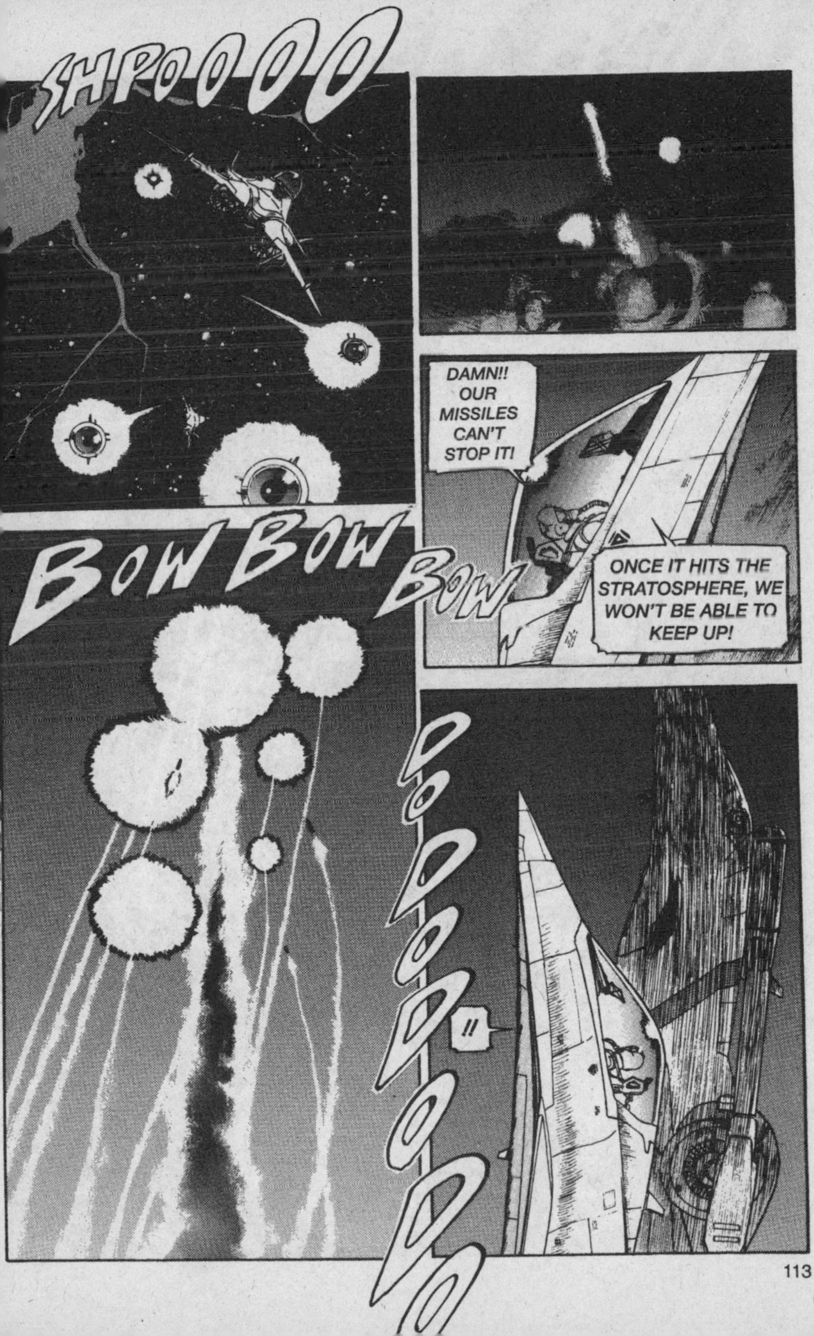
SHPOOOOO
DAMN!! OUR MISSILES CAN'T STOP IT!
ONCE IT HITS THE STRATOSPHERE, WE WON'T BE ABLE TO KEEP UP!
BOW BOW BOW BOW
!!
DOOOOOOOOO

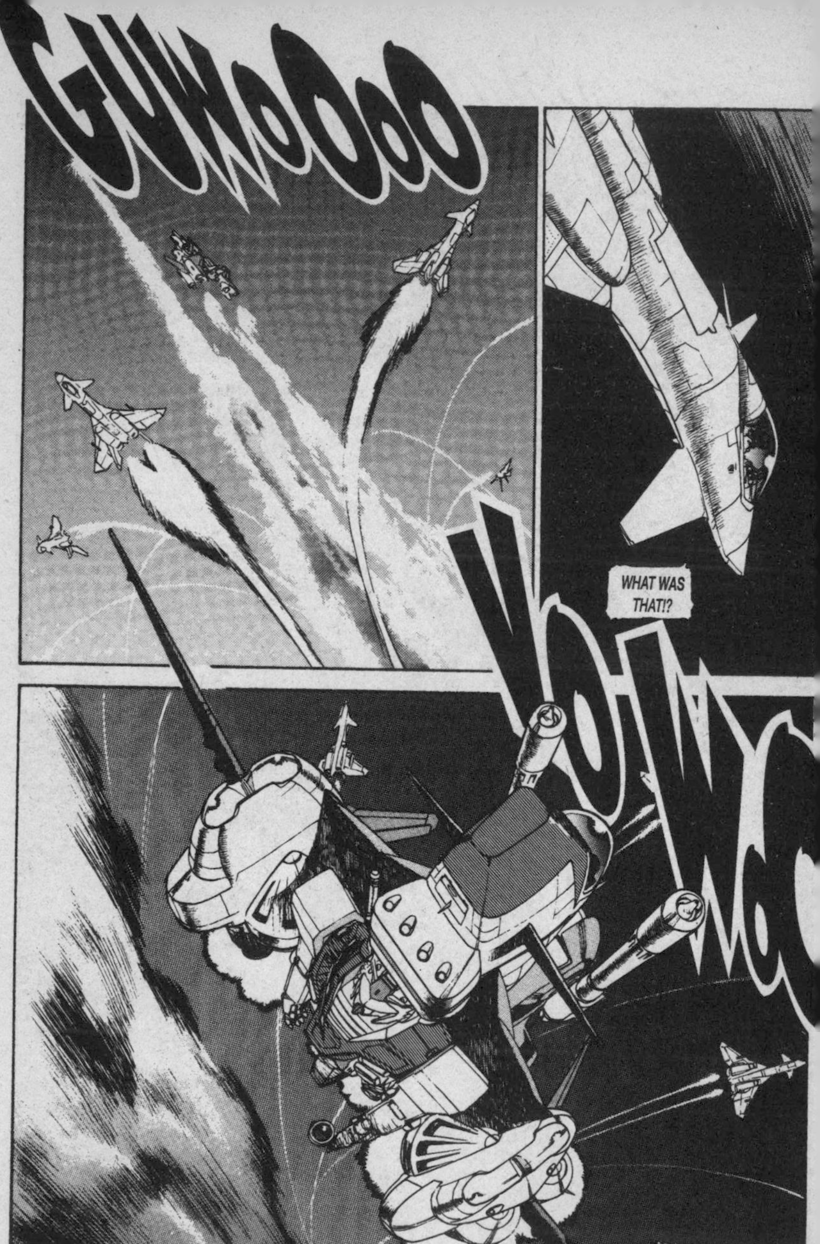
GUWOOOO
WHAT WAS THAT!?

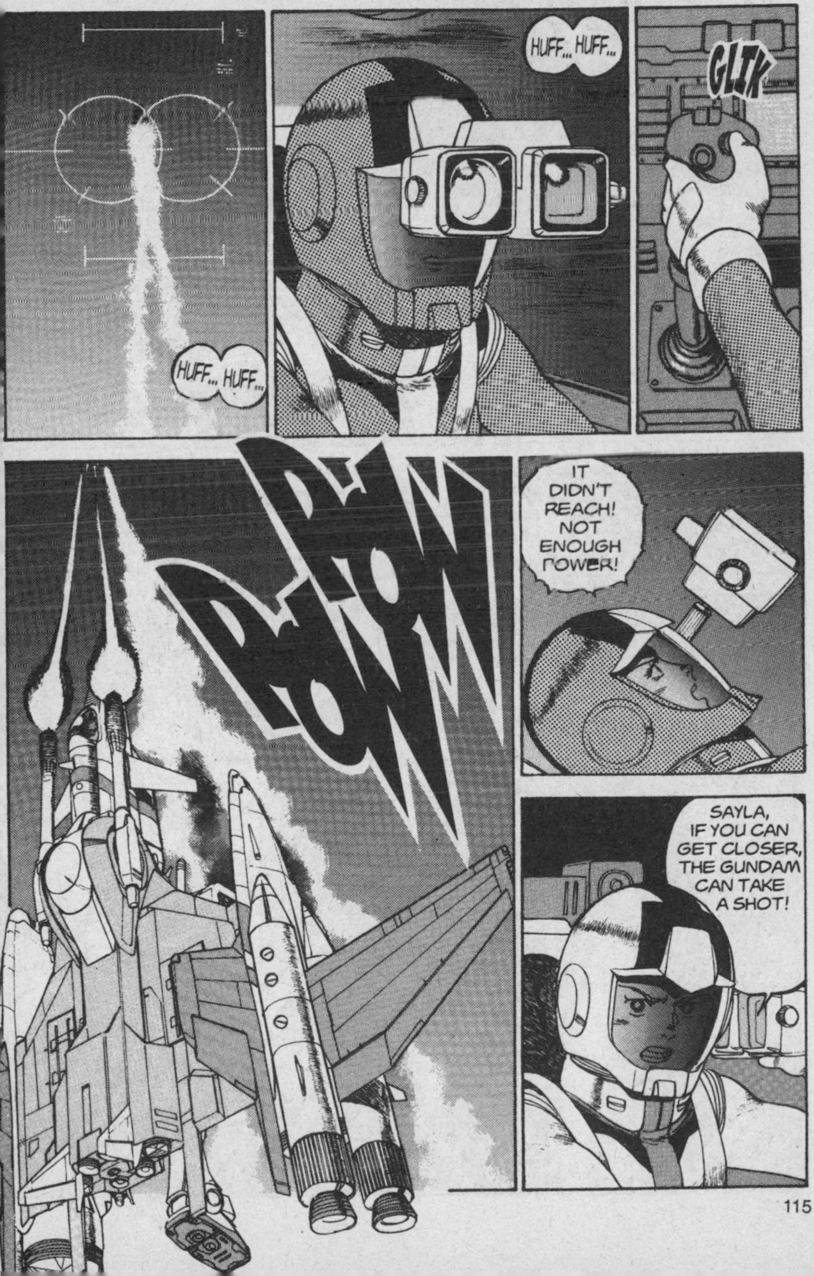
HUFF... HUFF...
HUFF... HUFF...
GLIK
BLOOM BOOM
IT DIDN'T REACH! NOT ENOUGH POWER!
SAYLA, IF YOU CAN GET CLOSER, THE GUNDAM CAN TAKE A SHOT!

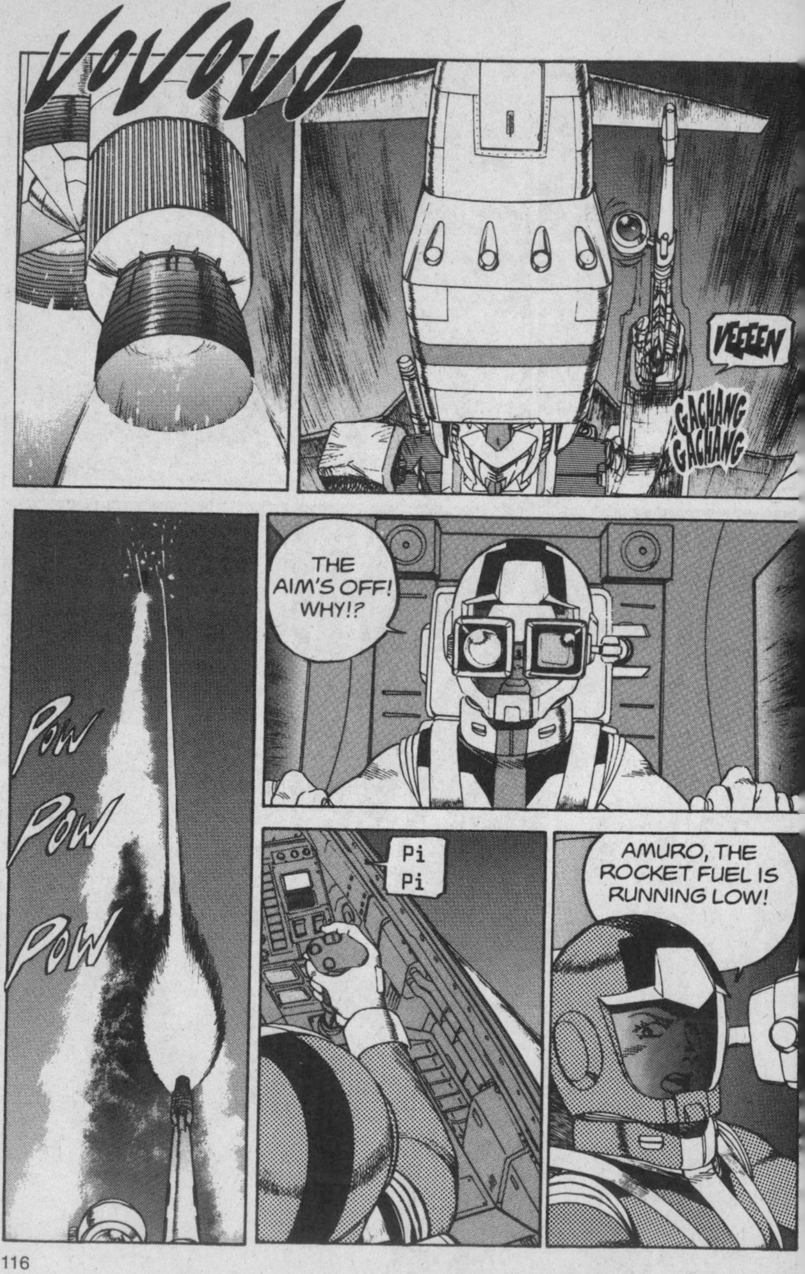
VOVOVO
VEEEEN
GACHANG GACHANG
POW POW POW
THE AIM'S OFF! WHY!?
Pi Pi
AMURO, THE ROCKET FUEL IS RUNNING LOW!

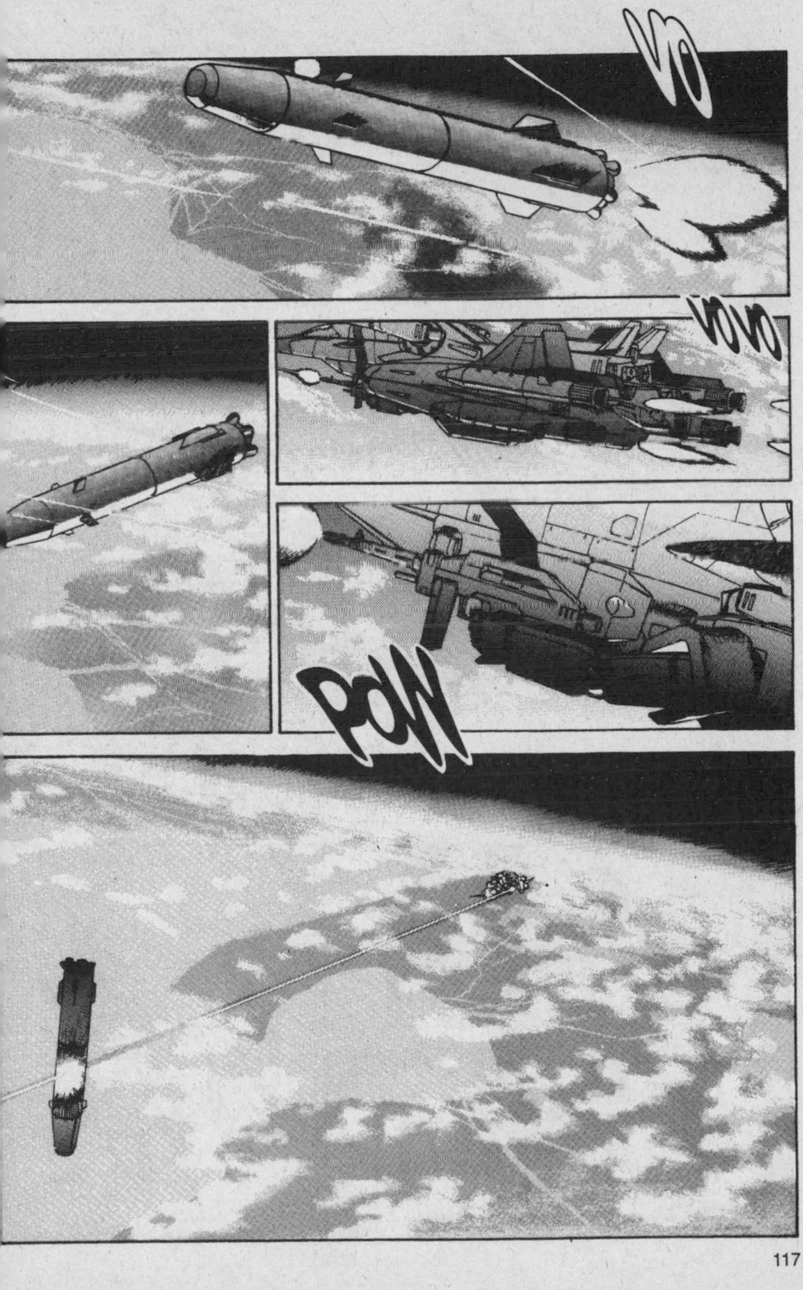
VO
VOVO
POW

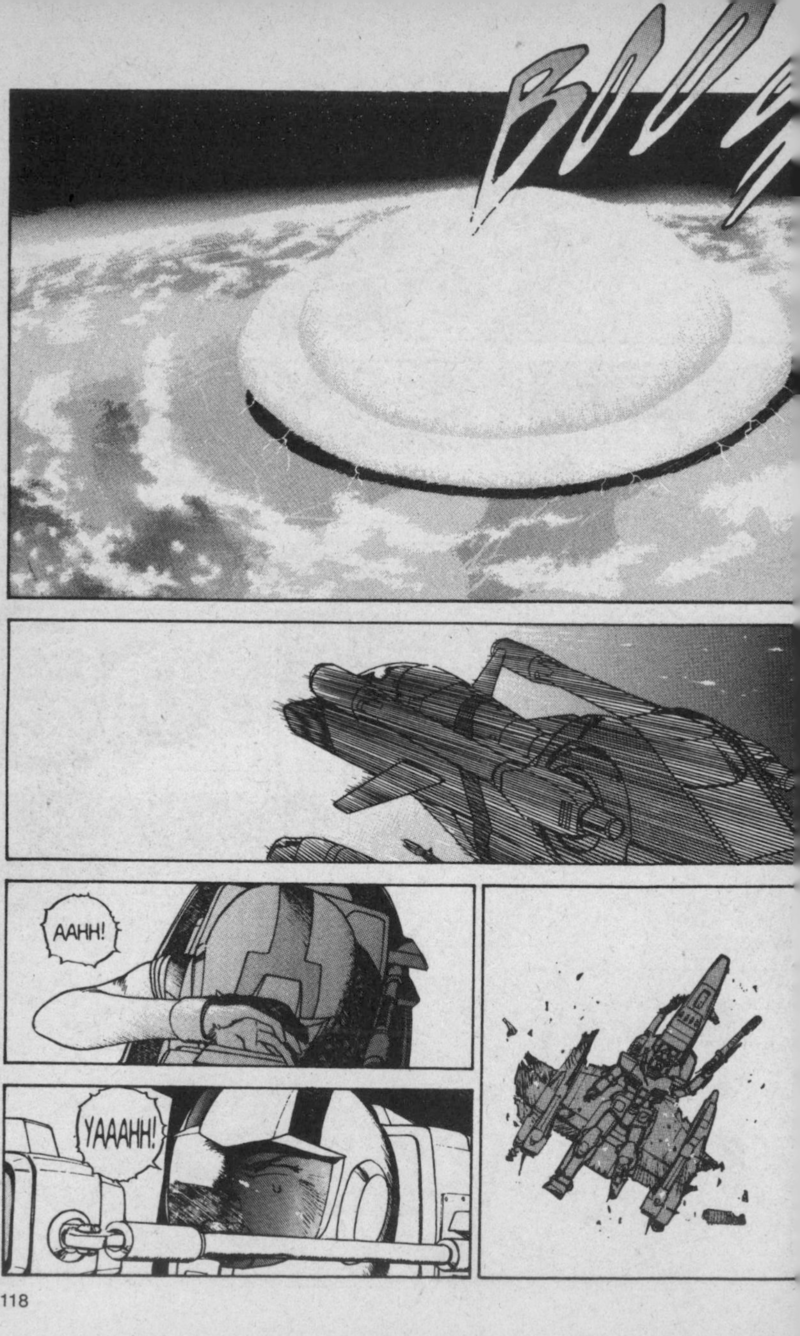
BOO
AAHH!
YAAAHH!

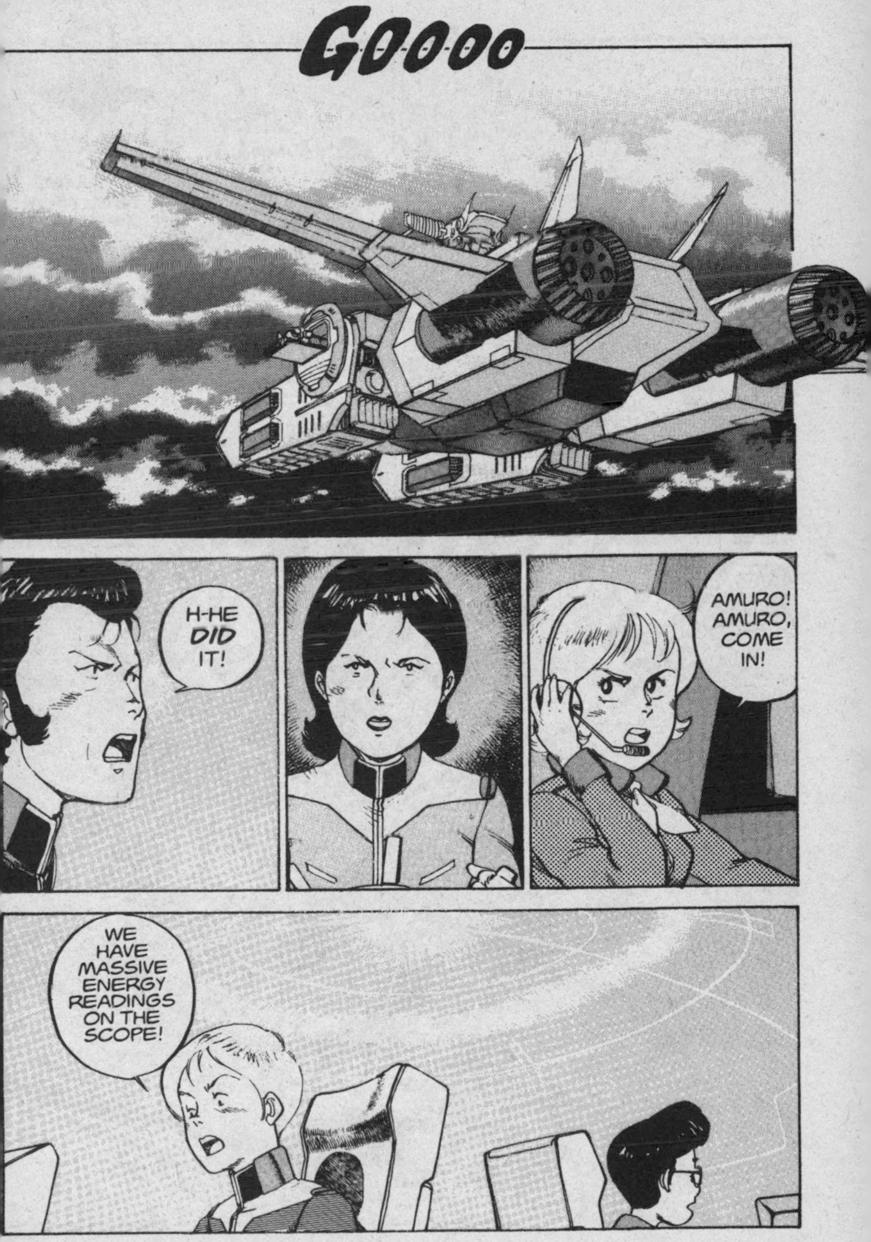
GOOOO
H-HE DID IT!
AMURO! AMURO, COME IN!
WE HAVE MASSIVE ENERGY READINGS ON THE SCOPE!

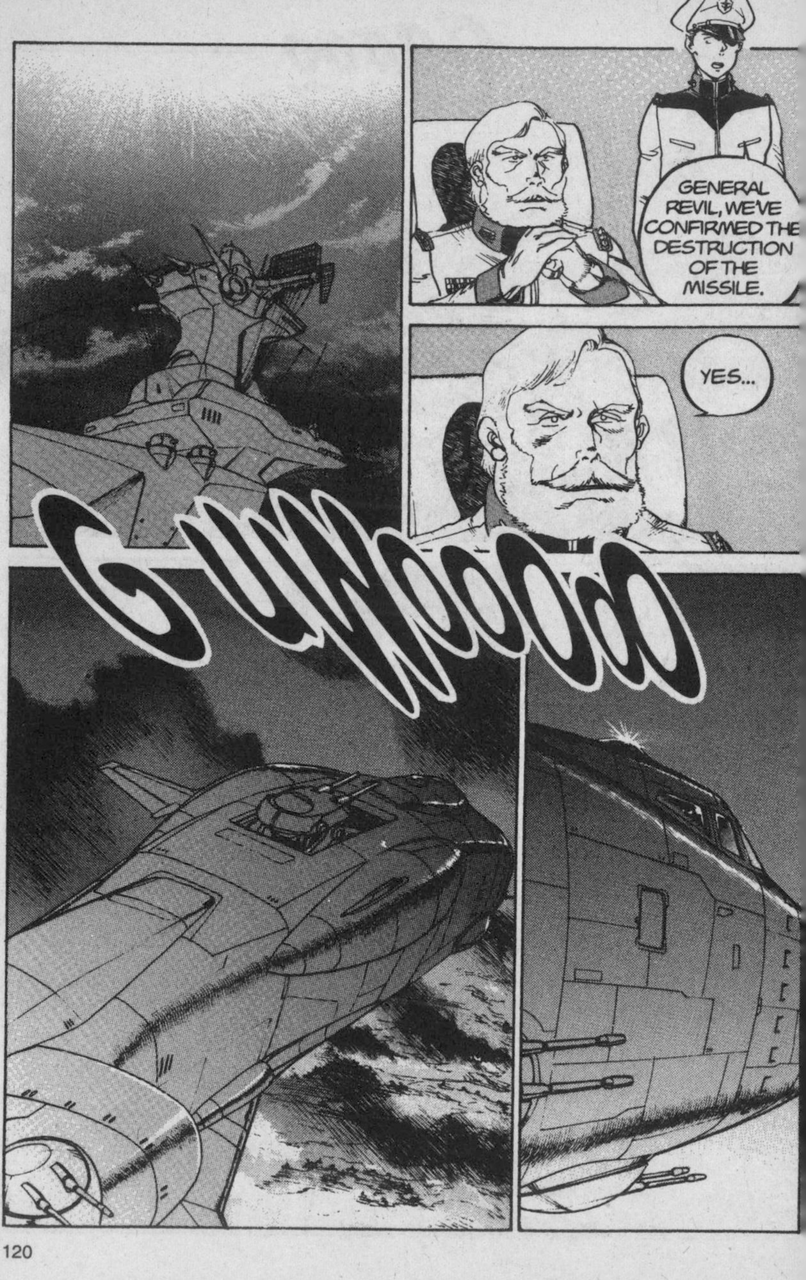
GENERAL REVIL, WE'VE CONFIRMED THE DESTRUCTION OF THE MISSILE.
YES...

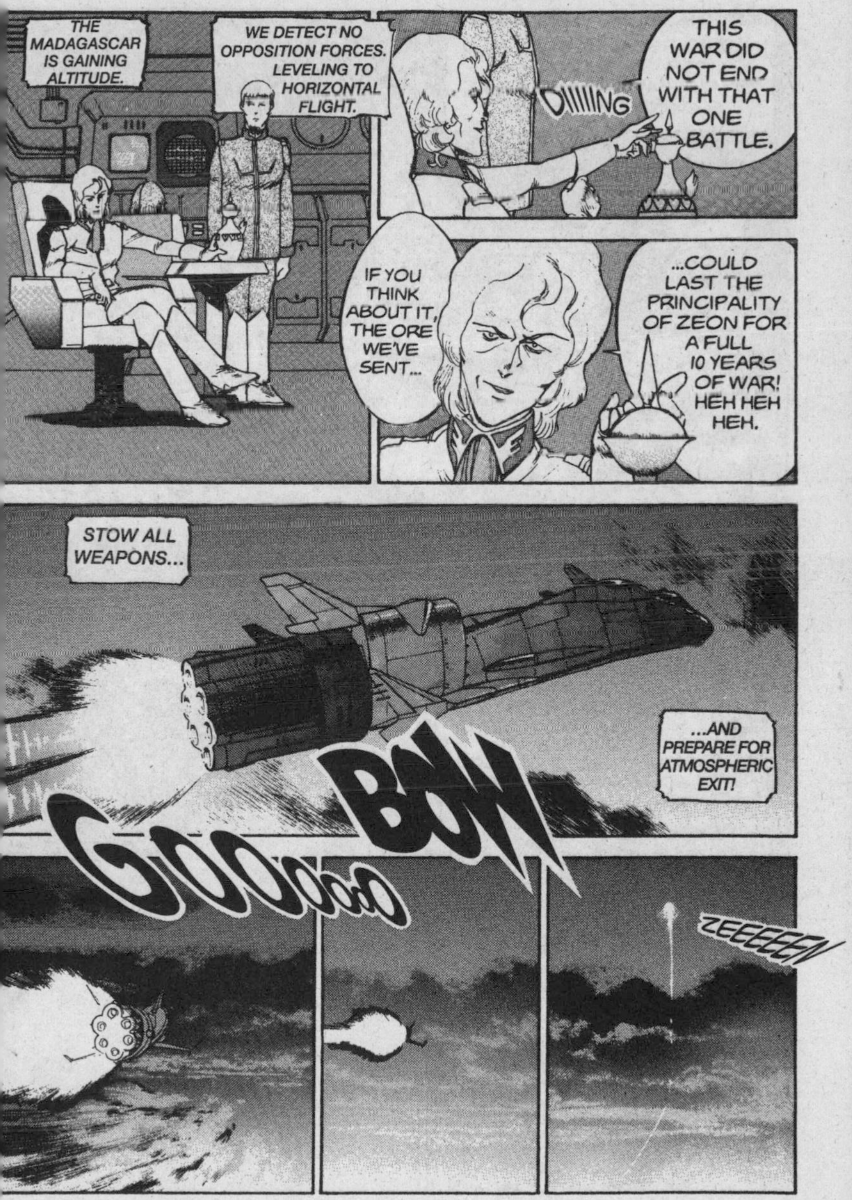
THE MADAGASCAR IS GAINING ALTITUDE.
WE DETECT NO OPPOSITION FORCES. LEVELING TO HORIZONTAL FLIGHT.
DIIIING
THIS WAR DID NOT END WITH THAT ONE BATTLE.
IF YOU THINK ABOUT IT, THE ORE WE'VE SENT...
...COULD LAST THE PRINCIPALITY OF ZEON FOR A FULL 10 YEARS OF WAR! HEH HEH HEH.
STOW ALL WEAPONS...
...AND PREPARE FOR ATMOSPHERIC EXIT!
GOOooo
BOW
ZEEEEEEN

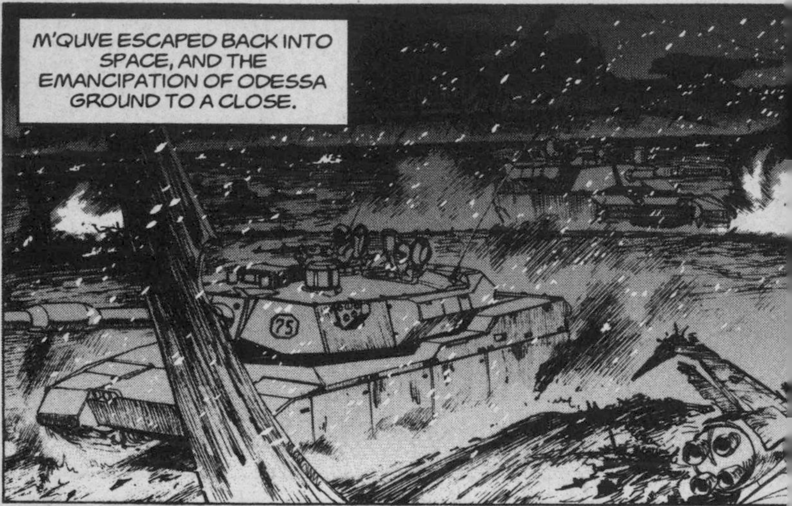
M'QUVE ESCAPED BACK INTO SPACE, AND THE EMANCIPATION OF ODESSA GROUND TO A CLOSE.

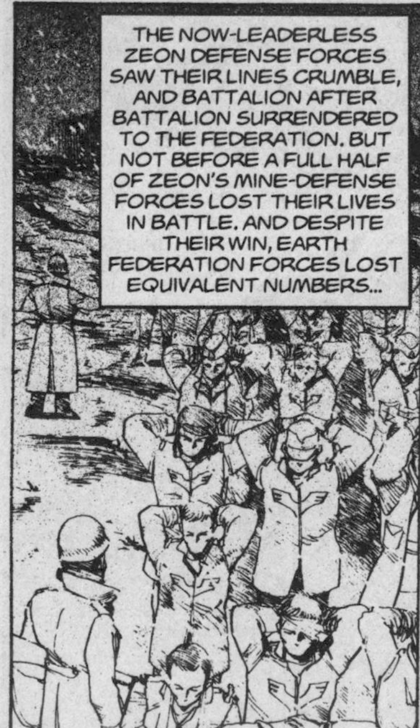
THE NOW-LEADERLESS ZEON DEFENSE FORCES SAW THEIR LINES CRUMBLE, AND BATTALION AFTER BATTALION SURRENDERED TO THE FEDERATION. BUT NOT BEFORE A FULL HALF OF ZEON'S MINE-DEFENSE FORCES LOST THEIR LIVES IN BATTLE. AND DESPITE THEIR WIN, EARTH FEDERATION FORCES LOST EQUIVALENT NUMBERS...

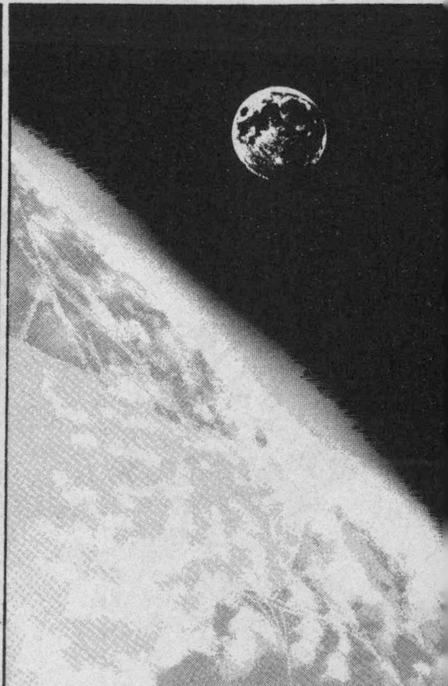

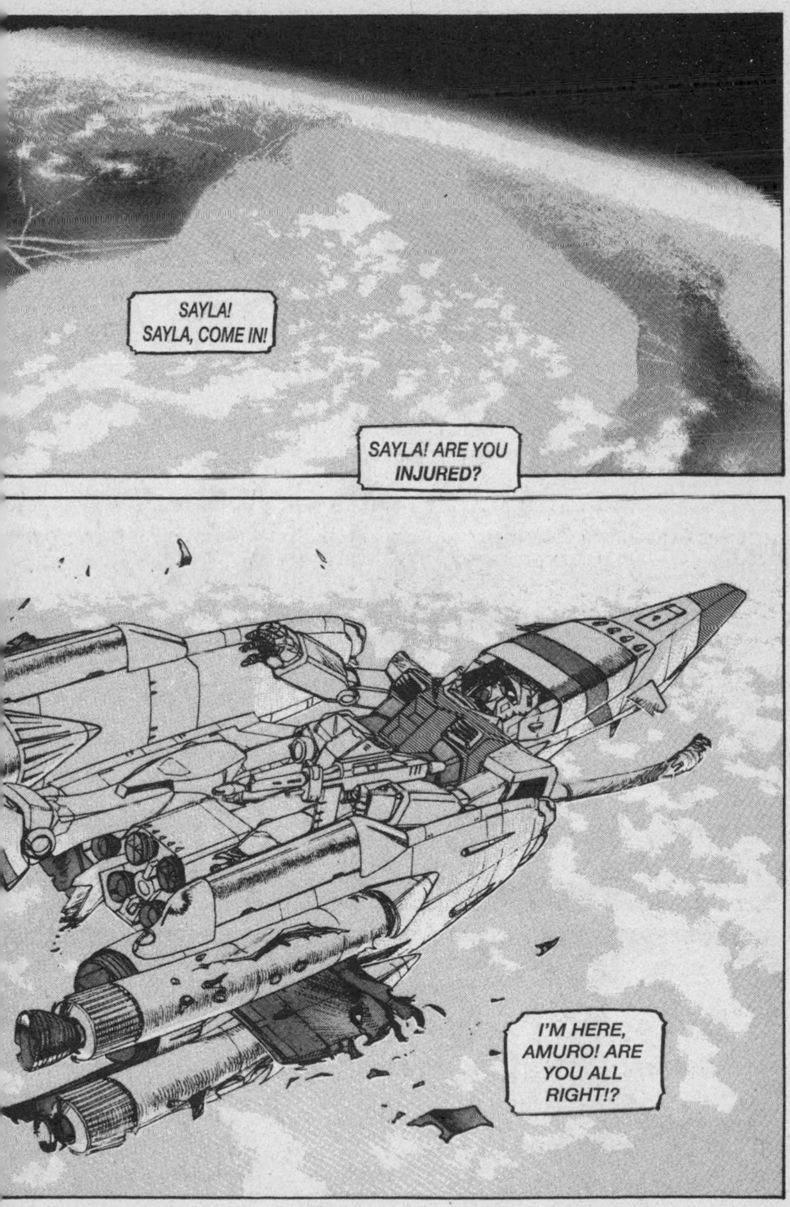
SAYLA! SAYLA, COME IN!
SAYLA! ARE YOU INJURED?
I'M HERE, AMURO! ARE YOU ALL RIGHT!?

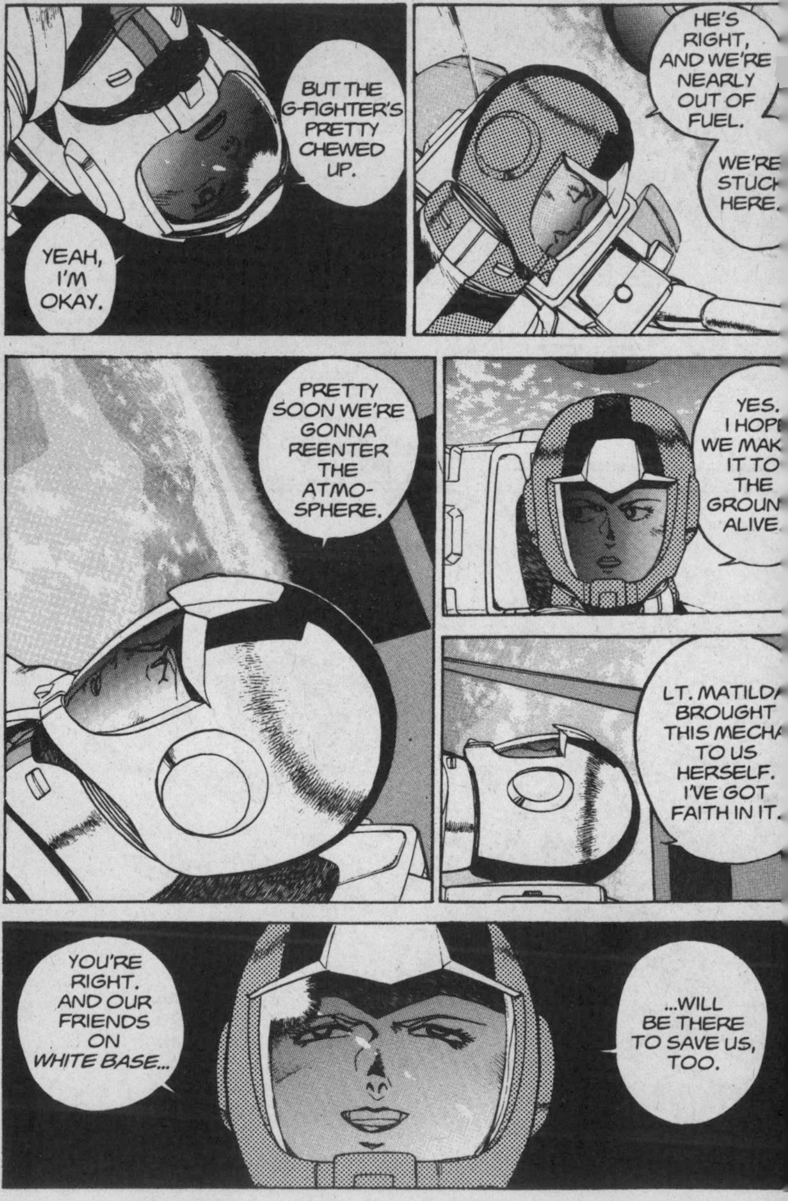
BUT THE G-FIGHTER'S PRETTY CHEWED UP.
YEAH, I'M OKAY.
HE'S RIGHT, AND WE'RE NEARLY OUT OF FUEL.
WE'RE STUCK HERE.
PRETTY SOON WE'RE GONNA REENTER THE ATMOSPHERE.
YES. I HOPE WE MAKE IT TO THE GROUND ALIVE.
LT. MATILDA BROUGHT THIS MECHA TO US HERSELF. I'VE GOT FAITH IN IT.
YOU'RE RIGHT. AND OUR FRIENDS ON WHITE BASE...
...WILL BE THERE TO SAVE US, TOO.

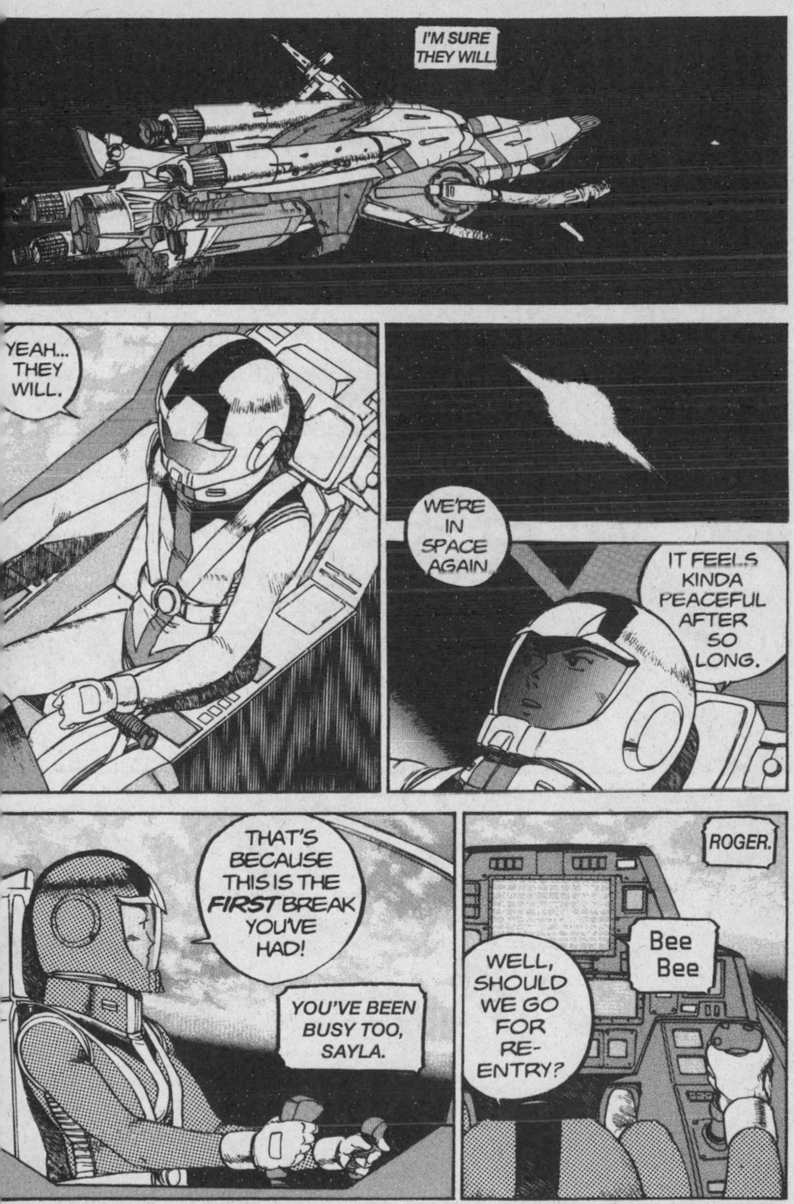
I'M SURE THEY WILL.
YEAH... THEY WILL.
WE'RE IN SPACE AGAIN
IT FEELS KINDA PEACEFUL AFTER SO LONG.
THAT'S BECAUSE THIS IS THE FIRST BREAK YOU'VE HAD!
YOU'VE BEEN BUSY TOO, SAYLA.
ROGER.
Bee Bee
WELL, SHOULD WE GO FOR RE-ENTRY?

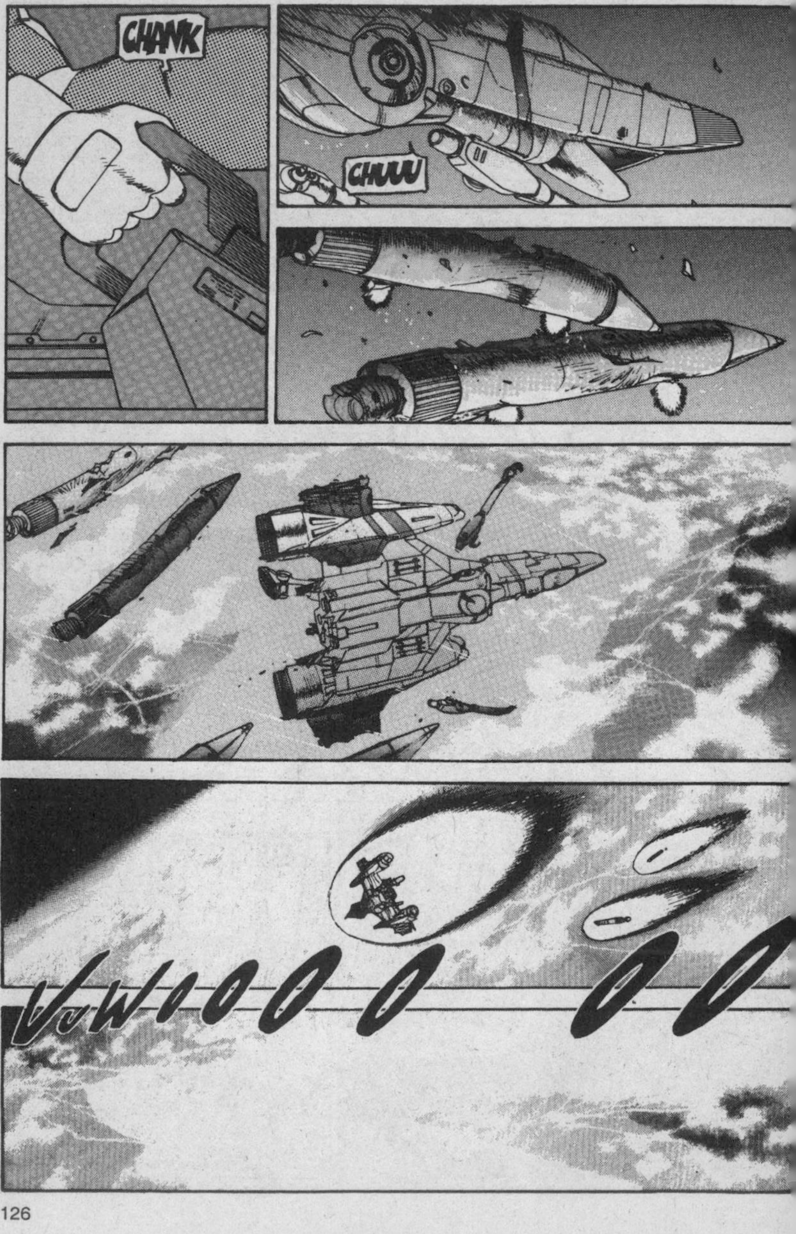
CHANK
CHUUU
VWIOOO OOO

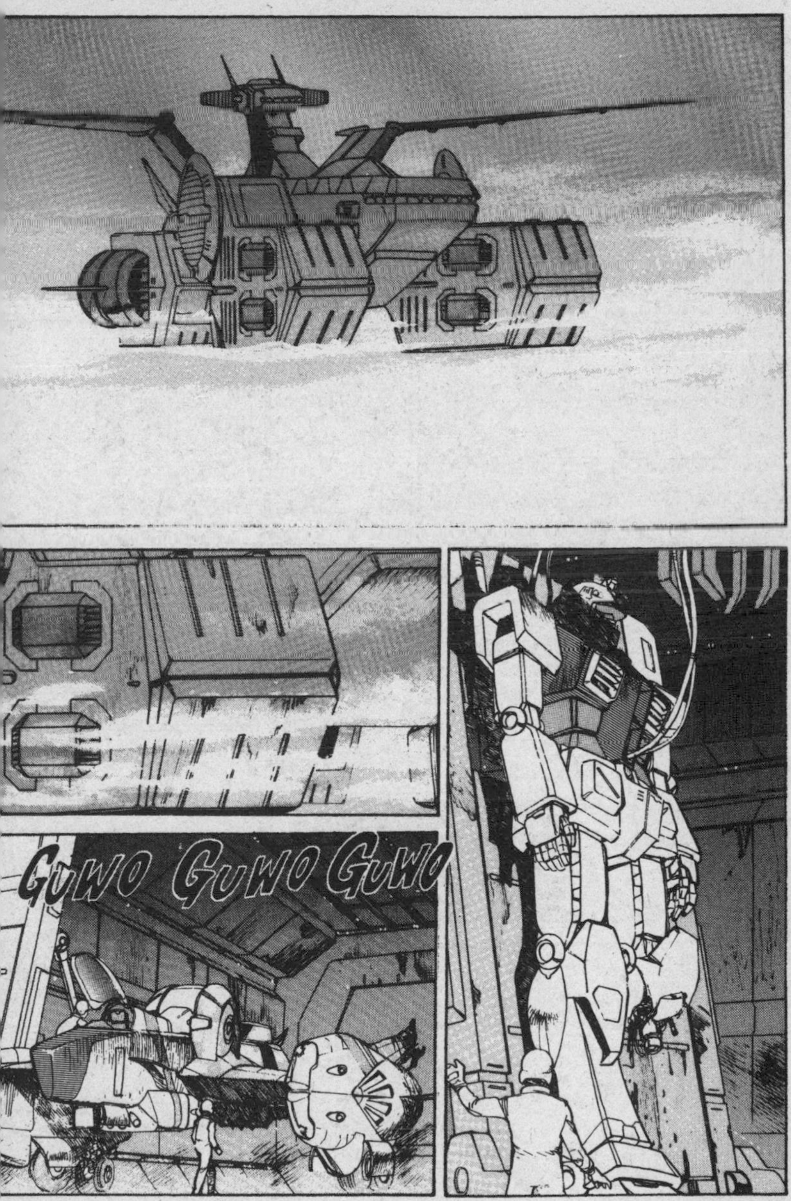
GUWO GUWO GUWO

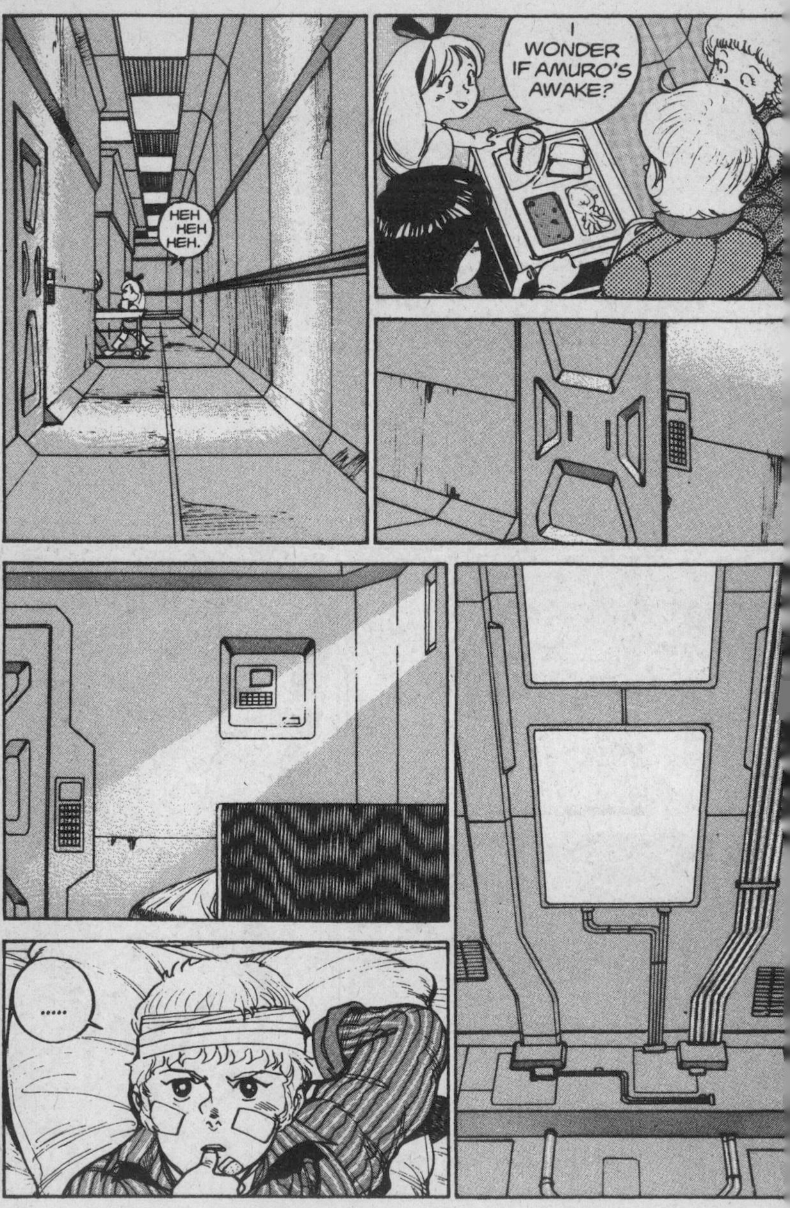
HEH HEH HEH.
I WONDER IF AMURO'S AWAKE?
......

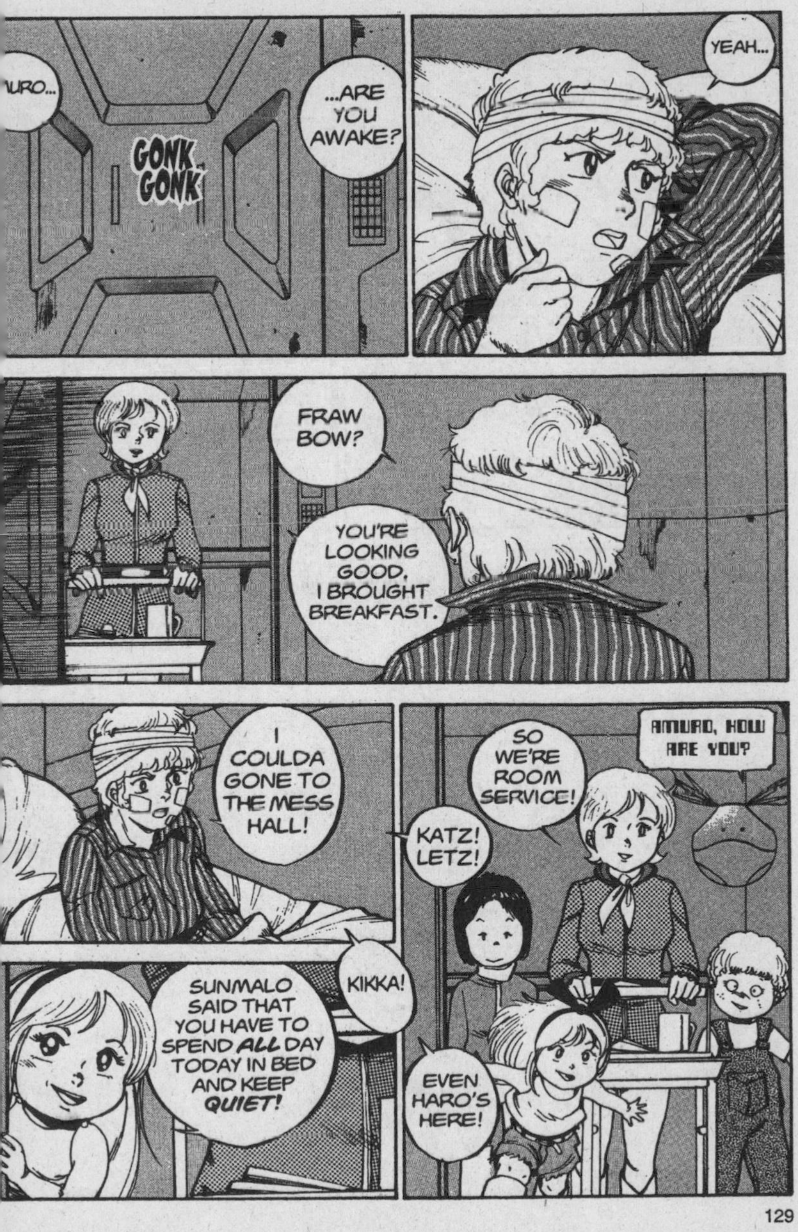

...URO...
GONK GONK
...ARE YOU AWAKE?
YEAH...
FRAW BOW?
YOU'RE LOOKING GOOD. I BROUGHT BREAKFAST.
I COULDA GONE TO THE MESS HALL!
SO WE'RE ROOM SERVICE!
AMURO, HOW ARE YOU?
KATZ! LETZ!
KIKKA!
SUNMALO SAID THAT YOU HAVE TO SPEND ALL DAY TODAY IN BED AND KEEP QUIET!
EVEN HARO'S HERE!

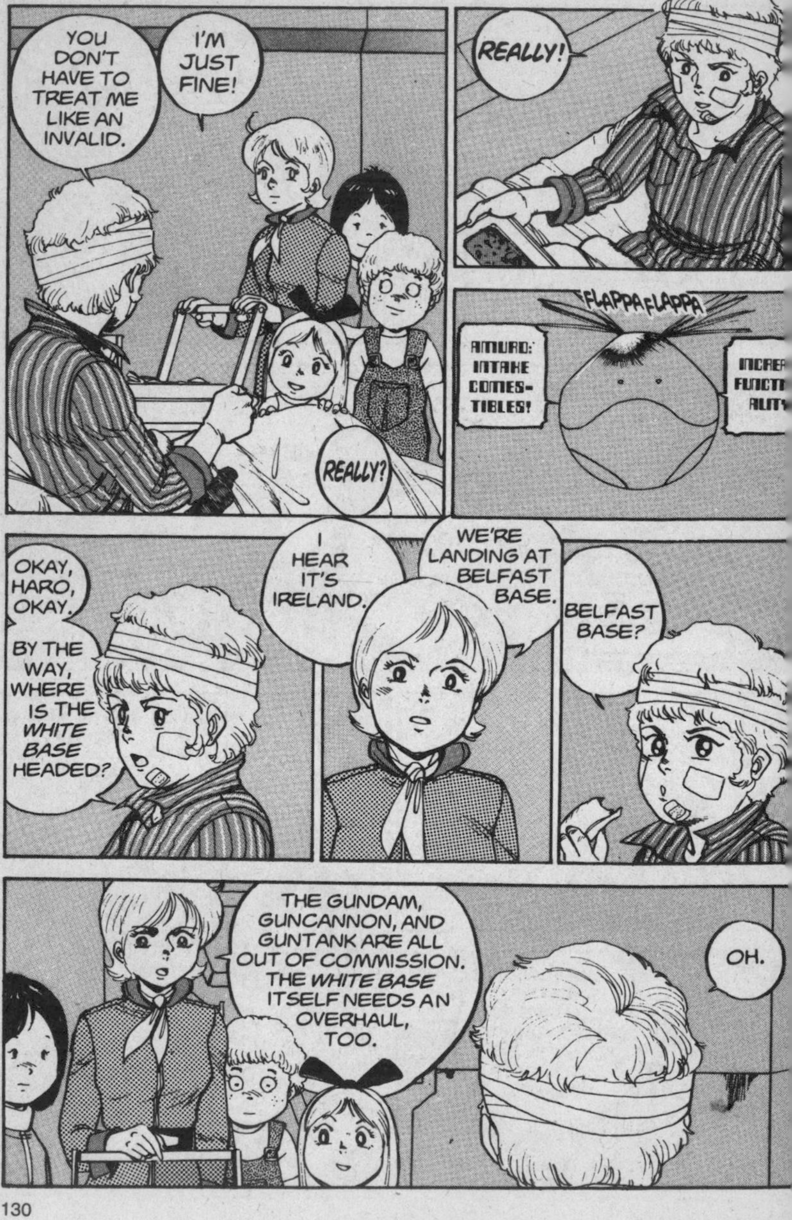
YOU DON'T HAVE TO TREAT ME LIKE AN INVALID.
I'M JUST FINE!
REALLY?
REALLY!
FLAPPA FLAPPA
AMURO: INTAKE COMES-TIBLES!
OKAY, HARO, OKAY.
BY THE WAY, WHERE IS THE *WHITE BASE* HEADED?
WE'RE LANDING AT BELFAST BASE.
I HEAR IT'S IRELAND.
BELFAST BASE?
THE GUNDAM, GUNCANNON, AND GUNTANK ARE ALL OUT OF COMMISSION. THE *WHITE BASE* ITSELF NEEDS AN OVERHAUL, TOO.
OH.

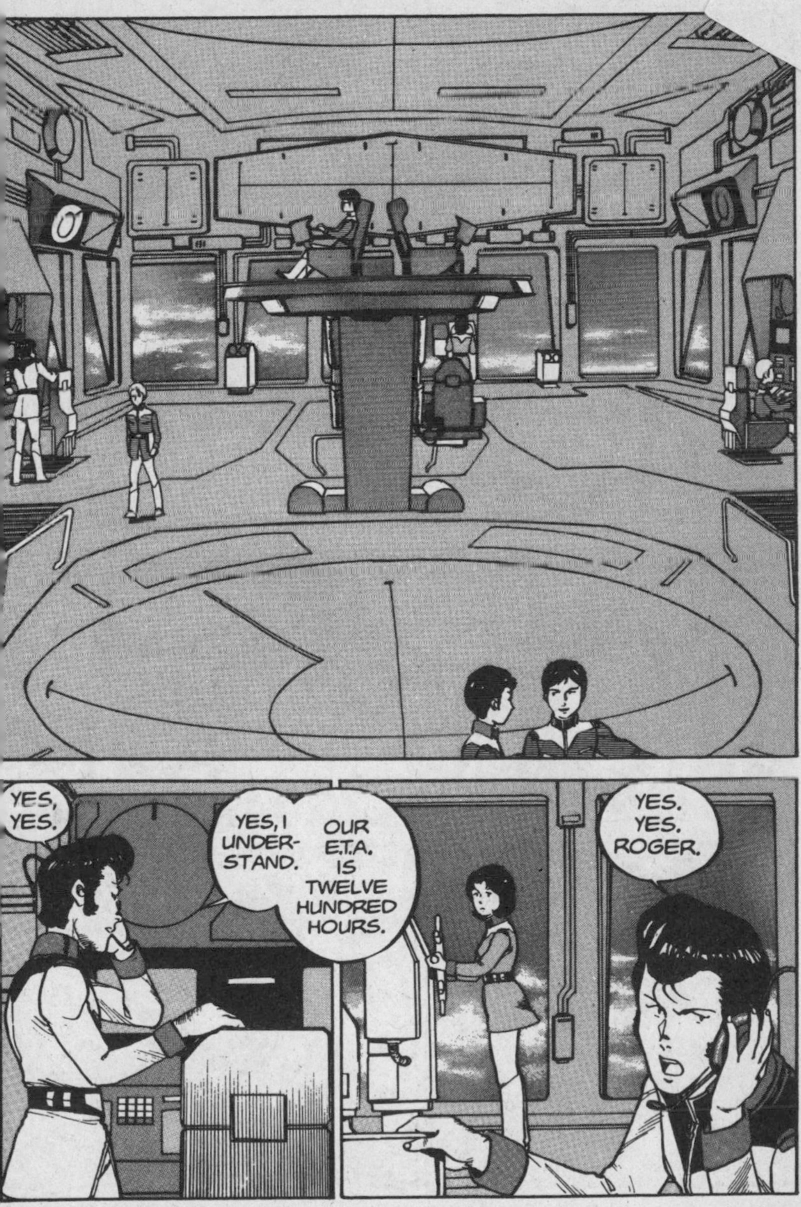
YES, YES.
YES, I UNDER-STAND.
OUR E.T.A. IS TWELVE HUNDRED HOURS.
YES. YES. ROGER.

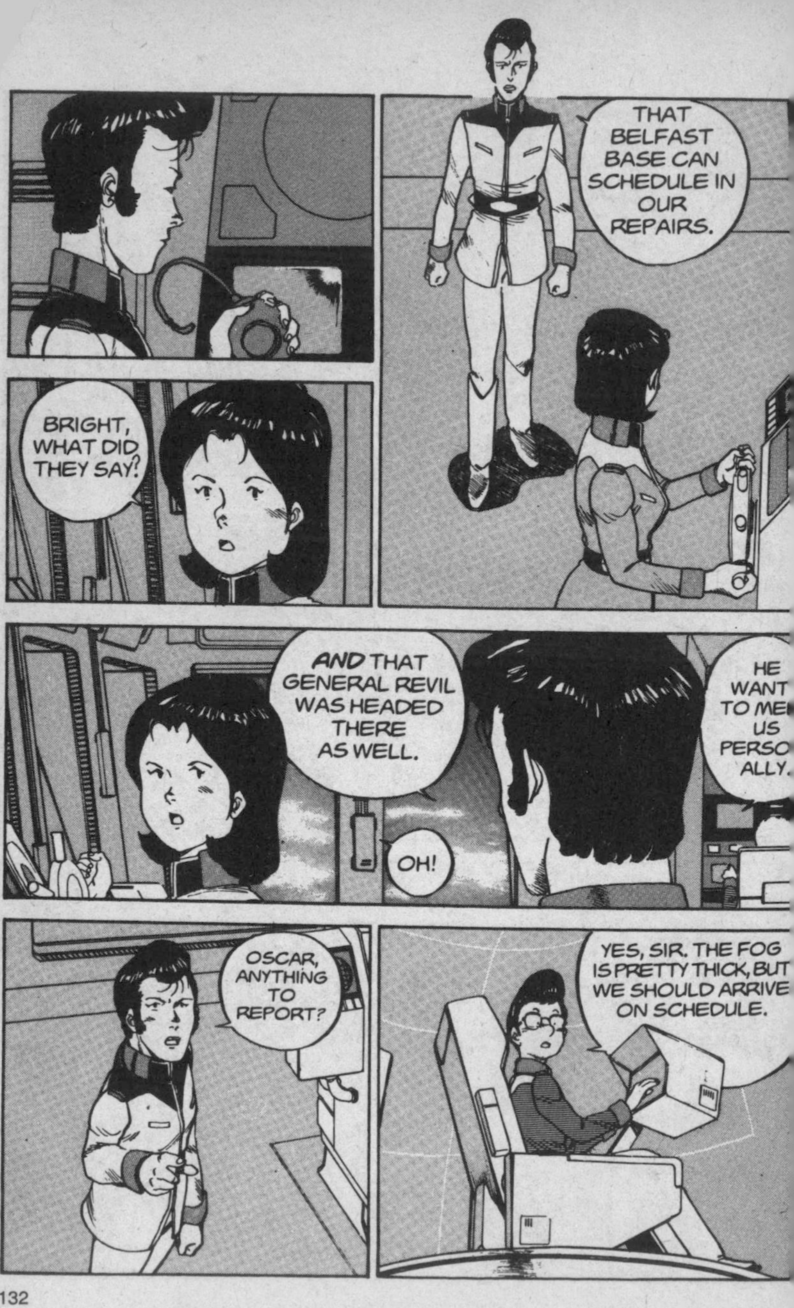
THAT BELFAST BASE CAN SCHEDULE IN OUR REPAIRS.
BRIGHT, WHAT DID THEY SAY?
AND THAT GENERAL REVIL WAS HEADED THERE AS WELL.
OH!
HE WANT TO ME US PERSO ALLY.
OSCAR, ANYTHING TO REPORT?
YES, SIR. THE FOG IS PRETTY THICK, BUT WE SHOULD ARRIVE ON SCHEDULE.

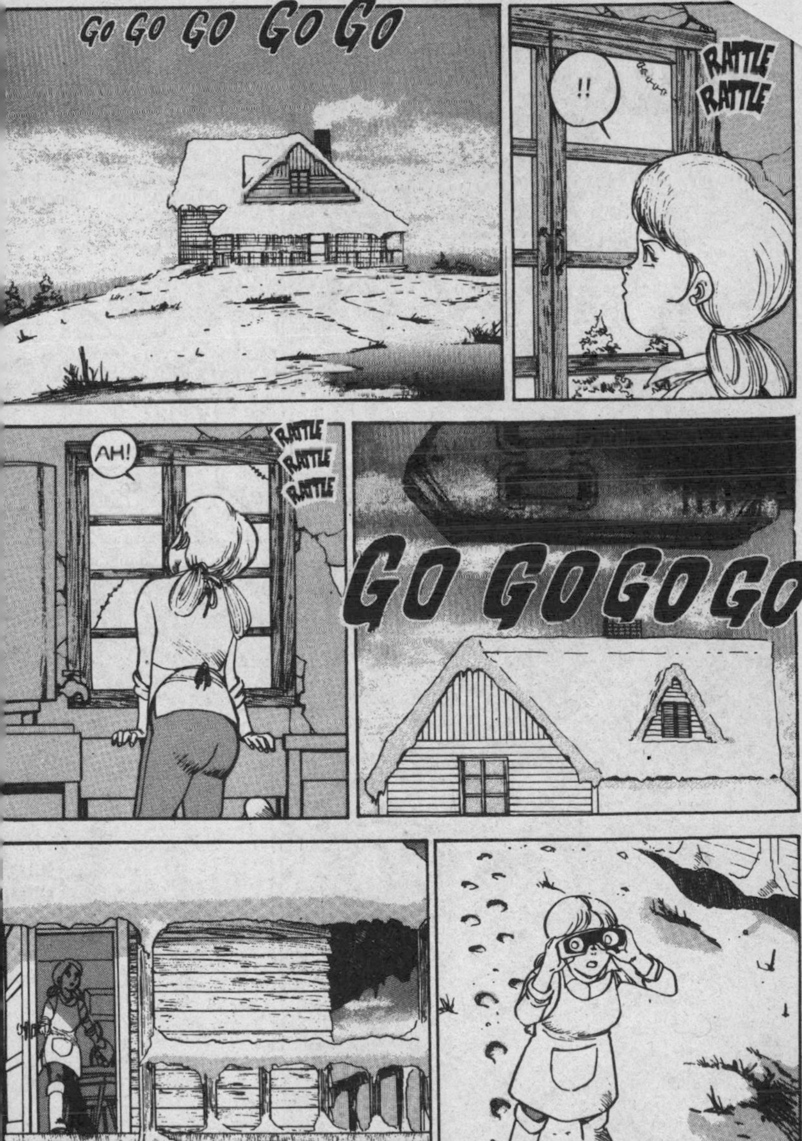

GO GO GO GO GO
!!
RATTLE RATTLE
AH!
RATTLE RATTLE RATTLE
GO GO GO GO

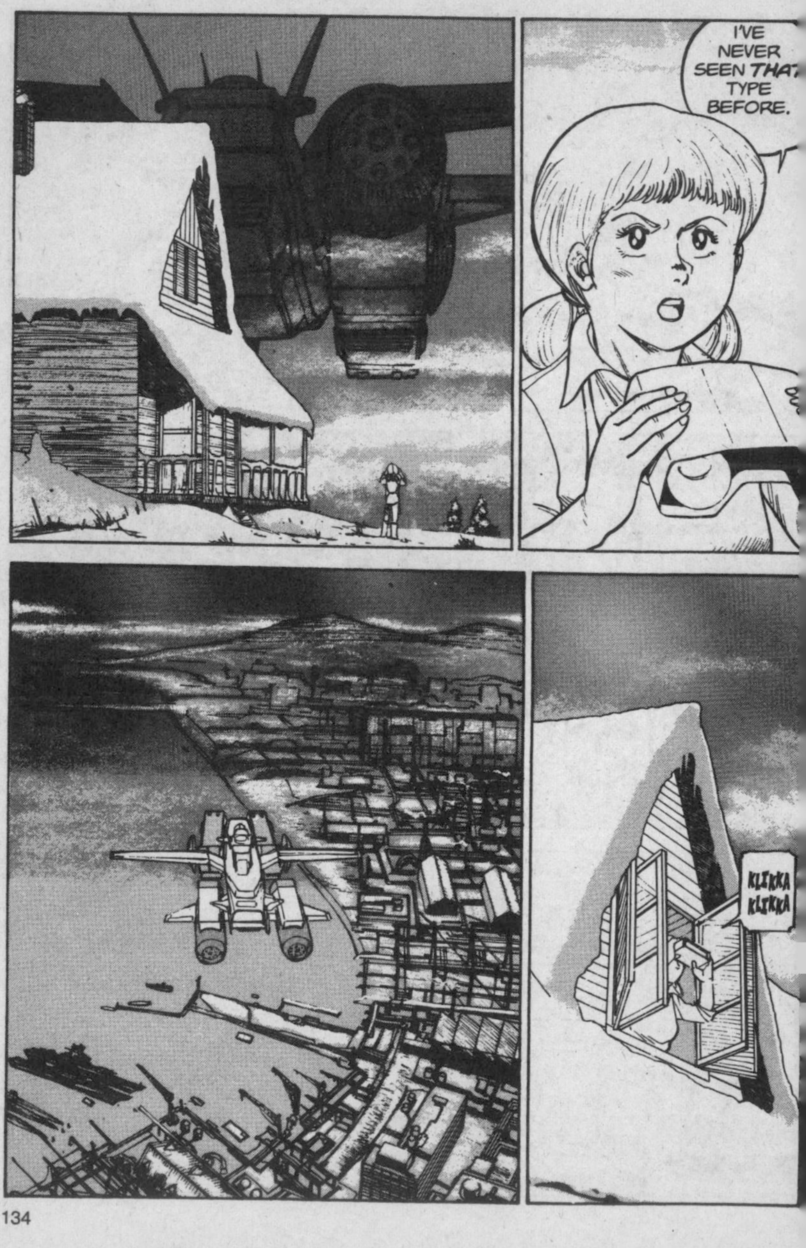
I'VE NEVER SEEN THAT TYPE BEFORE.
KLIKKA KLIKKA

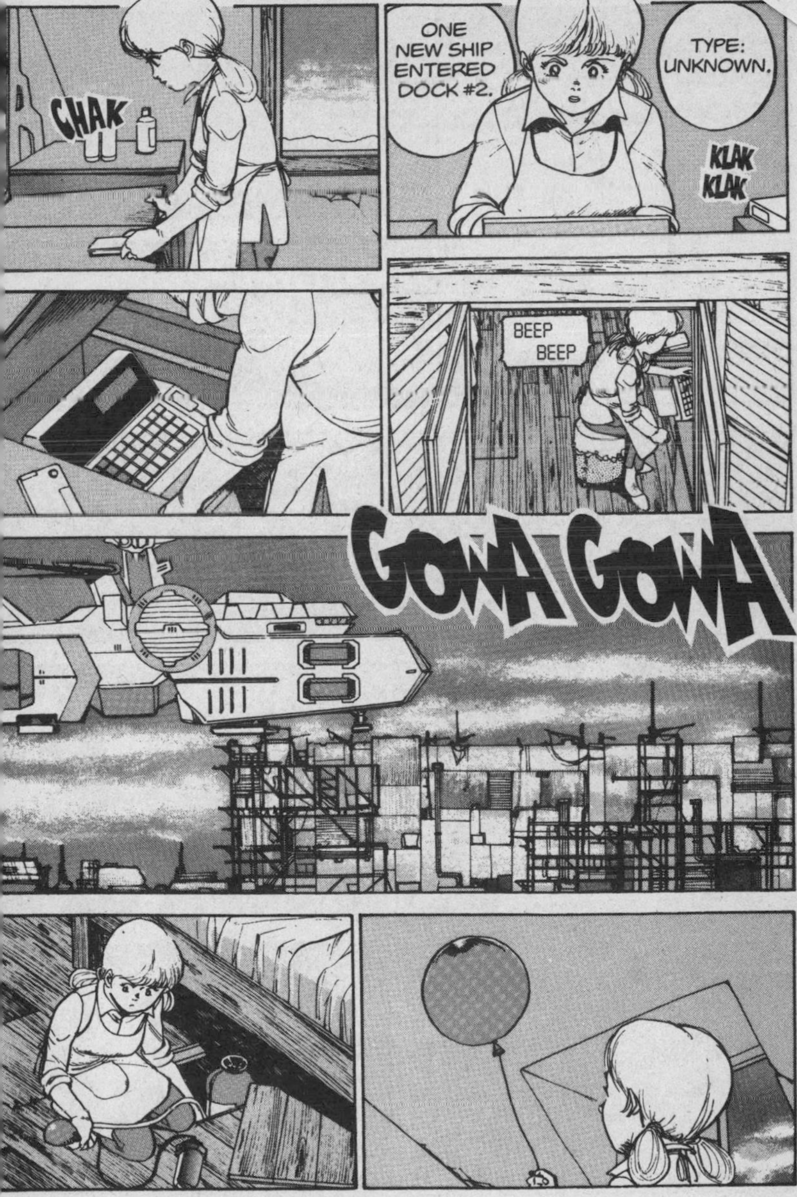
CHAK
ONE NEW SHIP ENTERED DOCK #2.
TYPE: UNKNOWN.
KLAK KLAK
BEEP BEEP
GOWA GOWA

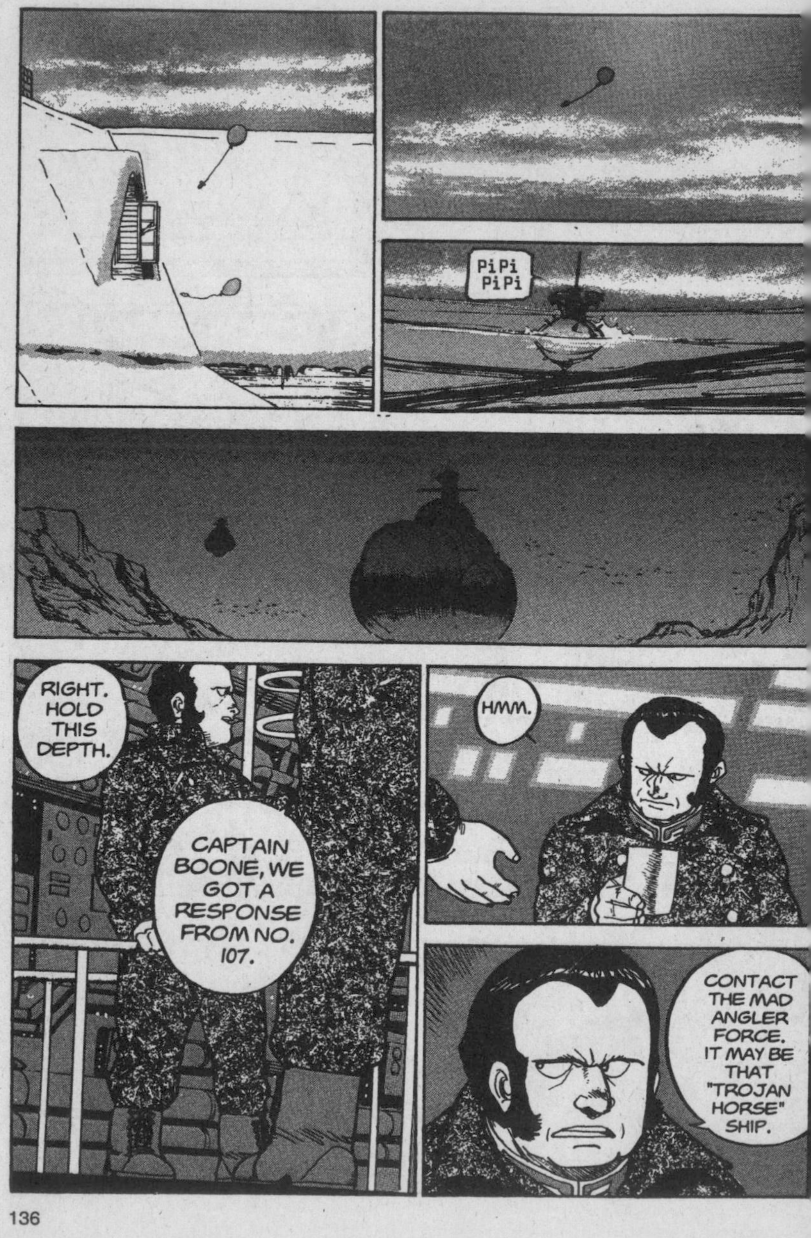
PiPi
PiPi
RIGHT. HOLD THIS DEPTH.
CAPTAIN BOONE, WE GOT A RESPONSE FROM NO. 107.
HMM.
CONTACT THE MAD ANGLER FORCE. IT MAY BE THAT "TROJAN HORSE" SHIP.

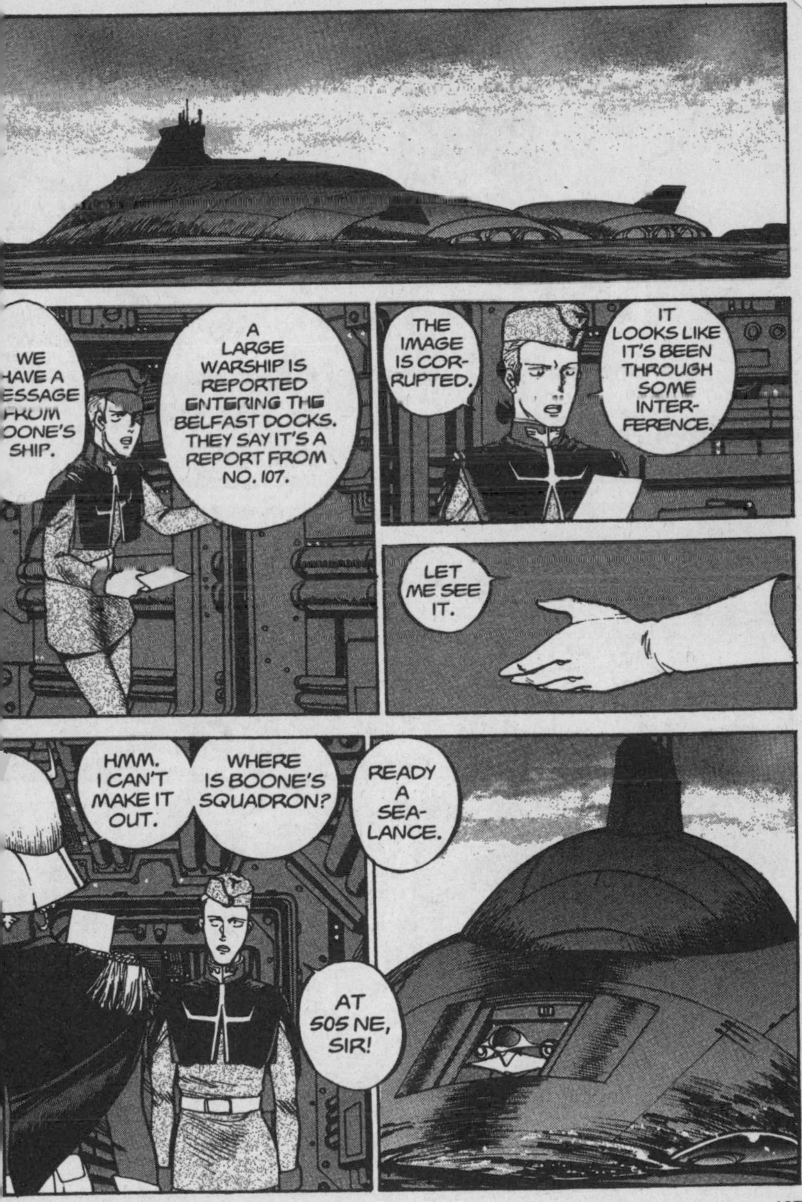
WE HAVE A ESSAGE FROM OONE'S SHIP.
A LARGE WARSHIP IS REPORTED ENTERING THE BELFAST DOCKS. THEY SAY IT'S A REPORT FROM NO. 107.
THE IMAGE IS CORRUPTED.
IT LOOKS LIKE IT'S BEEN THROUGH SOME INTERFERENCE.
LET ME SEE IT.
HMM. I CAN'T MAKE IT OUT.
WHERE IS BOONE'S SQUADRON?
AT 505 NE, SIR!
READY A SEA-LANCE.

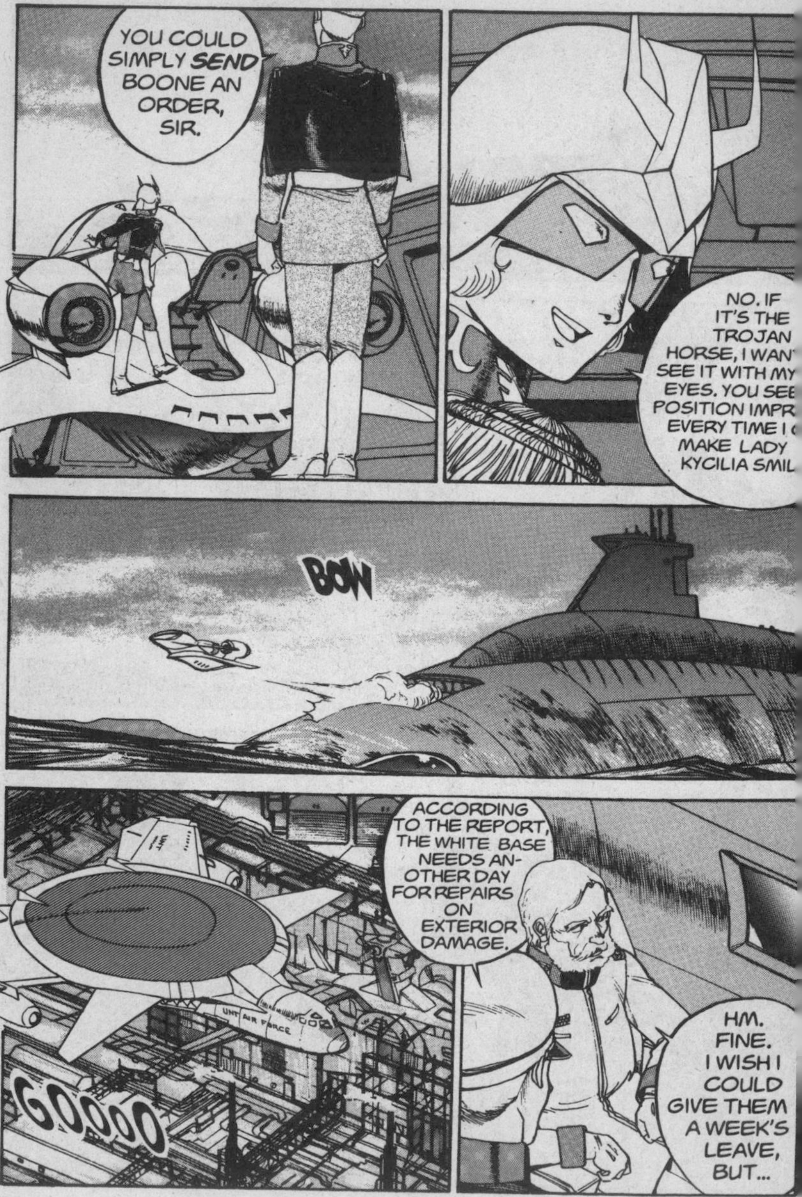
YOU COULD SIMPLY SEND BOONE AN ORDER, SIR.
NO. IF IT'S THE TROJAN HORSE, I WAN SEE IT WITH MY EYES. YOU SEE POSITION IMPR EVERY TIME I MAKE LADY KYCILIA SMIL
BOW
ACCORDING TO THE REPORT, THE WHITE BASE NEEDS ANOTHER DAY FOR REPAIRS ON EXTERIOR DAMAGE.
GOOOO
HM. FINE. I WISH I COULD GIVE THEM A WEEK'S LEAVE, BUT...

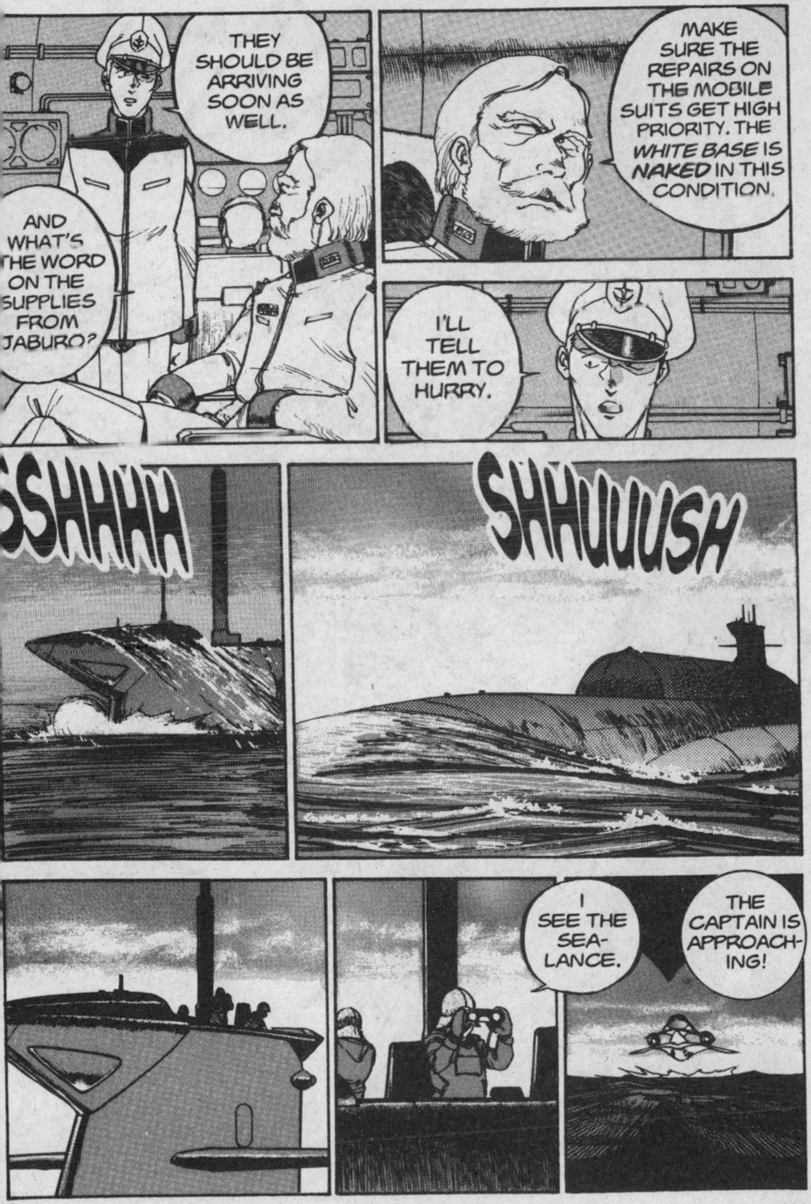
THEY SHOULD BE ARRIVING SOON AS WELL.
AND WHAT'S THE WORD ON THE SUPPLIES FROM JABURO?
MAKE SURE THE REPAIRS ON THE MOBILE SUITS GET HIGH PRIORITY. THE *WHITE BASE* IS *NAKED* IN THIS CONDITION.
I'LL TELL THEM TO HURRY.
SSHHHH
SHHUUUSH
I SEE THE SEA-LANCE.
THE CAPTAIN IS APPROACH-ING!

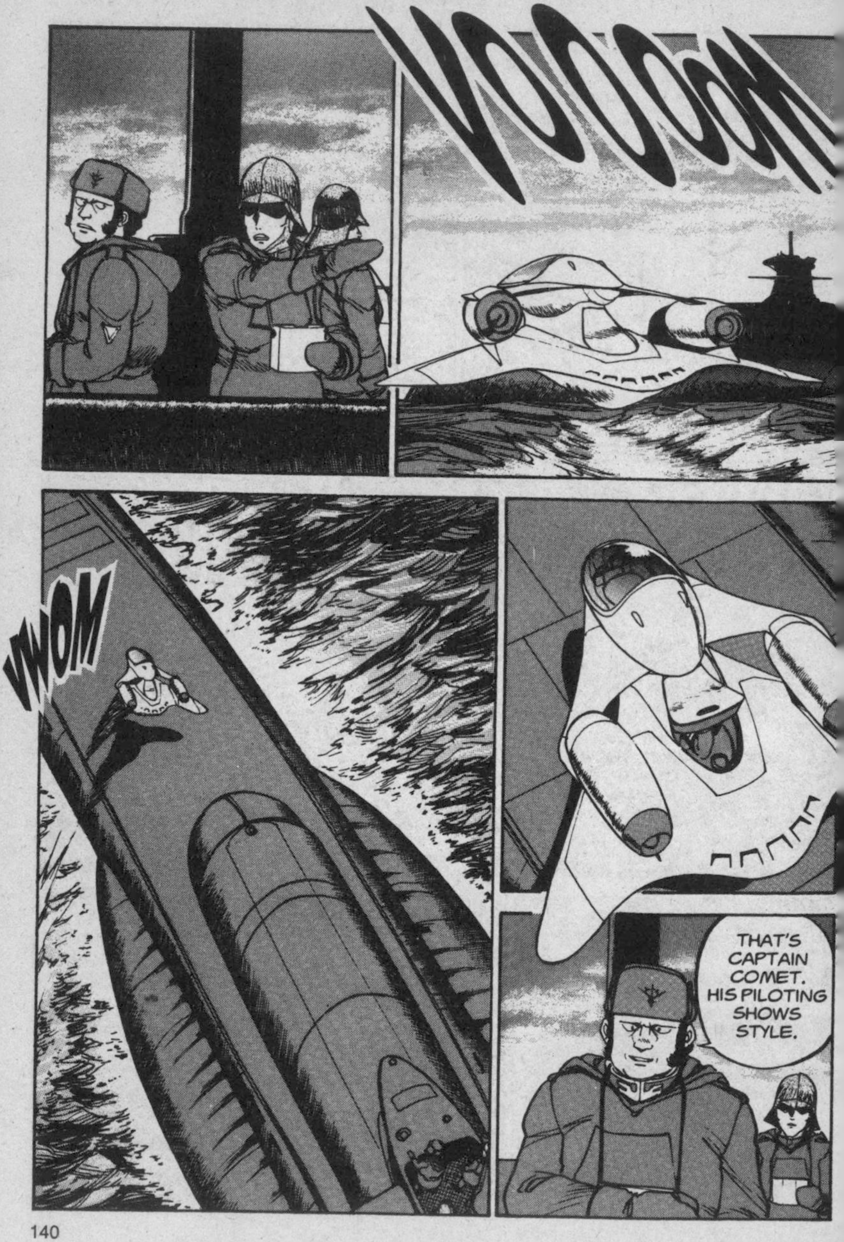
VOOOOOM
VWOM
THAT'S CAPTAIN COMET. HIS PILOTING SHOWS STYLE.

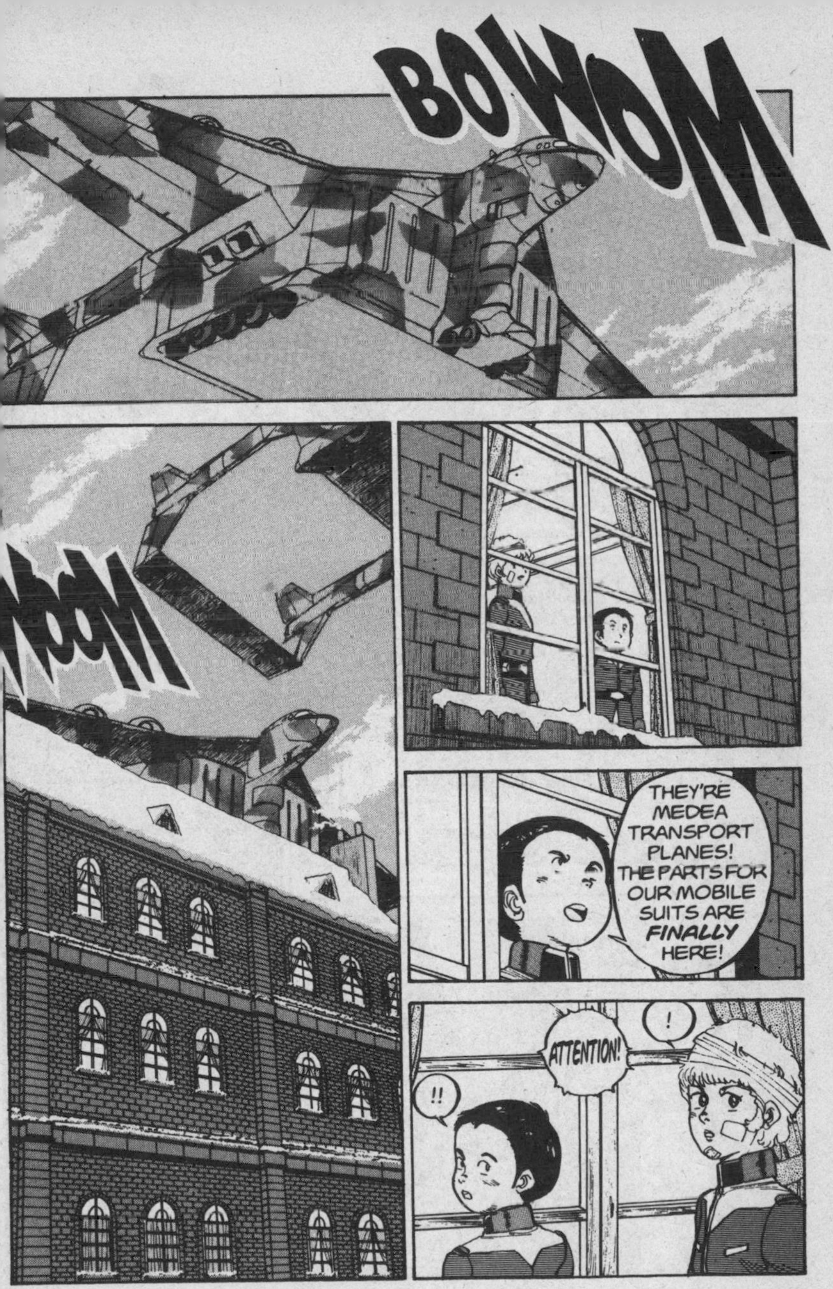
BOWOOM
WOOM
THEY'RE MEDEA TRANSPORT PLANES! THE PARTS FOR OUR MOBILE SUITS ARE FINALLY HERE!
ATTENTION!
!
!!

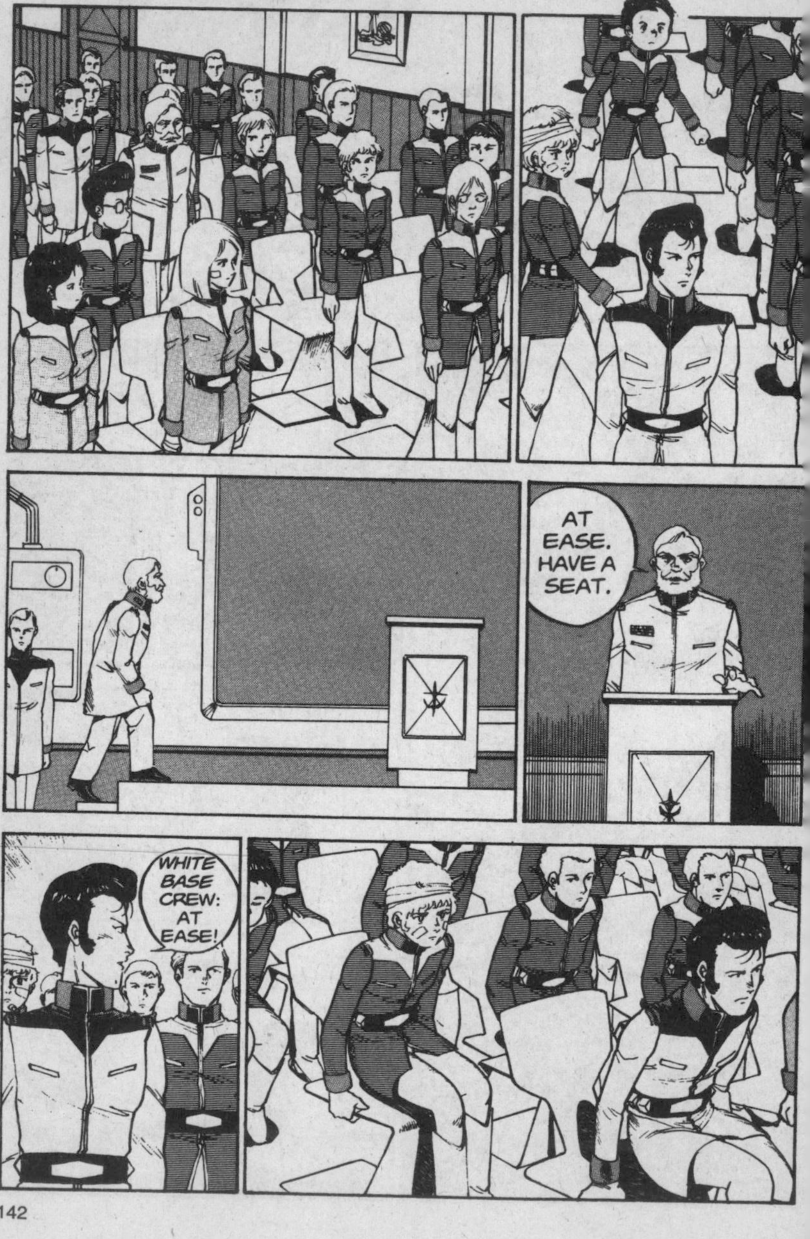
AT EASE. HAVE A SEAT.
WHITE BASE CREW: AT EASE!

AHEM

THERE AREN'T WORDS TO THANK YOU ENOUGH FOR ALL YOU'VE DONE SINCE YOU EMBARKED FROM SIDE 7.

WE WILL MAKE THE REPAIR OF THE *WHITE BASE* AND YOUR MOBILE SUITS OUR TOP PRIORITY.

ONCE REPAIRED, YOU WILL HEAD TO OUR JABURO BASE IN SOUTH AMERICA.

UMM... EXCUSE ME...

YES? WHAT IS IT?

SIR... WHAT ABOUT THOSE PEOPLE...

...WHO DON'T *WANT* TO JOIN THE MILITARY?

I'D SAY THAT YOU ARE *ALREADY* FINE SOLDIERS, BUT FOR THOSE WHO WISH TO LEAVE...

...WE'D HAVE TO DETAIN YOU IN PRISON FOR A TERM OF ONE YEAR.

WHAT!? THAT'S INSANE!

FROM THE MOMENT YOU STEPPED ABOARD THE *WHITE BASE*, YOU BECAME PRIVY TO SOME OF THE FEDERATION'S BEST KEPT SECRETS.

YOU WERE ON THE VERGE OF BEING IMPRISONED FOR *LIFE!*

SO... WE'RE SOLDIERS?

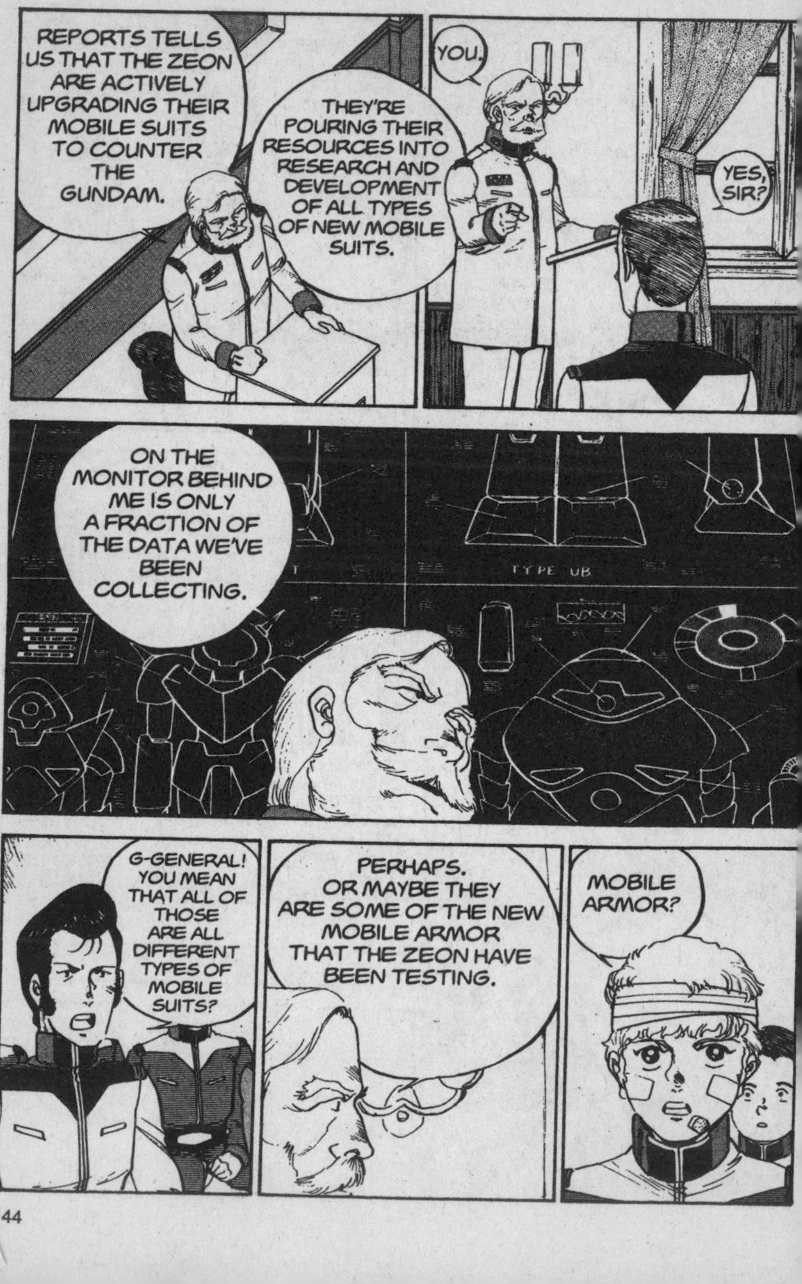
REPORTS TELLS US THAT THE ZEON ARE ACTIVELY UPGRADING THEIR MOBILE SUITS TO COUNTER THE GUNDAM.
THEY'RE POURING THEIR RESOURCES INTO RESEARCH AND DEVELOPMENT OF ALL TYPES OF NEW MOBILE SUITS.
YOU.
YES, SIR?
ON THE MONITOR BEHIND ME IS ONLY A FRACTION OF THE DATA WE'VE BEEN COLLECTING.
TYPE UB
G-GENERAL! YOU MEAN THAT ALL OF THOSE ARE ALL DIFFERENT TYPES OF MOBILE SUITS?
PERHAPS. OR MAYBE THEY ARE SOME OF THE NEW MOBILE ARMOR THAT THE ZEON HAVE BEEN TESTING.
MOBILE ARMOR?

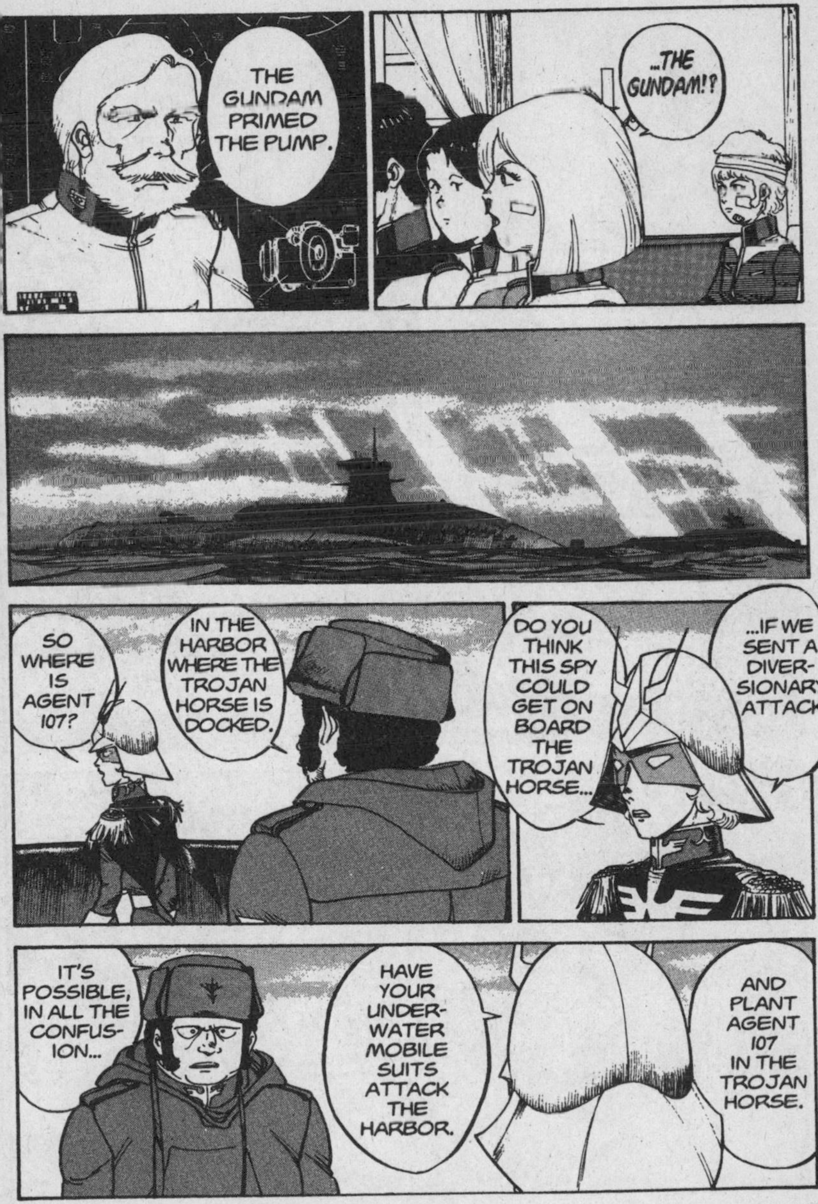
THE GUNDAM PRIMED THE PUMP.
...THE GUNDAM!?
SO WHERE IS AGENT 107?
IN THE HARBOR WHERE THE TROJAN HORSE IS DOCKED.
DO YOU THINK THIS SPY COULD GET ON BOARD THE TROJAN HORSE...
...IF WE SENT A DIVERSIONARY ATTACK?
IT'S POSSIBLE, IN ALL THE CONFUSION...
HAVE YOUR UNDERWATER MOBILE SUITS ATTACK THE HARBOR.
AND PLANT AGENT 107 IN THE TROJAN HORSE.

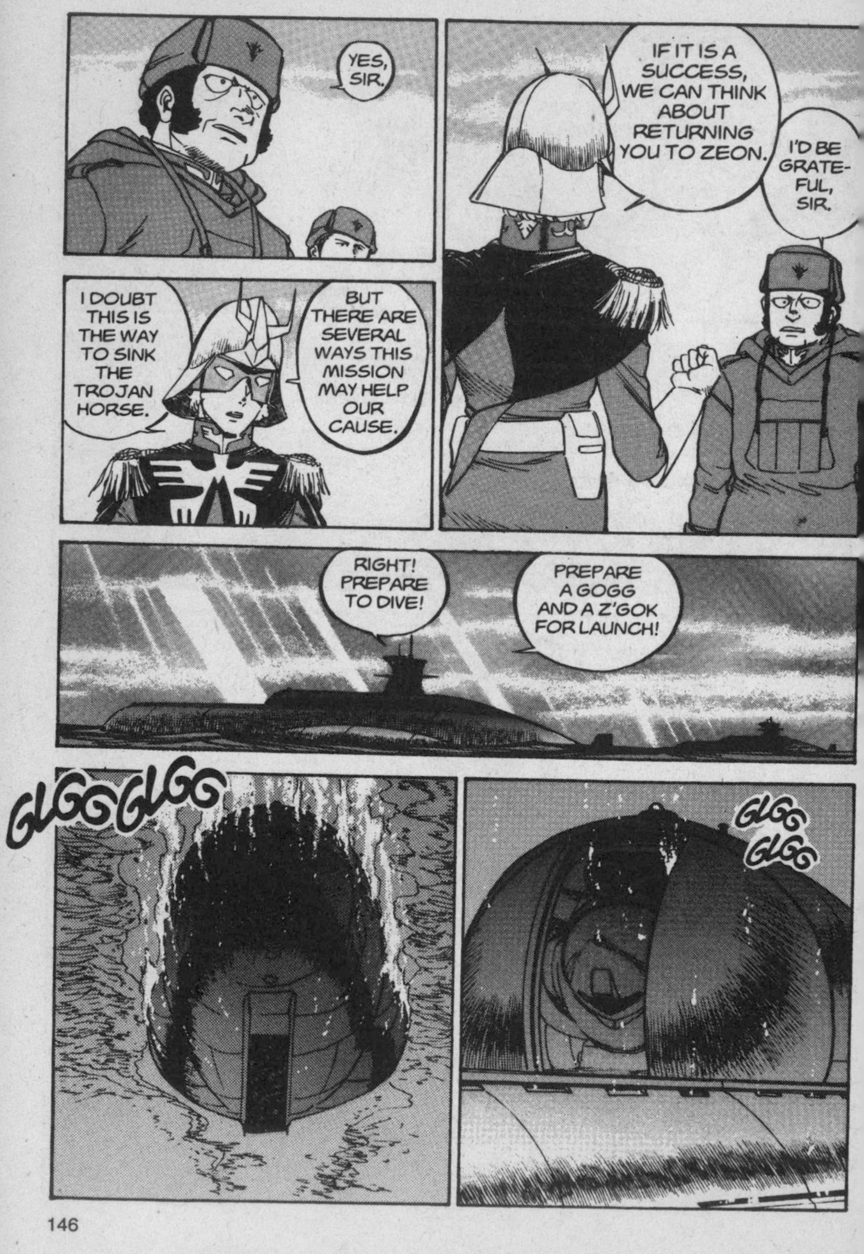
YES, SIR.
IF IT IS A SUCCESS, WE CAN THINK ABOUT RETURNING YOU TO ZEON.
I'D BE GRATE-FUL, SIR.
I DOUBT THIS IS THE WAY TO SINK THE TROJAN HORSE.
BUT THERE ARE SEVERAL WAYS THIS MISSION MAY HELP OUR CAUSE.
RIGHT! PREPARE TO DIVE!
PREPARE A GOGG AND A Z'GOK FOR LAUNCH!
GLGG GLGG
GLGG GLGG

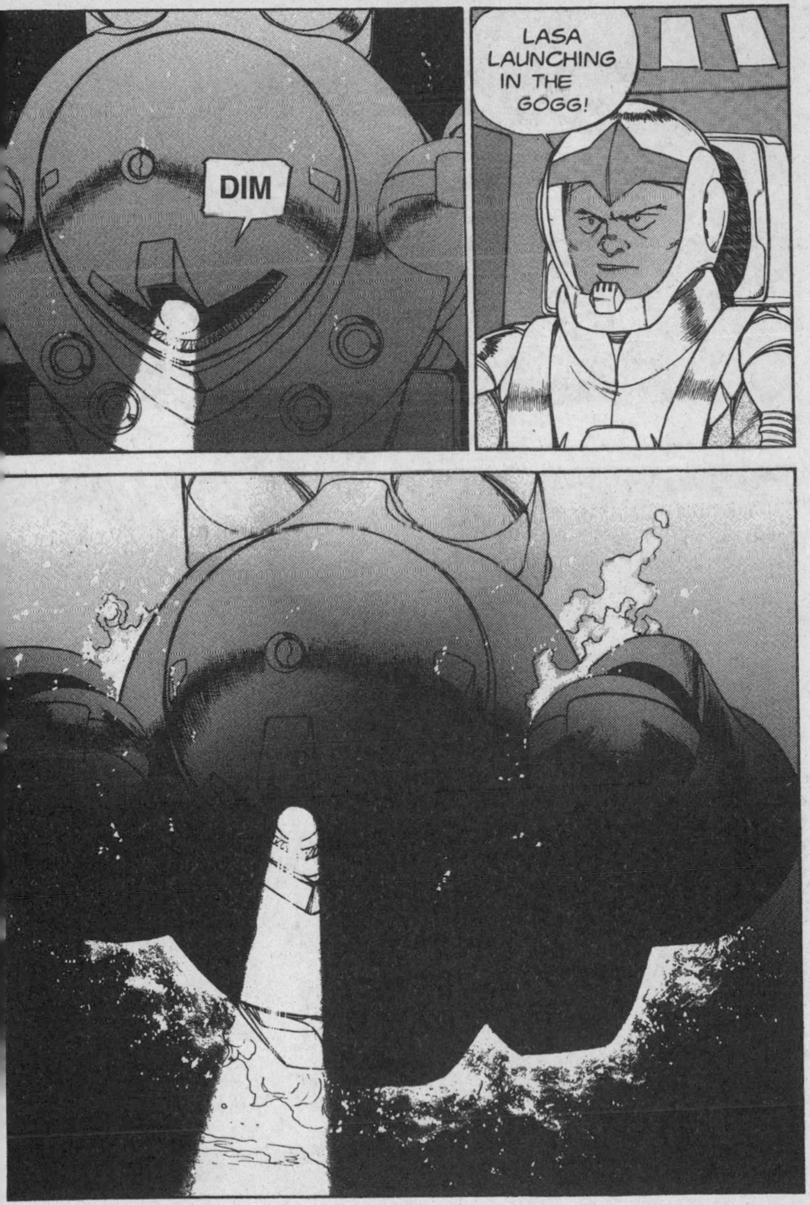
DIM
LASA LAUNCHING IN THE GOGG!

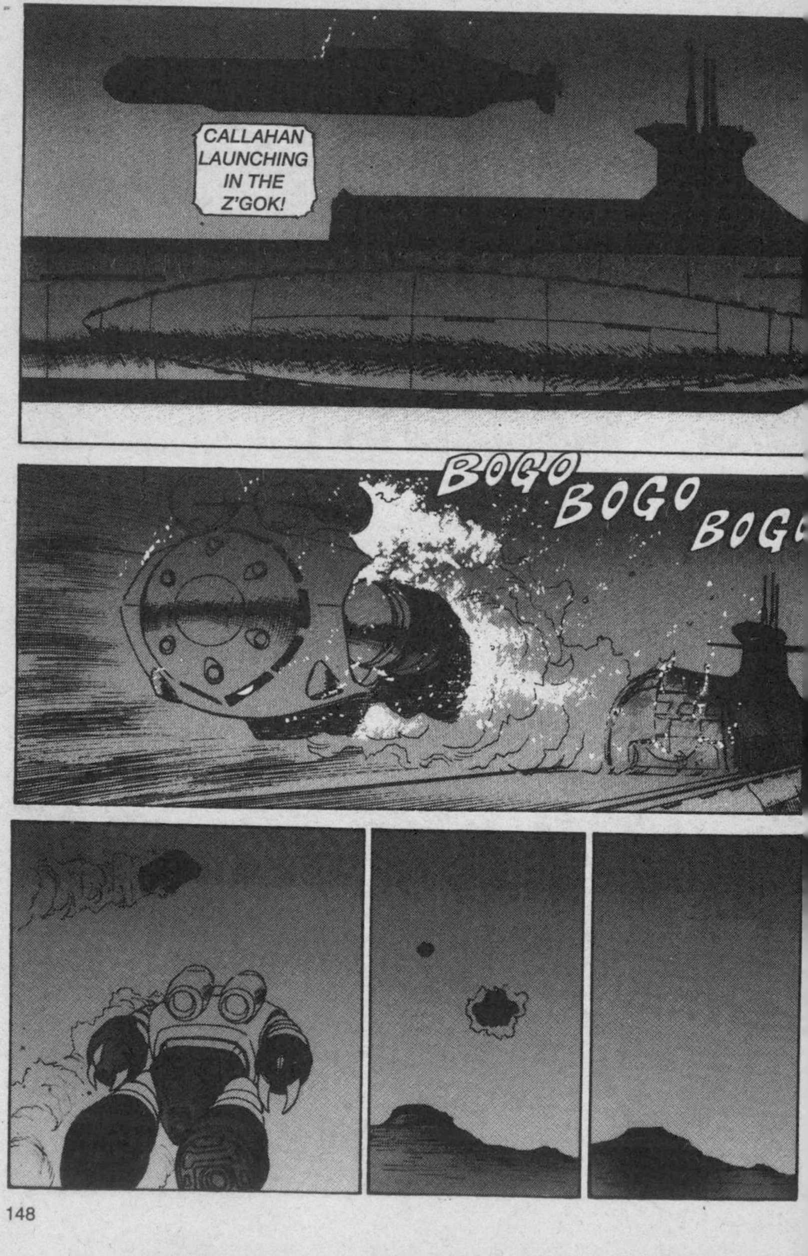
CALLAHAN LAUNCHING IN THE Z'GOK!
BOGO
BOGO
BOGO

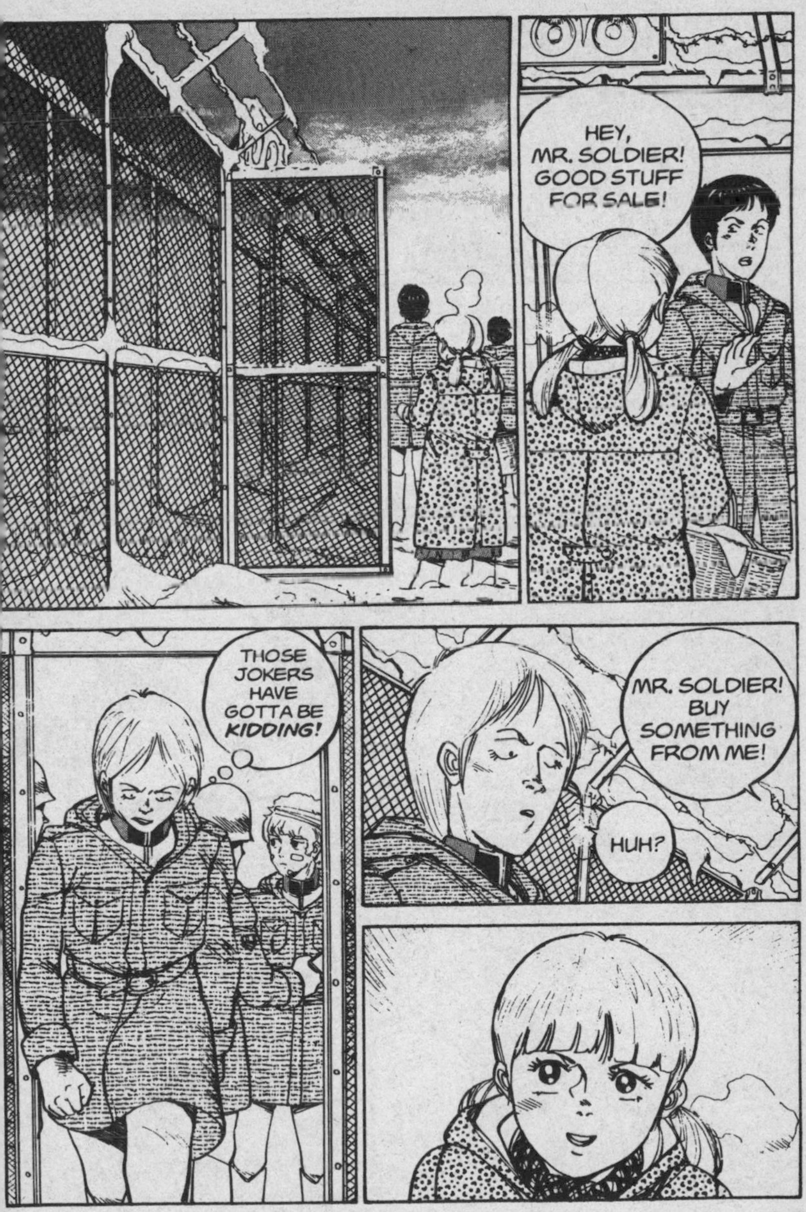
HEY, MR. SOLDIER! GOOD STUFF FOR SALE!
THOSE JOKERS HAVE GOTTA BE *KIDDING!*
MR. SOLDIER! BUY SOMETHING FROM ME!
HUH?

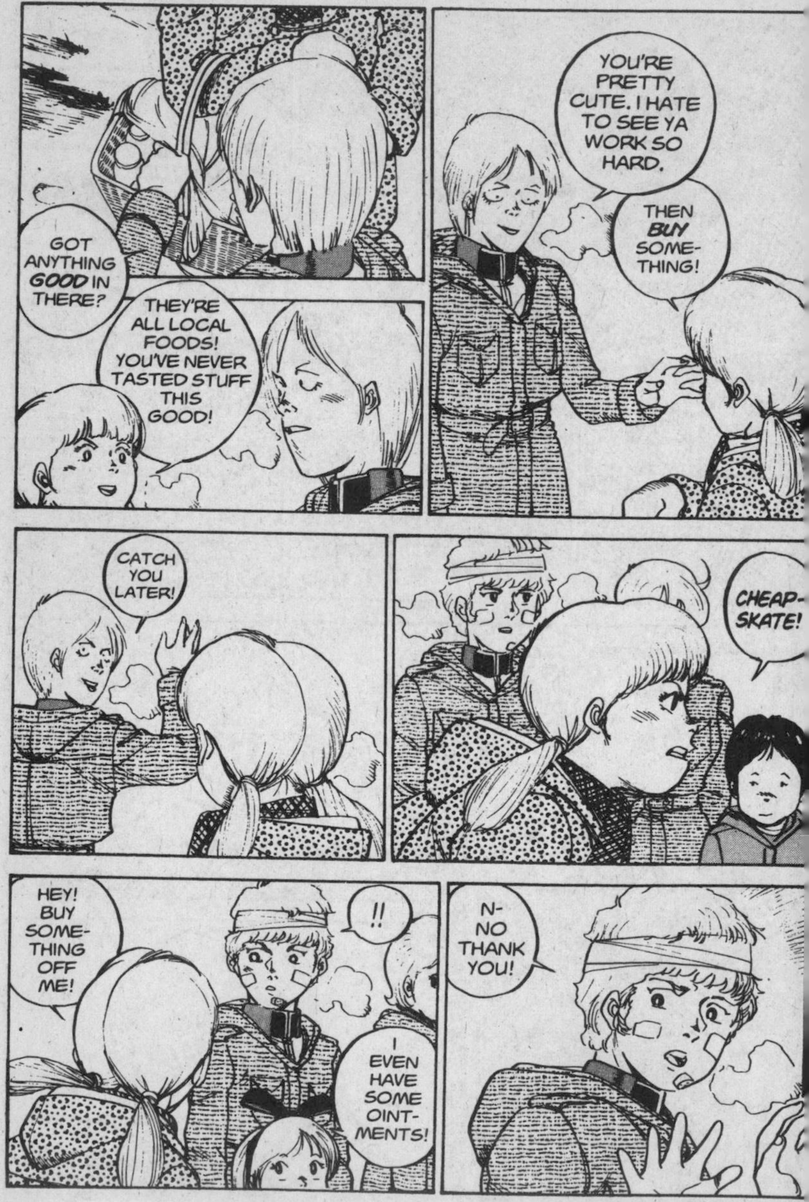
GOT ANYTHING GOOD IN THERE?
THEY'RE ALL LOCAL FOODS! YOU'VE NEVER TASTED STUFF THIS GOOD!
YOU'RE PRETTY CUTE. I HATE TO SEE YA WORK SO HARD.
THEN BUY SOME-THING!
CATCH YOU LATER!
CHEAP-SKATE!
HEY! BUY SOME-THING OFF ME!
!!
I EVEN HAVE SOME OINT-MENTS!
N-NO THANK YOU!

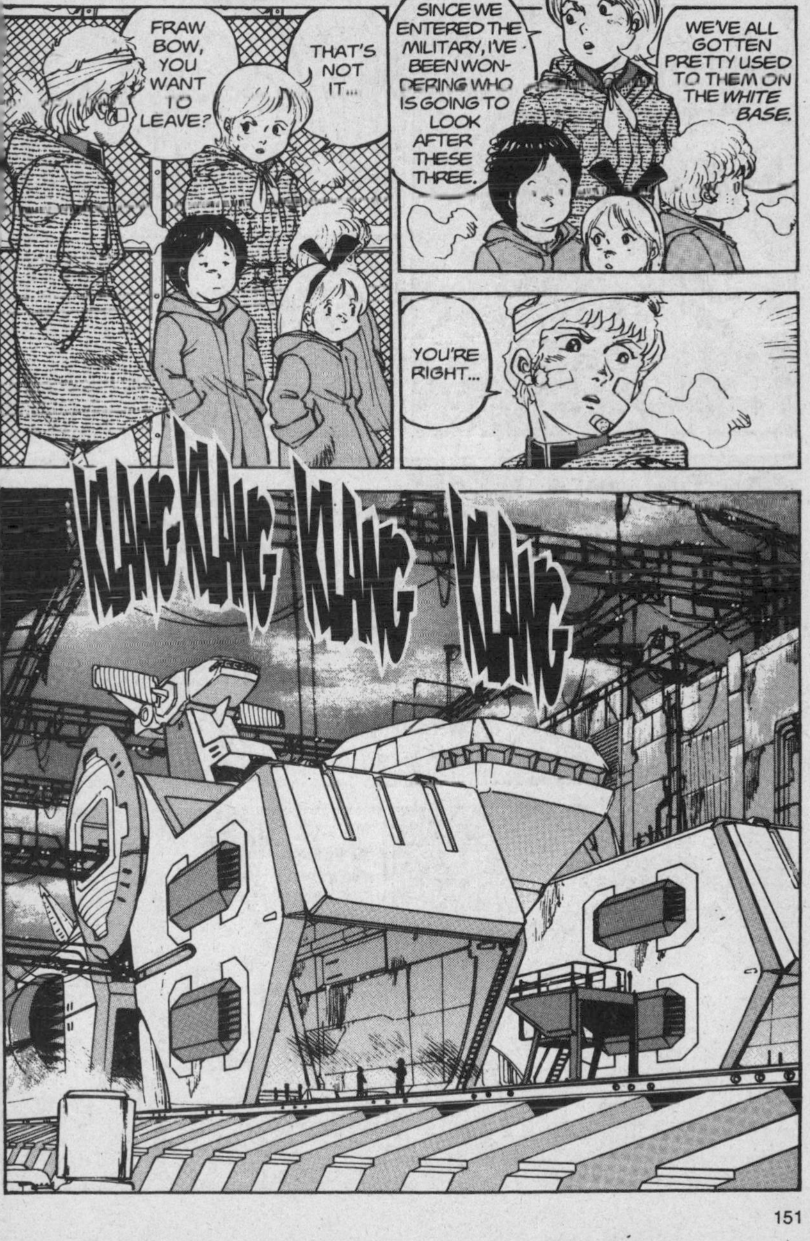
FRAW BOW, YOU WANT TO LEAVE?
THAT'S NOT IT...
SINCE WE ENTERED THE MILITARY, I'VE BEEN WONDERING WHO IS GOING TO LOOK AFTER THESE THREE.
WE'VE ALL GOTTEN PRETTY USED TO THEM ON THE *WHITE BASE*.
YOU'RE RIGHT...
KLANG KLANG KLANG KLANG KLANG

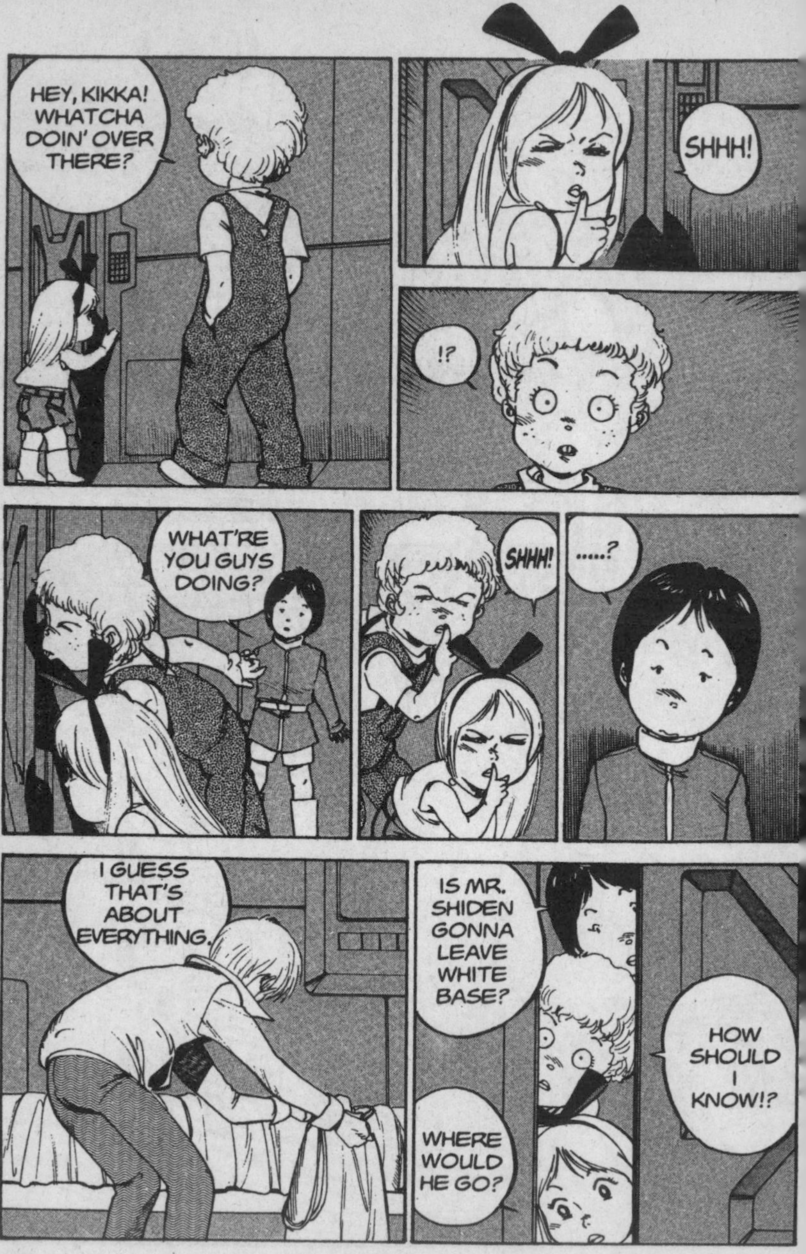
HEY, KIKKA! WHATCHA DOIN' OVER THERE?
SHHH!
!?
WHAT'RE YOU GUYS DOING?
SHHH!
.....?
I GUESS THAT'S ABOUT EVERYTHING.
IS MR. SHIDEN GONNA LEAVE WHITE BASE?
WHERE WOULD HE GO?
HOW SHOULD I KNOW!?

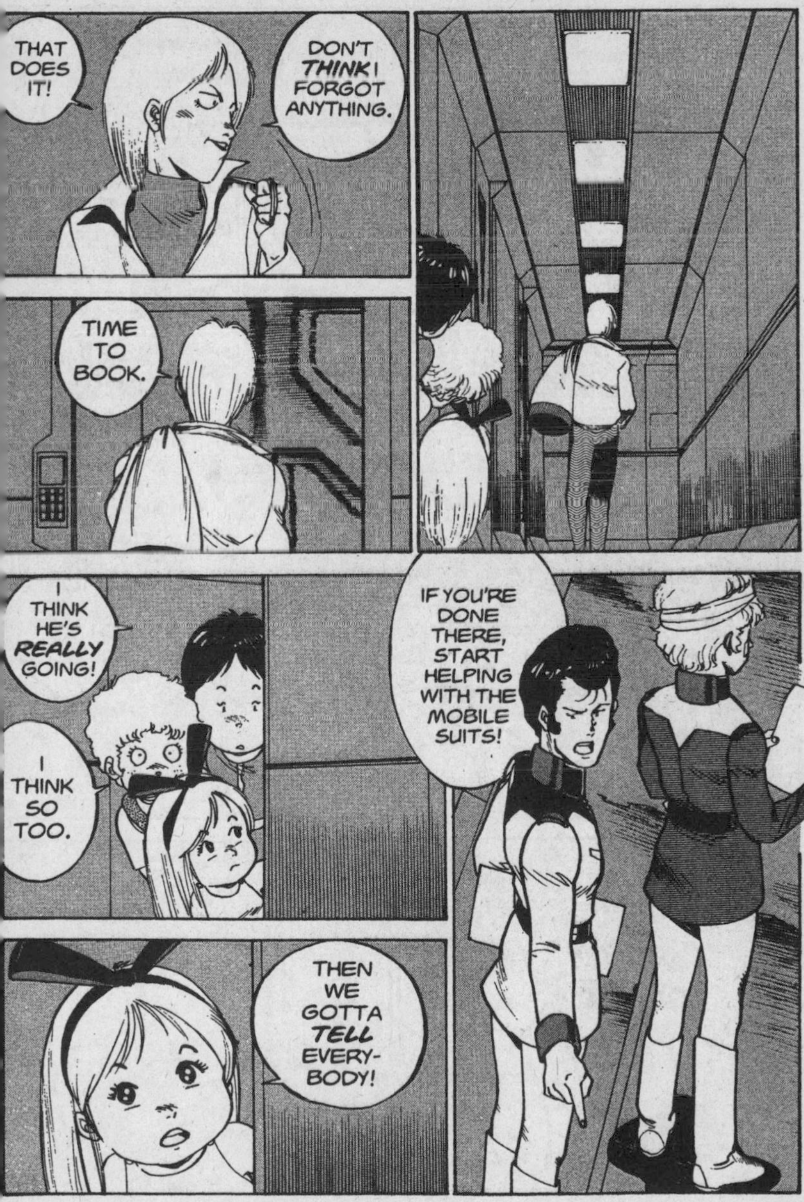
THAT DOES IT!
DON'T *THINK* I FORGOT ANYTHING.
TIME TO BOOK.
I THINK HE'S *REALLY* GOING!
I THINK SO TOO.
THEN WE GOTTA *TELL* EVERY-BODY!
IF YOU'RE DONE THERE, START HELPING WITH THE MOBILE SUITS!

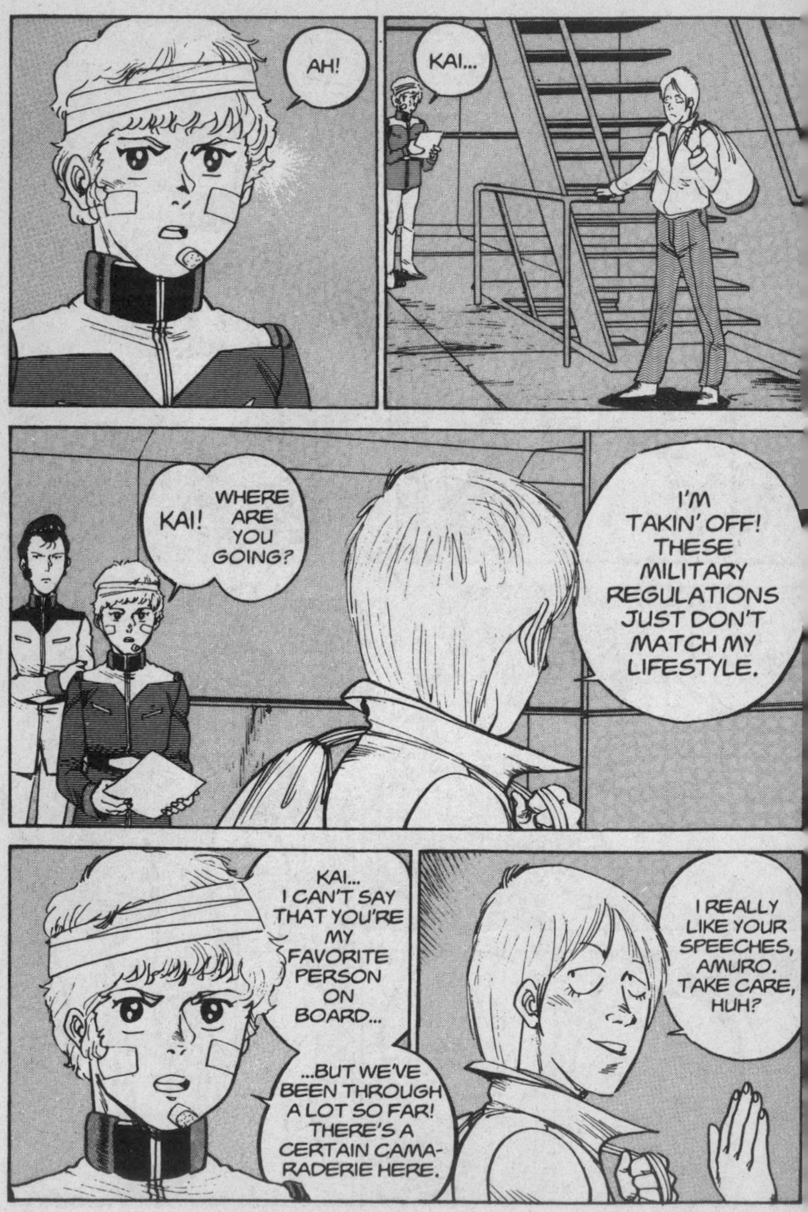
AH!
KAI...
KAI! WHERE ARE YOU GOING?
I'M TAKIN' OFF! THESE MILITARY REGULATIONS JUST DON'T MATCH MY LIFESTYLE.
KAI... I CAN'T SAY THAT YOU'RE MY FAVORITE PERSON ON BOARD...
...BUT WE'VE BEEN THROUGH A LOT SO FAR! THERE'S A CERTAIN CAMARADERIE HERE.
I REALLY LIKE YOUR SPEECHES, AMURO. TAKE CARE, HUH?

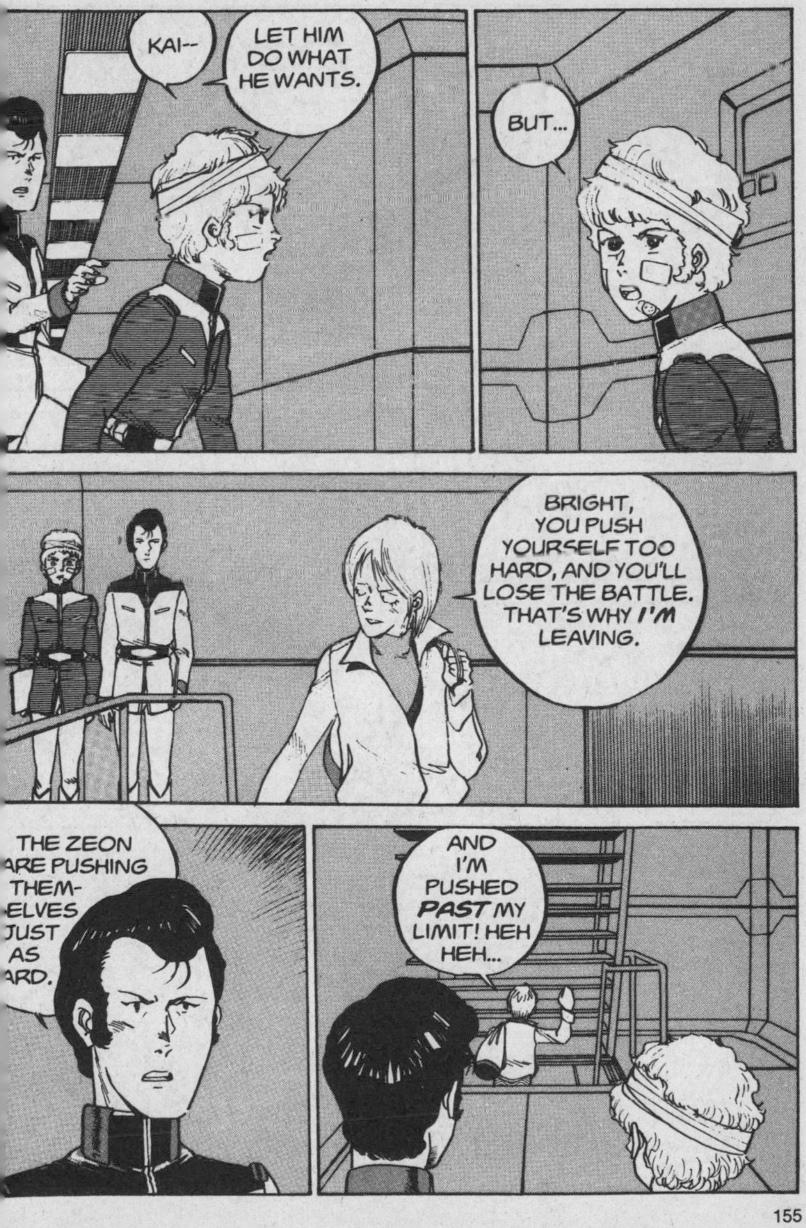
KAI--
LET HIM DO WHAT HE WANTS.
BUT...
BRIGHT, YOU PUSH YOURSELF TOO HARD, AND YOU'LL LOSE THE BATTLE. THAT'S WHY I'M LEAVING.
THE ZEON ARE PUSHING THEM-ELVES JUST AS ARD.
AND I'M PUSHED PAST MY LIMIT! HEH HEH...

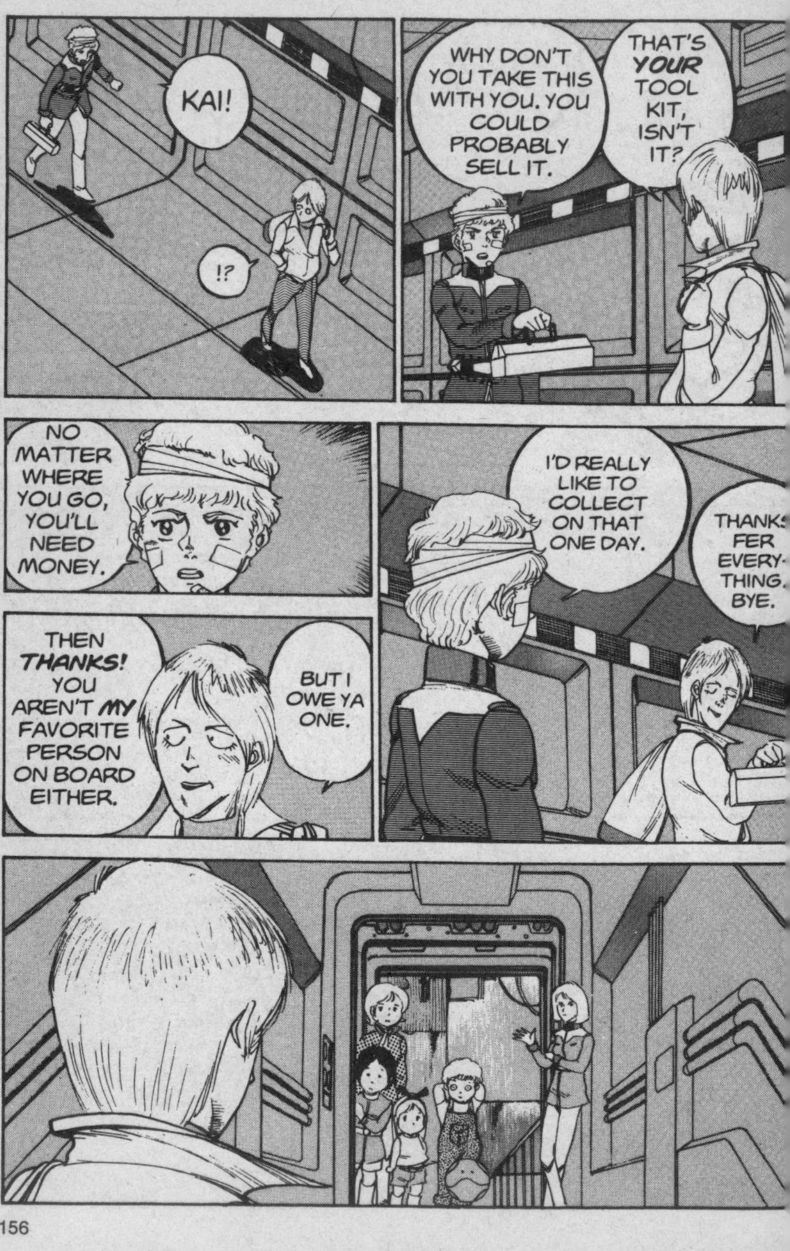
KAI!
!?
WHY DON'T YOU TAKE THIS WITH YOU. YOU COULD PROBABLY SELL IT.
THAT'S ***YOUR*** TOOL KIT, ISN'T IT?
NO MATTER WHERE YOU GO, YOU'LL NEED MONEY.
THEN ***THANKS!*** YOU AREN'T ***MY*** FAVORITE PERSON ON BOARD EITHER.
BUT I OWE YA ONE.
I'D REALLY LIKE TO COLLECT ON THAT ONE DAY.
THANKS FER EVERY-THING. BYE.

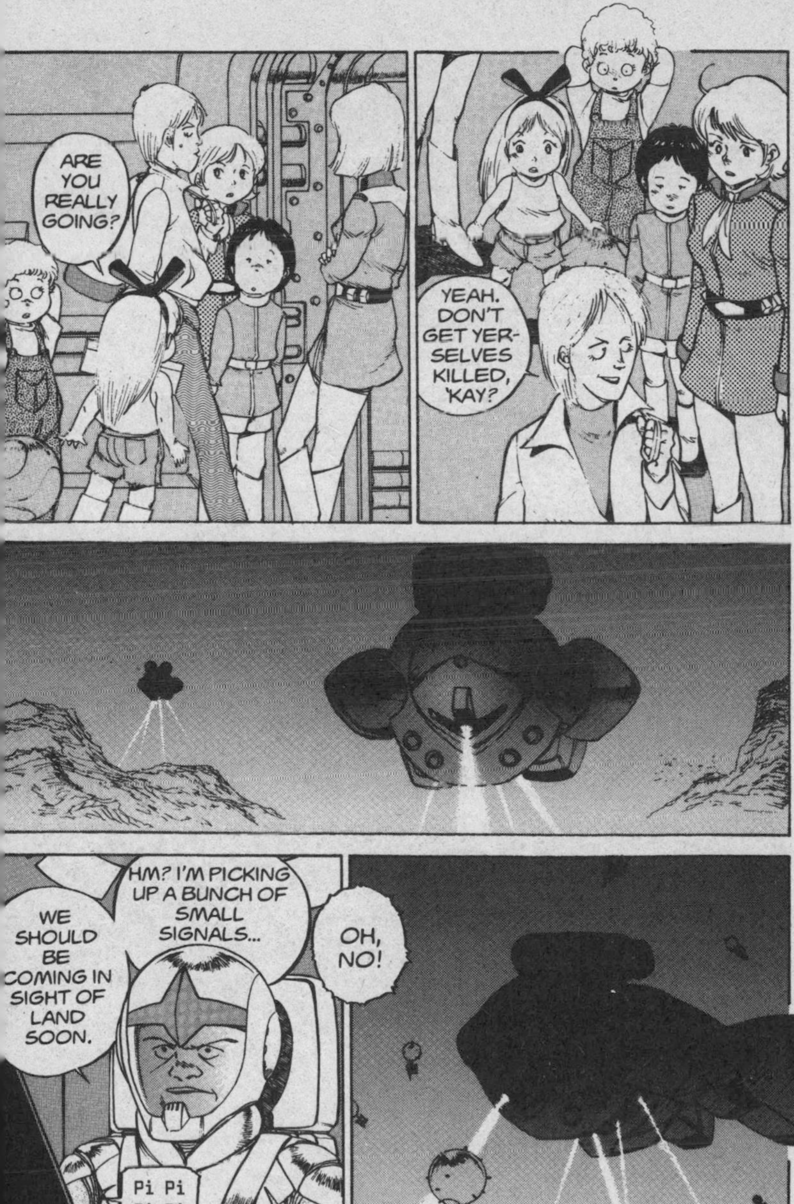
ARE YOU REALLY GOING?
YEAH. DON'T GET YER-SELVES KILLED, 'KAY?
WE SHOULD BE COMING IN SIGHT OF LAND SOON.
HM? I'M PICKING UP A BUNCH OF SMALL SIGNALS...
Pi Pi Pi Pi
OH, NO!

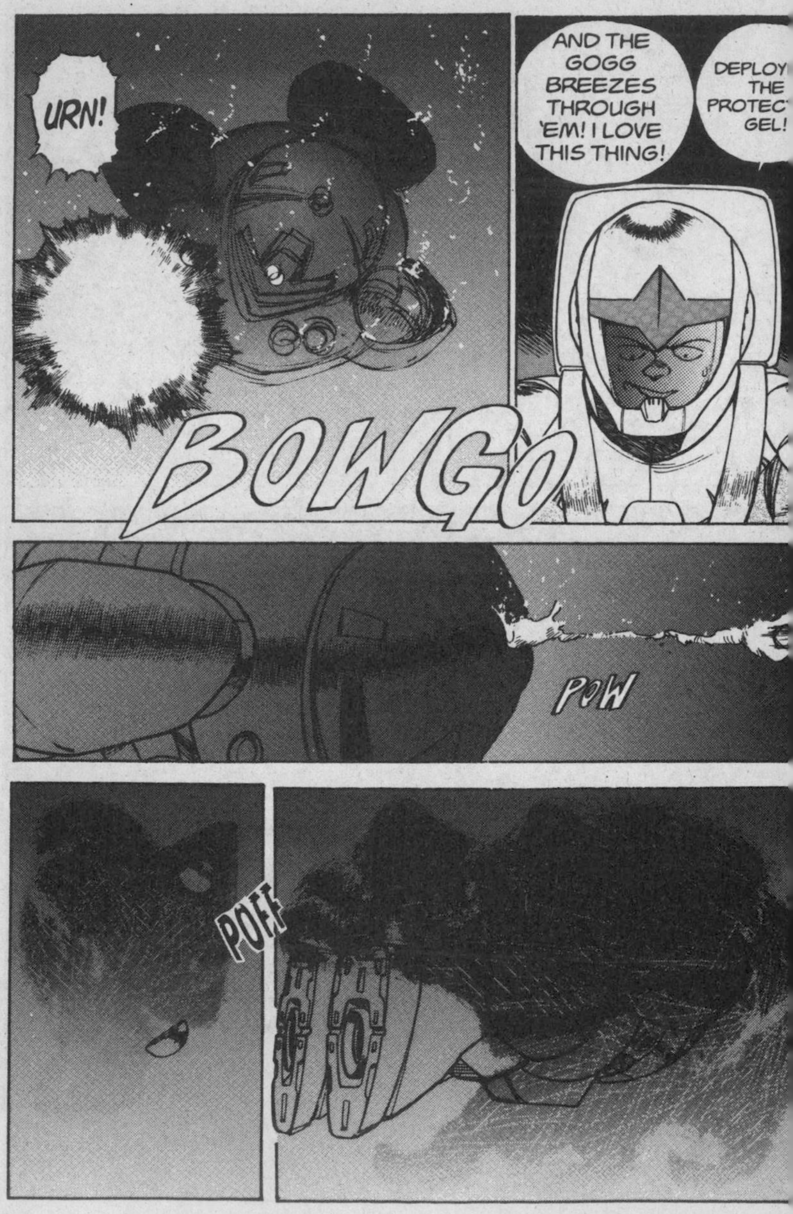
URN!
BOWGO
AND THE GOGG BREEZES THROUGH 'EM! I LOVE THIS THING!
DEPLOY THE PROTEC GEL!
POW
POFF

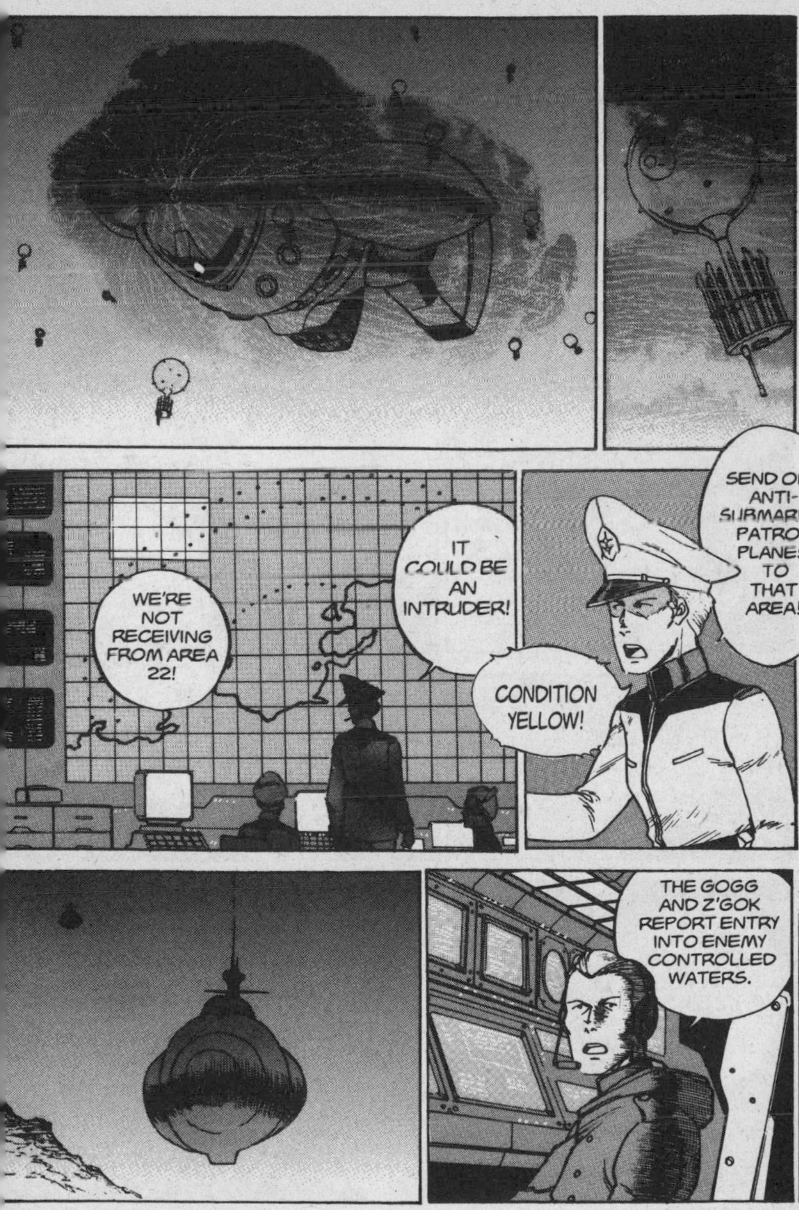
WE'RE NOT RECEIVING FROM AREA 22!
IT COULD BE AN INTRUDER!
SEND OUT ANTI-SUBMARINE PATROL PLANES TO THAT AREA!
CONDITION YELLOW!
THE GOGG AND Z'GOK REPORT ENTRY INTO ENEMY CONTROLLED WATERS.

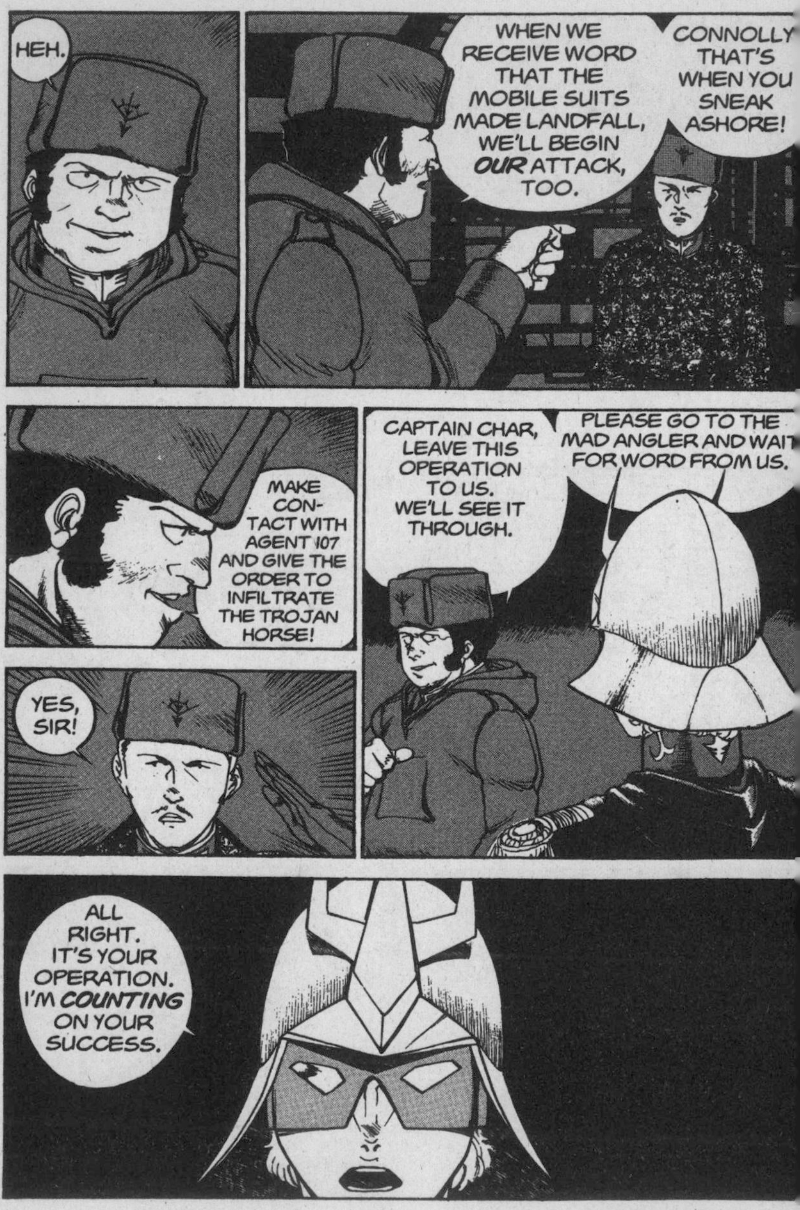
HEH.
WHEN WE RECEIVE WORD THAT THE MOBILE SUITS MADE LANDFALL, WE'LL BEGIN *OUR* ATTACK, TOO.
CONNOLLY THAT'S WHEN YOU SNEAK ASHORE!
MAKE CON-TACT WITH AGENT 107 AND GIVE THE ORDER TO INFILTRATE THE TROJAN HORSE!
YES, SIR!
CAPTAIN CHAR, LEAVE THIS OPERATION TO US. WE'LL SEE IT THROUGH.
PLEASE GO TO THE MAD ANGLER AND WAIT FOR WORD FROM US.
ALL RIGHT. IT'S YOUR OPERATION. I'M *COUNTING* ON YOUR SUCCESS.

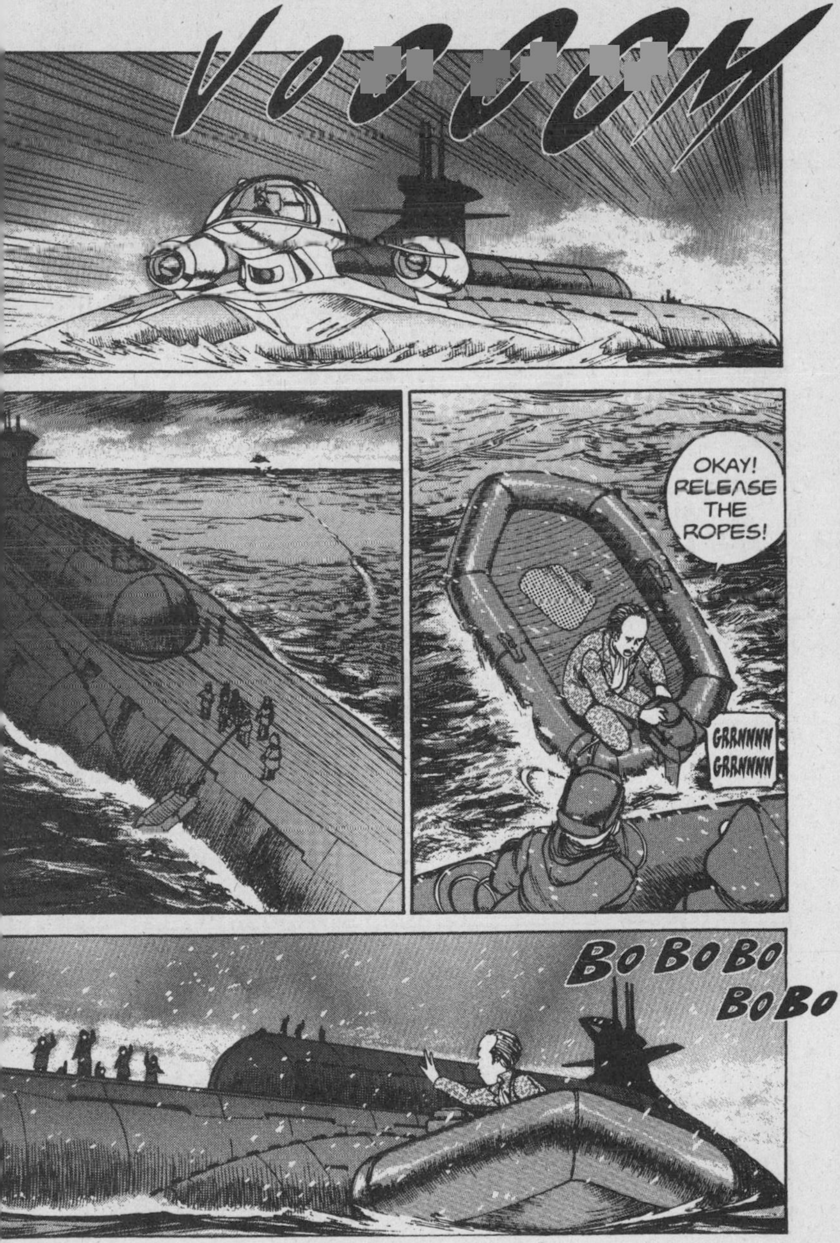
VOOOOM
OKAY! RELEASE THE ROPES!
GRRNNNN GRRNNNN
BoBoBo BoBo

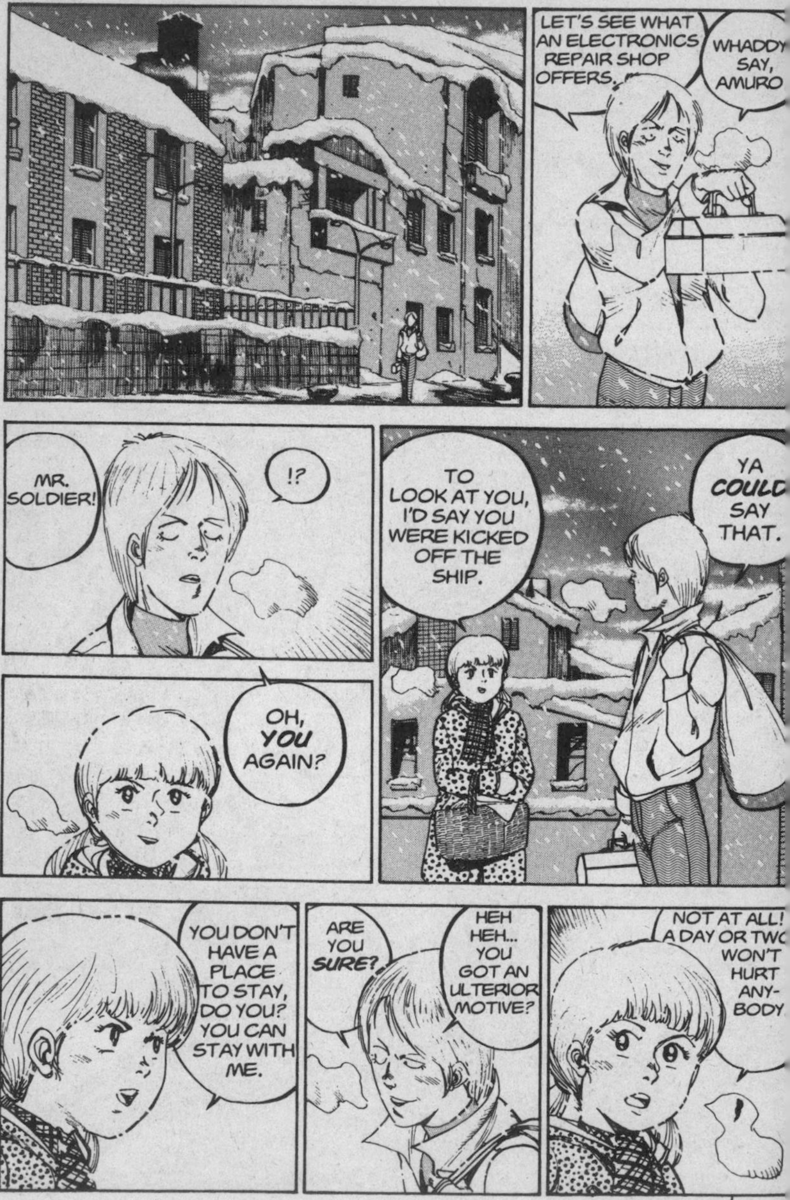
LET'S SEE WHAT AN ELECTRONICS REPAIR SHOP OFFERS...
WHADDY SAY, AMURO
MR. SOLDIER!
!?
OH, YOU AGAIN?
TO LOOK AT YOU, I'D SAY YOU WERE KICKED OFF THE SHIP.
YA COULD SAY THAT.
YOU DON'T HAVE A PLACE TO STAY, DO YOU? YOU CAN STAY WITH ME.
ARE YOU SURE?
HEH HEH... YOU GOT AN ULTERIOR MOTIVE?
NOT AT ALL! A DAY OR TWO WON'T HURT ANYBODY

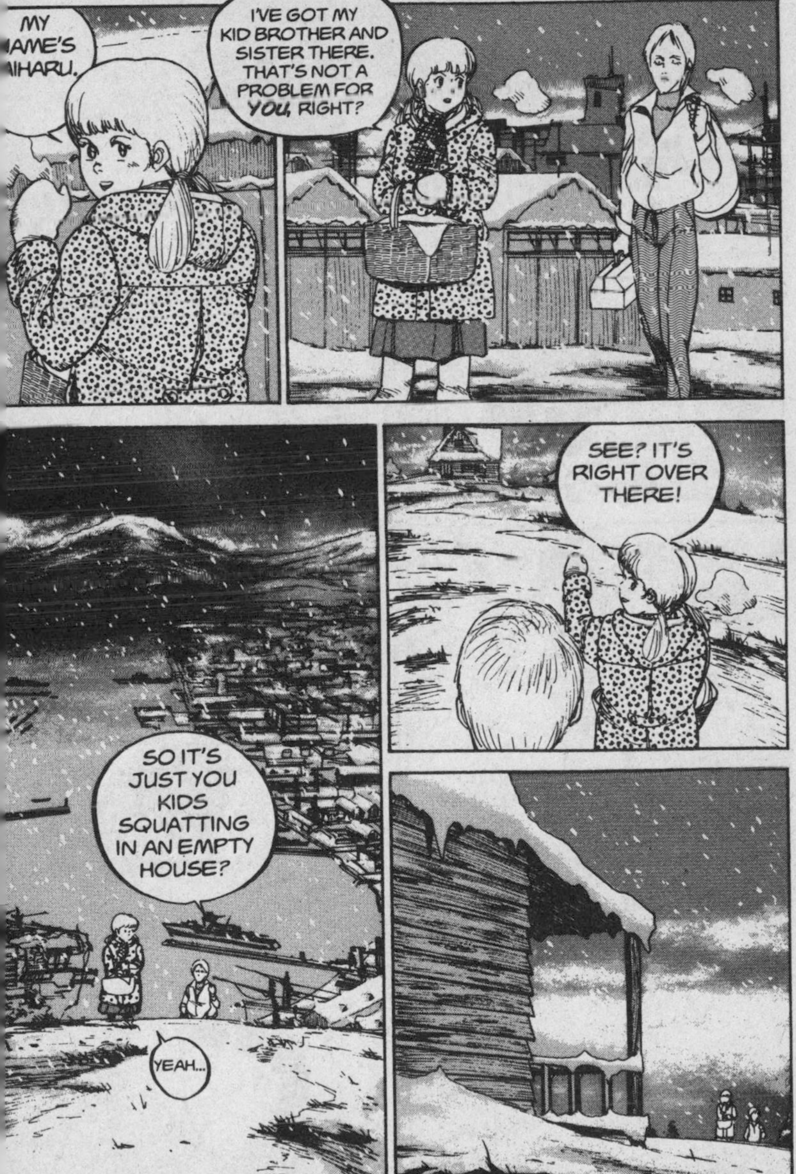
MY
NAME'S
MIHARU.
I'VE GOT MY KID BROTHER AND SISTER THERE. THAT'S NOT A PROBLEM FOR YOU, RIGHT?
SEE? IT'S RIGHT OVER THERE!
SO IT'S JUST YOU KIDS SQUATTING IN AN EMPTY HOUSE?
YEAH...

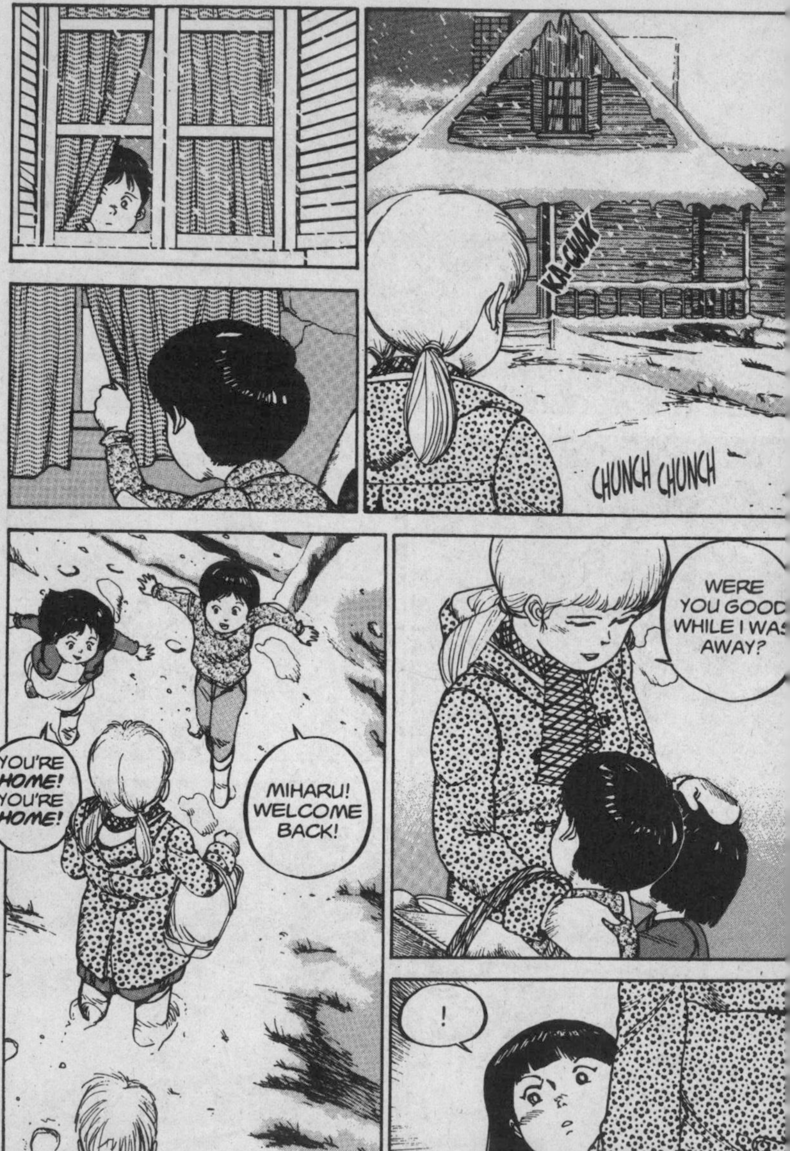
KA-CHAK
CHUNCH CHUNCH
YOU'RE HOME! YOU'RE HOME!
MIHARU! WELCOME BACK!
WERE YOU GOOD WHILE I WAS AWAY?
!

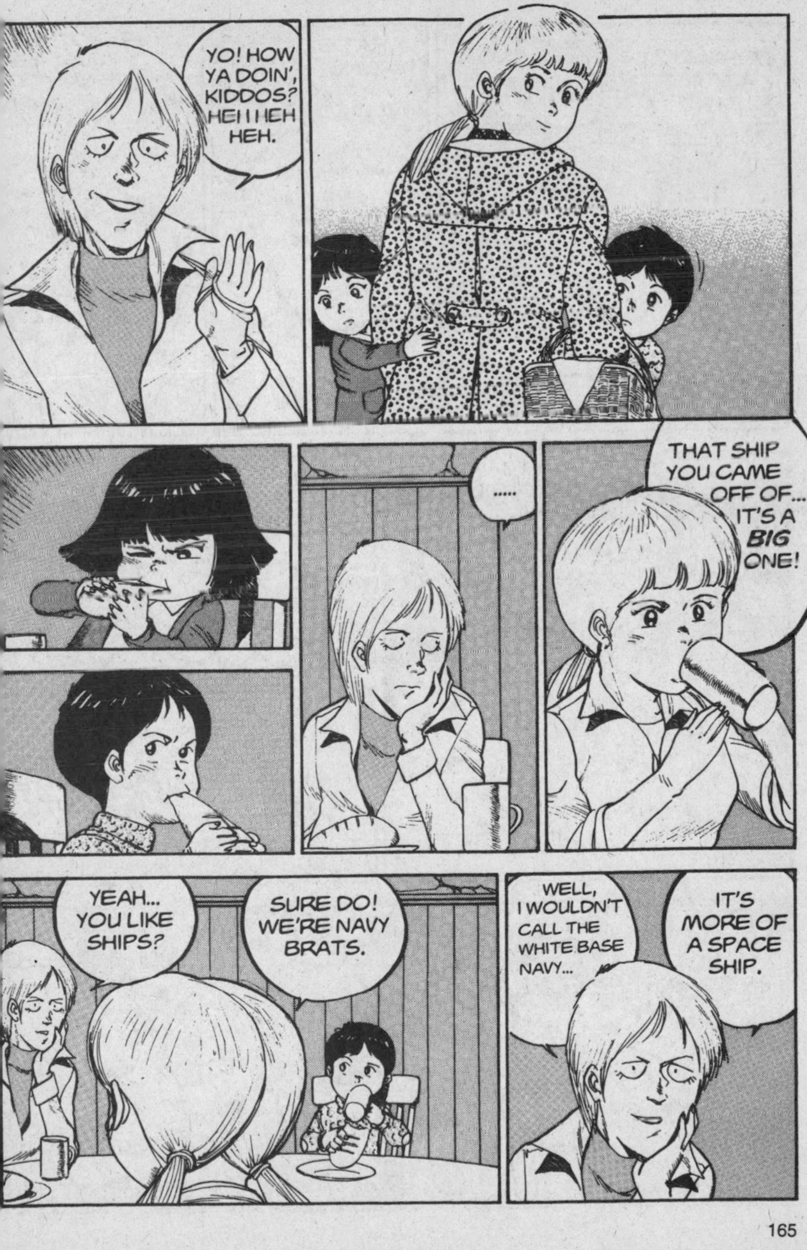
YO! HOW YA DOIN', KIDDOS? HEH HEH HEH.
.....
THAT SHIP YOU CAME OFF OF... IT'S A **BIG** ONE!
YEAH... YOU LIKE SHIPS?
SURE DO! WE'RE NAVY BRATS.
WELL, I WOULDN'T CALL THE WHITE BASE NAVY...
IT'S MORE OF A SPACE SHIP.

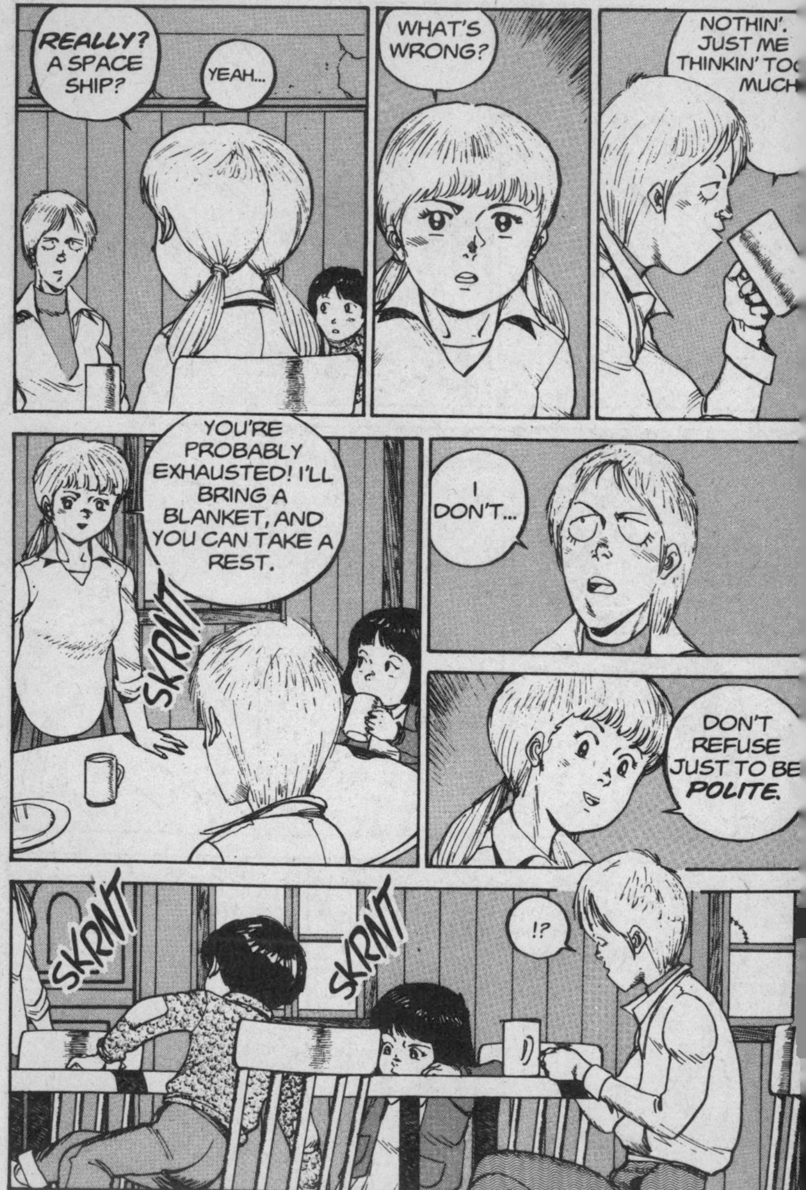
REALLY? A SPACE SHIP?
YEAH...
WHAT'S WRONG?
NOTHIN'. JUST ME THINKIN' TOO MUCH
YOU'RE PROBABLY EXHAUSTED! I'LL BRING A BLANKET, AND YOU CAN TAKE A REST.
SKRNT
I DON'T...
DON'T REFUSE JUST TO BE POLITE.
SKRNT
SKRNT
!?

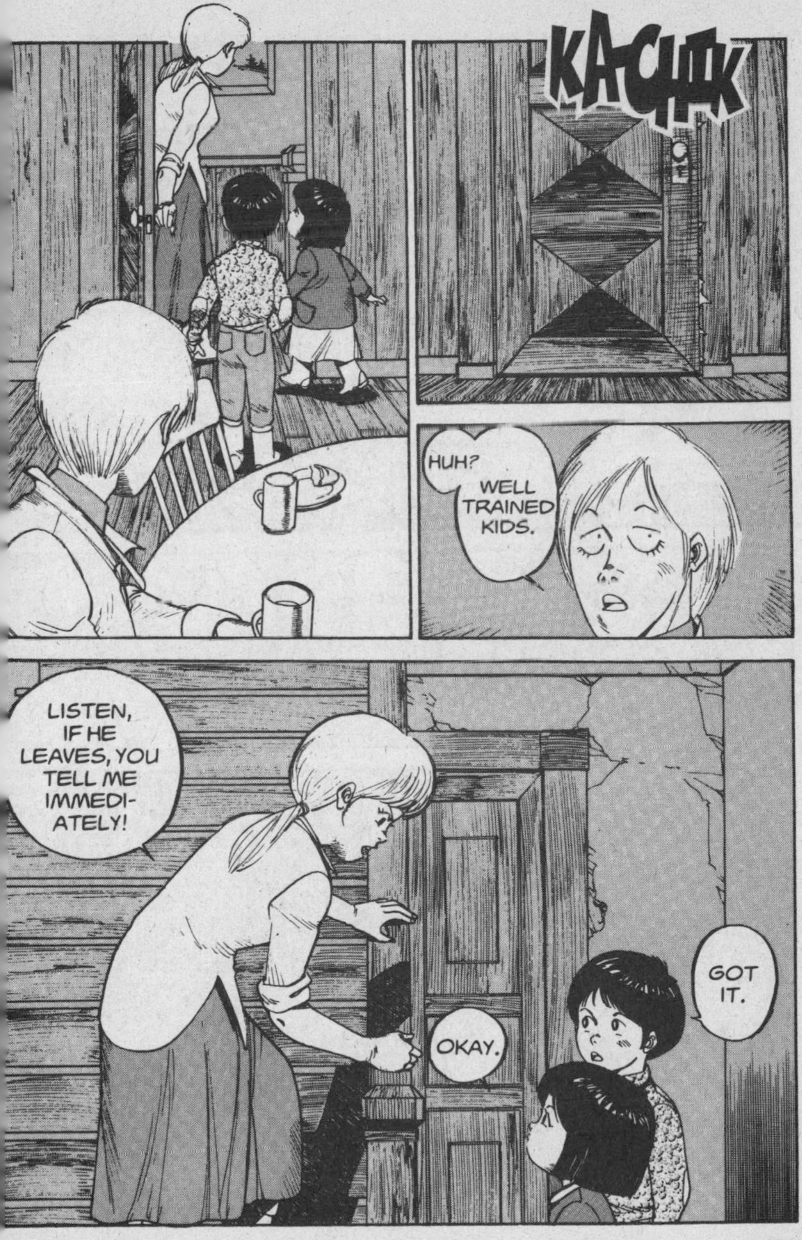

KA-CHIK
HUH?
WELL TRAINED KIDS.
LISTEN, IF HE LEAVES, YOU TELL ME IMMEDI-ATELY!
OKAY.
GOT IT.

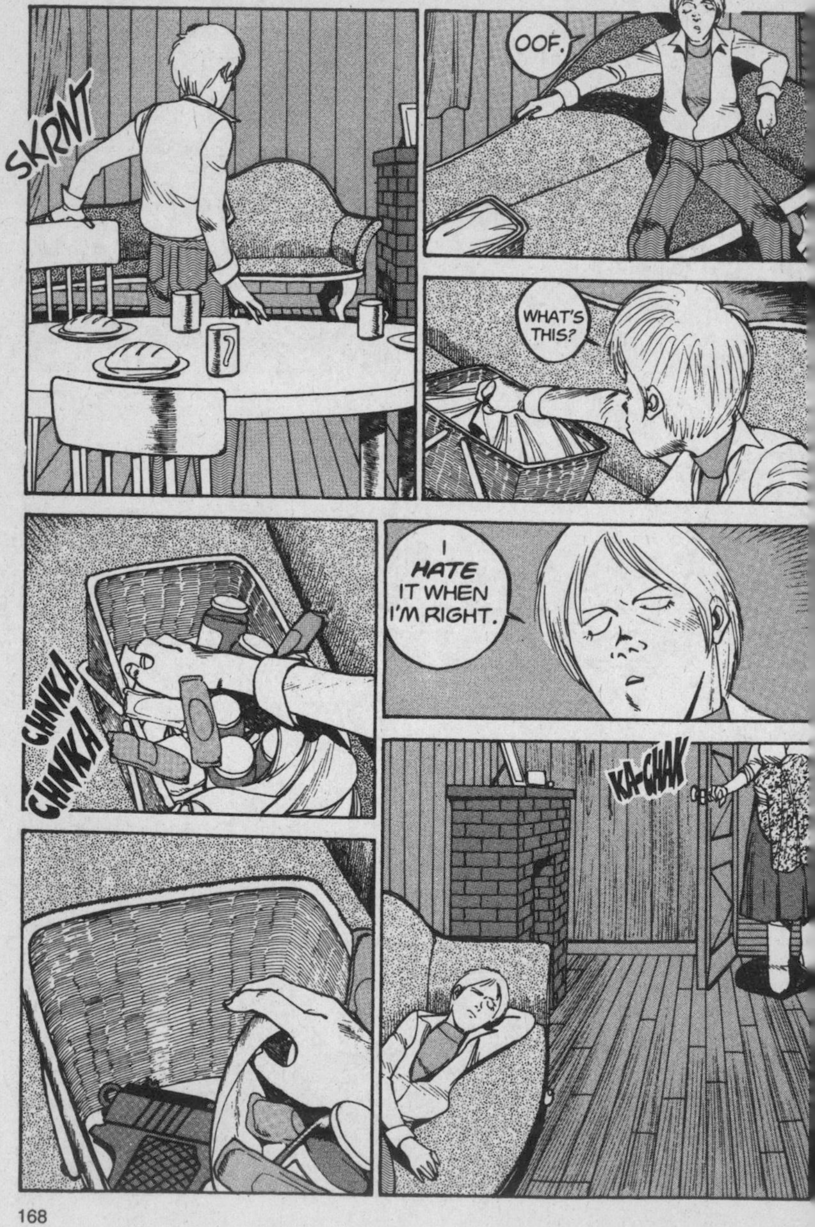
SKRNT
OOF.
WHAT'S THIS?
CHNKA CHNKA
I *HATE* IT WHEN I'M RIGHT.
KA-CHAK

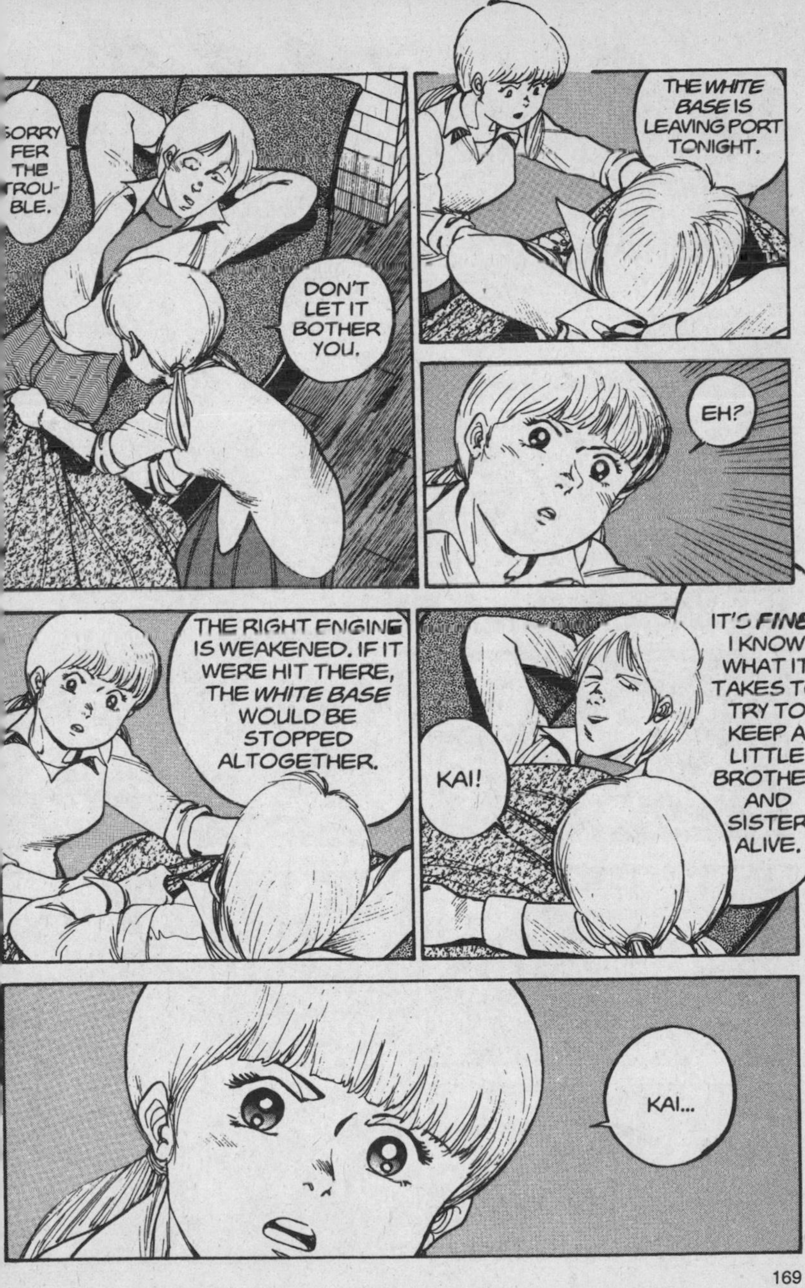
SORRY FER THE TROUBLE.
DON'T LET IT BOTHER YOU.
THE *WHITE BASE* IS LEAVING PORT TONIGHT.
EH?
THE RIGHT ENGINE IS WEAKENED. IF IT WERE HIT THERE, THE *WHITE BASE* WOULD BE STOPPED ALTOGETHER.
KAI!
IT'S *FINE!* I KNOW WHAT IT TAKES TO TRY TO KEEP A LITTLE BROTHER AND SISTER ALIVE.
KAI...

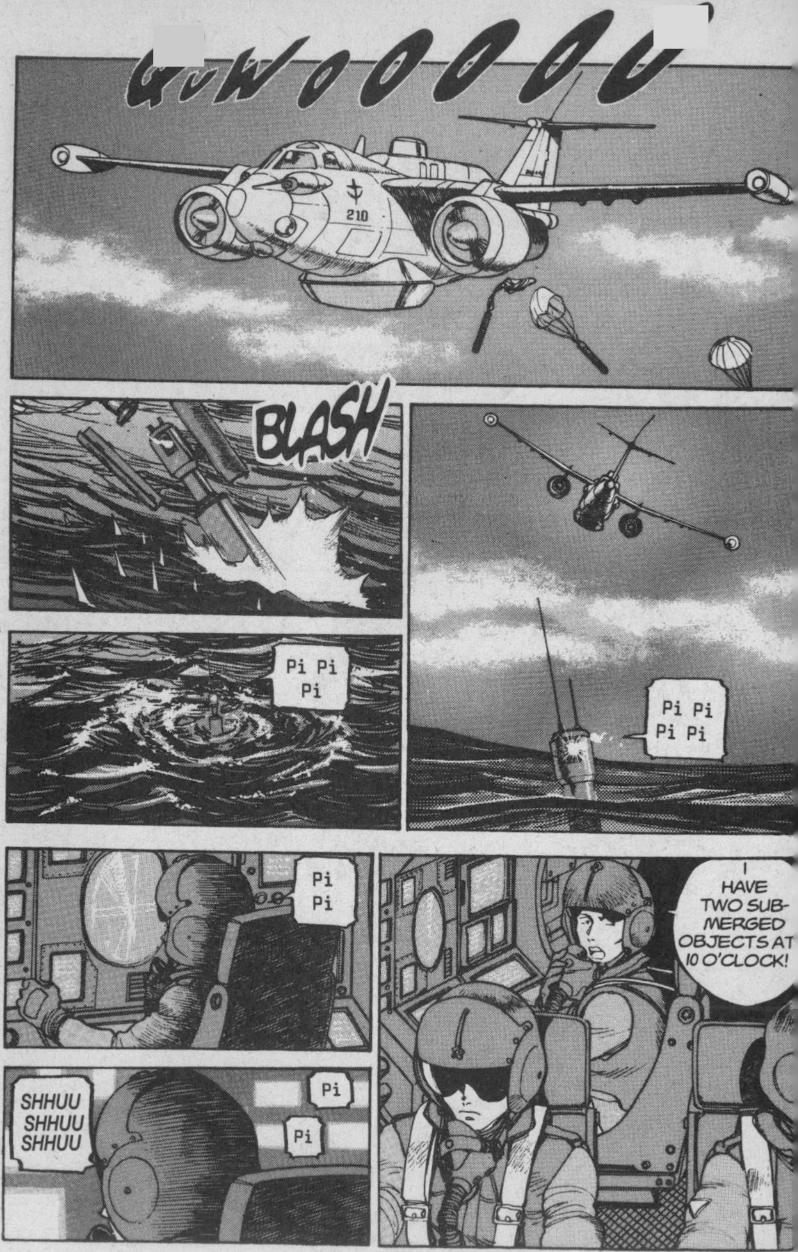
BLASH
Pi Pi Pi
Pi Pi Pi Pi
Pi Pi
SHHUU SHHUU SHHUU
Pi
Pi
I HAVE TWO SUB-MERGED OBJECTS AT 10 O'CLOCK!

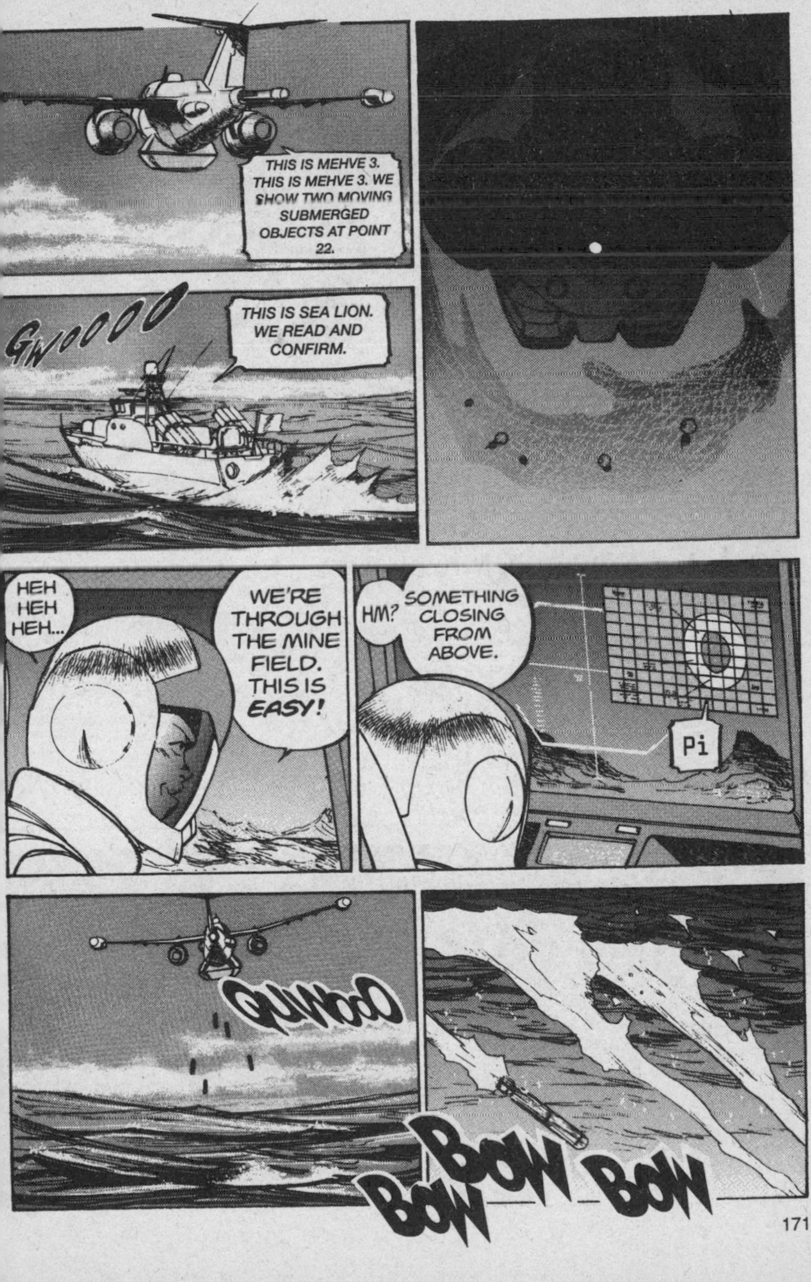
THIS IS MEHVE 3. THIS IS MEHVE 3. WE SHOW TWO MOVING SUBMERGED OBJECTS AT POINT 22.
GWOOOOO
THIS IS SEA LION. WE READ AND CONFIRM.
HEH HEH HEH...
WE'RE THROUGH THE MINE FIELD. THIS IS *EASY*!
HM?
SOMETHING CLOSING FROM ABOVE.
Pi
GUWOOO
BOW BOW BOW BOW

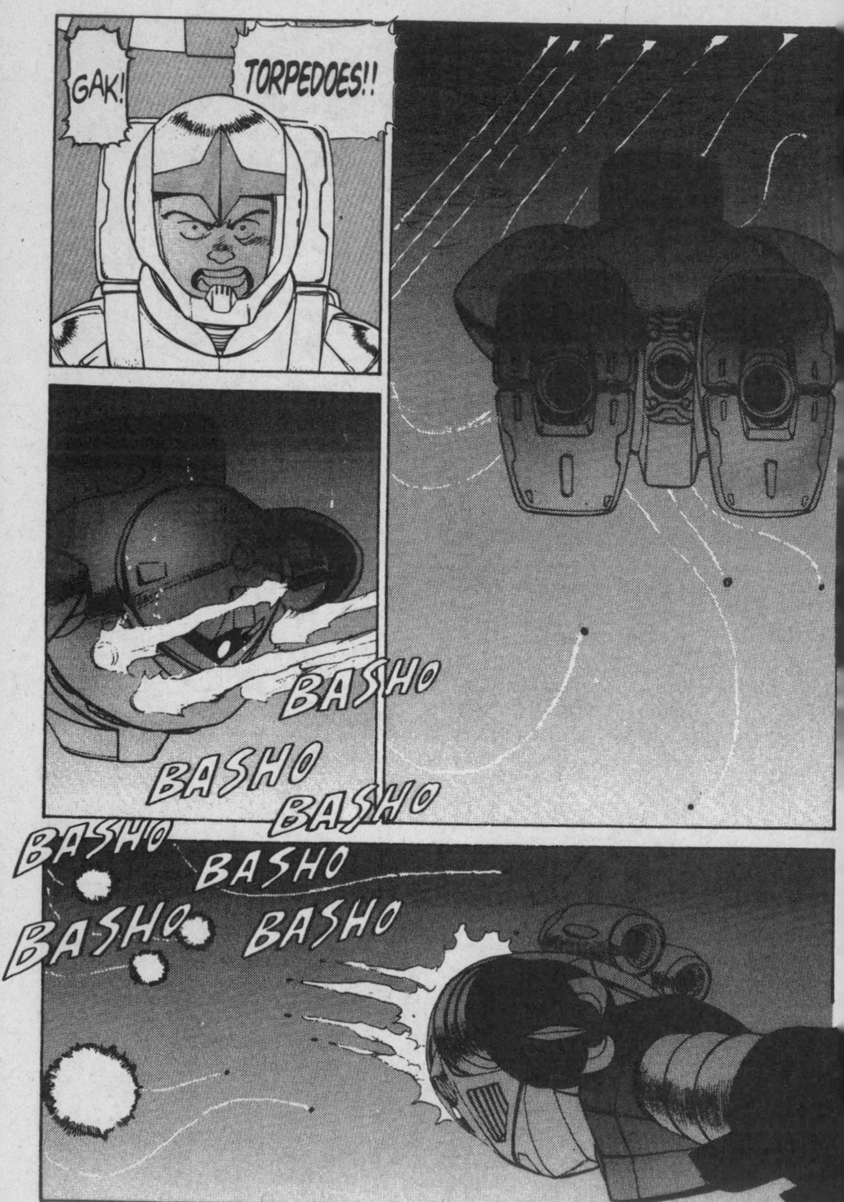
GAK!
TORPEDOES!!
BASHO
BASHO
BASHO
BASHO
BASHO
BASHO
BASHO

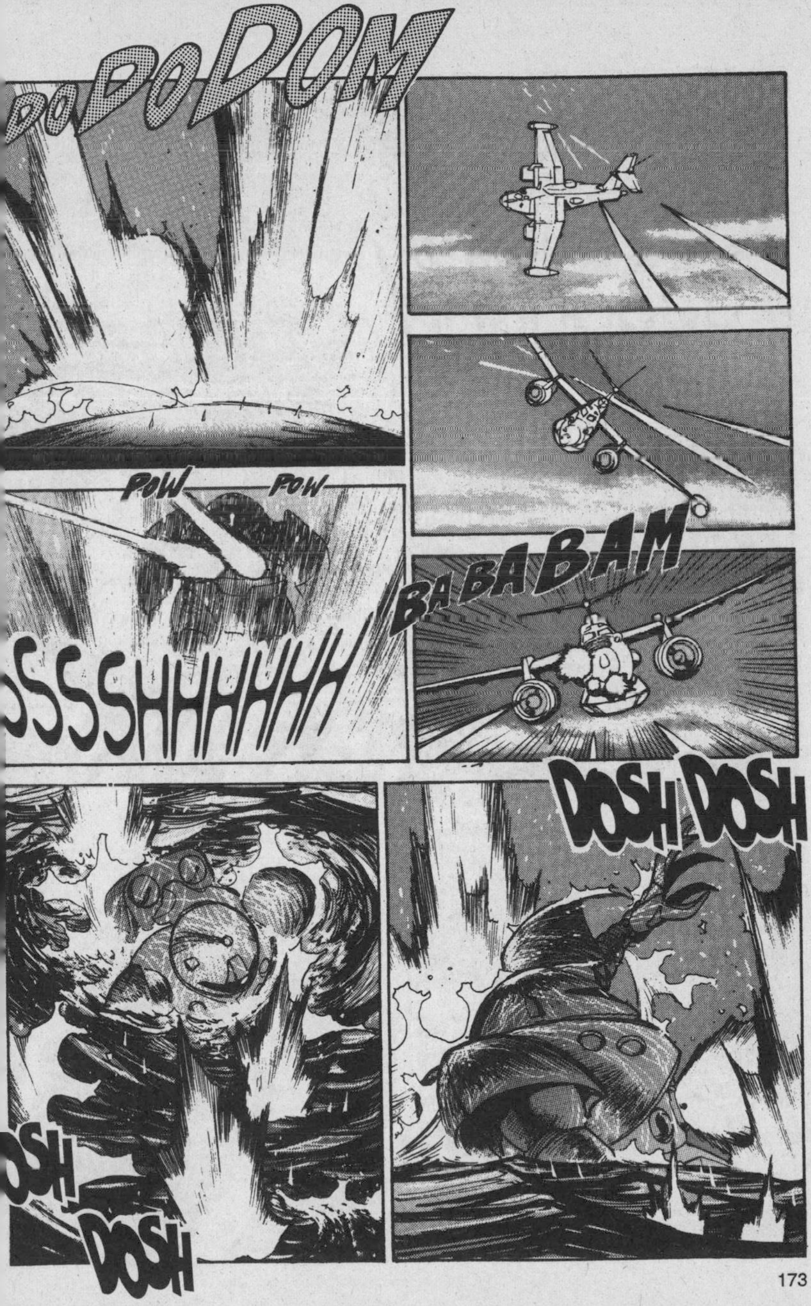
DODODOM
POW POW
BABABAM
SSSSHHHHHH
DOSH DOSH
DOSH DOSH

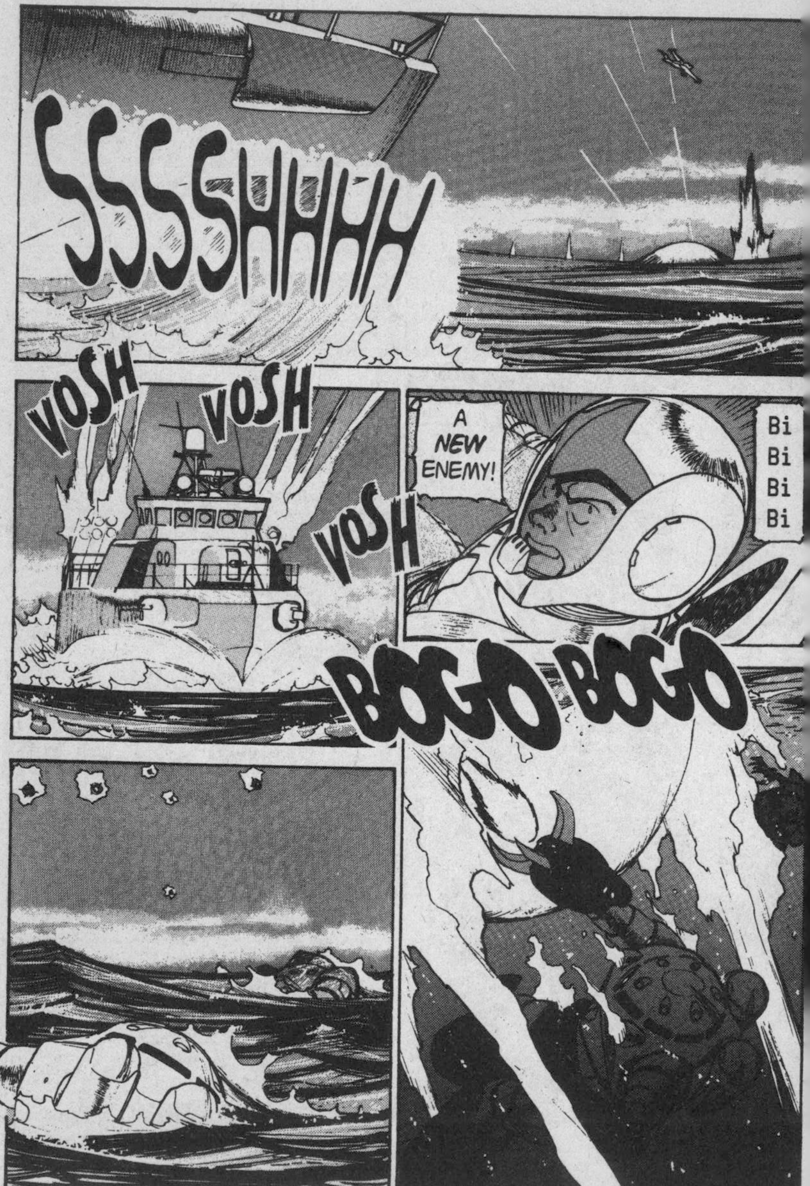
SSSSHHHH
VOSH
VOSH
VOSH
A NEW ENEMY!
Bi Bi Bi Bi
BOGO BOGO

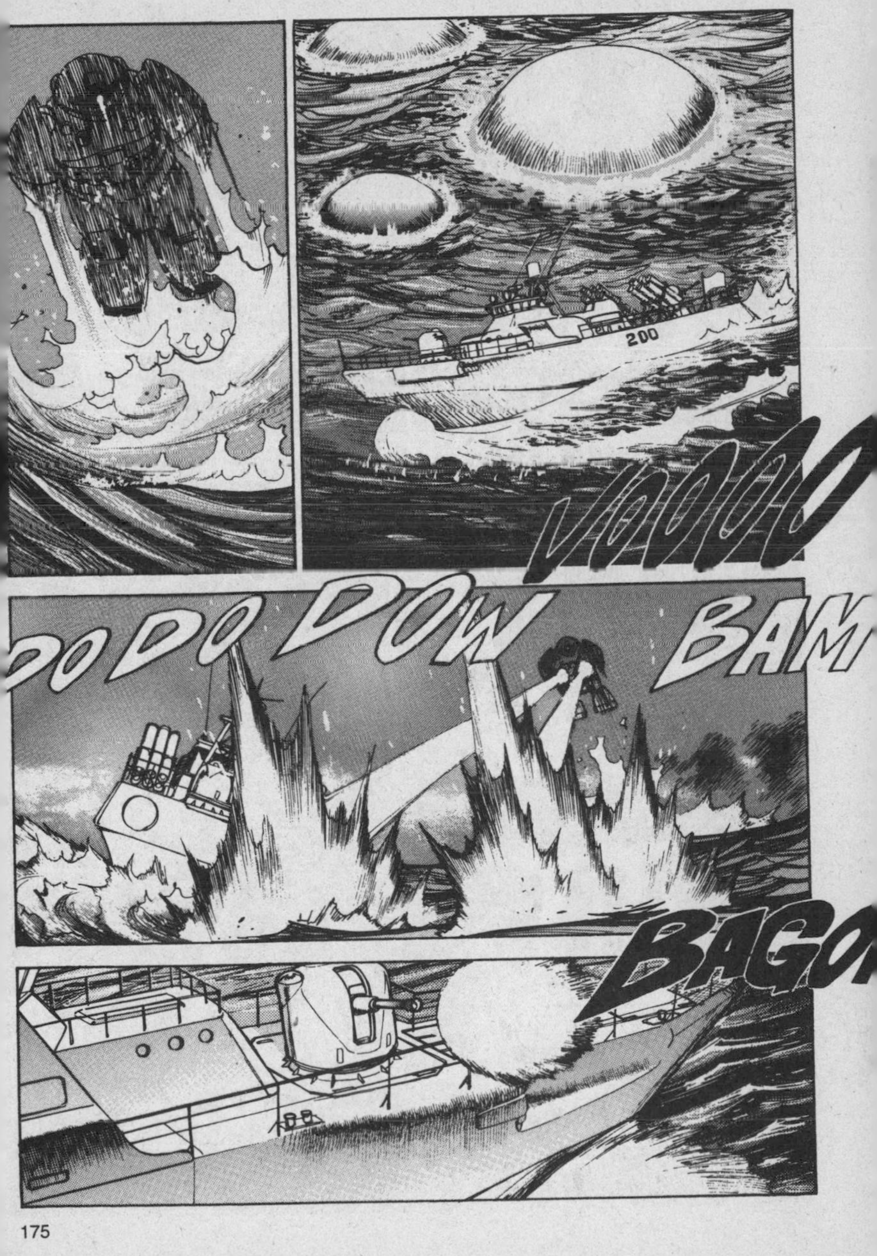

200
VOOOOO
DODODO DOW
BAM
BAGO

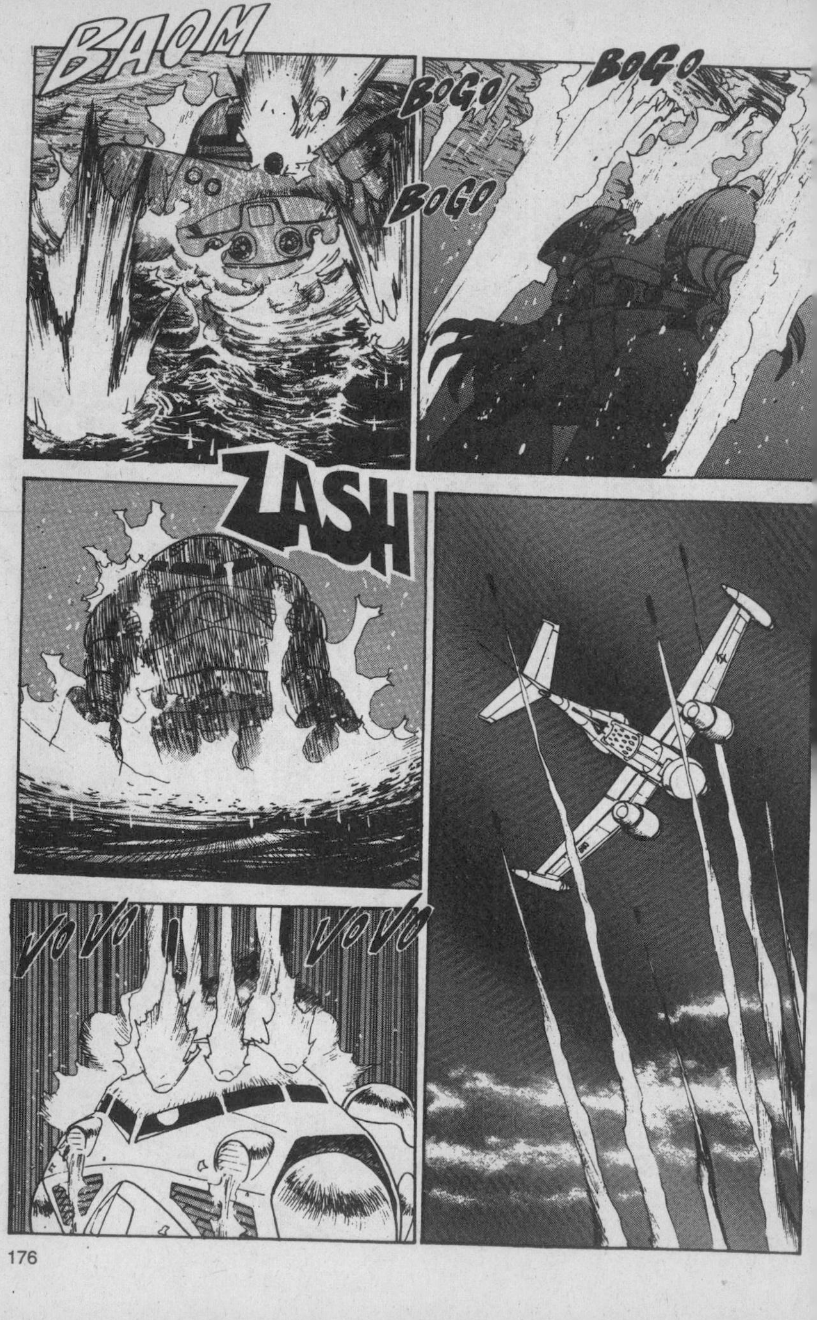
BAOM
BOGO
BOGO
BOGO
ZASH
VOVO
VOVO

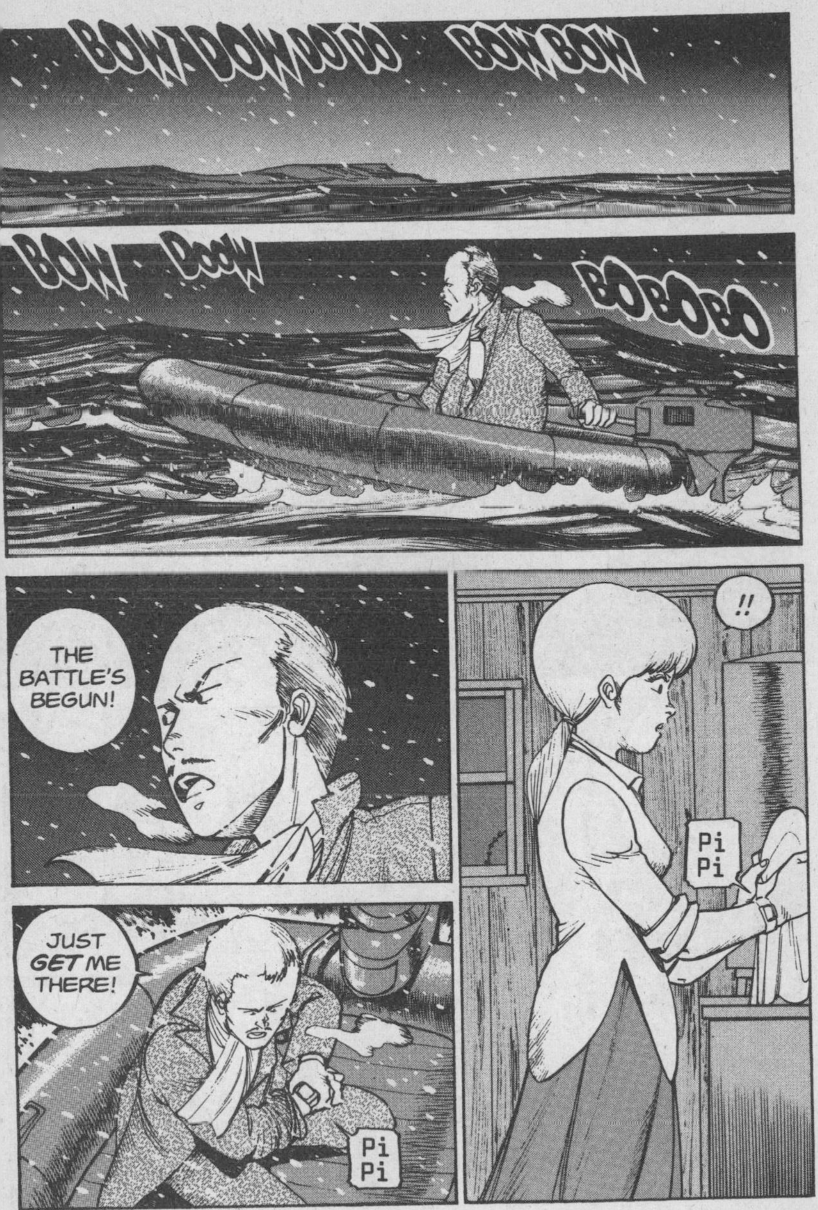
BOW DOW DO DO
BOW BOW
BOW
DOOW
BOBOBO
THE BATTLE'S BEGUN!
!!
JUST GET ME THERE!
Pi Pi
Pi Pi

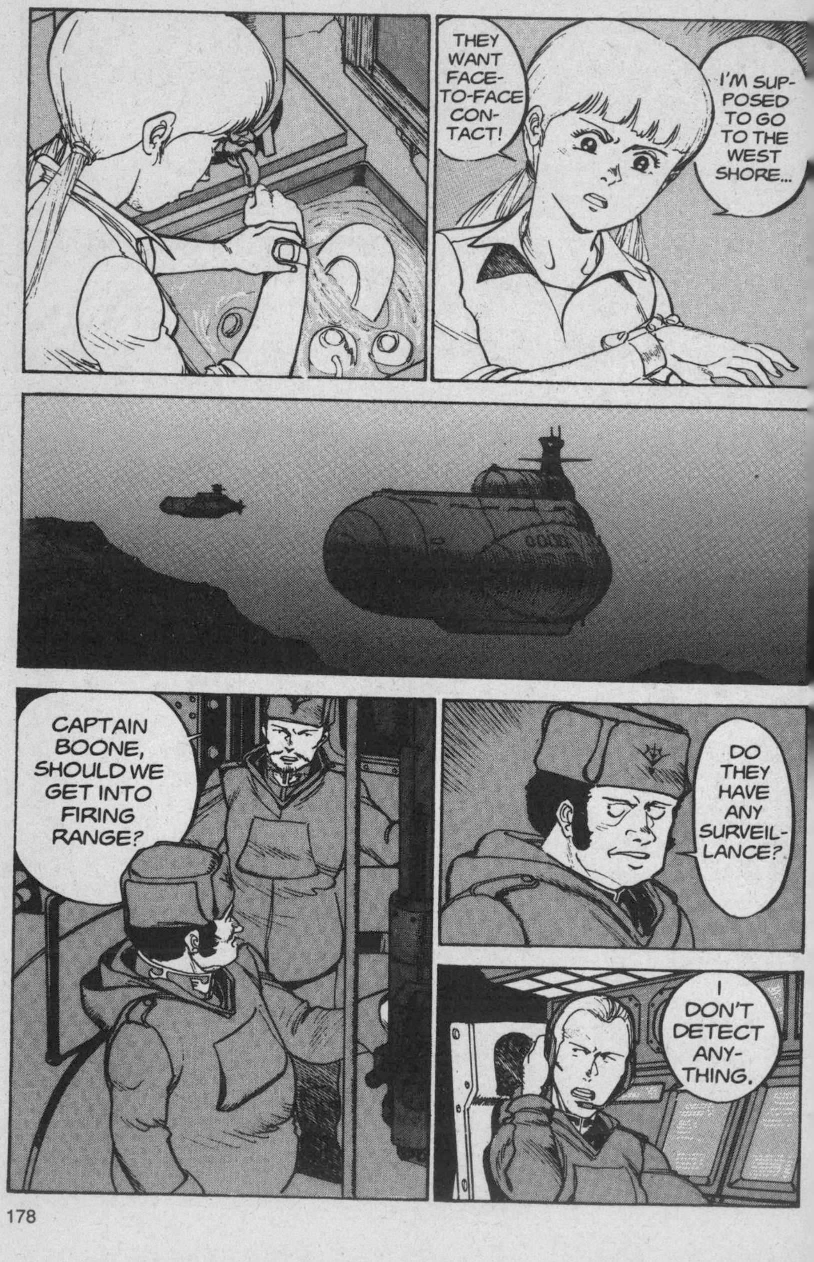

THEY WANT FACE-TO-FACE CONTACT!
I'M SUPPOSED TO GO TO THE WEST SHORE...
CAPTAIN BOONE, SHOULD WE GET INTO FIRING RANGE?
DO THEY HAVE ANY SURVEILLANCE?
I DON'T DETECT ANYTHING.

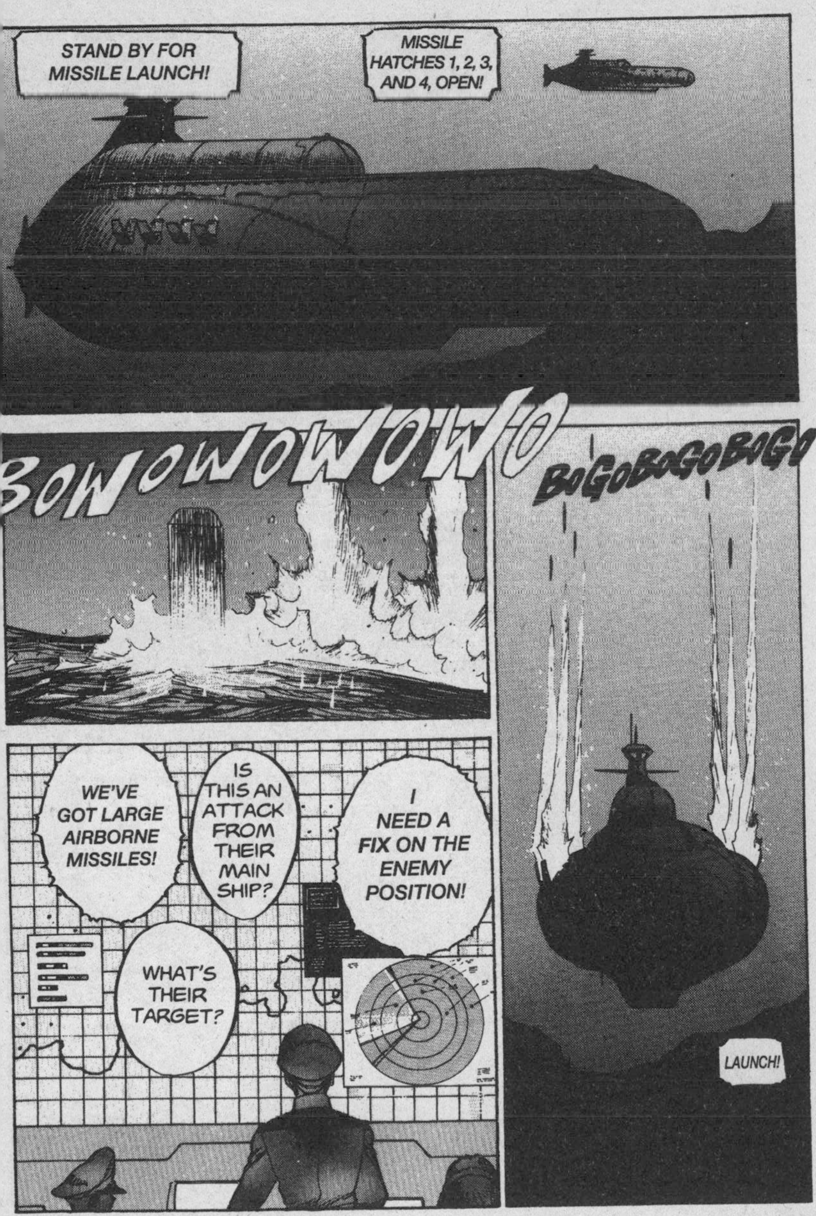
STAND BY FOR MISSILE LAUNCH!
MISSILE HATCHES 1, 2, 3, AND 4, OPEN!
BOWOWOWOWO
BOGOBOGOBOGO
WE'VE GOT LARGE AIRBORNE MISSILES!
IS THIS AN ATTACK FROM THEIR MAIN SHIP?
I NEED A FIX ON THE ENEMY POSITION!
WHAT'S THEIR TARGET?
LAUNCH!

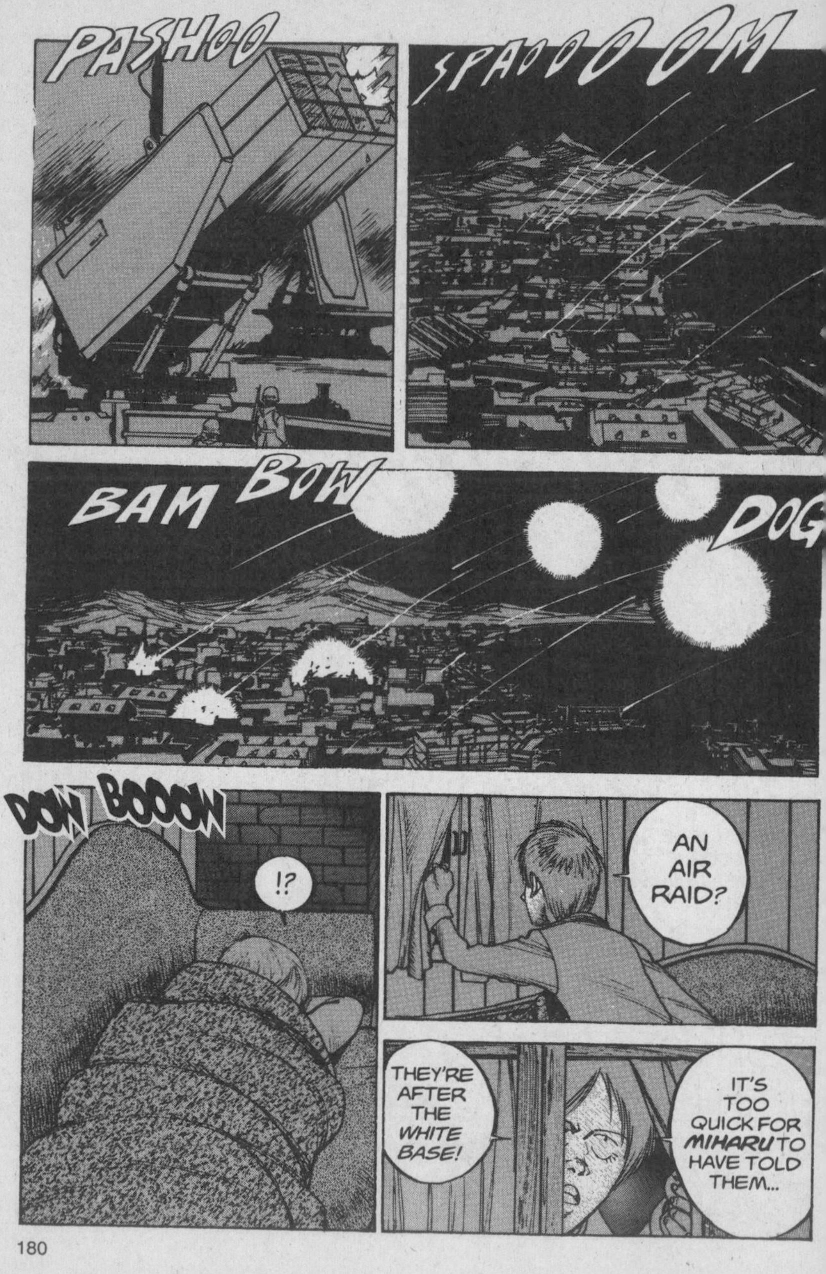
PASHOO
SPAOOOOOM
BAM
BOW
DOG
DOW
BOOOW
!?
AN AIR RAID?
THEY'RE AFTER THE WHITE BASE!
IT'S TOO QUICK FOR MIHARU TO HAVE TOLD THEM...

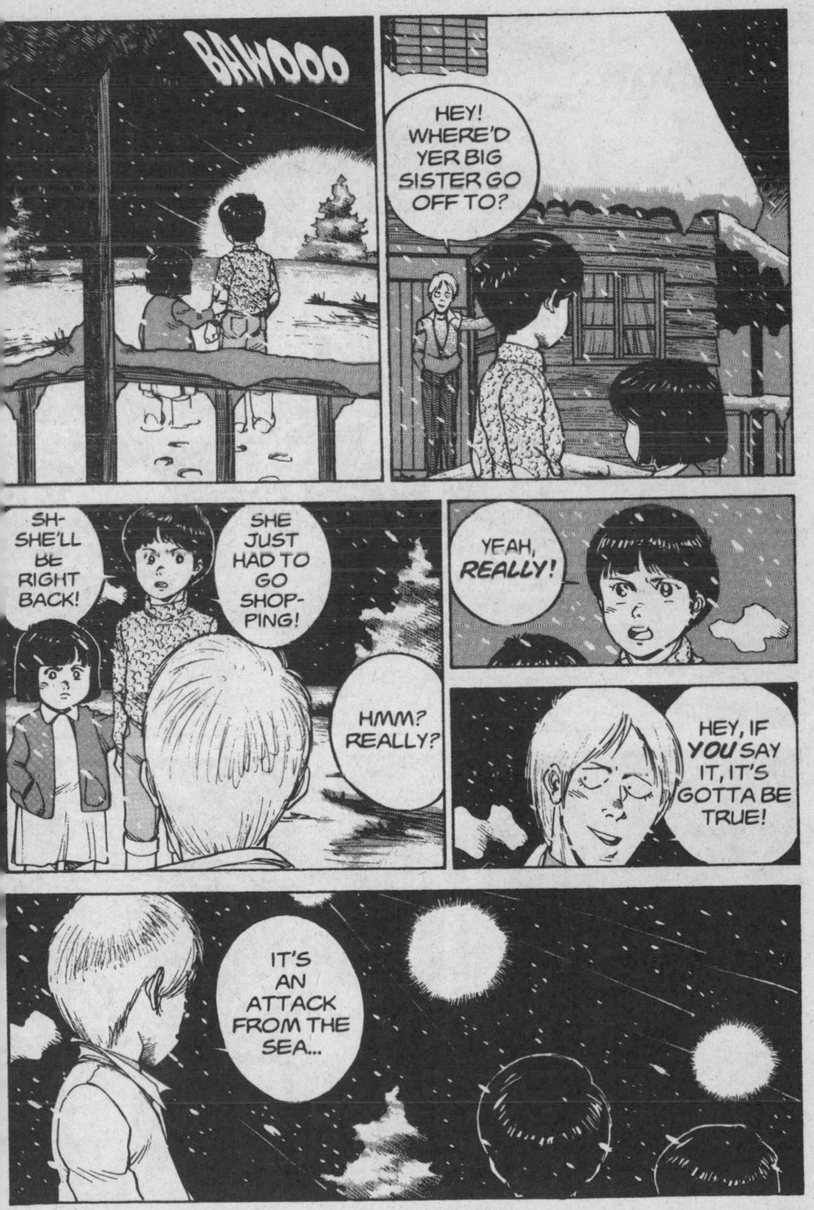
BAWOOO
HEY! WHERE'D YER BIG SISTER GO OFF TO?
SH-SHE'LL BE RIGHT BACK!
SHE JUST HAD TO GO SHOP-PING!
HMM? REALLY?
YEAH, *REALLY*!
HEY, IF *YOU* SAY IT, IT'S GOTTA BE TRUE!
IT'S AN ATTACK FROM THE SEA...

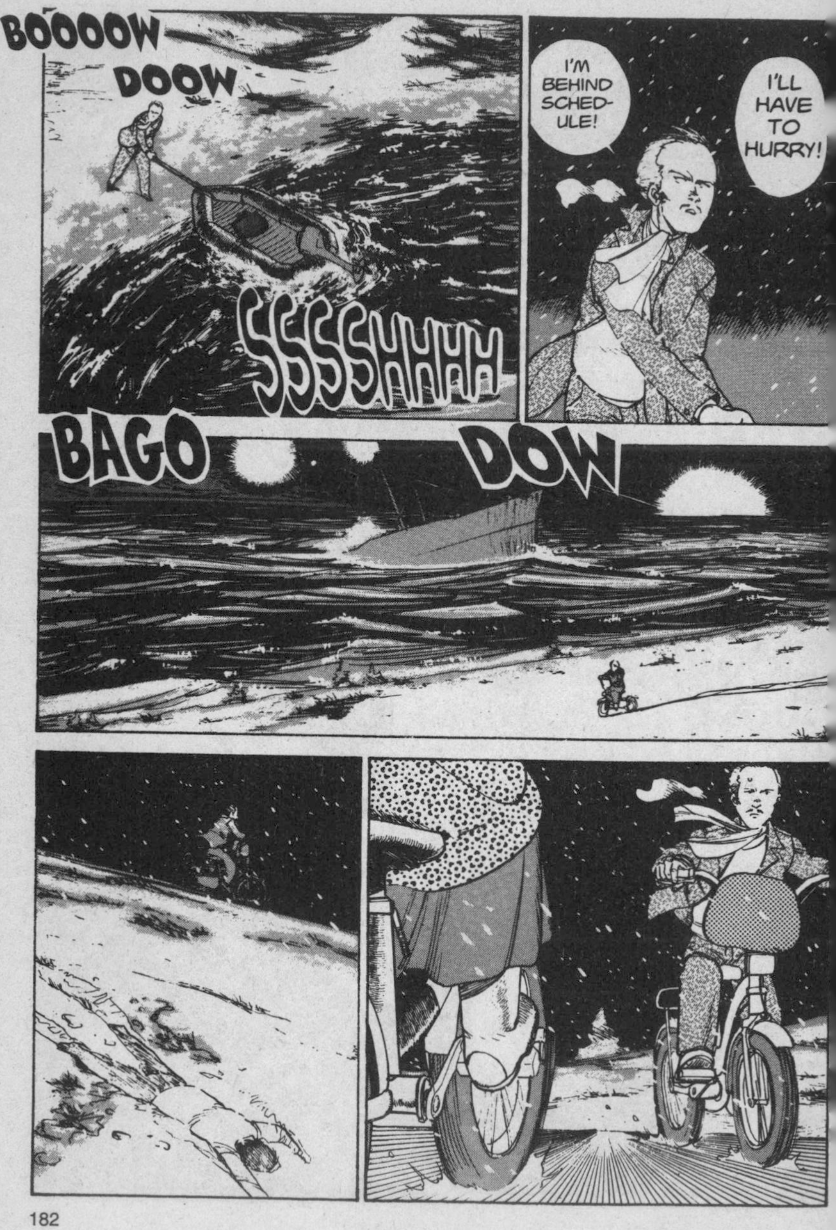
BOOOOW
DOOW
SSSSHHHH
I'M BEHIND SCHED-ULE!
I'LL HAVE TO HURRY!
BAGO
DOW

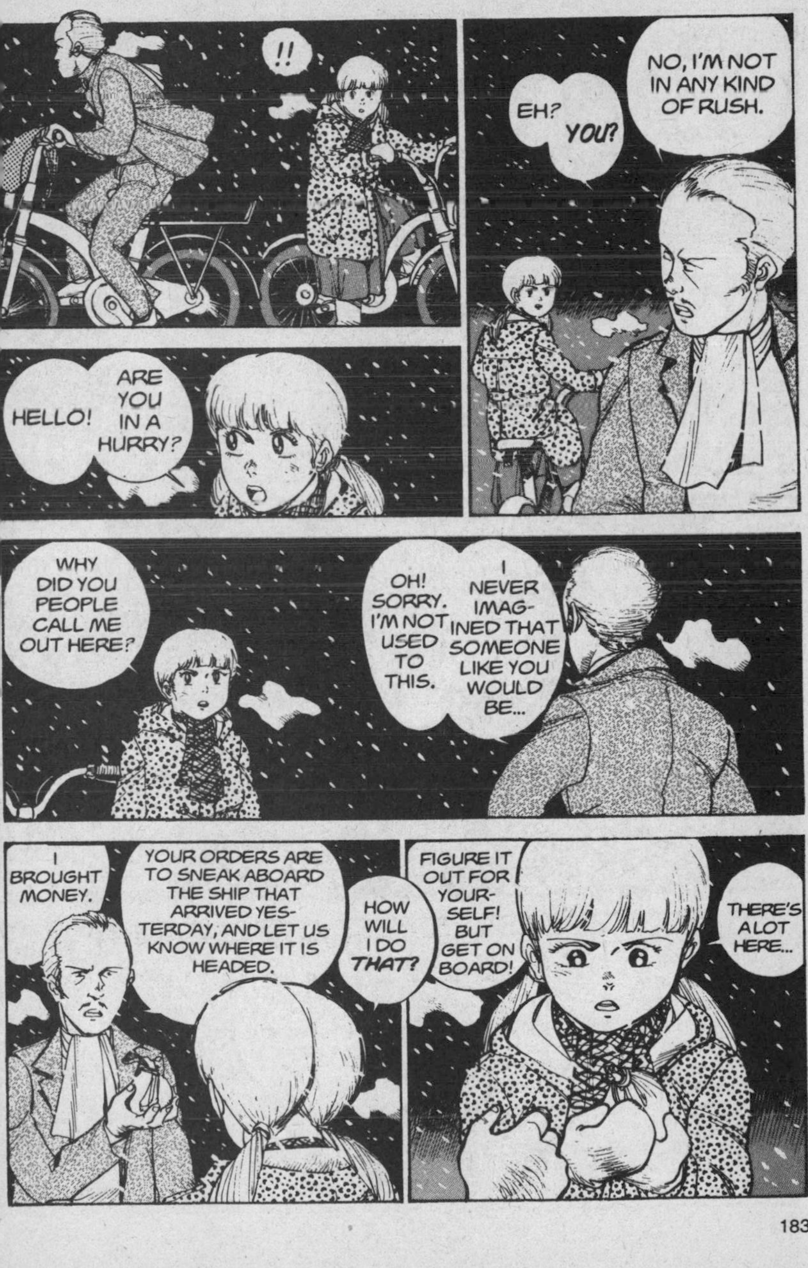
!!
HELLO!
ARE YOU IN A HURRY?
EH? *YOU?*
NO, I'M NOT IN ANY KIND OF RUSH.
WHY DID YOU PEOPLE CALL ME OUT HERE?
OH! SORRY. I'M NOT USED TO THIS.
I NEVER IMAGINED THAT SOMEONE LIKE YOU WOULD BE...
I BROUGHT MONEY.
YOUR ORDERS ARE TO SNEAK ABOARD THE SHIP THAT ARRIVED YESTERDAY, AND LET US KNOW WHERE IT IS HEADED.
HOW WILL I DO *THAT?*
FIGURE IT OUT FOR YOURSELF! BUT GET ON BOARD!
THERE'S A LOT HERE...

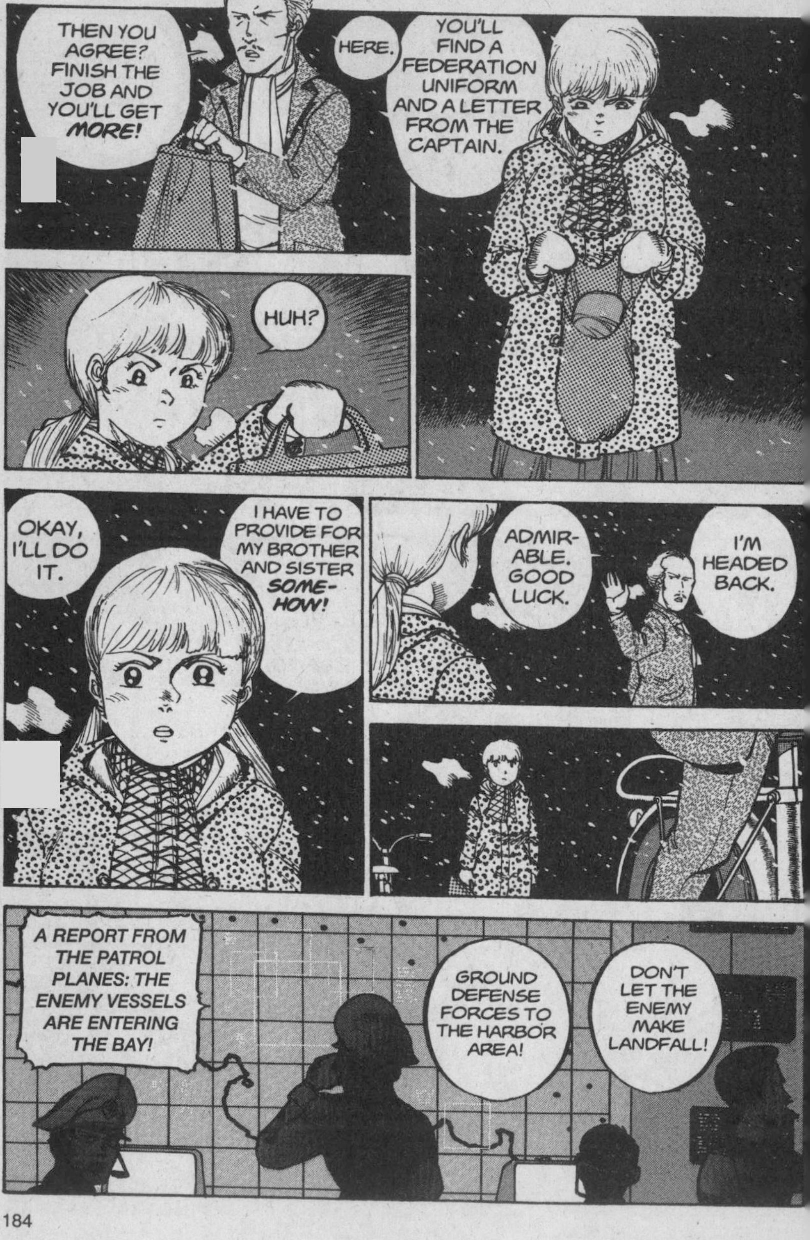
THEN YOU AGREE? FINISH THE JOB AND YOU'LL GET MORE!
HERE.
YOU'LL FIND A FEDERATION UNIFORM AND A LETTER FROM THE CAPTAIN.
HUH?
OKAY, I'LL DO IT.
I HAVE TO PROVIDE FOR MY BROTHER AND SISTER SOME-HOW!
ADMIR-ABLE. GOOD LUCK.
I'M HEADED BACK.
A REPORT FROM THE PATROL PLANES: THE ENEMY VESSELS ARE ENTERING THE BAY!
GROUND DEFENSE FORCES TO THE HARBOR AREA!
DON'T LET THE ENEMY MAKE LANDFALL!

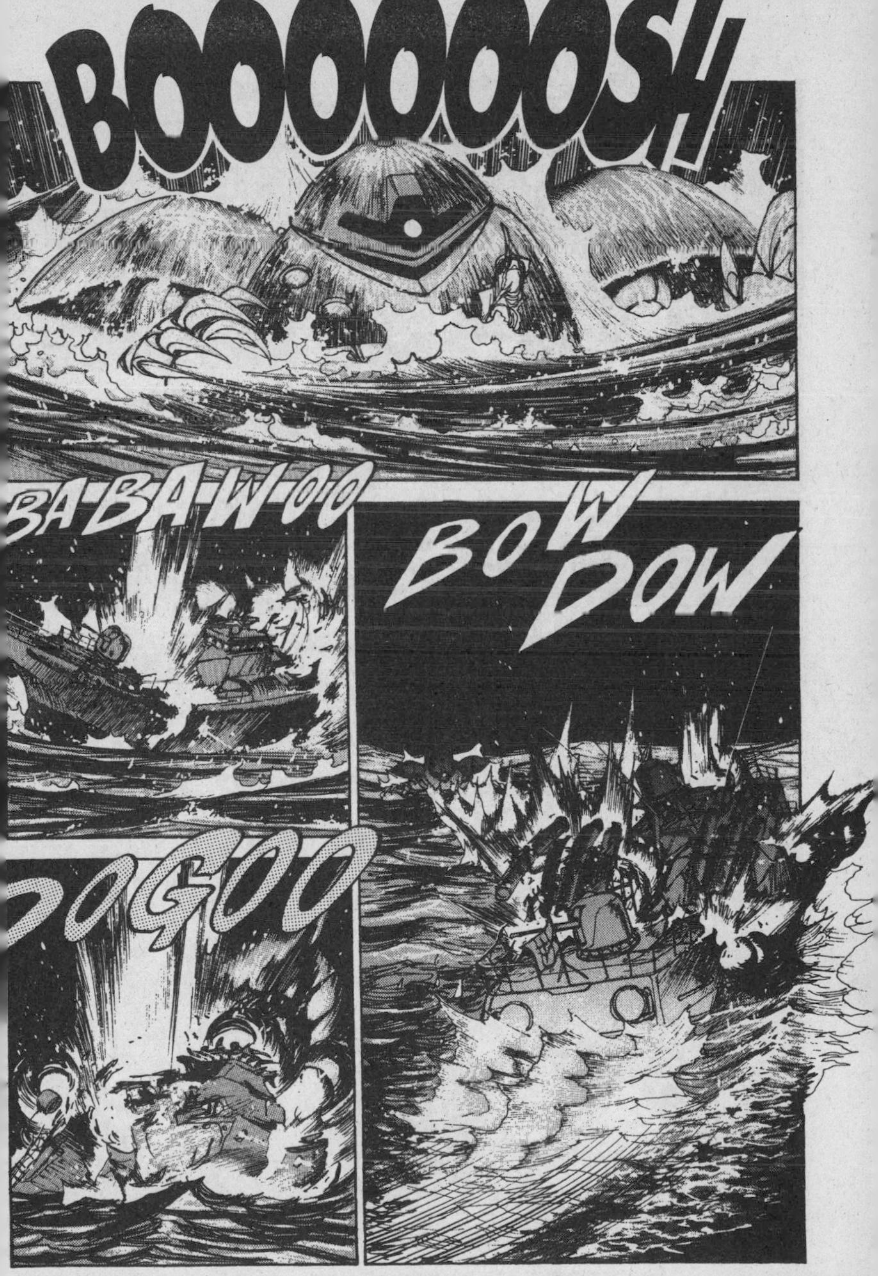
BOOOOOOSH
BABAWOO
BOW DOW
DOGOO

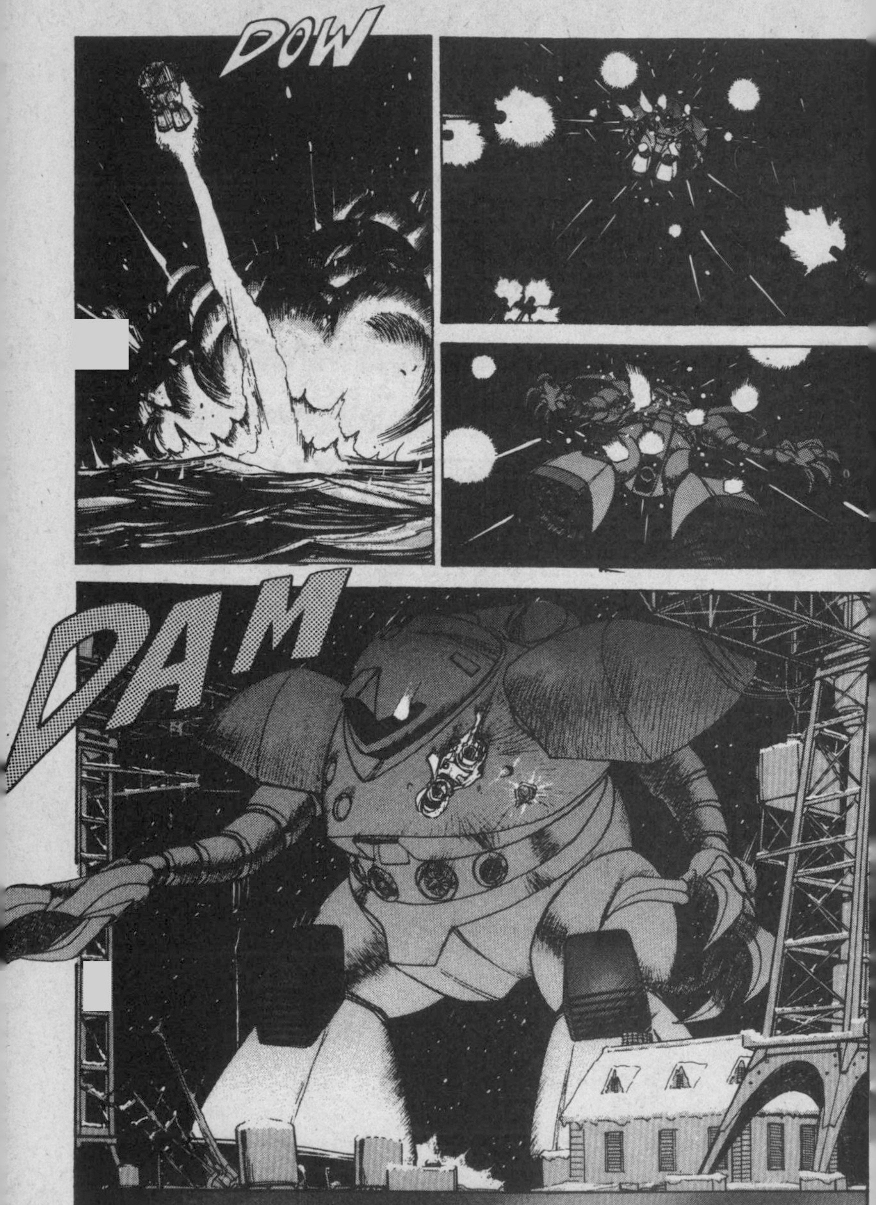
DOW
DAM

TO BE CONTINUED IN VOLUME 6!

THE PRINCIPALITY OF ZEON

he Principality of Zeon is the rebel nation of space colonists which now challenges the Earth ederation. The space colonies of Side 3 declared their independence in the year U.C. 0058, under ne leadership of Zeon Zum Deikun, but ten years later Deikun died and the reins of leadership assed to his aide Degwin Sodo Zabi. In U.C. 0069, Degwin declared himself Sovereign of the rincipality of Zeon and began making plans for a full-scale war against the Federation.

On January 3, U.C. 0079, the conflict later known as the "One Year War" began as the Principality unched simultaneous attacks against the other space colonies, wiping out most of the Federation's pace fleet. As the war continued, the Zeons invaded Earth, seizing control of much of the planet's urface. By mid-September, when our story begins, the Principality's military forces are organized nto three main branches, each controlled by one of the Zabi children, and all reporting to Degwin's ldest son Gihren.

Sovereign
Degwin Sodo Zabi
Commander in Chief
Admiral Gihren Zabi
Administrative Agencies
Royal Guard
Principality Forces General Headquarters
Intelligence Bureau
Public Security Bureau
Research & Development Bureau
Space Attack Force
Vice Admiral Dozle Zabi
Mobile Assault Force
Rear Admiral Kycilia Zabi
Earth Occupation Force
Captain Garma Zabi
Solomon Defense Forces
Colony Expeditionary Forces
A Baoa Qu Forces
Strategic Naval Intelligence Corps
Lunar Orbital Forces
Lunar City Defense Forces
Flanagan Institute
European Forces
North American Forces
Far Eastern Forces
African Forces

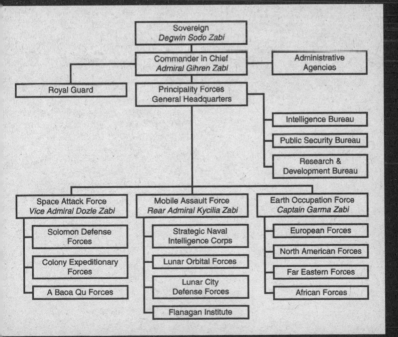

PRINCIPALITY OF ZEON: SUBMARINE FLEETS

After the Principality of Zeon successfully captures more than half of Earth's land surface, it sets out to gain control of the planet's oceans as well. However, as a nation of space colonists, the Zeons have very little experience with marine environments, and it's only in the last months of the war that Zeon's submarine fleets begin to play a major role.

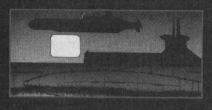

Jukon

These submarines, the backbone of Zeon's naval power, are redesigned versions of Federation vessels captured during the Earth invasion. In addition to its torpedo launchers and missile silos, the standard Jukon can carry a pair of mobile suits in the hangar beneath its bridge.

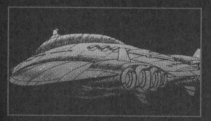

Mad Angler

This huge submarine mothership serves as the command center of Captain Char Aznable's Mad Angler squadron. Lurking deep beneath the oceans, it coordinates the movements of Char's submarine fleet, and dispatches amphibious mobile suits and mobile armors to harass the Federation Forces.

Sealance

The Sealance is a small hovercraft used for ferrying personnel between the vessels of Zeon's submarine fleet. It can travel at high speeds by skipping across the water's surface.

PRINCIPALITY OF ZEON: AMPHIBIOUS MOBILE SUITS

With its invasion of Earth, the Principality of Zeon demonstrates that its Zaku mobile suits - weapons originally developed for space combat - are effective on the ground as well. However, the Zaku proves less adaptable to underwater operations, and the Zeons ultimately create a completely new series of amphibious mobile suits for this purpose.

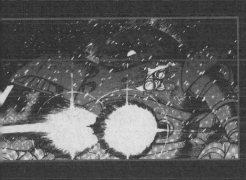

MSM-03 Gogg

The Gogg is the first of Zeon's amphibious mobile suits to enter production. Its heavy armor allows it to resist the water pressure of the deep sea, and it can retract its limbs to change into a streamlined cruising mode. As well as powerful claws and a battery of torpedo launchers, the Gogg is armed with a pair of built-in mega particle cannons, charged by the large water-cooled fusion reactor in its torso.

MSM-07 Z'Gok

The Z'Gok is a more advanced model of amphibious mobile suit, whose performance on land is superior to that of the Gogg. Its arm-mounted mega particle cannons and 360-degree mono-eye sensor allow the Z'Gok to fire in any direction. The Z'Gok is also armed with a set of missile launchers in its head, which can be used against air, ground, and underwater targets alike.

EARTH FEDERATION: BELFAST BASE

After the completion of the Odessa offensive, the battle-weary White Base continues on to an Earth Federation base in Belfast, Ireland. Here the crew at last meet with General Revil and receive orders for the next stage of their journey. However, this coastal base soon comes under attack by Zeon's amphibious mobile suits.

Mehve 3

While Zeon's submarine fleets have become a serious threat to the Federation's naval vessels and coastal bases, the Federation isn't completely defenseless. The Belfast base is protected by anti-submarine patrol aircraft like the Mehve 3, which can seek out undersea intruders, bombard them with torpedoes, and summon patrol boats to join the battle.

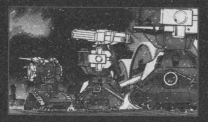

RGT-76 Guntank I

Last seen in Vol. 2, these crude mobile suits are a mass-produced version of the RX-75 Guntank that travels aboard the White Base. Though it lacks the prototype's Core Block system, the Guntank I can swivel at the waist. Three of these machines are stationed at the Belfast base; these are configured for defense, with anti-ground missile launchers and 80mm gun turrets.

RMV-1 Guntank II

This huge machine, nicknamed "Mammoth" by the Federation's soldiers, is a larger version of the Guntank with greater firepower; the "tusks" on its head are 200mm cannons. However, few are produced before the battlefield shifts back to space. One of these machines is currently stored at the Belfast base.

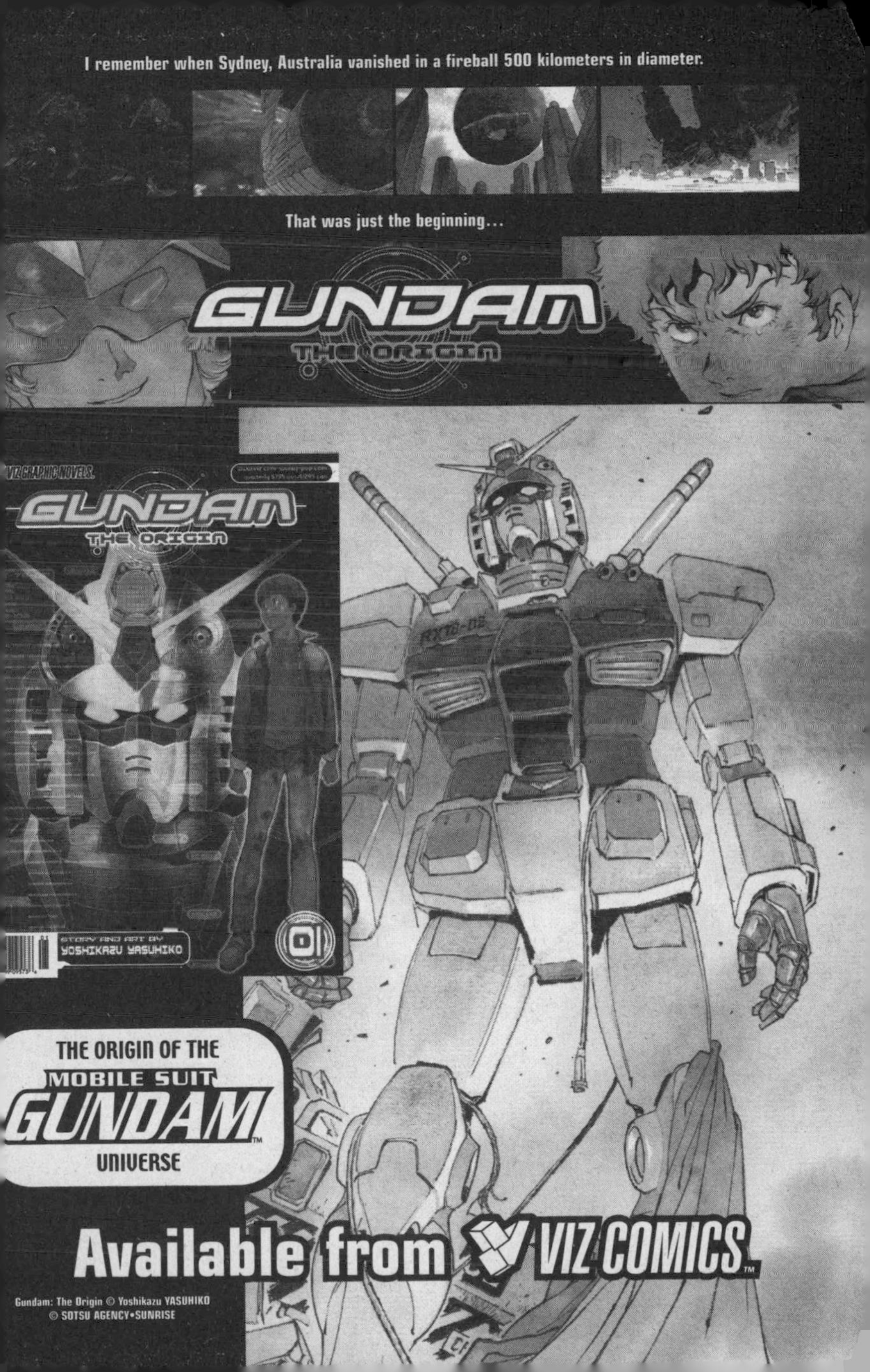
I remember when Sydney, Australia vanished in a fireball 500 kilometers in diameter.
That was just the beginning...
GUNDAM
THE ORIGIN
VIZ GRAPHIC NOVELS.
GUNDAM
THE ORIGIN
STORY AND ART BY
YOSHIKAZU YASUHIKO
01
THE ORIGIN OF THE
MOBILE SUIT
GUNDAM™
UNIVERSE
Available from VIZ COMICS™
Gundam: The Origin © Yoshikazu YASUHIKO
© SOTSU AGENCY•SUNRISE